PROSE SKETCHES

and *Poems*

D1453034

A Southwest Landmark

NUMBER SIX

Lee Milazzo, General Editor

ALBERT PIKE
PROSE
SKETCHES

and Poems

WRITTEN IN
THE WESTERN COUNTRY
(With Additional Stories)

Edited by

DAVID J. WEBER

TEXAS A&M UNIVERSITY PRESS

College Station

Originally published in 1834 by Light & Horton, Boston
Republished in 1967 by Calvin Horn, Publisher,
with design by Arthur Lites

The paper used in this book meets the minimum requirements of the
American National Standard for Permanence of Paper for Printed Library
Materials, Z39, 48–1984. Binding materials have been chosen
for durability.

Library of Congress Cataloging-in-Publication Data
Pike, Albert, 1809–1891.
Prose sketches and poems, written in the Western
country.

Reprint. Previously published: Albuquerque, N.M.:
C. Horn, 1967.
Includes index.
1. Southwestern States—Literary collections.
I. Weber, David J. II. Title.
PS2585.A4 1987   818'.309   86–29994
ISBN 0–89096–305–3
ISBN 0–89096–323–1 (pbk.)

Contents

Editor's Preface

Two decades ago, Albuquerque publisher Calvin Horn decided to add Albert Pike's *Prose Sketches and Poems, Written in the Western Country,* to his impressive list of reprints of Southwestern Americana—reprints that, until that time, had appeared under the imprint of Horn & Wallace. I learned of Calvin Horn's project through a mutual friend, James Toulouse, who arranged for us to meet. I hoped to persuade Mr. Horn to put aside the idea of producing a simple facsimile of Pike's book, for the first and only edition had appeared in 1834 in very small typeface, and a photocopy would be difficult to read. More important, it seemed to me that Pike's significant book had failed to win a wide readership not only because it was extremely rare, but also because in it Pike had eccentrically combined a variety of genres: prose, poetry, and a memoir. A new edition, I believed, required an introduction that would explain the significance of the work. Although I had not yet completed my doctoral studies, I hoped to convince Calvin Horn that I was the person to write such an introduction. To my delight, he graciously agreed.

Calvin Horn's edition appeared in 1967. It was set in new type and contained my introduction and notes, plus long-lost fiction by Pike that had not appeared in his original book. Reviewers praised the Horn edition and it sold out quickly. Calvin Horn and I were delighted, then, when Lee Milazzo and Texas A&M University Press agreed to bring this handsome book into print once again.

Recalling one's earlier work can be chastening (I now see, for example, that Pike's word *pelayos* was a poor rendering of *pelados*—p. 40, n. 17). But the passage of two decades since I wrote the first introduction to this book pales in comparison to Pike's own recollections of the journey to Santa Fe that prompted him to write *Prose Sketches.* In a poignant letter written in

vii

1890, which I came across only after the publication of the Horn edition, Pike looked back across six decades. T. B. Mills of New Mexico had sent Pike a copy of a newly published biography of the colorful frontiersman "Uncle Dick" Wootton. Pike, who was then in his eighty-second year and only one year from death, answered Mills in a letter published on August 1, 1890, by the *Daily Optic* of Las Vegas, New Mexico. Wootton's book, he wrote,

> has re-called to my mind recollections and associations connected with New Mexico when I was there in 1831 and 1832, and went out, from St. Louis, in August, 1831, with a "train" of ten ox-wagons, belonging to Charles Bent, the captain, Holliday, and I knew Bill Williams well, he being one of the first persons I met in Taos when I arrived there on the 11th of November, 1831, and in September, 1832, we being in the same party, got up to trap the San Saba river, and going together from Taos far into the Llano Estacado.
>
> The life that Uncle Dick describes, the Indian tribes have for me the great charm of familiarity. I have seen much of the same country, lived much in the woods, killed many a buffalo and seen millions of them and many a herd of elk and of wild horses.
>
> Santa Fe, Taos, Sevolleta, San Miguel, Jemez, and other places in New Mexico I remember as if it were only yesterday that I was there, and I well remember the night that I camped, with one hired Mexican, a night at the Las Vegas hot springs, where and in the neighborhood no one then lived.
>
> I thank you for giving me a great pleasure.
> Truly and fraternally yours,
> ALBERT PIKE

David J. Weber
Southern Methodist University

December, 1986

Introduction

ALBERT PIKE'S *Prose Sketches and Poems, Written in the Western Country*, defies classification as fiction, poetry, or reminiscence, for it is all of these. In employing two of these literary forms, based on first-hand experience, Pike may be considered New Mexico's first Anglo-American poet and its first Anglo-American short story writer. The narrative portion of Pike's book is one of the earliest American travel accounts in the Mexican Borderlands. Pike's pioneering role in the development of a Southwestern literature has often been over-looked, however, for *Prose Sketches and Poems*, originally published in 1834, is a scarce book. Only fourteen copies are listed with the National Union Catalogue of the Library of Congress; at wholesale prices on today's market, a copy of the first, and heretofore only, edition would bring upwards of two hundred and fifty dollars, could a copy be found. It is, then, a valuable and unique item of Southwestern Americana—no less unique, however, than its author.

The historian who termed Albert Pike "one of the most remarkable and interesting characters in the annals of the Southwest,"[1] was guilty of no exaggeration. During his long life Pike's talents were recognized in many areas—as a poet, lawyer, translator, military man, and Masonic leader and scholar. Although a minor character in United States history, writers have found his life of sufficient interest and importance to make it the subject of two books, two doctoral dissertations, one thesis and a number of articles.[2]

1. Grant Foreman, *Pioneer Days in the Early Southwest* (Cleveland, 1926), p. 203.
2. Frederick William Allsopp, *The Life Story of Albert Pike* (Little Rock, 1920); Robert Lipscomb Duncan, *Reluctant General: The Life and Times of Albert Pike* (New York, 1961); Susan B. Riley, "The Life and Works of Albert Pike to 1860," (unpublished Ph.D. dissertation, George Peabody College for Teachers, Nashville, Tennessee, 1934); Walter Lee Brown, "Albert Pike, 1809-1891" (unpublished Ph.D. dissertation, University of Texas, 1955); and Custer Kidd,

ALBERT PIKE, from a painting by Charles Loring
Elliott, original in the House of the Temple of the
Southern Scottish Rite, Washington, D.C. Photograph
courtesy of the J. N. Heiskell Historical Collection,
University of Arkansas at Little Rock Archives.

A romantic youth with pretentions to literary fame, Albert Pike seemed a most unlikely figure to find his way into the rugged frontiers of Mexico and the United States. Born in Boston, in December of 1809, Pike's precociousness as a child was soon apparent, but the modest means of his family prevented him from being educated beyond the public schools. At age sixteen Pike had prepared himself well enough to pass Harvard's admission exam for entrance into the junior year, and had saved enough money to pay tuition, but school officials demanded that he pay back tuition for the skipped freshman and sophomore years. This, Pike could not afford. Bitterly disappointed, he turned his attentions and talents to various teaching positions, while writing essays and poetry in his spare time. One of the magazines to which Pike contributed, *The Essayist,* was edited by George W. Light who would publish Pike's first book—*Prose Sketches and Poems, Written in the Western Country.*[3]

During his years as a New England schoolmaster, Pike wrote his best poetry and achieved some local fame. But publication of poetry was not highly remunerative—Pike grew increasingly restless. When he fell in love with one of his students, Elizabeth Perkins, but found himself too poor to marry her, Pike decided to move West, thereby fulfilling a dream he had long entertained. In March of 1831 he left Newburyport, the scene of his youth, with two companions, Rufus Titcomb and Luther Chase. Both accompanied him as far as New Mexico, although neither of their names appears in *Prose Sketches.* Joseph M. Titcomb, to whom Pike dedicated this volume, is probably the brother of Rufus.[4]

"Life of Albert Pike with an Introduction to His Poetry" (unpublished M.A. thesis, Southern Methodist University, 1927). A brief biography in article form is Harvey L. Carter's, "Albert Pike," in LeRoy R. Hafen, *The Mountain Men and the Fur Trade of the Far West* (Glendale, 1965), II, 265-274. In sketching Pike's life in this introduction, I have relied heavily on the dissertations of Riley and Brown.

3. Brown, "Albert Pike," pp. 11-24.

4. Brown, "Albert Pike," pp. 26-28. In other reminiscences Pike says that Titcomb went to Santa Fe and also joined the trapping party to the Staked Plains in the fall of 1832 (Riley, "Life and Works of Albert Pike," I, 110). Chase also reached Santa Fe, but he and Pike may have separated there. "Luther Chaes" secured permission from Mexican authorities in February of 1832 to accompany

Pike hoped to find in the West the opportunities that had eluded him in New England. Unable, however, to find even a teaching position, he lamented:

> I thought that I was finally educated and that, therefore, my opportunities would be greatly improved. When I got out West I found my education did not amount to much. It was not practical and what a man needed out there more than a school education was practical, common sense.[5]

Thus, Pike soon found himself at the edge of the American frontier and without a job. At St. Louis, faced with the choice of taking a steam-boat up the Missouri to the Yellowstone, or joining a trading party to Santa Fe, Pike settled on the latter. On the tenth of August, five months after his departure from Newburyport, Pike started for Santa Fe with Charles Bent's trading party of thirty men. The Santa Fe Trail had been open to American commerce a scant ten years when Pike set out; that very spring Comanches ended the life of the great pathfinder, Jedediah Smith, on the road to Santa Fe. Although Pike failed to realize it, his was an historic trip. David Lavender has pointed out that on this journey "for the first time a Santa Fe train was pulled entirely by oxen."[6] A year later, in 1832, caravan-leader Charles Bent would begin the construction of Bent's Fort on the Arkansas, making him one of the most powerful merchants in northern Mexico and eventually the first American Governor of New Mexico Territory, in 1846.

In 1831 these things meant little to young Albert Pike. Suffering from want of warm clothing (which Pike claimed Bent had told him would not be necessary), weary from standing nightly watches which he wrongly viewed as a mere formality,

---

some Mexican citizens on a trapping expedition (copy of a letter to Charles Bent, February 27, 1832, in the book of *Decretos* of the Governor of New Mexico, February 16, 1832 through August 8, 1833, Mexican Archives of New Mexico, State Records Center, Santa Fe, New Mexico). One contemporary remembered that Chase returned to St. Louis in 1832 in the employ of Charles Bent and Ceran St. Vrain—see William Waldo, "Recollections of a Septuagenarian," Missouri Historical Society *Glimpses of the Past*, V, 4-6 (April-June, 1938), 91. Chase later settled in Arkansas where he and Pike resumed their friendship.

5. Pike's autobiography in *New Age Magazine*, XXXVII, p. 468, quoted in Brown, "Albert Pike," pp. 30-31.

6. David Lavender, *Bent's Fort* (New York, 1954), p. 128.

(and even wearier after Indians had made off with his horse), Pike had little respect for Charles Bent. An account of Pike's journey from St. Louis to Santa Fe appears in the three "Crayon Sketches" which are included in the Appendix to this volume. Further of Pike's adventures on the outward trip are related in his "Narrative of a Journey on the Prairie." This first "Narrative," however, focuses chiefly on the journey of Aaron B. Lewis from Fort Towson, then in Arkansas Territory, to Taos, New Mexico. Lewis took the seldom-used route along the Washita and Canadian Rivers, but since he and Pike were traveling to New Mexico at the same time, Pike often notes where his party was in relation to that of Lewis and describes similarities in their experiences. Pike and Lewis later left New Mexico in the same party and struck up an acquaintance which lasted through Pike's first years in Arkansas. There Pike asked Lewis to write the account of his travels which Pike incorporated into his "Narrative."[7] Lewis' adventures also included a trapping expedition in the southern Rockies with a group of mountain men under the colorful Peg-leg Smith.

When Charles Bent's trading party approached the Sangre de Cristo Mountains, a few of the men—Pike among them—left the Trail and rode ahead into Taos. Their arrival there was noted by Mexican officials on November 28th.[8] One contemporary who met Pike about this time described him as

> tall, slim and of sallow complexion, with nothing remarkable in his appearance, but a large rolling black eye; he was shabbily dressed, in a well worn seal cap . . . which may have cost when new, fifty cents, and other clothing to match, and everything about the young man's appearance, indicated both destitution and despondency.[9]

7. Riley, "Life and Works of Albert Pike," I, 156, 179-180; Allsopp, *Life Story of Albert Pike*, pp. 33-34. Both of Pike's narratives are also published as "Narrative of a Journey in the Prairie," *Publications of the Arkansas History Association* (Conway, 1917), IV, 66-139.

8. Pike records reaching a still house three miles from Taos on the evening of the 28th. In his third "Crayon Sketch," he says he reached Taos proper on the 29th. He may have arrived there earlier, however, for a letter of November 28, 1831, reports the arrival of four foreigners at Taos in apparent reference to Pike's party. Book of Correspondence to the Comandante General, January 15 to December 29, 1831, Mexican Archives of New Mexico.

9. Waldo, "Recollections," p. 91.

This "destitute" and "despondent" young man's first impressions of Taos, a popular gathering place for American trappers and traders, are recorded in his story of "The Inroad of the Nabajo." Pike remained in Taos for only a week, then moved south to Santa Fe, a journey which he recounts at the beginning of his story of "Refugio." Pike apparently remained at this capital throughout his stay in New Mexico, except for a spring side trip farther west to Jemez Pueblo, which he describes in his "Journey to Xemes."[10]

Unlike most of the Americans who traveled west on the Santa Fe Trail during the first years of its existence, Albert Pike had a knack and a desire for literary expression. Although he remained in New Mexico for less than a year, his name has been perpetuated in the Far Southwest while those of most contemporary visitors have been forgotten. Pike must have done a considerable amount of listening both in English and in Spanish while in New Mexico, for he carried away a good understanding of the land and its people. Most of Pike's observations on New Mexico found their way into the short stories which he wrote upon his return to the United States. Three of these appear in *Prose Sketches and Poems* and four more have been added to the Appendix.[11] Not the least interesting aspect of these stories is that their author is the first Anglo-American visitor to New Mexico to use the region as the setting for published fiction. Previous to Pike's writing only Timothy Flint's *Francis Berrian,* published in 1826, had employed a Southwest background for prose literature.[12] Flint, however, had never entered the Spanish borderlands where his novel takes place. It was, then, with considerable justification that David Lavender commented that with the arrival of Albert Pike in New Mexico "the literary discovery of the Southwest had begun."[13]

10. In this story Pike claims to have gone to Jemez in July, but his poems written there are dated April. Possibly he went on two trading expeditions in that direction.

11. Of the eight items in the Appendix only four have plots and can be considered stories.

12. Edwin W. Gaston, Jr., *The Early Novel of the Southwest* (Albuquerque, 1961), p. 33.

13. Lavender, *Bent's Fort,* p. 130.

Like other American visitors of his time, Pike was surprised by what he saw in New Mexico. He later commented that "the first sight of these New Mexico villages is novel and singular ...a different world." Indeed it was. The New Mexico settlements that Pike describes, like those on the American side of the Santa Fe Trail, were rude frontier communities. Their unique adobe architecture gave them the appearance, as Pike recorded, of towns of "brick kilns." Although many New Mexico villages were well over a century old when Pike saw them, Indian depredations, the poverty of the countryside, and the area's isolation from the mainstream of Mexican life served to keep New Mexico in a perpetual frontier condition. Pike's observation, in "San Juan of the Del Norte," that New Mexico was "the Siberia of the [Mexican] Republic," was scarcely an exaggeration.

Along with such other literate visitors to New Mexico as Zebuloñ Montgomery Pike, Thomas James, James Ohio Pattie, Rufus B. Sage and Josiah Gregg, Pike enjoyed many of the prejudices and preconceptions common to Americans of his day. He had little respect, for example, for Roman Catholicism or its priests. One of these becomes the villain in "A Mexican Tale." In "A Journey to Xemes" Pike draws the stereotype of Mexicans as a "lazy, gossipping people, always lounging on their blankets and smoking cigarrillos." Unlike most visitors, he seems to have found the woman unattractive. Critical of their dress and dirty shoeless feet, he opined that "the New Mexicans are peculiarly blest with ugliness." In "A Mexican Tale" Pike concluded that New Mexico was "a country in which every man, though he be a fool, has a small sprinkling of the knave." He was harshest, however, on the politicians, defining an *alcalde* as "a greater knave with a better opportunity." In his story of "Refugio" Pike names (quite accurately) a group of Santa Fe *politicos* and ascribes to them a multitude of sins (probably also quite accurately). Pike's stories bristle with ethnocentricity to the point where he imbues some of his Mexican characters with a dislike for their own people and a warm admiration and envy of the "superior" Americans. Thus, at an early date, Pike anticipated the Anglo-American attitudes of cultural superiority toward Mexicans which would find final expression in the twin concepts of Manifest Destiny and Mission, and result in the loss of Mexico's far northern frontier to the United States.

Harsh as Pike's judgments of New Mexican society were, their frankness scarcely exceeded that of many contemporary Mexicans who often expressed painful awareness of the poverty and backwardness of their own frontier culture.[14] While recognizing their own inadequacies, few New Mexicans held the Americans in the high esteem that Pike records. One New Mexico official complained that the Americans "avail themselves of a familiarity they ought not to have here, no more than in their own land . . . they act as if they owned the Courts and Justices." Another official complained that in the courts the foreigners "stretch themselves or recline on the seats," and answer questions from that position with their hats still on.[15] While respecting their technical expertise, New Mexicans probably viewed Americans with a contempt equal to that which the Americans held for them.

Despite his prejudices, Pike could often be a sympathetic observer. Occasionally he reveals that he is charmed by the New Mexican countryside and its inhabitants, and he once generously admitted that "whatever vices that people may possess, they are at least hospitable." More important than being a sympathetic observer, however, Pike was an accurate one. He kept no journal, but his prodigious memory, for which he would later become famous, enabled him to recall correctly the names of persons, towns, distances, and dates. His use of Spanish terms and place names required little editing for Pike had studied that language while still in Massachusetts and was apparently quite fluent in it by the time he left New Mexico. Pike's gift for languages would serve him well in later years.

14. See, for example, the comments of Antonio Barreiro in his *Ojeada Sobre Nuevo Mexico* (1832), which forms part of *Three New Mexico Chronicles*, tr. and ed. by H. Bailey Carroll and J. Villasana Haggard (Albuquerque, 1942), and Melquiades Antonio Ortega to Banco de Avio Para Fomento de Industria Nacional, Santa Fe, January 31, 1831, in *New Mexico Historical Review*, XXIV, 4 (October, 1949), 336-340.

15. Remarks of Miguel Sena and Santiago Abreu in the session of August 20, 1832, Santa Fe Ayuntamiento Journal, 1829-1836, Coronado Room, Zimmerman Library, University of New Mexico.

As early as his first year in Arkansas, after returning from New Mexico, Pike advertised in a local newspaper that he would translate Spanish and French legal documents.[16]

Written in the Romantic style of the day, Pike's stories still hold charm for the modern reader. His plots maintain suspense, his descriptions capture the beauty of the country he passed through, and he writes with good humor and grace. If his characters are external and undeveloped, his dialogue formal and stilted, and his plots dependent on coincidence, so were those of his better known contemporaries, Washington Irving and James Fenimore Cooper. Few modern readers will be impressed by Pike's "literary" allusions and his comparisons—of the prairie, for example, to the Dead Sea or the Sahara. Those who have not visited the Old World landmarks to which Pike refers should be comforted by the knowledge that Pike had not seen them either. Susan B. Riley, who has made the most extensive study of Pike's literary abilities, makes this assessment:

> It is to be regretted that Pike ... did not turn his attention more during his stay in New Mexico to prose records of the life around him. The sketches which he did write are vivid in their pictorial quality. There are occasional touches of realism which show that the author might have done really significant work in the field of the literature of locale if he had cared to develop his ability. . . . But he never seemed to regard this work as highly as he did his poetry, and with the small circulation that his prose had in magazines and the long out-of-print *Prose Sketches* his contribution in recording frontier life in the early part of the nineteenth century has gone practically unnoticed.[17]

Aside from their importance as representative period pieces, Pike's autobiographical poems are chiefly valuable in providing insights into his own moods and nature, for they are highly introspective. He was moved by the beauty of the prairie and the grandeur of the Southwest, but he wrote few descriptive poems. In his "Lines Written in the Vale of the Picuris," Pike

16. Riley, "Life and Works of Albert Pike," I, 101-102, 196.
17. *Ibid.*, I, 138-139.

begins with local description, but ends by praising New England. A poem such as "The Robin: Written in New Mexico, on hearing a red-breast sing, the only one that I ever heard there," reveals the extent of Pike's homesickness. Only his "War Song of the Comanche," "Song of the Nabajo," and his "Lines" and "Dirge," written in honor of dead companions, were inspired entirely by events in the Southwest. These poems are less "literary" than the others in this volume and the "Dirge" is thought by some critics to be "one of the best."[18]

No attempt has been made to edit Pike's poetry, a task which is outside this editor's area of competence. It should be noted, however, that Pike's contemporaries considered him an outstanding poet and his work appears in several anthologies of the day.[19] Edgar Allen Poe thought highly of Pike's verse, claiming that "there are few of our native writers to whom we consider him inferior." One of Pike's later poems, "To Isadore," is believed to have influenced Poe's famous "The Raven."[20] In retrospect, however, Pike's reputation as a poet is somewhat tarnished. Riley, for example, recently termed Pike "a minor poet with an occasional good moment."[21]

Pike's poetry is usually thought of as highly imitative of the British Romantics—especially Coleridge, Shelley, Keats, and Byron—almost to the point of plagiarism, of which he was accused on occasion. Susan B. Riley explains, however, that Pike's borrowings and imitations were not surreptitious. Rather, they were "an open, almost boastful, acknowledgment that he knew and admired their works." Much of the melancholy mood evoked by Pike's poems was doubtless genuine, reflecting his disappointment at failing to win the hand of Elizabeth Perkins. He also languished for a second love, Ann Condry of New-

18. Mabel Major, Rebecca W. Smith and T. M. Pearce, *Southwest Heritage, a Literary History with Bibliography* (rev. ed. Albuquerque, 1948), p. 77.

19. See, for example, the most important nineteenth century anthology, Rufus W. Griswold (ed.), *The Poets and Poetry of America* (Philadelphia, 1842), p. 425.

20. Susan B. Riley, "Albert Pike as an American Don Juan," *Arkansas Historical Quarterly*, XIX, 3 (Fall, 1960), 211. Jay B. Hubbell, *The South in American Literature, 1607-1900* (Durham, 1954), p. 644.

21. Riley, "Albert Pike as an American Don Juan," p. 224, Pike's finest poetry, it should be noted, does not appear in this volume.

buryport, to whom he addressed three of the poems in this
volume. Some of Pike's melancholy, however, may have been
self-induced. Riley suggests that Pike

> found some recompense in the picture of himself as an
> unhappy lover and that his romantic soul revelled poeti-
> cally in the pathos and melancholy of the situation.

Yet, this melancholy introspection was the source of much of
Pike's inspiration. As this diminished with age, so did the
quality and quantity of his verse.[22]

In autumn of 1832, having had enough of New Mexico, Pike
joined a trapping party destined for the Red and Washita
Rivers in Texas and Oklahoma. His adventures with this group,
and his subsequent trek to Arkansas Territory, are related in
his "Narrative of a Second Journey in the Prairie." Pike's
reminiscence provides the only contemporary account of a
New Mexico-based trapping party attempting to operate in
Texas and its value has long been recognized by fur trade
historians. "Tales of Character & Country. No. X," which is
included in the Appendix, describes a trapping party on the
Cimarron and was apparently inspired during the early part of
Pike's journey out of New Mexico. In his second "Narrative,"
Pike provides us with unique pen portraits of such well-known
characters as Old Bill Williams and Peg-leg Smith.[23] Pike's
was one of the first Anglo-American groups to cross the Llano
Estacado, or Staked Plains, of West Texas. His comments on
the Comanches, the Comanche traders or *Comancheros,* and
the topography and routes across this country are, therefore, of
particular interest. Pike's wanderings took him through a remote area of West Texas that would not be charted for another
generation. Few people, however, profited from his pioneering
trek except, perhaps, George Wilkins Kendall, who relied on

22. *Ibid.,* p. 209; Riley, "Life and Works of Albert Pike," I, 105-106, 176;
II, 394.

23. Pike was fascinated by the trapper's life. In *North American Magazine,*
VI, XXXI (July, 1835), 102-108, Pike published "The Trapper's Journal," which
recounts the activities of a group of trappers on the Grand River in April of
1834. I am indebted to Arthur Woodward, of Patagonia, Arizona, for calling this
little-known item to my attention.

Pike and Josiah Gregg in preparing his map of the area "between the Cross Timbers and the settlements of New Mexico."[24]

Albert Pike never returned to his native New England. He had planned to go to Louisiana, amass a fortune there, then travel to South America. But on a cloudy day, as his trapping party neared civilization, it missed the road to Fort Towson, traveling sixteen miles before realizing the mistake. Too weary to retrace their steps, the trappers continued to Fort Smith, Arkansas. Pike made Arkansas his permanent home, becoming so associated with the South that in later life his New England origins were nearly forgotten.

During his first year in Arkansas, Pike schemed to raise "a company to go to the heads of the Brazos and rob the Comanches of their horses," as well as a "half a dozen scalps."[25] When this plan fell through, for reasons unknown, Pike settled down to a more conventional existence. Penniless and proud, Pike was unable to return to Massachusetts. Following brief employment as a woodchopper and two equally short stints as a rural schoolmaster, Pike landed a job as Assistant Editor of the *Arkansas Advocate*, at Little Rock, in October of 1833. In this newspaper Pike published four of the stories of his Western adventures which are herein republished, for the first time, in the Appendix. Pike's two "Narratives," which constitute the first part of *Prose Sketches and Poems,* appeared in the *Advocate* in 1835.

Pike apparently wrote his *Prose Sketches and Poems* almost immediately upon reaching Arkansas. By May of 1833, the manuscript was sent to his friend, in Boston, George Light for publication. Pike showed a great eagerness to have his book in print and in one letter to Light revealed his motives with candor, if not modesty:

> You observe a change in the character of my poetry—It has grown from a boy's to a man's—and if God gives me life for ten years more I will tear fame and honor from the world

24. George Wilkins Kendall, *Narrative of the Texan Santa Fé Expedition.* . . . (2 vols. New York, 1844), I, ii.

25. Pike to George Light, May 25, 1833, Van Buren, Arkansas Territory, quoted in Riley, "Life and Works of Albert Pike," I, 163. See also the final poem in this volume which was written on the same day as the letter to Light.

—I have been tossed about wearily on its waves—and treated roughly enough by its breakers—The poems which I send you shall be my first stepping ground—Let me get hold once more—and I will have what I want from the world.

A year passed, however, before Pike heard from his friend. Pike learned from his sister that Light had received the manuscript and had answered Pike's letter, but Pike heard nothing. In May of 1834, Pike again wrote to Light. Displaying anxiety about the fate of his book, he promised Light a novel—"Scene in N. Mexico 16th Century—War &c," of which he claimed to have already completed one hundred and fifty pages.[26] This manuscript, if it ever existed, has not yet been located.

On August 18, 1834, *Prose Sketches and Poems* was finally published, receiving favorable notices in several Boston journals. *The New England Magazine* (July, 1835), however, accused the author of the very affectation which he denied in the book's preface. Even less fond of criticism than most people, Pike replied in the January, 1836 issue of *The American Monthly Magazine*:

Sir, it is easy for men who dwell in New England to chide the luckless wanderer of the desert and sojourner in solitude—for gloom and despondency; I hope that those who blame me may never suffer what I have suffered. Part of that book I wrote in a foreign country, while travelling about, *alone,* among men of a different language—part in the lodge of the Wild Indian—part in the solitudes of the mountains; on the loneliness and danger of the desert; in hunger and watching and cold and privation—part in the worse loneliness of a schoolroom—all in poverty, trouble and despair. It is easy to imagine a desolation of the heart; I *know* what it is.[27]

In the relatively primitive society of Arkansas Territory, the success of Pike's first book had little effect on Pike's rise to eminence. Fame and wealth Pike achieved in other ways. As

26. Pike to Light, May 26, 1833, and May 9, 1834, quoted in Riley, "Life and Works of Albert Pike," I, 165-168, 231-232.
27. *Ibid.*, I, 236. Riley comments: "Certainly an effective reply, for no one can argue with a man, especially a romantic poet, about how lonely he is."

editor and eventual owner (due to his fortuitous marriage) of a newspaper, Pike's outspoken opinions won him considerable notoriety. By 1836 he became the first reporter of the Arkansas Supreme Court. The next year he sold his newspaper to devote full time to a nascent law practice. Self-taught, as was the custon of the time, Pike had read only the first volume of Blackstone when, as Pike later told it, a judge of the Territorial Supreme Court "gave me a license to practice law, saying it was not like giving a medical diploma; because as a lawyer I could not take anyone's life."[28] Despite any deficiencies in his training, however, Pike "made a meteoric rise in the legal profession. At thirty years of age he was recognized as one of the outstanding lawyers of the Southwest."[29]

Although Pike was a prominent attorney and a popular and effective orator, he never held public office. A Whig since his association with the *Arkansas Advocate,* Pike stood no chance of election in Democratic Arkansas. In 1854, like so many members of his party, Pike joined the Know-Nothings, became their chief organizer in Arkansas and was active in that party's national convention of 1856.[30]

The most controversial aspect of Albert Pike's life was his military career, which began when Pike was made captain of an ornamental home guard in 1842. This office required little time or sacrifice until the outbreak of the Mexican War. Then, the Little Rock Guard voted to march to Mexico, and its captain, although reluctant to leave his flourishing law practice and not completely in sympathy with the war, was forced to go along. Pike participated in the Battle of Buena Vista but came nearest to losing his life upon return home when he challenged another officer, who had questioned his courage, to a duel. In this confrontation, in which neither man was wounded, Pike's old traveling companion from Newburyport, Luther Chase, acted as his second. Following the War, Pike amassed a sizeable

28. John Hallum, *Biographical and Pictoral History of Arkansas* (Albany, 1887), p. 216.

29. Brown, "Albert Pike," p. 160.

30. The finest treatment of Pike's later life is William L. Brown's dissertation, "Albert Pike," which I have used as the basis for the last part of this brief summary.

fortune as attorney for the Creeks and Choctaws in their claims against the federal goverment. At the height of his career, just preceding the Civil War, Pike was in a genuine quandry over the issue of secession. In danger of losing his influential friends in Washington or his friends and property in Arkansas, Pike finally spoke for secession.

In March of 1861 Pike accepted the position of Confederate Commissioner to the Indians, soon effecting treaties with a number of tribes in the Indian Territory of Oklahoma. By summer he was appointed Brigadier-General in command of all Indian troops in the service of the Confederacy. Pike had hoped that the Indians would be used only to defend their own country, but he was obliged to lead them in the Battle of Pea Ridge in March of 1862. In this losing battle Pike gained a reputation in the North as a leader of bloody savages while Southerners questioned his bravery and intelligence. Dissatisfied with the course of the War in the area under his command and embittered toward his superiors, Pike resigned his commission in 1863. So intense was his quarrel with his fellow officers that he was ordered under arrest for a time. In retrospect, Pike's only success in the Great War was to have written the verse for the finest version of "Dixie" in 1861.[31] One writer has pointed out that Pike "had earned the dubious distinction of being accused as traitor by both sides during the Civil War.[32]

Following a brief stay in Canada, Pike received a pardon from President Andrew Johnson for his part in the Civil War. Settling in Memphis, Pike resumed practice of the law and edited the *Memphis Appeal* for a short time. In 1868 he moved to Washington, D. C., where he made his home for the remainder of his life. There his law practice soon gave way to his activities in the Scottish Rite of the Masonic Order. In 1859 Pike had become Sovereign Grand Commander of the Supreme Council, Southern Jurisdiction of the United States, a position that he held until his death in 1891. By 1880 he was known, both at home and abroad, as the foremost Scottish Rite Mason

31. Louis Wann, *The Rise of Realism: American Literature from 1860 to 1898* (New York, 1938), pp. 137, 767; Hubbell, *The South in American Literature*, p. 646.

32. Duncan, *Reluctant General*, pp. 12-13.

in the world, winning recognition for his scholarly activity on behalf of the order.[33]

Albert Pike's long and eventful life, which has only been briefly sketched in this introduction, has tended to make obscure his early contribution as an interpreter and booster of the area that would become the American Southwest. Pike displayed considerable foresight and an unusual modesty when he wrote, in his "Journey to Xemes:" "there is a great field in that land for the painter and the antiquarian. I can not enter it—but would that I could excite some friend to do it." Perhaps he did more than he knew.

Prose Sketches and Poems, Written in the Western Country, is here reproduced in its entirety. Editorial comment is designed to elucidate the text for the modern day reader. Pike's occasional footnotes have been numbered along with my own and may be distinguished by the appearance of his name at the end of the note. Pike often borrowed from his rich poetic vocabulary to add "literary effect" to his prose. Words such as "certes" (meaning certainly), or "contemn" (meaning condemn), have been clarified only if their meaning was not clear in context. The same policy has been applied to Spanish words or phrases. I have chosen to retain the character of the original manuscript by not providing accent marks where Pike omitted them. Quaint spellings which seem phonetically clear, such as "Nabajo" (Navaho), "Semaron" (Cimarron), "Caiawa" (Kiowa), or "Eutaw" (Utah), have received no editorial comment. Pike's system of punctuation, which today seems curious, has also been retained. In all but four of the items in the Appendix, for example, Pike affects the British system of enclosing the primary quotation within single quotes. Only on rare occasion have I corrected obvious printer's errors. Otherwise, corrections and clarifications appear in square brackets or through the use of a *sic.* The reader is free to enjoy Pike's grammatical eccentricities without excessive editorial interference.

33. Pike's numerous writings are listed in William L. Boyden, *Bibliography of the Writings of Albert Pike: Prose, Poetry, Manuscript* (Washington, D.C., 1921).

In editing this volume a wide variety of source material has been consulted, almost all of which was available at the Zimmerman Library of the University of New Mexico. There, Miss Carol Thomasson, Special Collections Librarian of the Coronado Room, and Miss Dorothy Wonsmos, inter-library loan librarian, were particularly helpful. For help in solving various problems posed by Pike, I am especially grateful to Donald Cutter, Robert Dykstra, and Marc Simmons, of the history department at the University of New Mexico, and to Janet Lecompte and Harvey Carter of Colorado Springs. The publisher, Calvin P. Horn, has been most gracious in allowing me to expand Pike's original book. As always, the contribution of my wife, Carol, is inestimable.

David J. Weber
San Diego State College

September, 1967

PROSE SKETCHES

AND

POEMS,

Written in the Western Country,

BY ALBERT PIKE.

BOSTON:
LIGHT & HORTON
1834.

TO

JOSEPH M. TITCOMB,

of NEWBURYPORT.

My Dear Friend:

As a token of ancient fellowship and friendship, I beg you to allow me to dedicate to you what will probably be my last (as it is my first) attempt at authorship, in the shape of a book. Names more widely known than yours it were easy to find; but none possess in a higher degree than yourself that unsullied honesty and perfect goodness of heart, which render your memory so dear to the old friend who addresses you. Farewell:—may the world frown less upon you than it has, and may you keep a corner in your heart for the author.

A. P.

Preface

WITH RESPECT to the Prose part of this book I have nothing to say, except that such portions of it as purport to be true, are actually and truly facts. With respect to the Poems, the kind public will indulge me in saying a brief word. For them I have to ask no indulgence, and the public, I know, ought to have none to grant. It is not my intention to bespeak for them any degree of favor, but merely to mention, in passing, that if there be in them imitation of any writer, I trust that it extends only to the style; and I know that I have not wilfully committed plagiarism. It is possible that the imitation may extend farther than I suppose. It is some time since I have seen the works of any poet; and the things of memory have become so confused with those of my own imagination, that I am at times, when an idea flashes upon me, uncertain whether it be my own, or whether, like the memory of a dream, it has clung to my mind from the works of some of the poets, till it has seemed to become my own peculiar property.

If I am accused of affectation, I needs must deny the charge. What I have written has been a transcript of my own feelings—too much so, perhaps, for the purposes of fame. Writing has been to me, always, a communing with my own soul. These Poems have been written in desertion and loneliness, and sometimes in places of fear and danger. My only sources of thought and imagery have been my own mind, and nature, who has appeared to me generally in desolate fashion and utter dreariness, and not unfrequently in the guise of sublimity.

I have acquired, by wild and desolate life, a habit of looking steadily in upon my own mind, and of fathoming its resources; and perhaps solitude has been a creator of egotism. Of this, the public will judge. By all whom I number as my friends, the faults of this book will be forgiven; and if there be in it no *vatis spiritus,* those who knew me will at least recognise it as the breathings of one who has departed from among them—as the expression of his feeling, and as such they will love them. Fame is valueless to me, unless I can hear it breathed by the lips of those I love. To the world, therefore, and to my old Mother City, I bequeath my last gift. If unworthy of her, let her re-member, that poor and weak though it be, the tribute of the heart is not to be despised.

Ark. Territory, 1st May, 1833.   A. P.

PROSE
SKETCHES
and Poems

Narrative of a
Journey in the Prairie

His breast was armed 'gainst Fate, his wants were few;
Peril he sought not, but ne'er shrank to meet:
The scene was savage, but the scene was new;
This made the ceaseless toil of travel sweet,
Beat back keen winter's cold and welcomed summer's heat.

BYRON.

THE world of prairie which lies at a distance of more than three hundred miles west of the inhabited portions of the United States, and south of the river Arkansas and its branches, has been rarely, and parts of it never, trodden by the foot or beheld by the eye of an Anglo-American. Rivers rise there in the broad level waste, of which, mighty though they become in their course, the source is unexplored. Deserts are there, too barren of grass to support even the hardy buffalo; and in which water, except in here and there a hole, is never found. Ranged over by the Comanches, the Pawnees, the Caiwas, and other equally wandering, savage and hostile tribes, its very name is a mystery and a terror. The Pawnees have their villages entirely north of this part of the country; and their war parties—always on foot—are seldom to be met with to the south of the Canadian, except close in upon the edges of the white and civilized Indian settlements. Extending on the south to the Rio del Norte,[1] on the north to a distance unknown, eastwardly to within three or four hundred miles of the edge of Arkansas Territory, and westwardly to the Rocky Mountains, is the range

1. Known today as the Rio Grande, this river was then commonly called the Río Del Norte in New Mexico. Río Bravo and Río Grande were also used. See Josiah Gregg, *Commerce of the Prairies,* edited by Max L. Moorhead (Norman, 1954), p. 101.

3

of the Comanches. Abundantly supplied with good horses from the immense herds of the prairie, they range, at different times of the year, over the whole of this vast country. Their war and hunting parties follow the buffalo continually. In the winter they may be found in the south, encamped along the Rio del Norte, and under the mountains; and in the summer on the Canadian, and to the north of it, and on the Pecos. Sometimes they haunt the Canadian in the winter, but not so commonly as in the summer.

It is into this great American desert[2] that I wish to conduct my readers—first solemnly assuring them that what I am about to relate is perfectly the truth, and that nothing is exaggerated or extenuated in the narration.

In the month of September, 1831, Aaron B. Lewis,[3] residing at the time near Fort Towson, on Red River, in the territory of Arkansas, was induced to undertake a journey to the province of New Mexico, allured by the supposed immense riches in that country, and the opportunity which he imagined there was of making a fortune there. He looked upon New Mexico as a sort of Utopia, a country where gold and silver were abundant and easily obtained. In short, his ideas of it were precisely such as the word Mexico generally suggests to the mind. Neither has he been alone in his delusion. With a blindness unaccountable, men still continue rushing to Santa Fe, as if fortunes were to be had there for the asking. Men, who by hard and incessant labor have amassed a little money, laying that out to the last farthing, and in addition, mortgaging perhaps their farms to obtain farther credit, convey the goods thus obtained to Santa Fe, hoping thus and there to gain a fortune, notwithstanding they have seen numbers returning poor and impoverished, after starting, as they are doing, with high hopes and full wagons. Here and there an individual, by buying beaver or trading to Sonora and

2. Pike was repeating a phrase coined by Major Stephen H. Long, in 1821, for the area between the 98th meridian and the Rocky Mountains, although the idea of a Great American Desert originated with the earlier expedition of Zebulon Montgomery Pike.

3. Little more is known of Aaron B. Lewis than that which appears subsequently in Pike's account. A biography of Lewis, by Harvey L. Carter, will appear in vol. V of LeRoy R. Hafen (ed.) *The Mountain Men and the Fur Trade of the Far West*. (Glendale, in press).

California for mules, returns home a gainer, but generally the case is far otherwise.[4]

Lewis, however, was far from knowing all this, and accordingly on the 3d of Sept. 1831, with a good horse, gun, pistols, and plenty of clothes, ammunition and blankets, he left the United States, and bent his course to the mountains. He left Arkansas in company with two other Americans and eleven Cherokees, who were headed by a chief commonly called Old Dutch, and whose object was hunting and trapping on the Fore Washita.[5] Besides these, there was a young doctor by the name of Monro, and his wife, who were to accompany Lewis to New Mexico. Chambers, one of his companions, was a middling-sized young man, a very good fellow on the prairie, but of very little use there. George Andrews, the other, was a big, obstinate, cowardly Dutchman, of no use to himself or any one else, and of no character except a bad one.[6] Lewis himself is a large, very

4. For example:—I knew one honest and excellent man from Missouri: he had been a hard-working mechanic and farmer, and had raised sufficient money and credit to obtain a stock of goods to take to Santa Fe. The St. Louis cost of his goods was 1750 dollars; the duties at the custom house were 2104 dollars, and a gratuity to the interpreter of 250 dollars. His stock of goods was sold in the course of a year, at 30 cents per yard, measuring and including domestic cloth, silks, and in fine, his whole stock, except ribands. The result was, after paying the custom house, 1500 dollars with which to pay the cost of his goods and his expenses in transporting them.

The duties on common domestic—in fact, on domestic of all qualities, is 21 cents per yard. Those who take in shoes, silks, coffee and tobacco, which are contraband, are almost, the only men who make anything.

I have given elsewhere a description of the character of a few of the New Mexicans. As a circumstance, I may mention that the regular duties for the year 1831 which ought to have been paid to the Mexican government from Santa Fe, were nearly 200,000 dollars. Only 30,000 was forwarded from Santa Fe; and the rest found a way into the pockets of individuals.

Perhaps the reader is at a loss to imagine how such a result is produced. Reader—the bills are reduced to one third (generally) of their original amount, and thus passed through the custom house; and the interpreters and custom house officers share the gratuity paid by the merchants for this favor and service. —PIKE.

5. Today's Washita, then known as the Faux Ouachita or False Washita, to distinguish it from the Ouchita in Arkansas and Louisiana.

6. I have been unable to further identify Doctor Monro. Chambers may be the son of Samuel Chambers—see note 29. George Andrews is the victim of a one-sided account by Lewis, whose examples of Andrews' "cowardly" character appear in this narrative. Andrews was born in Pennsylvania, perhaps of a Pennsylvania Dutch family. He had come to New Mexico at least as early as 1828, for in October of that year, at age twenty-six, he was baptized at Taos. The following

large and tall man, red faced, of undaunted bravery, coolness, and self-possession, an excellent hunter, and of constant good humor.

The course which they intended to pursue, was to follow the Fore Washita to its head, and then to cross to the Canadian, and follow it to the wagon road [The Santa Fe Trail]. As I shall have frequent occasion to speak of these rivers, I may as well at once give a description of them. No maps describe the Red River and the Colorado correctly. The Canadian fork of the Arkansas rises near the head of the Arkansas itself, runs south to within seventy miles of Taos, and then takes a course a little south of east. It is there called Red River by the Spaniards and traders. The North Fork of the Canadian heads about fifty miles to the north-east of Taos, in two hills, which are called by the Spaniards Las Orejas, and by the Americans the Rabbit Ears. The North Fork itself is called there Rabbit Ears' Creek. The Fore Washita heads about three hundred miles to the east of Taos, in some prairie hills, and a man can travel in half a day from the head of the principal branch of it to the Canadian, at a large bend of the latter. Red River rises in the prairie not far south of Santa Fe, and between one and two hundred miles east of it. The heads of it are salt, and, as well as the Colorado, it has a wide, sandy bed, and but little water until it reaches nearly to the Cross Timbers, within three hundred miles of the settlements of the whites. I shall describe the Colorado or the Brazos hereafter.[7]

I have never seen the Fore Washita far above the Cross Timbers. It is, above them, a small clear stream of water, always running. Where I crossed it, it was perhaps one hundred yards wide, deep, and with not very bluff banks. Above this it is bor-

---

spring, on March 3, 1829, he married María Luz Hurtado at Taos. Fray Angélico Chávez, "New Names in New Mexico, 1820-1850," *El Palacio*, 64, 9-10 (September-October, 1957), 294.

7. Pike's geographical knowledge was excellent for his time. The headwaters of the Canadian are not, however, near those of the Arkansas. The headwaters of the north fork of the Canadian is not Rabbit Ears Creek (today's Seneca Creek), but Corrumpa Creek. Pike had a good idea of the location of the headwaters of the Red River, a problem which would not be solved until 1852 with the exploration of Randolph B. Marcy. See also George Wilkins Kendall, *Narrative of the Texan Santa Fé Expedition. . . .* (2 vols. New York, 1844), I, 218.

dered by a strip of timber, generally from one eighth to a quarter of a mile wide, and on the outside of this, a prairie bottom, half a mile, and in some places a mile wide, of exceedingly rich land. These bottoms extend to the distance of more than a hundred and fifty miles above the Cross Timbers. It is indeed the best hunting ground of the west for deer, buffalo, and bear, and the trees are abundantly stored with delicious honey. The timber is chiefly oak, walnut, and pecan, and close to the bank cottonwood and sycamore.

Of the early part of his route—that is, from Fort Towson to the Cross Timbers—Lewis can give but a vague and confused account. Most of the time he was sick, and in addition to this, the Cherokees, whose purpose was hunting, loitered along so slowly—killing deer as they went—and accommodated their course so constantly to this pursuit, that there could be but little possibility of remembering the route distinctly. What I know about it is derived rather from my own passage through the same part of the country, than from that of Lewis. Leaving Fort Towson, as before stated, on the 3d of September, they took the road, which, crossing the Kiamesia, goes on to the ford of Boggy—a branch of Red River—running into it below the Washita.[8] The country is beautifully diversified—hills covered with oak and hickory, rolling prairies with their tall swarthy grass waving in the wind, and here and there creek bottoms, flush with greenness. In parts, however, the country has a bleak and barren appearance, which becomes much more marked when the sun scorches up the prairies, and the hot fire runs over them, leaving only bleak, black and barren wastes, undulating in gloomy loneliness, and here and there spotted with a clump of trees, leafless, gray and gnarled, perhaps scorched with the fire which has gone over the prairie.

As they proceeded farther to the west, the prairies became larger, and bore in a greater degree that look of stern silence which hardly ever fails to impress itself on any one who at first enters a plain to which he can see no bounds. Crossing Boggy at the ford below the Forks, just beyond which the road lost

8. Lewis' party apparently followed a military road part of the way. His approximate route is traced on the map which accompanies this volume.

itself in the prairie, they kept on to the ford of the creek called Blue, or Blue-water—crossed it, and in a few days entered the hills of the Fausse or Fore Washita, on the north side of that river—high, broken, and precipitous elevations, in which they were entangled for the space of two or three days. Where I afterward passed through these hills, they are devoid of timber; but where Lewis went through on his outward trip, they were, generally, thickly covered with low shrub oaks and briers, forming, as it seemed, a portion of the Cross Timbers into which they entered as soon as they left the hills. Passing through the Cross Timbers—in width, there, about fifteen miles—they struck, for the first time, the Fore Washita.

These Cross Timbers are a belt of timber, extending from the Canadian, or a little further north, to an unknown distance south of Red River. The belt is in width from fifteen to fifty miles, composed of black-jack and post oak, with a thick undergrowth of small bushy oak and briers, in places absolutely impervious.[9] About this time Lewis lost his horse, which wandered off one night, and was never found again. He was now, like Andrews and Chambers, on foot. Just beyond the Cross Timbers, Monro and his wife left him and returned to the white settlements, weary of the journey. It was well that they did so.[10]

Fifty miles above the Cross Timbers, upon the Washita, and on the morning of the twelfth of October, Lewis and his two companions parted from the Cherokees, though with the utmost reluctance on the part of the latter, who were urgent for them to remain and trap with them. Thus far there had been to them, and there is to any man, but little danger. The Pawnees are sometimes, but very seldom, found below the Cross Timbers —the Comanches never. Now, however, commenced the danger. The heads of the Washita and the western part of the Canadian are the homes of the latter tribe. It was not the nature, however,

9. The Cross Timbers was an outstanding landmark for the prairie traveler. Early accounts of this area have been compiled by Mrs. Carolyn Thomas Foreman, *The Cross Timbers* (Muskegee, Oklahoma, 1947).

10. It has been asserted that there is danger from the Pawnees and Comanches to the Cherokees and Choctaws in their new country. Now, reader, the case is far otherwise. The Pawnees come in to the bounds of the Osage nation, at times; but even they, the cowardly Osages, whip them. As to the Comanches, there is no earthly danger, for they never come within the Cross Timbers.—PIKE.

of either Lewis or Chambers to fear, and they, encumbered by Andrews, pushed on boldly up the river. The country was now changed. On each side of the river, after leaving the bottom, there was the high, level and dry prairie, where grass grows only to the height of two or three inches, and, by the month of October, is scorched, curled, and gray, affording little or no sustenance to anything but the buffalo.

No man can form an idea of the prairie, from anything which he sees to the east of the Cross Timbers. Broad, level, gray, and barren, the immense desert which extends thence westwardly almost to the shadow of the mountains, is too grand and too sublime to be imaged by the narrow-contracted, undulating plains to be found nearer the bounds of civilization.[11]

Imagine yourself, kind reader, standing in a plain to which your eye can see no bounds. Not a tree, not a bush, not a shrub, not a tall weed lifts its head above the barren grandeur of the desert; not a stone is to be seen on its hard beaten surface; no undulation, no abruptness, no break to relieve the monotony; nothing, save here and there a deep narrow track worn into the hard plain by the constant hoof of the buffalo. Imagine then countless herds of buffalo, showing their unwieldy, dark shapes in every direction, as far as the eye can reach, and approaching at times to within forty steps of you; or a herd of wild horses feeding in the distance or hurrying away from the hateful smell of man, with their manes floating, and a trampling like thunder. Imagine here and there a solitary antelope, or, perhaps, a whole herd, fleeting off in the distance, like the scattering of white clouds. Imagine bands of white, snow-like wolves prowling about, accompanied by the little gray collotes [coyotes] or prairie wolves, who are as rapacious and as noisy as their big-ger brethren. Imagine, also, here and there a lonely tiger-cat,[12] lying crouched in some little hollow, or bounding off in tri-umph, bearing some luckless little prairie-dog whom it has caught straggling about at a distance from his hole. If to all

11. Antedating the publication of Washington Irving's *A Tour on the Prairies* by one year, Pike must be regarded as one of the earliest travelers to record the spell of the prairie. Further impressions appear in Pike's first and sec-ond "Crayon Sketches" which are included in the Appendix of this volume.

12. Pike's "tiger-cat" is probably a bobcat.

this you add a band of Comanches, mounted on noble swift horses, with their long lances, their quiver at the back, their bow, perhaps their gun, and their shield ornamented gaudily with feathers and red cloth, and round as Norval's,[13] or as the full moon; if you imagine them hovering about in the prairie, chasing the buffalo or attacking an enemy, you have an image of the prairie, such as no book ever described adequately to me.

I have seen the prairie under all its diversities, and in all its appearances, from those which I have described to the uneven, bushy prairies which lie south of Red River, and to the illimitable Stake Prairie which lies from almost under the shadow of the mountains to the heads of the Brazos and of Red River, and in which neither buffaloes nor horses are to be found. I have seen the prairie, and lived in it, in summer and in winter. I have seen it with the sun rising calmly from its breast, like a sudden fire kindled in the dim distance; and with the sunset flushing in its sky with quiet and sublime beauty. There is less of the gorgeous and grand character, however, belonging to them, than that which accompanies the rise and set of the sun upon the ocean or upon the mountains; but there is beauty and sublimity enough in them to attract the attention and interest the mind.

I have seen the *mirage,* too, painting lakes and fires and groves on the grassy ridges near the bounds of Missouri, in the still autumn afternoon, and cheating the traveller by its splendid deceptions. I have seen the prairie, and stood long and weary guard in it, by moonlight and starlight and storm. It strikes me as the most magnificent, stern, and terribly grand scene on earth —a storm in the prairie. It is like a storm at sea, except in one respect—and in that it seems to me to be superior. The stillness of the desert and illimitable plain, while the snow is raging over its surface, is always more fearful to me than the wild roll of the waves; and it seems unnatural—this dead quiet, while the upper elements are so fiercely disturbed; it seems as if there ought to be the roll and the roar of the waves. The sea, the woods, the mountains, all suffer in comparison with the prairie—that is, on

13. A reference to either young or old Norval in John Home's popular play, "Douglas," written in 1756. See Hubert J. Tunney, "Home's Douglas," *Bulletin of the University of Kansas Humanistic Studies,* III, 3 (November, 1924).

the whole—although in particular circumstances either of them is superior. We may speak of the incessant motion and tumult of the waves, the unbounded greenness and dimness, and the lonely music of the forests, and the high magnificence, the precipitous grandeur, and the summer snow of the glittering cones of the mountains: but still, the prairie has a stronger hold upon the soul, and a more powerful, if not so vivid an impression upon the feelings. Its sublimity arises from its unbounded extent, its barren monotony and desolation, its still, unmoved, calm, stern, almost self-confident grandeur, its strange power of deception, its want of echo, and, in fine, its power of throwing a man back upon himself and giving him a feeling of lone helplessness, strangely mingled at the same time with a feeling of liberty and freedom from restraint. It is particularly sublime, as you draw nigh to the Rocky Mountains, and see them shot up in the west, with their lofty tops looking like white clouds resting upon their summits. Nothing ever equalled the intense feeling of delight with which I first saw the eternal mountains marking the western edge of the desert. But let us return to Lewis.

After leaving the Cherokees, he and his companions kept up the Washita for eight days, until it became so small that they could step across it, and branched out into a number of small heads, coming down from different parts of the prairie. In these eight days they traveled two hundred and fifty miles. Lewis was loaded with his heavy gun, his saddle-bags full of clothes, and generally from ten to forty pounds of buffalo meat. Game was abundant thus far, and they suffered nothing but fatigue.

OCT. 20.—On this day, in the morning, they left the main Washita, now very small, and struck a course nearly west, two degrees north, through the prairie. After traveling in a treeless and broken prairie until midnight, they came upon a deep hollow, near the head of it, in which water was running towards the main Washita, and encamped under a big elm.

21.—Started again, and traveled all day directly towards the dividing land between them and the waters of the Canadian, and at midnight came to the head of another hollow similar to the one of the night before. This Lewis takes to be the head of the longest branch of the Fore Washita. From this head of the Washita to the Cross Timbers is probably three hundred and forty miles, not calculating the bends of the river, but keeping a course nearly straight.

22.—This morning they left the head waters of the Washita, and, after traveling about twenty miles in a course west, two degrees north, they came upon a hollow from which a little branch ran to the Canadian. All this day it rained. The country between the head waters of the Washita and this part of the Canadian, is a high, broken, uneven prairie. Here they killed a bear, cut up the meat, and built a fire under it to dry and preserve it. This day I was traveling upon Semaron, a branch of the Arkansas to the south, between it and the Canadian. I was in a company of thirty men guarding ten wagons.[14]

23.—This morning the adventurers left their camp and kept their course for about four miles, when they struck the Canadian and crossed it, and in the evening, thinking that they would obtain no water, they altered their course, turned to the south-west, and, crossing the river again to the south, encamped on the bank. Lewis computes this day's travel at eighteen miles.

24.—Left camp and traveled about six miles up the Canadian on the south side, then crossed it to the north, and left it, keeping their regular course west, two degrees north. They soon came into high sand hills, and encamped at night, finding no water. About midnight Lewis insisted on starting and finding water, and they did so, and in the morning came upon a large creek running into the Canadian.

25.—After staying an hour or two at the water, left it and kept their course all day, and at night, owing to a large bend in the Canadian, they came upon it again, and encamped on the river. It had snowed all day, but ceased at sunset. This day our company reached the middle spring of the Semaron, and the last

14. This river Semaron is a branch of the Arkansas on the South. It is a singular river. You may see it one day running flushly in one part of it, and sinking, below, entirely in the sand, and the next day the case will be reversed. The dry place will then run water, and the place which was before running will be dry as a desert. The bed of the river and its banks are covered with salt; not like the salt of the Brazos, pure muriate of soda, but bitter and precisely the same effect as the latter substance. This river is a great haunt of the Comanches, heads in the mountains, and has beaver at its heads.—PIKE.

watch this night, of eight hours, belonged to me. Stood it without fire for three hours, and then built me a fire of the buffalo ordure which we had gathered for mess fuel. During my watch a horse froze to death.

26.—They traveled all day again, and encamped at night on a small creek half a mile from the main river. The weather was very cold in the morning, but moderated towards night. Country, as before, broken, uneven prairie, covered with oak bushes about a foot and a half high.

27.—They traveled all day, and encamped in the prairie, and melted snow in a tin kettle, which Chambers carried. Still kept their course west, two degrees north.

28.—Traveled all day, and encamped again in the prairie, at a hole where buffalo had been rolling, called by hunters a buffalo wallow, and containing water.

29.—Traveled all day, and encamped on a little fork of clear water running to the north—a branch, probably, of the Semaron, or, perhaps, of the north fork of the Canadian.

30.—Traveled all day, and at night encamped on another little fork running north.

31.—Traveled all day in a high, barren, undulating prairie: found water once or twice during the day; but at night slept in the prairie without a drop. This is the beginning of what Lewis calls the water scrape.

Nov. 1.—Started in the morning early, and traveled all day without water; likewise traveled all night without rest or cessation.

2.—High, barren prairie; all day no water. They traveled constantly and eagerly until about two of the afternoon on their course, and then changed it and traveled a due south course. Night came, but did not delay them, and it was not till the morning star rose, that, weary and tormented with thirst, they lay down and slept.

3.—Towards day they arose, and started again in a course still due south. About ten in the morning, Lewis threw away his saddle-bags, pistols, blankets, and about forty weight of buffalo meat. Chambers had thrown his meat down the evening before, and Lewis had added it to his load. Early in the morning Chambers went ahead, promising to keep the course, and whenever he reached water to return with a bucket full to Lewis and Andrews. After leaving them he saw an antelope, and went out of his course to kill it for the sake of drinking the blood. He thus lost the course and his companions. Towards evening Lewis killed an antelope and drank the blood.[15] It drank like new milk, but increased the thirst ten fold. All night they kept slowly along the dry prairie without water, till about two hours before day, when they lay down and slept. Lewis had now become so weak as to be unable to shoulder his gun except by placing one end on the ground and getting under it; and he went staggering along through the prairie like one who had long been sick.

4.—Started again at daylight, and proceeded slowly along the plain, and about the middle of the forenoon descried the high, broken country of the Canadian. About two of the afternoon they reached the river, almost exhausted. As Lewis drank he forced himself to vomit, and the water came from his stomach as cold as it entered it. He tells me that he is certain of having drunken at least three gallons of water. This day, after seeing the river, they fired the prairie as a signal to Chambers. He saw it, but supposing it to proceed from Indians, was afraid to approach it. He struck the river early in the morning, about ten miles above the place where Lewis and Andrews came upon it.

5 and 6.—Lay by at the same place, in order to gather strength for traveling. Killed a fat cow.

7.—They made preparations for going back to find the articles which they had thrown away. Lewis took four gallons and a half of water in a cased deer skin, which he had been carrying, and as Andrew insisted on going ahead and keeping the course, he allowed him to do so. In the afternoon, finding that they had lost their course, they returned to their camp again.

8.—Started again this morning, Lewis going ahead and bearing the water. They traveled all day, and at night encamped in the prairie, with no water except what they bore with them.

9.—Traveled still north until about noon, when, despairing of finding their property, and fearing to suffer again from thirst,

15. This was not an unusual expedient on the Plains, but the buffalo was a more common victim.

they turned their course to the south west, and at night encamped on the head of a large creek running toward the main Canadian.

10.—Followed the creek down for about ten miles, and encamped in a grove of cottonwood, on the same creek.

11.—Left the creek and traveled west all day, until late in the evening; they struck the Canadian again, and saw Chambers's track on the river bank. They had supposed him to be dead.

From this to the sixteenth they kept up the river slowly, and Lewis has but a confused remembrance of this part of the trip. On the sixteenth it commenced raining in the morning, and towards night they crossed the Canadian by wading, and found a cave in the bluff bank, in which they could be sheltered, and, rolling a large pine root to the mouth of it, they were very comfortable all night, though but poorly clad, and with no blankets. Lewis's dress consisted of a pair of thin linen pantaloons and a shirt, with a pair of deerskin moccasins. It hailed towards night severely, and about midnight cleared off very cold.

17.—Started very late, and went down the creek about half a mile, and encamped again in a cottonwood grove, where Andrews killed, for the first time, something to eat, viz. a little 'puck [buck].' All this day the cold was intense.

18.—Started in the morning in a snow storm, and traveled nearly all day. In the evening they encamped in a bleak place, and made a fire with cedar, which was thinly scattered about on the bluff banks of the river. The snow round the fire melted, and the mud was soon knee-deep. When, during a lull in the storm, Lewis saw up the river about half a mile a grove of cottonwood, and proposed going and camping there, George answered that, 'py Cot, it was petter here as there, and he would not co.' 'Stay, then,' was the answer of Lewis, and taking his gun and a brand of fire, he went on, but had not proceeded more than a hundred yards, when, looking back, he saw Andrews puffing along behind him. They soon made a large fire, raked away the snow, and sat out the night by their fire—*comfortable*—as Lewis says.

I met this storm at the Point of Rocks,[16] about sixteen miles
to the north east of the Canadian, at the crossing of the wagon
road under the mountain. This Point of Rocks is a high ridge
of mountain which, dividing at this place and jutting out into
the prairie in three spurs, ends abruptly, making a high and im-
posing appearance in the boundless plain in which they stand.
Between these three points two cañons ran up into the bosom
of the ridge—(by which word cañon the Spaniards express a
deep, narrow hollow among the mountains). We arrived here
on the eighteenth, after the first storm, and seeing indications
of another approaching, we encamped early, running our
wagons in a straight line across the mouth of the northern
cañon. Our mess pitched our tent on the south end of the line—
fronting the line—and we then employed ourselves all the afternoon in cutting and bringing from the sides of the mountain
the small rough cedars, which grow there in abundance; and
we soon gathered huge piles on the outside of the wagons. Our
oxen and the one or two horses yet left, were driven far up the
hollow, and about ten of the evening I ascended the side of the
hollow and stood guard two hours—which standing guard consisted in wrapping myself in a blanket and lying down under
the lee of a rock. When my guard was off, Schench [Schenck]
and myself retired to our tent, and I slept out the night under
two buffalo robes and two blankets. He, poor fellow! is since
dead.[17]

Two or three hours before daylight the storm commenced
with terrific violence, and I never saw a wilder or more terrible
sight than was presented to us when day came. The wind swept
fiercely out of the cañon, driving the snow horizontally against
the wagons, and sweeping onward into the wide prairie, in
which a sea of snow seemed raging. Objects were not visible at
a distance of twenty feet, and when now and then the lull of
the wind permitted us to look further out in the plain, it only
gave us a wider view of the dim desolation of the tempest. There
was small comfort at the fires, immense though they were; for as

16. A prominent point on the Cimarron cutoff of the Santa Fe Trail.
17. The news of his death moved Pike to write the poem "Lines on the
Death of William R. Schenck."

gust after gust struck the wagons, the snow blew under them and piled around us, while the cold seemed every moment to increase in intensity. For some time in the morning we were crowded together in our tent, but while eating our breakfast in it, the pins gave way, and we were covered with snow. We then pitched it again in the lee of the wagons, with its mouth to the prairie. In the evening we all turned out, although the cold was hardly supportable, and cut and carried wood to a sheltered place on the side of mountain, where our sapient captain had directed us to stand guard. We then stuffed boughs of cedar under the wagon, in the lee of which our mess-fire was built, and also built us a shelter at each end of the wagon, and managed to enjoy some small degree of comfort.

19.—We left the Point of Rocks in spite of the deep snow and the intense cold, leaving also some six or eight oxen frozen to death, and although I ran backward and forward in the track of the wagons all day, still I froze my feet before I stopped at night. Such was the weather in which Lewis and Andrews lay without a blanket or a coat by a fire in the open air. There is but small comfort in the prairie in such a storm, even when a man has blankets and clothes in abundance; but when he is nearly naked, and sits all the long night shivering by the fire which is the only barrier between him and death, it requires the greatest fortitude to bear the feelings of utter misery and desolation which throng upon the heart.

Lewis and Andrews traveled this morning four or five miles, and stopped in a grove of cottonwood. After making a fire, Andrews shot a turkey, and called to Lewis to run to catch it. Lewis did so, and was hotly engaged in the chase of the turkey, when he came upon an old buck, and shot him. Andrews, however, was enraged, and 'would rather have his turkey as fifty pucks.'

20.—This day Lewis left the Canadian, and followed a small southern branch of it which heads within five miles of the junction of the Demora and Sepellote, (branches likewise of the Canadian), which junction takes place on the wagon road within fifty miles of San Miguel,[18] and within fifteen miles of

18. Pike is referring to the junction of Mora River and Sapello Creek at present-day Watrous, a point on the Santa Fe Trail. Mora River originally was

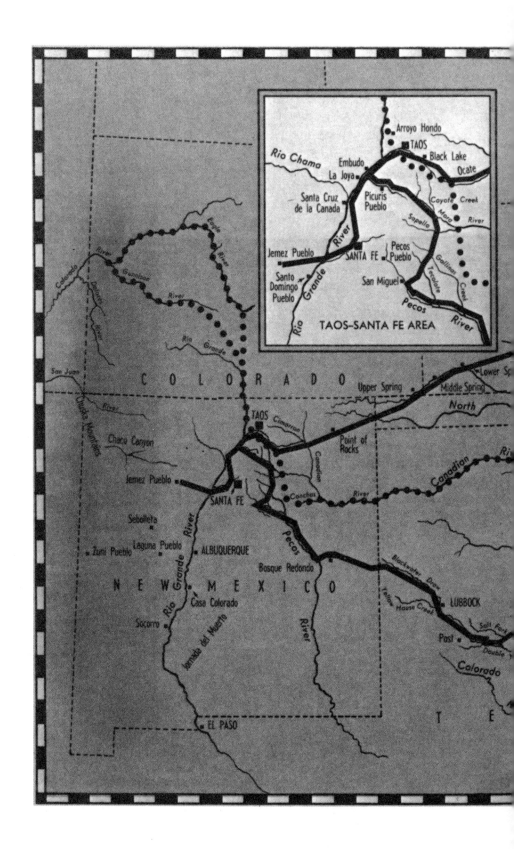

TAOS–SANTA FE AREA

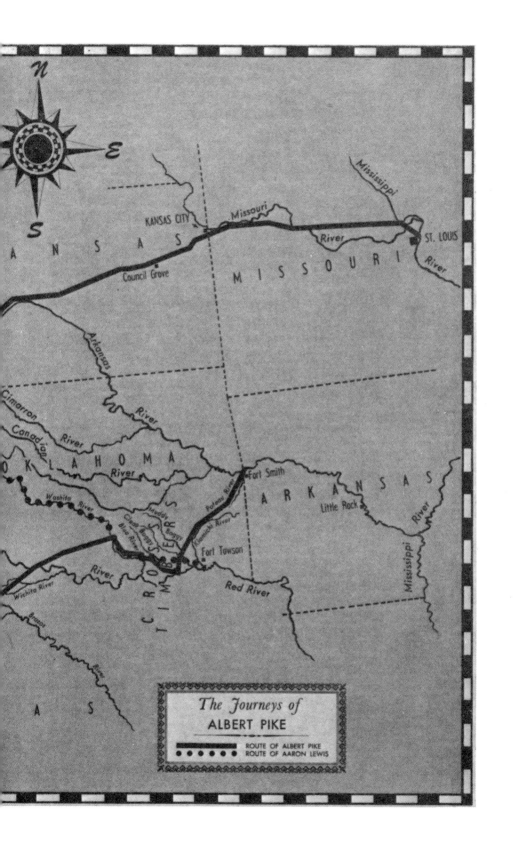

The Journeys of
ALBERT PIKE

ROUTE OF ALBERT PIKE
ROUTE OF AARON LEWIS

the Galimas [Gallinas] branch of the Pecos, which is itself a branch of the [Rio Grande] Del Norte.

The progress of Lewis was now slow, owing to Andrews, who pretended great fatigue and incapability of walking. They traveled this day about six miles, and encamped in a cliff of rocks on the creek.

21.—This day they ascended the first bench of mountain, and came into prairie again; traveled about ten miles in the whole, and found water in a hollow rock.

22.—They started, aiming to go to a long mountain covered with timber, which lay in the course. In the afternoon Lewis saw a piece of timber to the left, and thinking it impossible to reach the timbered hill, proposed going and encamping in the nearer timber. Andrews was, as Lewis expressed it, 'for fooling along and killing antelope.' They held a long confab, and at length Andrews agreed to go to it. But after turning towards the timber and proceeding a short distance, they saw a smoke in it, and Andrews again refused to go thither, alleging that it was Indians; and Lewis, enraged, went on without him, saying that he would go thither if there were five hundred Indians in the timber. Andrews followed. On arriving at the edge of the timber, Lewis stopped, primed his gun anew, and picked the flint. Andrews by this time had come up, and observed, with some surprise, 'that Lewis did allow to fight.' A little further, and they saw a track. It was that of Chambers. They were within five steps of him before he knew it. He had always supposed them dead, but they had seen his track along at intervals, and even that day, going to the right of them. Reader, you can imagine their joy at meeting.

Chambers, as Lewis says, 'never expected to get no place, and had only concluded to keep going until he died.' He had killed a panther that night—after being encamped here a day or two —and all the three now feasted on panther meat.

23.—Lay by, in a snow storm.

24.—Moved camp about half a mile to better timber, and

called Río de lo de Mora, from which Pike derived his "Demora." The "small southern branch" of the Canadian that Lewis took can not be identified with certainty. Perhaps it was the Conchas River.

encamped again. Our wagons, in the mean time, had crossed the Canadian, and were encamped about twenty miles beyond, in a grove of pine timber, within seventeen miles of the foot of the first high mountain on the road to Taos.

25.—The storm ceased, and the weather was intensely cold. This day Lewis and his small party moved two miles, and stopped for fear of freezing; encamping on the same little creek [?] which I have mentioned before. This day a party of us left the wagons and went into Taos. The blue mist hung about the mountains, and gathered into icicles on our beards and blankets; and the snow was knee-deep. The climate in which I was born is cold enough, but I never experienced anything equal to the cold of this day. All of our party except one or two froze their feet. This was the kind of weather in which Lewis traveled with a pair of linen pantaloons, a shirt, a deerskin on his breast with the hair in, and one on his back with the hair out, and a pair of thin moccasins. We this day traveled twenty-five miles, a part of which was up one of the highest mountains to be seen around us, and encamped in a grove of hemlock and pine, which the reader will hereafter find mentioned as the encamping ground of Lewis.[19] There were two pack mules ahead of us, and we walked all day in their steps, which was the only path. It was no strange thing that Lewis could not travel.

26.—Lewis this day traveled about four miles, and encamped in the snow on the head of a hollow in pine timber.

27.—Our adventurers traveled this day about nine miles, and came upon the waters of the Demora, that is, upon a small branch running towards this creek. This day our party from the wagons reached the foot of the last mountain on the road to Taos.

19. Pike's party crossed the Sangre de Cristo Mountains into Taos, via the Ocaté Creek route which Joseph C. Brown, who accompanied the United States survey party of 1825, delineated. See the endpapers of Kate L. Gregg (ed.), *The Road to Santa Fe, The Journal and Diaries of George Champlin Sibley* (Albuquerque, 1952). This route, which was more level than the Cimarron River crossing of the mountains, took Pike along the Ocaté to its headwaters, down into the valley of Coyote Creek near Black Lake, then up this valley and over the mountains again, apparently by way of Old Taos Pass, and down the Río Fernando de Taos into Taos. This route would, as will be seen, overlap in a number of places with Lewis' trail into Taos.

28.—Lewis this day traveled all day, and gained about four miles; in the evening they killed an old buffalo, and, finding his flesh too poor to be eaten, they cleansed and ate the entrails; encamping at night on the same branch of the Demora. This day about ten in the evening our party reached the still house in the valley, within three miles of Taos.[20]

29.—This day they traveled about eight miles, and in the middle of the afternoon stopped on the main Demora, where, in a few minutes, Lewis killed two black-tailed deer. I have often mentioned these deer. They are larger than the deer which are found in the United States, and in fact their skin sometimes is so large that it might be mistaken for an elk-skin. They are of a darker color than our deer, more clumsily made, and not so fleet; neither is their flesh so good, but their skins are much better.

30.—This day they lay by.

Dec. 1.—Directly after starting, they came upon the road at the junction of the Demora and Sepellote [Mora and Sapello], which the reader will find mentioned hereafter, as the place whence I went into San Miguel. Had Lewis continued up the Demora to the old village, and thence through the pass of the mountains, he would have found a broken trail, and would have gone in with much more ease.[21] He wished to do so; Andrews, however, who had been in Taos before, and in fact had a wife there, assured him that they could not go in that way for the snow, but that they must go to a timbered hill which lay to the right, and can be seen from the junction of the roads; and that beyond this they would find a mule-path leading from the ford of the Canadian to San Fernandez. They accordingly traveled three or four miles in the direction of the timbered hill, and encamped.[22]

2.—Traveled this day three or four miles, and encamped on the timbered hill.

20. Lewis eventually reached the same still house which is subsequently discussed.

21. Pike here refers to the trail that he later took in leaving New Mexico, crossing the Sangre de Cristo range between Picuris Pueblo and the Mora River. See note 6 of the second "Narrative."

22. Andrews, it would appear, led Lewis overland, to the west of the Turkey Mountains, eventually reaching Ocaté Creek.

3.—Traveled this day about the same distance upon the hill, and encamped on it again in a deep cañon. While sitting in camp this morning, ready to start, two deer came running up towards them, and stopped. Lewis shot and brought one down, and was followed by Andrews, who killed the other. Chambers and Andrews then insisted upon stopping and eating, to the great anger of Lewis, who hated losing time.

4.—Traveled all day and encamped at night on the upper end of the mountain.

5.—This morning Lewis issued the last meat, being a piece for each man about as large as his two fingers. The reader will remember that though they killed two deer, they were too weak to pack much of it. Andrews this morning alleged that he could carry his gun no further, and that they must stop till he could rest a day or two and gain strength. What was to be done? Lewis was forced to lay by and starve, or carry his own gun and that of Andrews likewise. Either gun is extremely heavy. Andrews had long been burdensome by delaying his companions, and once Lewis had threatened to throw him into the fire, and would have done so had he not, as Lewis calls it, 'backed out.' This day they reached a small creek within six miles of the foot of the mountain, which I have said we ascended on the twenty-fifth. The road goes by the creek, but the snow which had fallen after we went in, had erased the tracks completely, and there was no vestige of a road.[23]

6.—Left Cache Creek, and traveled toward the mountain. After ascending it about half way, and coming upon a small platform on the side of it, Andrews insisted on encamping, and they did so. A fire was made, and they were standing by it, when Lewis observed that he still had a great mind to go on. 'I wish that you would,' said Andrews, 'for then you could tell them to send for me.' A word was enough for Lewis, and, shouldering his gun and taking a brand of fire, he went on up the mountain alone. He had a day or two before given his thin moccasins

23. This must be Ocaté Creek. Pike next refers to it as Cache Creek, which may have been its American name. In July of 1831, Santa Fe officials had caught American smugglers in the act of caching goods on the Río de Ocaté. Santiago Abreu to Agustín Durán, Santa Fe, July 5, 1831, Mexican Archives of New Mexico, State Records Center, Santa Fe, New Mexico.

to Andrews, who complained bitterly of his feet, and he was himself now equipped with a pair made of the raw hide of a buffalo.

The few days' journey which are left now, I shall give in his own words; that is, as far as the words of an uneducated man can be written without giving the world cause for supposing that one is aiming at burlesque. If I retain his own peculiar phrases, it will be because he can express himself by them more forcibly than I can by any language of my own. Henceforward, then, the reader will understand him as speaking in the first person, and any remark which I have to make for the purpose of explanation will be placed in parenthesis.

After reaching the top of the mountain, I saw before me the wide prairie through which I had to travel about six miles to timber. My thin pantaloons were torn into strips everywhere, and there was hardly a place where you could put your finger down without touching flesh. Added to this, about ten inches of my legs above my moccasins were entirely bare. The snow through the prairie was generally about to my middle, and whenever I missed the road, which was beaten hard underneath, though covered with soft snow above, then I took it plump to my neck, and had all sorts of kicking to get out of it at all. The air kept growing colder as I went, and I thought that the timber receded. I was sure that some power or other was holding back my feet. My heart leaped when I got into the timber and heard the tall trees singing above me. I turned in and blowed up my chunk of fire, packed big logs and made a pretty good fire. Then I took off one of my raw deer-skin, spread it out and sat down upon it, and there I sat all night, turning every now and then, as some side of me would get to freezing. I had nothing else to do but to watch the stars, whenever the snow ceased blowing on me from the mountains, except making the old pines and hemlocks smoke.

7.—Just after daylight the wind began to blow. It knows exactly *how* to blow, and where to hit to cut deepest. But it was death or victory, and I was obliged to start any how. I gathered my chunk, looked at my fire awhile, and started. I used to hate to leave my fire in the morning, not knowing where the next fire was to be. After traveling about three hundred yards, I came upon a little hollow, where I could see mule sign. (They had been out to our wagons). I could see where they had sunk to their bellies, and as they raised their knees, had pushed up the big pieces of crusted snow on end. But I was glad to see any sign of the road, for I never knew whether I was in it or out of it. Andrews had given me all the directions he could about the road, but he could not find the way in himself, much less tell me. I had not got fifteen steps across the hollow, when I came to a big hemlock, which was lying in the edge of a thicket of mountain cottonwood and hemlock. I found I was freezing to death, and had to stop. I tumbled old brindle (his gun) to the ground, and tried to drop my chunk, but I could not do so for some time, my fingers were so froze. I got it down at last, and tried to straighten out my fingers by rubbing them up and down my legs, but I could not do it, and had to pick up chunks between my two fists, and pack them to my fire along side of the hemlock. There like to have been no calling of the dogs that time. I laid here till I got thawed out a little, and then moved further down among the hemlock, where I made me a real comfortable place to stay in all day. I had not been there long before I shot a white wolf, intending to eat him, but he went tumbling over and over, till he got out of the way. I did not care much about it, though, for I was not hungry at all. I had other things to think of than getting hungry. It clouded up towards morning, and just after the sun rose it began to snow.

8.—I was right glad to see it turn warm enough for snow to fall; so I shouldered old brindle, gathered a chunk and started. In traveling about eight miles I came to the edge of what Andrews had described to me as the Black Lake.[24] It is a hollow prairie, where water is sometimes. I do not know how far it is across it, for I took no notice of the distance. When I got into it I never expected to see any other place. It heads all cold places I ever saw, at any rate; and I think it is about six miles across it. Just as I entered it, I found I was freezing, and stopped in a cliff of rocks, and made a little fire of choke-cherry bushes. I could

24. Lewis had apparently crossed the mountains near the headwaters of Ocaté Creek to Black Lake.

have put the whole of it in my hat. I pulled off my moccasins, and began to thaw them; but before they were half thawed, my feet began to swell, and I was obliged to put on my hard moccasins again. I stayed here about an hour, and then I took a few sprigs of choke-cherries and lighted them. It was snowing violently. I had got so as not to care much about life now, and I did not take any particular pains to keep my sprigs alive as I walked, and had they gone out, I never should have struck fire again. I had not gone more than half a mile, when I reached a clump of eight or ten pine trees, and determined on stopping here. I gathered a few pieces of pine, and blowed up my sprigs, now almost extinguished. After setting my pieces of wood afire, I had ten minds not to put anything more to it, where I had one to do so. All that I could see about me was two big logs on the side of the little rise, and I concluded to give them a try. I carried my fire to the side of the lower one, and then turned in to rolling the upper one down along side of it. I made half-a-dozen trials, and then gave it up. I did not believe then that half-a-dozen oxen could have stirred it. I went and laid my gun on a high stump, so that Andrews and Chambers might see it, and sat down by the fire again. I would have died then, willingly. After a while, I thought that I would take another try, and went to the log again. I gave one lift, but it was in vain. Rage and despair urged me on again, and I lifted with a strength which seems astonishing to me now—and I felt it move. I tried again, and out it came; and as I raised this last time, I saw the fire flash out of my eyes, and felt the joints of my back snap together. I rolled it down along side of the other, and they made a most glorious fire, which was burning when Chambers and Andrews came by, the next day. Here I lay, that is to say, sat up on a deer-skin, about as big as the brim of a hat, all night. It cleared off in the night, but did not grow so much colder as I expected.

9.—This morning I took my chunk of fire, and put out again. I had not taken my moccasins off here, for fear of never getting them on again; and in half an hour they were froze stiff again. I thought, just after starting, that I never would get across the Black Lake, and turned back and went half a mile, intending to lay at my fire until Chambers and Andrews came up; for there was no kind of a track in the lake, and I did not know whether I was going right or wrong. I again summed up resolution, and turned my face to Taos again, and by good luck kept the right course. I made three fires this day before I stopped at night, and after all, came nigh giving up the ghost several times. I wished heartily to die, but hated to kill myself, and so kept moving. When I got into the narrow cañon, beyond the Black Lake, I saw a mule-track or two again, and again thought I might get some place. After leaving the cañon, I encamped on the head of a spring, not many miles this side of the last mountain, and was more comfortable here than anywhere in the mountains. There was an old pine fallen, and I stripped some big pieces of the bark off, put one under me, one edgeways by my back, and one at my head, as well as one at my feet, and laid down. This was luxury. Still I felt no hunger, and still I kept my moccasins on.

10.—This morning I gathered me a chunk and started, concluding that this would be the last day I could hold out. I soon reached the foot of the mountain, and in the way, and during the ascent, I sat down several times, never intending to rise again. It seems a pretty bold thing to say, and hard to believe, but so it is. The thoughts of turning coward would raise me again, and I kept on until I reached the top of the mountain. You know what a dark, black-looking place it is on the other side, away down, down, in the depth of the valley. When I looked off from the summit of the mountain, and saw it, the thought flashed into my mind that this must be the Black Lake.[25] No man in the world can express the feelings which came over me then. I still kept moving down the mountain, and when about half way down, I threw away my chunk of fire, and gave myself up to die; still, however, resolving to move as long as I had life. I had sat by my fire and wept at night, and had prayers in my heart, though I did not utter them; but I shed not a tear now. I kept on through the cañon, and towards noon reached

25. Lewis seems to be in the mountains to the northwest of Black Lake, looking across the valley formed by Tienditas Creek.

the forks of the cañon,[26] which I knew to be twelve miles from
the still house. I knew where I was now, and I found mule-
tracks here. Now I determined to go in or die; and in fact, as I
had thrown away my fire, I had no other chance, for I could not
have made fire. I could not use my hands a bit. I had gone but
a little way in the cañon, when I found a beaten track, and soon
got to the places where wood had been cut. My feet were now all
cut to pieces by my hard moccasins, and I could hear the blood
splash in them as I walked, as though they were full of water,
while the snow would gather in the heels of them until the
hinder part of my foot would be four inches, sometimes, from
the moccasin. After a while, I saw a cow: it was the pleasantest
sight I ever saw in my life; and just as I had concluded not to
walk more than half an hour longer, and as I went staggering
along, so sleepy that I could hardly move, I heard a chicken
crow. How it waked me up!—and I soon after came in sight of
the old mud still house. I went round to the lower end of it, and
two or three dogs came out and began upon me. In a minute,
I could see two men looking through the hole in the door. I
could have shot both their eyes out with one bullet. 'Hallo!'
said I; and they pushed the door partly open, and stood looking
at me. They took me, as they said afterwards, to be a Comanche,
who had come in ahead of a party, to take the still house,—and
no wonder! for the pine smoke had made me as black as you
please, and my hair was perfect jet. Long was the best soldier,[27]
and he stepped out and walked round me, keeping a good distance though, and with his eye fixed upon the door. The dogs
were still baying me; and I, at length enraged, spoke in good

26. The junction where Tienditas Creek and La Jara Creek flow into the
Río Fernando de Taos. Lewis followed this latter stream into Taos.

27. Horace Long, who was later baptized on January 1, 1840, as "Jorge," or
George Long, and was thereafter known in New Mexico by either name. Chávez,
"New Names in New Mexico," *El Palacio*, 64, 9-10 (September-October, 1957),
316. Born about 1804, Long seems to have come to New Mexico from his native
Kentucky in 1830 or 1831. In 1839 he was listed as a distiller, living at "Des
Montes de Taos." A later contemporary remembered that Long was still operating
a distillery at Taos in 1858: "This whiskey was as good as any except that it
lacked color & age; they drank it up about as fast as he could make it." Report
of the foreigners in the Department of New Mexico, March 20, 1839, Ritch
Papers, no. 175, Huntington Library, San Marino, California. Albert William
Archibald to Francis Cragin, Trinidad, Colorado, December 25, 1907, notebook
XI, p. 40, Cragin Papers, Pioneers' Museum, Colorado Springs, Colorado.

plain English:—'Call off your dogs, or I will put a bullet through one of them.' Hearing me speak, they soon drove away their dogs, and told me to come in. I did so, sat down by the fire, and after thawing out my hands, began ripping open my moccasins with my knife. In the mean time Conn[28] and Long, who are both the best fellows in the world, began to recover the power of speech. They stood and looked at me awhile, and then Conn inquired—'Where, in the name of Heaven, are your from?'

'From the United States.'

'What company did you come with?'

'I came with a company of my own—of three men.'

'Where are they?'

'Behind, in the mountains.'

'Are these all the clothes you have got?'

'Yes, they are so.'

'What! and have you no blankets?'

'No, not one.'

'Have you eaten anything to-day?'

'No, not for five days.'

'What! are you not hungry?'

'No.'

They drew me about half a pint of whiskey, which I barely tasted, and then Conn brought me a bit of meat, about as big as my two fingers, and a like bit of bread. In vain I told them that I would not thank them for that little, and begged for more. When it touched my stomach, my hunger became ravenous; but finding I could get no more, I submitted, and turned in to ripping my moccasins again. In ten minutes after the moccasins were off, my feet were swelled as big as four feet ought to be. I could have cried with the pain; and while I sat bearing it as well as I could, an old Spaniard came in—old Señor San Juan. The old fellow started back when he saw me, lifted up his hands with a stare of terror and surprise on his dried-up face, and uttered the ejaculation, Adios! In two minutes, he had half a bushel of onions in the ashes, and as soon as

28. Perhaps Francis Conn of Kentucky who was baptized at Taos in January of 1834. In 1831 he was about 27 years of age. Chávez, "New Names in New Mexico," *El Palacio*, p. 302.

they were roasted, he swathed my feet up with a parcel of them. I could not have lifted one of my feet with both hands. They were bigger than a bull's head. The old man stayed with me all night, changing the onions for fresh ones at intervals, and I have no doubt that it was old Mr. St. John who saved my feet for me. During the night Conn gave me a little bit of meat and bread at intervals, and in the morning he was about serving me the same way; but I uptripped him this time, and declared my resolution of eating breakfast with him and Long. I ate all I could get, though it was not half enough, and during the day I ate about fifteen times. I thought while I was there, that I never would get out of the sound of a chicken's voice again. This day I sent word to Kincaid and old Chambers,[29] that Andrews was in the mountains, and they informed his father-in-law,[30] who immediately went out for him, and found him and Chambers at the forks of the cañon. They were both better dressed than I, and had thin moccasins; in consequence they froze their feet but very little. In fact, Andrews said that 'he pelieved he could have cone in petter as I.' And sure enough; the rascal had only been possumming the whole time, and was better able to travel than I was, but wanted me to break the way and pack his gun.

Lewis lay at the still house six weeks before he was able to go to San Fernandez, a distance of three miles. While there, he was visited frequently by the Indians of the Pueblo of Taos, and presented by them with cakes, dried fruit, &c. They wished to convey him to their village, but he could not go. At length, at the expiration of six weeks, he was lifted on a horse and taken to the Rio Hondo [Arroyo Hondo], as it is called, a little settlement four or five miles from San Fernandez, in the same valley of Taos. In the mean time, the skin had peeled off from the

29. Probably Mathew Kinkead and Samuel Chambers. Both were partners in a proposed distillery venture in Taos in 1826. David J. Weber, "A Letter from Taos, 1826, William Workman," *New Mexico Historical Review*, XLI, 2 (April, 1966), 156. A biography of Kincaid by Janet Lecompte appears in LeRoy R. Hafen (ed.), *The Mountain Men and the Fur Trade of the Far West* (Glendale, 1965), II., 189-199. Samuel Chambers was a long-time resident of Mexico having first come to Santa Fe in 1812 as a leader of a trading party, then remaining until 1820 as a captive. The Chambers who accompanied Lewis may have been a son of this "old Chambers."

30. See note 5.

whole of his body, and the flesh had come from parts of his feet, so that the bones and leaders [tendons] were bare. He was soon after attacked with the pleurisy; and, to use his own expression, the thing was near dead out with him. He recovered, however, although it was not until April that he became perfectly well. After that he was the terror of the Spaniards, for he could have demolished them rapidly with his powerful arm, had they ever given him cause. He is not quarrelsome, however, even when he gets caught in what they call in the West, 'a spree.'

In the month of May, Lewis joined himself to a party of five men, including himself, headed by Tom [Peg-leg] Smith, the 'Bald Hornet,' for the purpose of trapping in the mountains to the north of Taos. They went out to the northwest, directly to the Elk Mountain, between the forks of Grand River, that is the Colorado of California, and there commenced trapping.[31] The first night that Lewis set his traps, he had entered a little narrow cañon, which had never been trapped, because a man could not ride up it. He took it on foot, with his six traps on his back, obtained a set for all of them, and went back to camp, about fifteen miles. He there borrowed all the spare traps, returned the next morning, and, finding four beaver in his traps, set the ten which he had brought, and went back to camp again with four beaver. On returning again the next morning with a companion, he found eight more beaver in his traps, and was sure of making, as he says, an independent fortune. The whole party, of five, then moved there, and trapped the creek. I am almost afraid to describe the manner of catching this animal, but it may be new to some of my readers. You find the place where the animal comes out of the water, that is, if you can, and set your trap in his path, about four inches under water, fastening your chain to a stake, which you put as far out in the water as its length will allow; sometimes you put your trap behind a bank, sometimes you cover it with moss or something

31. Harvey L. Carter, in his previously cited biography of Aaron Lewis, places them in the area between the Colorado and the Gunnison Rivers. Elk Mountain remains unidentified. Pike is the only contemporary to term Peg-leg Smith the "Bald Hornet." Indeed, Smith was bald. For a little known description of Smith see Pike's "Tales of Character and Country, No. X," in Appendix. Although a book length study has appeared, the best account of Smith's life is Alfred Glen Humphreys' biography in Hafen (ed.), *The Mountain Men*, IV, 311-330.

else. This depends on the nature of the settlement of the beaver, whether it has been often trapped or not. You then dip a little twig in your bait, (that is, in dissolved castor), and stick this twig sometimes within the jaws of the trap, and sometimes just outside of them. The beaver goes to the smell of the castor, and is generally caught by the fore feet, and, flouncing over, is drowned in the water. If the place has been long trapped, they are too old to be caught by bait. Lewis once set his traps five nights for an old beaver, and for four nights the old fellow took away his bait-stick without springing the trap. On the fifth night, Lewis placed his trap still deeper under the water, and covered it with moss, placing no bait-stick. He then washed away all trace of himself, and in the morning he had the beaver. He was an immense old fellow, and had got out on the bank, where he lay puffing and shaking the water. Lewis laid down his gun and pistols, and then creeping up to him, caught him by the hind leg. The beaver tried to bite him, but was unable to do it, until Lewis, putting his knee on the trap, loosened his paw from it, and dashed his brains out with it.

It is no uncommon thing to see trees, three and four feet in diameter, cut down by these animals, cut up into lengths of about eight feet, and taken lengthways to their dam.

They had only caught about forty beaver in this mountain, when the Eutaws came upon them, in number about three hundred, and wished to rob them. They are in the habit of doing so to the Mexicans; but they, to use another western phrase, 'barked up the wrong tree,' when they got hold of Tom Smith. The Bald Hornet is not easily frightened, if he *has* a wooden leg. The old chief sat down in their camp, and after various threats, shot his gun at the ground, as a sign that they would kill all the party immediately. Tom was undaunted: he told the chief that he might kill them, but could not rob them; that his heart was big as the sky, and defied the old chief to attack them. All this time, he was keeping Lewis off, who had drawn his pistol when the chief shot his gun into the ground, and would have killed him, had not Tom interfered. The consequence of their boldness was, that the Eutaws went off without molesting or robbing them. They then immediately moved camp.

While upon the Elk mountain, they killed several mountain

sheep and white bear. The former animal is larger than a deer, and is like a common sheep in appearance—of a dirty light color—very fleet, and a great lover of rocks and precipices, in which, as well as in its speed and faculty of smell, it equals the chamois. Their horns are like those of the domestic sheep, but much larger and stronger. They will often fall thirty or forty feet, strike upon their horns, and rise and go off, as if nothing had happened to them. You may see them standing with all their feet together, and that in a place where they scarcely have foothold. Lewis was out, after leaving the Elk mountain, in company with Alexander,[32] one of his companions, and an excellent hunter. They came upon a flock of perhaps sixty or seventy of these sheep. Lewis shot, struck one, and he fell. Alexander likewise fired, but missed entirely. They then ran about thirty yards further and stopped again. Being now about one hundred and seventy yards from them, Alexander was for creeping nearer, but Lewis determined to shoot from the place in which they were. 'Shoot, then,' said Alexander, '*I* cannot hit one at this distance.' 'Do you see that bunch of heads together?' said Lewis; 'I will shoot at the upper head.' He did so, and the sheep fell, and lay kicking. Alexander ran and cut his throat, and then went to the first one which Lewis had shot, and was busy doing the same office for him, when the former rose and made off over the rocks. Alexander rose also, and was hardly off the other sheep, when it likewise rose and followed its companion, and they lost both. The party laughed heartily at Alexander, for acting the doctor, and bleeding mountain sheep. The meat of these animals is excellent, and their skins are thin, when dressed, and soft as velvet.

From the Elk mountain they crossed to the main branch of Grand River, and came within a few days' journey of the heads of the Columbia. They then left this branch, after trapping a time upon it, and crossed to the head of Smith's fork of the same river,[33] and thence to the heads of the Arkansas, where they trapped again, and then crossed to the heads of the Del Norte;

32. This was apparently Cyrus Alexander who would soon become an early pioneer of California. See Donald C. Cutter and David J. Weber, "Cyrus Alexander," in Hafen (ed.), *The Mountain Men*, V, in press.
33. Harvey Carter, in note 6 of his biography of Lewis, identifies this as the Eagle River of today.

and came in to Santa Fe. The last forty days they had only one bag of dried meat to live upon, and it was during this time that they shot and lost the two sheep. They killed nothing at all in that time. They bought a dog or two in the time from the Eutaws, and ate them. Grand River, on which they mostly trapped, has been, and still is, excellent hunting ground. It has been supposed that there is much beaver below the place where Lewis trapped, and in a cañon through which the river runs for a distance of two or three hundred miles. I think that the trappers compute the length of the cañon at three hundred. The river, where it emerges, is half a mile wide, and yet you may stand on the edge of the fissure in the solid rock which forms the cañon, and the river, a hundred feet below, looks like a thread. It is a terrible place, and once in it, there is no egress except at the lower end of it. Some Spaniards unwittingly entered it once in a canoe, and were carried violently down it about forty miles. There they fortunately reached an eddy, produced by a bend in the sides of the cañon, stopped the canoe, and climbed up the sides of the cañon, which were there less precipitious than usual, leaving canoe, beaver, guns, &c. all in the cañon to find a way through it.[34]

It was on the heads of the Del Norte, that General [Zebulon Montgomery] Pike, then a lieutenant, was taken by the Mexicans. Has it ever been satisfactorily known why he was there? I think not. *He could not have been mistaken in the river.* He knew it not to be the Arkansas, and he knew himself to be in the Mexican territory. Was he not seeking a place for the army of Aaron Burr to enter and subdue Mexico? He was no traitor, I know; and neither, in my opinion, was Burr. Neither ever aimed to raise a hand against our own country. I find some proof of Pike's intentions in his book.[35]

34. Pike is describing the famous Grand Canyon of the Colorado, about which little was then known.

35. Pike here takes sides in an ongoing historical controversy. Despite the recent publication of Zebulon M. Pike's journals and letters, edited by Donald Jackson (2 vols. Norman, 1966), historians remain in disagreement. Some, like Albert Pike, believe that Zebulon Pike knew he was on the Rio Grande. Most historians, however, take him at his word and believe that he had become lost. Aaron Burr's conspiratorial activities were shrouded in a haze of secrecy so that any good Republican, as Pike was, could continue to believe in his innocence.

Narrative of a Second
Journey in the Prairie

AFTER Lewis had returned to Taos from his trapping expedition in the mountains, I first became acquainted with him. In the month of August [of 1832], I heard that Mr. John Harris, of Missouri,[1] was collecting a party for the purpose of entering and trapping the Comanche country, upon the heads of Red River and the Fore Washita; and I was induced, by the prospect of gain, and by other motives, to go up from Santa Fe to Taos, and join him. After my arrival, however, I thought it best to buy an outfit of Mr. Campbell,[2] who was going into the same country, and to join him, and did so. The only Americans in our party, were Mr. Campbell, a young man who came with me from Santa Fe, and myself. There was likewise a Frenchman. I bought my outfit—one horse, one mule, six traps, and plenty of powder, lead, and tobacco, and went out to the valley of the Picuris,[3] a distance of about thirty miles, over the hills and among the pine woods. Here and there was a little glade, among the hills, grassy and green; but generally it was all a bleak and unproductive country. The pine trees were stripped of bark to the height of six or eight feet by the Apaches, who prepare the inner coat of the bark in some manner, and eat it; and I ob-

1. John Harris had entered the Santa Fe trade as early as 1829, in company with a Robert Harris who was apparently his son. In the fall of 1831 John Harris led a group of French and Mexican trappers north from Taos to the Shoshone River. My biography of John Harris will appear in a forthcoming volume of LeRoy R. Hafen (ed.), *The Mountain Men and the Fur Trade of the Far West*.

2. Richard Campbell, whose first name Pike later supplied in a letter "To the Public" in the *Arkansas Advocate* of March 7, 1834, was a prominent Taos trapper and trader. In 1827, Campbell was the first mountain man to find his way from New Mexico to California. A brief biography is John E. Baur, "Richard Campbell," in Hafen (ed.), *The Mountain Men*, III, 69-70.

3. The valley of the Río de Peñasco where the Pueblo of San Lorenzo de Picuris is located.

served that it was only one particular kind of pine which they used, viz. the rough yellow pine. My friend and myself were alone, and in consequence, we soon lost our way; we traveled until nearly night, and then retraced our steps for about four miles, to a place where we had seen the remains of an Indian fire. Here we kindled a large fire, tied our horses, and laid down with our guns by our sides. We were awakened early in the morning by the howling of wolves close to us, which, however, was of short duration. We then mounted, and proceeded again towards Taos, but meeting a Mexican, who was going to our camp to recover a horse, which he said he lost, we turned back again, and about noon arrived at camp; where we staid four or five days, lounging about and quarrelling with the New Mexicans, for whom we had killed several oxen, and who disliked the idea of going to San Fernandez to receive their pay. On the fourth of September, those of our party and of Harris's for whom we had been waiting, came out from Taos. Both parties joined, made up between seventy and eighty men, of whom about thirty were Americans. One was a Eutaw, one an Apache, and the others were Mexicans. Among the men who came out on the fourth, was Lewis, who belonged to the party of Harris.

The reader need not expect much delineation of character. Trappers are like sailors; when you describe one, the portrait answers for the whole genus. As a specimen of the genuine trapper, Bill Williams certainly stands foremost. He is a man about six feet one inch in height, gaunt, and red-headed, with a hard, weather-beaten face, marked deeply with the small pox. He is all muscle and sinew, and the most indefatigable hunter and trapper in the world. He has no glory except in the woods, and his whole ambition is to kill more deer and catch more beaver than any other man about him. Nothing tires him, not even running all day with six traps on his back. His horse fell once, as he was galloping along the edge of a steep hill, and rolled down the hill with him, while his feet were entangled in the stirrups, and his traps dashing against him at every turn. He was picked up half dead, by his companion, and set upon his horse, and after all he outwitted him, and obtained the best set for his traps. Neither is he a fool. He is a shrewd, acute, original man, and far from illiterate. He was once a preacher, and afterwards an interpreter in the Osage nation.[4]

There was Tom Banks, the Virginian, with his Irish tongue, and long stories about Saltee, as he called Saltillo, and the three tribes of Indians, the Teuacauls, Wequas, and Toyahs, whose names were never out of his boasting mouth.[5] He claimed to have been prisoner among the Comanches three months; but he lied, for he could not utter a word of their language.

There were various others, better at boasting than at fighting; and a few upon whom a man might depend in an emergency.

We left the valley of the Picuris on the sixth of September, taking the pass which, following the river up, led out to the large valley of the Demora,[6] at which we arrived on the same day, and encamped near the Old Village—in it, in fact. These New Mexicans, with a pertinacity worthy of the Yankee nation, have pushed out into every little valley which would raise half a bushel of red pepper—some of them like this—on the eastern side of the mountains, thus exposing themselves to the Pawnees and Comanches, who, of course, use them roughly. The former tribe broke up the settlement in this valley about fifteen years ago, and the experiment has never been repeated,[7] though this valley, and that of the Gallinas, are great temptations to the Spaniards. The sole inhabitants of the Old Village now, are rattlesnakes, of which we killed some two or three dozen about the old mud houses. The third day brought us, by a roundabout course, to the junction of the creeks Demora and Sepellote, about fifty miles from San Miguel, and on the Missouri wagon road. Buffalo are frequently found in the winter not far from

4. Pike provides us with the best contemporary description of the well-known Old Bill Williams. A full-length biography is Alpheus H. Favour, *Old Bill Williams, Mountain Man* (Norman, 1962). Pike further describes Williams in "Tales of Character and Country, No. X," which appears in the Appendix of this volume.

5. I have been unable to identify these tribes which were apparently in the Saltillo area.

6. Pike's party traveled up the Río Pueblo, probably crossing the mountains to Agua Fria Creek, then following Encino Creek to the Mora River, which runs east into the Canadian.

7. The village which Pike found abandoned had been settled about 1819 and was apparently on or near the site of present-day Mora. See Fray Angélico Chávez, "Early Settlement in the Mora Valley," *El Palacio*, 62, 11 (November, 1955), 318-319.

here, namely, at the springs called 'Los Ojos de Santa Clara,'—
'The Eyes of Saint Clara,' distant a day's journey beyond. While
at the Old Village, the night before, a consultation had been
held, to determine what course we should pursue. Lewis advised
to cross to the main fork of the Canadian branch of the Arkansas, or, as it is commonly called, Little Red River, and then
following his trail, to go on to the Washita, trap it, and then to
the heads of Red River. But, acting under a wrong impression
and a radical mistake, this advice was rejected. It was supposed
by all of us, that Red River and all its main branches headed
into the mountains,[8] and that it was only necessary to keep under the mountains, and we should necessarily find beaver. It
was determined, then, to obtain an old Comanche, who had
been converted, and was married in San Miguel, as our guide,
and to go directly to the rivers which we supposed lay not far
to the south-east of us, and contained beaver. Accordingly, on
arriving, the next day, at the wagon road, it was agreed that the
party should go down the Gallinas a day or two, and cross over
to the Pecos, where I was to find them. For at that time we supposed that the Gallinas creek ran into Red River, while, on the
contrary, it runs into the Pecos. While they, therefore, followed
the course of the Gallinas, I, in company with three of our Mexicans, went into San Miguel to bring out the Comanche.[9]

The country is a rolling prairie for a part of the way between
the Demora and San Miguel. About noon we reached the Gallinas, where we rested and fed our mules. We then struck into
the hills, crossed the little creek called the Tecolote, (Owl) and
slept at night at the Ojo de Bernal, within seven miles of San
Miguel, where we arrived the next morning. That day and the
next we spent there, waiting the return of a messenger from
Taos, and purchasing a horse; and on the third day, late in the
morning, we left again the village of Saint Michael. Various
prophecies were uttered, all boding ill to us. The Comanches

8. This was a common mistake in Pike's day—one which Zebulon Montgom-
ery Pike had made over two decades earlier. By the time that Albert Pike reached
Arkansas, however, he had a good idea of the location of the headwaters of the
Red River. See note 6 of the first "Narrative."

9. Pike here took the Santa Fe Trail from Watrous to San Miguel del Vado,
roughly following the course of present-day United States highway 85.

were described as *diablos* and *infieles,* and the women in particular seemed to take a great interest in our well-being. In fact,
while we were at the Old Village of the Demora, there came
in some dozen Mexicans who had gone from Taos to Red
River, having hard bread and other 'notions,' to trade with the
Comanches. The Indians wisely concluded that it was better
to get it all for nothing, than to give in return their buffalo
robes and horses; and they accordingly took violent possession
of the mules and horses of the luckless pedlers, drove them off,
and kept their hard bread in spite of their bows and arrows.
Besides this, a new story had come in, that a man had been shot
by the Caiawas, about four days' journey out of San Miguel,
and found by some of the Puebis [Pueblos]. Accompanied by
many good wishes, prayers and benedictions, however, we left
the village on the twelfth, and reached that night a little village
below, on the Pecos, (whose course we followed) where we
slept. The next morning we bought a sheep, and started again.
At noon we heard that our party was about fifteen miles distant,
down the river. We were then at the last settlement, about forty
miles from San Miguel.[10] Beyond, there are some deserted
ranchos, as they are called—that is, sheep-pens and shepherd huts.
At night we reached the party, and right glad was I to be delivered from the peril of riding about in a dangerous country,
accompanied only by four Mexicans (for an old man who had
been sent from Taos to bear a letter to the Comanche went out
with us) and an old faithless Indian, of a tribe to which a white
man is like a smoke in the nostrils. A lone American has no
mercy from them, and little aid from the Mexicans who may
chance to be with him. Not long ago one Frenchman went out
from Taos in company with a hundred and fifty Mexicans, and
was by them given up to half their number of Comanches, to
be murdered. It was even said that the Spaniards danced round
his scalp in company with the Indians. One of these fellows
was with me, and another one was with the party. I knew it not
at the time, or the Señor Manuel Leal[11] should not have ac-

10. No permanent settlements are known to have existed this far down the
Pecos at this time. Perhaps Pike saw some temporary shepherd's structures.
11. Manuel Leal seems to have made a habit of accompanying American
trapping parties. That very summer, however, Leal had returned from a trap-

companied me. The Comanches have killed several of our countrymen when alone. Mr. Smith was out hunting antelope, when a body of them came upon him; he killed one woman and two men before they despatched him. They have his scalp now, and sold his saddle, gun, pistols, & c. to the Spaniards.[12] They killed another man the year before in the same way— blowing off half his head with a fusee. This winter, two hundred and fifty of them attacked a party of twelve men on the Canadian, killed two and wounded several of them.[13] Nor, though at peace with the Spaniards, do they serve them any better. On the fifth of July last, (1832) they killed the nephew of the Commandant Viscara, while out alone and unarmed, with the oxen of his uncle, about three miles from Little Red River, and with thirty or forty troops in sight. They gave him thirteen wounds, took off all his hair except the foretop, and still left him alive.

When Mr. Flint, in his Francis Berrian, described these Indians as noble, brave, and generous, he was immensely out in the matter. They are mean, cowardly, and treacherous. Neither (since I am correcting a gentleman for whom I have a great regard) is there any village of the Comanches on the Heads of the Arkansas.[14] Neither is the Governor's palace, in Santa Fe anything more than a mud building, fifteen feet high, with a mud-covered portico, supported by rough pine pillars. The gardens, and fountains, and grand stair-cases, &c., are, of course, wanting.

---

ping expedition to California (that of Ewing Young), and informed New Mexico officials that his new boss, David Jackson, was carrying contraband beaver fur. Testimony relating to the embargo of the furs of Ewing Young, Santa Fe, July 12-July 25, 1832, Mexican Archives of New Mexico, State Records Center, Santa Fe, New Mexico.

12. Pike here refers to the Comanche murder of the famous explorer, Jedediah Smith, on the Santa Fe Trail in late May of 1831. An account of this appears in Dale L. Morgan, *Jedediah Smith and the Opening of the West* (New York, 1953), pp. 329-330.

13. Pike provides more details in the final paragraph of this Narrative.

14. The Caiawas live not far from the heads of the Arkansas, but they are as far from being brave, faithful, &c. as the Comanches. Bill Williams says that no man on earth can learn to talk their language. He says that it is all like dropping stones in the water; punk! punk! punk! The Comanche tongue is easy to learn.—PIKE.

Pike is criticizing Timothy Flint's novel, *Francis Berrian, or the Mexican Patriot* (1826). Flint had never been to the southern Rockies or to New Mexico where the early part of his novel takes place.

The Governor may raise some red pepper in his garden, but he gets his water from the public spring. But to return.

The next day after my arrival, we kept on down the Pecos, agreeably to the direction of our guide, intending to follow the river as far as the Bosque Redondo, or Round Grove. This river Pecos, which derives its name from the Pecos tribe of Indians, rises in the same lake with the river of Santa Fe,[15] and, passing by San Miguel, keeps a south-easterly course. At a distance of about one hundred and twenty miles from San Miguel, it being there a deep stream about thirty yards wide, it bends to the south, and runs into a deep, narrow, and rocky cañon, in which it cannot be followed. I know not how far it goes in this cañon, but emerging from it below, it keeps on its course southwardly, and runs into the Del Norte near San Antonio.[16] It is a long but narrow river, and however important it may be to the people of San Miguel, it is of no great consequence in any other way.

On the fifteenth, we started, all together, down the Pecos; but early in the morning a dispute arose between Harris and Campbell, which ended in a separation. Harris was now for going on to Little Red River [the Canadian], through a dry prairie. We were for following our guide and the Pecos. We turned down to the river, and Harris kept on ahead, but soon followed our example by taking to the river. Campbell and myself were delayed, recovering a mule which had joined to those of Harris, and in the mean time our party encamped on the river. Harris went into the cañon of the river, and followed it down, and the next morning we turned to the hills above the cañon, and came upon the river below, leaving him struggling in it among the rocks. He was obliged at last, finding egress below impossible, to ascend the precipitous sides of the cañon and come out upon the hills. After this we never encamped together until we reached the Bosque Redondo, the point where we were to leave the river and strike into the prairie. We

15. Although their headwaters are close, these rivers do not begin at a common source. Josiah Gregg, it is interesting to note, repeated the same story in his *Commerce of the Prairies* (Norman, 1954), p. 101.

16. The distance is about one hundred and fifty miles.

were six days in reaching the Bosque, including the fifteenth, and during the time we traveled in a south-east direction. The country along the river was hilly, red, and barren, devoid of timber, except on the river. At the Bosque we encamped near some lodges of poles, the remains of an old Comanche camp, and Harris encamped half a mile or more above us.

The Spaniards who composed our party were now getting frightened. We had already had two alarms of Indians, which, although unfounded, still tended to dispirit the cowardly pelayos;[17] and, added to this, the name of the Llano Estacado, on whose borders we then were encamped, and which lay before us like a boundless ocean, was mentioned with a sort of terror, which showed that it was by them regarded as a place from which we could not escape alive. This Stake Prairie[18] is to the Comanche what the desert of Sahara is to the Bedouin. Extending from the Bosque Redondo on the west, some twenty days' journey on the east, northward to an unknown distance, and southward to the mountains on the Rio del Norte, with no game but here and there a solitary antelope, with no water except in here and there a hole, and with its whole surface hard, barren and dry, and with the appearance always of having been scorched by fire. The Comanche only can live in it. Some three or four human skulls greeted us on our passage through it; and it is said that every year some luckless Spaniard leaves one of these mementos lying in the desert. It is a place in which none can pursue. The Comanches, mounted on the best steeds which the immense herds of the prairie can supply, and knowing the solitary holes of water, can easily elude pursuit.

Just before encamping at the Bosque Redondo,[19] some of our Spaniards were met by a party of their countrymen, who had just returned from the Cañon del Resgate,[20] in the Stake

17. I have been unable to identify this word. Perhaps Pike meant *pellejos*, meaning *fools*.

18. The Llano Estacado was more commonly translated by Americans as the "Staked Plains." There is considerable disagreement over the meaning of the name of this prominent West Texas high plateau—see H. Bailey Carroll in the *Handbook of Texas* (2 vols. Austin, 1952), II, 69-70.

19. Near the later site of Fort Sumner (1851), Bosque Redondo achieved notoriety during the Civil War when Apaches and Navahos were relocated there.

20. This canyon of barter has been identified by David Donoghue, "Explora-

Prairie. They had been there to trade hard bread, blankets, punche, beads, &c., for buffalo robes, bear skins, and horses, and were returning with the avails of their traffic.

After night, Campbell and myself were called upon to attend a council of the Spaniards of our party. We accordingly went, and found Manuel, the Comanche,[21] acting as chief counsellor in the matter, and Manuel Leal and another of the fraternity officiating as spokesmen. They informed us that the traders had brought bad reports from the Comanches: that they and the hostile Caiawas were gathered in great strength in the Cañon del Resgate; that they had defeated the American wagons, taking fifteen hundred mules and one scalp, and lost several men in the contest; that they were much excited against the Americans, and had determined that none of us should trap in their country; and that they had sent word to Manuel, the Comanche, that if he entered their country guiding us, they would sacrifice both us and him. They likewise told us that there were no buffalo in the prairie; and though all the rest was a lie, this was indeed the truth. Manuel, the Comanche, then declared that he would not enter the Stake Prairie, if one American remained in the company, and all the Spaniards seconded him. Finding thus that they would not fight for and with us, that they would leave us to the mercy of the Comanches, or perhaps give us into their hands, it was determined to leave them on the next morning; and thus went my last good opinion of New Mexican char-

tions of Albert Pike in Texas," *Southwestern Historical Quarterly,* XXXIX, 2 (October, 1935), 136, as Blackwater Draw. I have relied heavily on this article in tracing Pike's route through Texas. Donoghue, however, failed to realize that Blackwater Draw is the name applied to the headwaters of the Double Mountain Fork of the Brazos and confused Yellow House Creek with the Double Mountain Fork to the east of Lubbock. Despite this confusion in names, Donoghue traces Pike's route most admirably. As Pike later points out, his route from the Bosque Redondo followed a *Comanchero* (Mexican traders who dealt with the Comanches) trail. It also followed a Comanche road—see the *Handbook of Texas,* I, 386.

21. Manuel may be the "old Comanche" whom Pike secured at San Miguel to guide his party. If so, he was not too old, for in 1840 "*Manuel el Comanche*" of San Miguel guided Josiah Gregg across the plains (Gregg, *Commerce of the Prairies,* p. 316, n. 1), and in 1849 Randolph B. Marcy found Manuel's services valuable on his return from Santa Fe through Texas. W. Eugene Hollon, *Beyond the Cross Timbers: The Travels of Randolph B. Marcy, 1812-1887* (Norman, 1955), p. 76.

acter. I had tried these men for the last; had put confidence in
them; and knew that if they were not worthy of it, there were
none in the country who were; and I found this last, best specimen of character, as mean, as treacherous, as cowardly, as any
other portion of the people of the province. A man does not
like to be made a fool of, and I felt ashamed of myself for ever
thinking again (after repeated proofs to the contrary) that any
New Mexican could be a man. I think I never felt so badly as
I did the next morning, when I stood a four hours' guard, in
company with four Mexicans, and in a camp of them where I
knew that not one would fight for me.

The next morning I went to the camp of Harris, and joined
his party. R—— and Pierre accompanied me, and Campbell returned to Taos. That day we lay by, and the next we entered
the Stake Prairie. I think it was the twenty-first of September
that we left the Pecos, leaving the party of Campbell waiting
for oxen on which to subsist. The Bosque Redondo is about one
hundred and twenty miles from San Miguel, or perhaps it may
be nearer one hundred and fifty. As I kept no journal, and am
writing merely from memory, I cannot certainly say; but I am
not far from the true distance.[22]

We entered the Llano Estacado by the road of the Comanches
and Comanche traders. We had been given to understand that
in the course of fourteen days we should arrive at a descent, or
falling off of the prairie to the east, and that there (rising out
of this ceja, or eye-brow, as they called it) we should find the
rivers Azul, (which we took to be Red River), San Saba, Javalines, Las Auces, and one other, whose name I have forgotten.
We had with us one man who had trapped on some of these
rivers, and who said that there was beaver on them. We never
were on the Rio Azul, to my knowledge, but I am inclined to
think that it is the main branch of the Colorado; the San Saba
is a southern branch of it, the Mochico is another, north of the
San Saba, and Javalines and Las Cruces are branches of the
San Saba. They all head near the same degree of longitude.[23]

22. Following the course of the river, Pike has made a good estimate.
23. With the exception of the San Saba, an affluent of the Colorado, I have
been unable to identify these streams on contemporary maps. The Río Azul,
which Pike mentions further on, may be the upper Colorado of Texas.

Oct. [Sept.] 21.—We left the Pecos, taking a course to the northward, in search of the road which was to lead us to the Cañon del Resgate. Our route lay, for about ten miles, across an uneven, dry, barren plain towards the edge of the Stake Prairie, which seemed like a low ridge before us. Reaching this about noon, we discovered that two of our Mexicans were missing, intending, as we supposed, to join the party of Campbell, through fear of entering the desert. Two or three of the party went back, accordingly, and brought them up. We then proceeded three or four miles, passing, on our way, a good sweet spring of water, where we first came into the road; and following up the branch which ran down by this spring, we encamped in a grassy meadow to the east of the stream. This day Bill Williams killed an antelope, which was divided among the whole party of forty-five men. Here we saw plenty of sign of wild horses.

22.—Left camp early, and followed the road, which now took a south-easterly direction. The day was exceedingly hot, and we were frequently tantalized by seeing at a distance ponds which appeared to be full of clear rippling water. The deception would continue until we were within a dozen rods of the place, and it would then be found to consist of merely a hollow, encrushed over with salt. About noon, thirst becoming excessive, two or three of us rode ahead. The prairie was still uneven and rugged. We passed through a body of sand-hills, and then descending from them, came upon a hollow where the earth appeared damp, and there were two or three old holes which had been dug either by the traders or by the Comanches. We here stopped and dug for water, obtaining enough to satiate our thirst. It was warm, but fresh. The eagerness with which our men drank, as they came up one by one, and threw themselves upon the ground, was amusing. Some of the party were for encamping here, but we overruled them, and went on. After traveling four or five miles, we came upon a large lake, and turning to the right of it, we found a spring by which we encamped. No antelope was killed to-day. Some of the party tried to kill cranes, and Bill Williams succeeded towards night in bringing one to camp. This day we saw two skulls bleaching in the sun. Traveled this day about eighteen miles.

23.—Started early again, and hunted the road an hour or two; in the mean time crossed a piece of marshy ground. Some of us here went ahead to hunt; killed nothing. Towards night we thought we saw buffalo at a distance upon a ridge; we went to it accordingly, but found it to be only weeds looming up in the distance; turned down to a piece of low ground, where there was water in holes, and encamped; found here the remains of a defeated party of Spaniards—old blankets, saddles, &c. Here, finding ourselves in danger of starving, Harris killed an old mare, in which our mess refused to be partakers. We had determined to starve two days longer before eating any of it. This day we traveled on the road about twelve miles. This road was now broad and plain, consisting of fourteen or fifteen horse trails side by side; its course still south-east.

24.—Early this morning Bill Williams killed an antelope, which was divided among the whole party. After eating, we started again, still keeping the road, still very hot, and no water on the road. Stopped at noon on a hill, and lay in the sun; saw horse tracks here. About the middle of the afternoon we reach-ed a low place fed by a spring which came out under limestone rocks; this was very good water. Here were plenty of old Coman-che lodge poles, sites of lodges, half burnt sticks, &c., and piles of buffalo bones. Wherever the Comanches kill buffalo they make piles of bones, for the purpose of appeasing the offended animals, and have ceremonies performed over them by their medicine men; and no matter how poor a fire they have, or how wet and cold it may be, they will not burn a bone, alleging that it would make them unlucky in hunting. A son of Harris[24] killed an antelope here, and our mess still ate no horse meat. We traveled this day about twelve miles, and still toward the southeast, following the road.

25.—Six of us, this morning, kept to the right of the party, for the purpose of hunting. About noon we reached a hole of water, at which we found the track of a buffalo bull. We sepa-rated, accordingly, three to the sand-hills on the left, and the others of us to those which lay to the right, along on the edge of a large dry salt lake. The idea of getting buffalo inspired us,

24. Probably Robert Harris—see note 1 of this Narrative.

and we pushed on cheerily with our jaded animals, now weary with running antelope. After traveling among the hills to the distance of a mile and a half from the place where we separated, we saw five bulls below us in a wide hollow, lying down. One of us went back then to the party, to bring more men and better horses, with which to run the buffalo, and in the mean time my companion and myself dismounted, and lay awaiting his return. In the course of an hour we were joined by some thirteen, including the three from whom we had separated. We approached warily to within a hundred yards of the animals, and then rushed upon them; and had I been mounted on anything but a slow mule, the chase would have been exciting. As it was, I was soon distanced; for though a buffalo appears, both standing and running, to be the most unwieldy thing in the world, I can assure my readers that they get along with no inconsiderable degree of velocity; and, strange as it may seem, no matter how old and lean a buffalo may be, no matter if he cannot run ten steps after he is up, still you can never see more than one motion when he rises; he is up and running in an instant. Shot after shot and shout after shout told the zeal of the hunters, and in a short time one buffalo fell about three miles from me. Thither I went, and while the hunters were busy cutting up the animal, Lewis and myself went in pursuit of another, which was wounded. Our expedition was unsuccessful; we accordingly followed the party, now in motion, and after traveling about eight miles through a dry plain, covered with scrub oak bushes, very small, we encamped at a spring near the road, and in the course of two hours the other hunters came in, having killed two more buffalo. Here was nothing to burn, not even the ordure of horses, which had hitherto never failed us; we could only make a blaze of tall weeds, and throw in our meat. I can conceive of nothing so disgusting. Lean, tough and dry, blackened with the brief blaze, impregnated with the strong filthy smoke of the weeds—and only half cooked—it required the utmost influence of that stern dictator, hunger, to induce us to eat it. The reader is not to imagine that the meat of the buffalo is all good. Oh no! The meat of the cow is, of a certainty, superior to any meat on earth; but even horse-meat is better than the flesh of a lean old bull. To add to our comforts, the ground here was covered with sand-burs which easily pierced through our thin moccasins, and kept us continually employed in picking them out of our feet. Traveled to-day about eighteen miles.

26.—This day I mounted my horse, determining not to be left behind again in a chase. Very windy. I have forgotten this day's journey entirely. We traveled, however, nearly all day, and must have made fifteen miles in a south-east direction.

27.—This day the road turned first north, and then nearly north-west, leading through a deep soft sand. About the middle of the afternoon, we came in sight of trees. These were the first we had seen since leaving the Pecos, and they were merrily hailed by all the party, as though they had been old friends. There is nothing adds so much to the loneliness of the prairie as the want of timber. Bill Williams, a Frenchman by the name of Gerand, and myself, were now ahead, pushing on to reach water and timber, for we were both tired and hungry. It was likewise very cold and windy, and the sand was continually blowing in our eyes. We had entirely lost the road, and when we at length ascended the highest sand-hill near us and saw an uneven plain extending in front of us, we found that we were not yet near the water. Antonio, our guide, indicated a place where he said he had once encamped, and where there was water, and while looking towards it, we thought we saw buffalo in the distance. We accordingly pushed on, leaving Antonio to wait for the pack mules, hoping ourselves to kill a cow before night. Arriving within half a mile of them, we found that they were horses, and at the same time that we were close upon a camp of the Comanches, around which the horses were feeding. We stood looking at the lodges until we were joined by half a dozen more of the party, who informed us that a young squaw was with the party. We all then returned to meet the pack mules; and to take measures for any emergency. On arriving at the party, Bill Williams insisted on shooting the woman who was riding towards the camp leading a horse packed with wood. Bill was actually senseless with fear, or he would not have done it. He drew his pistol, and was only deterred from shooting her by a threat of instant death if he did so. I do not think that we would have shot him for her; but he supposed that we would do it, and it answered our purpose. The girl went on, and we held a consultation upon the course to be pursued. Bill declared that he would sooner sleep three nights without water, than go to the village, and the silence of several others gave assent to what he said. But the rest of us overruled him, and we determined on proceeding and encamping at the water. Our Spaniards commenced firing off and reloading their guns; and in the mean time the Comanches began to come out, mounted, towards us. Three of them, including an old chief, first met us. We directed our interpreter to ask them if they were friends? They answered that they were—that they had shaken hands with the Americans, and were friends. Bill was again protesting that he would kill the chief, but was again hindered by the same significant threat as before. As they now began to come in greater force from the village, we directed the chief to order them to keep their distance, and we moved forward, agreeably to the request of the chief, who wished us to encamp near the village. Notwithstanding our former order, the Indians pressed upon us, all armed with spears and bows; and seeing that Antonio hestitated, through fear, to interpret for us, I directed the chief in Spanish (at which I was the only linguist) to send back his men, or we would fire upon them. This threat produced the desired effect, and we were molested no more until we reached the place for encamping, upon the edge of a marshy spot of ground, with here and there a hole of water. Just above us was the village, consisting of about twenty lodges, together with some additional minor edifices. A good Caiawa, or Comanche lodge, is about fifteen feet high, made with six or eight poles, and in the form of a cone, covered with dressed buffalo hides, which, when new, are perfectly white, but grow brown and smoky with age. Inasmuch as these Comanches are wandering Indians, and as it is seldom that they find themselves in a place where they can obtain lodge-poles, they are obliged to carry them wherever they go. Thus you may know their trail by the marks which the poles make as they are dragged along, suspended on each side of their horses. They likewise carry an abundance of stakes for securing their horses.

The Comanches are a nation entirely distinct from the Pawnees, with whom they are often confounded, because a part of
the western desert is common ranging ground for both nations.
Generally speaking, westwardly from the degree of longitude,
distant four hundred miles from the border of Arkansas Territory, and extending to the Rocky Mountains, and bounded on
the north by the upper branches of the Arkansas, and on the
south by the Rio del Norte, is the country of the Comanches.
Still, as I have mentioned before, the Pawnees do rob and murder along the mountains to a considerable distance south; and,
as well as the Caiawas and Arapehoes, are to be found on the
main Canadian, and to the south of it.

The Comanches are a part of the Snake or Shoshone nation,
and speak nearly the same language. They have no settled place
of abode, and no stationary villages. They follow the buffalo,
and are most commonly to be found, in the winter, along the
Pecos and del Norte; and in the summer, on the Canadian and
the Semaron; but even to this, there are exceptions. This last
winter, they were upon the Canadian, as they were likewise in
July, 1832. In the winter of 1831-2, they were not on that river
at all, but were gathered in numbers along the del Norte below
the Pass. As to their number of warriors, I doubt if any one
knows much about it. The country through which they range
is so large, and they are so liable to be confounded with other
tribes, that we are not likely to have any certain idea of their
numbers. I have heard the whole nation estimated at 10,000
warriors; but I am mistaken if they have more than five thousand. As we knew that the part of the Comanches living to the
south along the Presidio del Norte, and bordering on the Indians
of Texas, were, for all our purposes, entirely distinct from
the northern Comanches, we took great pains to find out to
which our present acquaintances belonged.[25] We knew that those

25. Pike's distinction between the northern and southern Comanches was
very perceptive for his time. Upon arrival at Arkansas he penned a letter, March
16, 1833, to Secretary of War, Lewis Cass (copy in the Chouteau Collections,
Missouri Historical Society, St. Louis, Missouri) suggesting that Aaron Lewis and
himself guide a treaty-making party to the Comanches. Pike criticized Sam Hous-
ton for trying to treat with the southern Comanches whom Pike maintained were
already friendly toward Americans. In this letter Pike estimated that there were
eight thousand Comanches. This agrees with current estimates. For a discussion

in the south were more friendly to the Americans, and less treacherous, than those in the north, who, although speaking a different language from the Caiawas, are still always allied with them, and are, like them, the deadly enemies of the Americans. They uniformly asserted that they were from the del Norte, and were friendly. In corroboration of this, they had a few red and green American blankets, which we thought they must have obtained from San Antonio in Texas. They might, however, have obtained them of the Snakes, as they do their guns; while the Snakes are supplied by the trappers and traders. Seeing but few warriors about, we inquired where they all were? They answered, 'To the north, hunting:' and this induced us to believe only that they were with the Caiawas on the track of the returning wagons. The old chief told us, too, that when he was in Santa Fe just before, he went thither for the purpose of making peace with the Americans there as he had done in San Antonio. If he was in Santa Fe, he and his party were the Indians who killed the nephew of Viscara. On the whole, we concluded to believe them to be hostile and northern Comanches, whom fear, and not their own good will, forced to keep peace with us. Soon after our arrival, the few young men who were in the village, mounted and went off in different directions, as the chief said, for the purpose of hunting—but, as we believed, to give intelligence to the other villages, and to the scattered warriors—and none were left in the village, except the old men, women and children. The people of this village appeared to be extremely poor. They had no blankets—no buffalo robes—no meat—and were dressed shabbily, and without any of that gaudiness which some Indians exhibit. A dirty and ragged dress of leather, and part of a ragged blanket, was the common apparel. They are, in fact, a very common-looking Indian, much inferior in person to the Osages, the Shawnees, the Delawares, or any of the Mexican tribes, except the Apaches.

---

of the various Comanche tribes and their total number see Rupert Norval Richardson, *The Comanche Barrier to South Plains Settlement* (Glendale, 1933), pp. 15-24. The Comanche villages which Pike encountered as he traveled down the Double Mountain Fork of the Brazos were, Pike told Cass, of northern Comanches who inhabit the "Valley of Traffic" from July through September, "while they are out hunting buffalo to the north."

I saw none of them possessing that acute and at the same time dignified look common to the Aboriginal. They are of middle height, and like all Indians, have good limbs, and long black hair, which they leave uncut. Some of them had their hair joined behind to buffalo or horse hair, and a rope of the latter depending from it, which nearly reached the ground. The old women, particularly, were hideously ugly. I imagine that there is no being on earth who would be as valuable to a painter desirous of sketching his satanic majesty, as an old Comanche woman. They reminded me strongly of Arab women, whom I have seen painted out in divers veritable books of travels. The same high cheek-bones—long black hair—brown, smoked, parchment-like skin—bleared eyes, and fiendish look—belong to the women of both nations. While looking at them, I could hardly help shuddering, as the thought would strike me, that possibly they might, ere long, have the opportunity of exercising the infernal ingenuity of their nature upon me. Several of us went to their village, distant from us perhaps three hundred yards, and bought wood and a little dried buffalo meat of them, with tobacco and vermillion. The young man, in particular, who was the only intelligent-looking Indian among them, took especial pains to obtain me some meat, and likewise offered me a good horse for red cloth enough to make me a pair of leggings. I had no such article, however. Horses are their only riches. There were about a thousand of them round this village, and a few mules. I particularly observed one mule in the mark of Agustin Duran, custom-house officer at Santa Fe.[26] In the evening, the same young fellow came down and invited Harris and his clerk, Bill Williams and myself, to go up and eat with him. Taking our guns, we went accordingly. We found the old chief and his family outside of the lodge, seated round a fire, over which a small brass kettle was hanging. On our arrival, we were motioned to our seats with true Indian gravity, and something of respect. The contents of the brass kettle were then emptied into a wooden bowl, and placed before us. It was the boiled flesh of a fat buffalo cow, perfectly fresh, having been killed that day

26. Pike's memory for names is astounding. Agustín Durán was in charge of the custom house at Santa Fe for many years.

—and a most delicious meal it was to us. Kettle after kettle was filled and emptied, between us and the family of the chief; for it takes but five minutes to boil this meat. A man never knows how much meat he can eat, until he has tried the prairie; but I assure the reader that four pounds at a meal is no great allowance, especially to a hungry man. On ending the supper, we paid them with tobacco and a knife or two, and returned to our camp—not, however, without that indispensable ceremony, a general smoke, in which my pipe went once or twice round the whole party, women and all. The next morning, the chief wished us to lay by a day or two, and hunt buffalo. He assured us that there was an abundance of buffalo cows on a lake about nine miles to the north-east, and that his young men should accompany our hunters thither. We declined remaining, chiefly through apprehension of treachery. Finding that we would not remain, he promised us that at the next village his son and daughter in law should join us and conduct us to the beaver. He said that we should find beaver in nine days.

28.—Gathered up our horses and left the camp of the Comanches, directing our course nearly due east, and following the trail by which the chief and his party had come a day or two before. Our route at first, lay through sand-hills, just before emerging from which, we found two or three hackberry trees, and several of us delayed, picking the berries. From the sandhills we now came again upon the prairie, and found much difficulty in tracking the marks of the lodge-poles along its hard surface—and in addition it began to rain. Just at night, we followed the path into a break in the prairie, which opened into a long hollow, in which we encamped by the side of a pond, which is the head of one of the chief branches of the Colorado or the Brazos de Dios river.

Lest I may be misunderstood, I will explain why I use both these names in speaking of this river. The reader, by consulting the map, will find two rivers running through Texas, of which the longer one is called (in most maps, if not in all) the Colorado. But I have been informed, that not long since the names were changed, and that the long river is now called the Brazos. The reason given me for the change, is this:—Some years ago there was a drought in Texas; the short river (Brazos) became dry, and the only water came down in the long river (or the Colorado). The pious Spaniards accordingly changed names, and called the long river the Brazos de Dios, (or the Arms of God), on account of the especial care which it took of them, and of the benefits which they received from it.[27] We were now in the Cañon de Resgate, and supposed ourselves to be on the heads of Red River,[28] but we began to question the probability of finding the immense quantities of beaver which we had anticipated. Still, however, we had abundance of hope, though it was at times mingled with a little distrust. Our beef, too, was nearly gone, but Bill Williams, fortunately, killed an antelope, which was divided as usual. Ducks were abundant in this pond, and one or two were killed. Yesterday we traveled about twenty miles north-east, and to-day twenty more, a little south of east, making in both days about forty miles.

29.—This day we followed the valley down for some distance. There was the bed of a stream, but water was not running. Here and there it stood in ponds and holes. The day was cold and windy, with a little rain. We then went out of the valley to the left, and traveled in the prairie, for the cañon was merely a break in the plain, of the width of two or three hundred yards, and as soon as you ascended the low sides of it, you were again on the illimitable plain; and, like a well in the desert, the valley cannot be seen until you are close upon it. About the middle of the afternoon we saw in the valley another encampment, and descended to it, for the purpose of procuring wood and water. On our approach, the women mounted their horses and took to the hills. A boy, whom they had taken prisoner from the Mexicans, came out and talked with us, and we sent him to assure the fugitives of our friendship. They soon returned, and as it was raining hard, we commenced trading for wood, and with difficulty bought enough to make fires. Bill Williams

27. The names of these streams were changed, but not as recently as Pike implies. The *Handbook of Texas*, I, 379, concludes that "the present names . . . were well established before the end of the Spanish period." The reason that Pike has given for the change is of interest, but may not have any validity.

28. Pike was on Blackwater Draw, the headwaters of the Double Mountain Fork of the Brazos River—see note 20.

then went over and obtained part of a lodge cover, and two of the ugliest old women I ever saw brought the lodge poles and put it up for him. One of our party was lame with the rheumatism, and we managed to keep him out of the rain in the lodge. We bought some more dried meat, some dried grapes and acorns, paying tobacco, as usual. The rain poured upon us all night, and almost every gun in camp was wet. We traveled this day about fifteen miles in a south-east direction.

30.—Left the valley and traveled in the prairie to the right of it. Late in the afternoon we turned down to timber, and found no water in the valley. Some of the party went to the distance of two miles above and below. Several of the party, among whom was myself, brought in terrapins [turtles] hanging to their saddles. Our meat was gone, and these animals cost no ammunition. Some, likewise, had killed prairie dogs. The little plot of hackberry and bitter cottonwood, where we encamped, appeared to have been a great haunt of the buzzards and crows, and just after sunset, the hawks began to gather in, and we commenced shooting them, and thus, by means of hard labor, managed to satiate our hunger. Hawks and prairie dogs do very well, but there is too little meat about a terrapin. Traveled eighteen miles to-day.

Oct. 1.—This day we again followed the road, which now kept down the valley, and after going about three miles we found rain-water standing in small holes. Soon after, we came to a miry branch, and gave our animals drink. Early in the day Bill killed an antelope, and about noon, as we ascended a hill upon the edge of a valley, (to the left of it), we saw two or three Indians on the other side in the prairie. Some of our party were behind. Bill gave the sign of Indians, by riding four or five times round in a circle of about ten feet in diameter; and when they rejoined us we all turned down to the valley again— still hunting terrapins—and at night we encamped on the creek at a large hole of water. Traveled this day about fifteen miles.

2.—About noon of to-day, reached the site of an old encamp-ment of the Indians; found some remnants of wood and a few acorns. We went, perhaps, a hundred yards beyond and en-camped at a clear pond of water. Towards night a Comanche came to us, armed with bow, arrows, spear and shield, the latter ornamented with feathers and red cloth. For his viaticum [provisions] he bore the mane-piece of a horse. He remained with us all night, and informed us that there was beaver below on the river; he said the water would run soon. Another antelope was killed this day. Traveled this day about twelve miles.

3.—Traveled for a time in the valley, and were rejoiced at finding the water begin to run; it was a shallow, clear stream of sweet water, about twenty yards wide, and we began to have hopes of beaver. About noon we ascended the hills to the right, (following the road,) and traveled in the prairie. We here found a few bushes of the mesquito [mesquite], the first we had seen. In the afternoon we saw below, in the valley, horses feeding, and we descended the hills with much difficulty into the cañon, and found another village. The valley was here wider, and was full of small hills interspersed with mesquito bushes, that is, a kind of prickly, green locust bush, which bears long narrow beans in bunches, of a very pleasant and sweet taste. In this village were about fifty lodges, much handsomer, too, than those in the other villages; and, as in the two former, there were multitudes of horses. I think that around the three camps there could not have been less than five thousand horses—and some of them most beautiful animals. Here, too, there was a medicine lodge of black skins, and closely shut up. We bought some meat and mesquito meal, made by grinding the beans between two stones. Here, also, there were no warriors. Several of the women had their legs cut and mangled by knives, as in the first village, where they had disturbed us all night by their lamentations. I know not how they had lost the men for whom they were mourning, but at the time I supposed that it had been done in the attack on the wagons. This day we traveled about sixteen miles, perhaps more.

4.—About two miles below the village we came to a large lake, and here Antonio wished us to leave this river and go to the south, until we struck the Mochico, crossing which, he assured us that in four or five days we would come upon the San Saba.[29] Harris, however, who seemed destined always to go

29. Perhaps this was the upper Colorado.

wrong, determined on following down the river on which we then were, and which he very wisely took to be the south fork of the Canadian.[30] We traveled this day about fifteen miles, and encamped on the creek. The water was still fresh and running. Course still south-east.

5.—This day we killed another antelope, and encamped early, upon the creek. While I was on the first guard, the hunters brought in a Comanche horse which they had found, blind of one eye. At their approach, almost every animal in company broke their ropes or drew their stakes. Had a yell been raised then, we should not have saved one animal. Traveled this day about ten miles.

6.—This day we passed an old camp of the Comanches, and followed their trail down the bed of the river, which here was dry. Encamped at night in a thicket of mesquito bushes, near a large pond of water, and where, for the first time, the river water was salt. It likewise began to wind around, keeping, however, its general course to the south-east. Traveled this day about fifteen miles.

7.—Started late, crossed the fork we had been so long traveling on, went over to the other, and encamped. These two forks are nearly of the same size.[31] In going from one to the other, we passed through a large level prairie, covered with tall mesquito bushes; and finding some very large, deep purple, prickly pears, Lewis and myself ate of them, and the consequence was, a terrible ague all night. The river bottom where we encamped was wide and grassy, and shaded with large cottonwood. Traveled this day near twenty miles, in a due south-east course. At night, killed the Comanche horse which had been brought in. Of this I partook, but just before dark two or three deer were killed close to camp. Encamped at the junction of the two forks.

8.—Lay by this day.

9.—Left early in the morning, crossed the river, and struck into the hills. The valley and the prairie had now disappeared,

30. Pike is here being sarcastic.
31. Pike apparently crossed over to the south fork of the Double Mountain Fork of the Brazos in the area of present-day Post, Texas. Donoghue, "Explorations of Albert Pike," p. 137.

and we were in a country of broken, red, barren hills and deep gullies, then dry, but which must, in the spring, carry the whole water of the prairie into the branches of the Brazos and Red River. Lewis, Irwin and myself lost the company. We were on the right of the river. After waiting for the party for some time, we turned down to the river, but found no trail. We then went into the hills again, and followed the river up, and met with Bill Williams and seven or eight others, all lost. We traveled up the river till night, and then encamped together. We had plenty of meat, however. The next morning we separated again from Bill, took to the hills on the right, and followed down the river, nearly to a high hill which we had seen the day before. Finding still no trail, and not imagining that the party had been farther from the river than we had, and had struck in again between us and the hill, we turned back and went up nearly to our old camp. Here we struck the trail and followed it till dark, and encamped within about four miles of the party, without water or food, having traveled that day nearly forty miles, through the worst country upon earth. We could hardly go five rods at a time without crossing a gully, and were often obliged to dismount, and sometimes we lost an hour in going up and down one of them, to find where to cross it. Just after dark we heard three guns fired in the direction of the river, and answered them by three more. This day we had seen a large signal-smoke rise to the right behind a mountain, and another still farther below answered it.

11.—Went down to the river and found the party, got break-fast, scolded awhile with Harris, and started. We still kept down the river—though not following all its windings—and encamped on the southern bank of it. Traveled this day, in a south-east direction, about eighteen miles.

12.—This day we crossed the river several times in the course of the forenoon; dug for water, which was, as usual, salt. About noon five of us left the party, turned into the hills on the north-east side of the river, and left this fork of the Brazos forever. Striking our course for a hill which we saw at a distance, we traveled about twelve miles after leaving the party, and en-camped by a hollow of water and among some mesquito bushes.

Traveled to-day in the whole, about twenty-two miles.

On reviewing our route thus far, it will appear that about two hundred and sixty miles to the south-east of San Miguel, or three hundred and ten from Santa Fe, is the head of the branch of the Brazos upon which we had been traveling; that, keeping down this river to the distance of seventy-eight miles, still south-east, and then striking a due south course from the pond below the last Comanche village, we should have reached the small creek Mochico in three days—that is, in the distance of forty miles; that, crossing this branch, which also runs a south-east course, we should have reached, in five days more, (seventy miles) the Rio Azul, a river of clear running water, running also to the south-east, and which is, without any doubt, the main branch of the Brazos; that, keeping down this six or eight days, we should have reached the point where the San Saba joins it, turning up which river we should have passed the mouths of three branches running into it. Thus much we were informed by Manuel, the Comanche, before we left him, and it was corroborated by Antonio. One hundred and forty-six miles below the head of the branch on which we traveled (on the Del Resgate) another fork came in from the north and joined it; and one hundred and eighty-four miles from the head of it, or four hundred and ninety-four miles, nearly, south-east of Santa Fe, we left the Del Resgate. It was here about fifty yards wide, containing water only here and there in holes.

The country upon which we entered after leaving the river, was hilly, red and barren, thinly covered with mesquito bushes, and in the hollows with hackberry trees. At almost every step you could see marks of water, although at this time it was perfectly dry and hard. These general marks of inundation, the numerous gullies at every step, and the rough, washen appearance of the red hills, all prove that, in the spring, the rush of water through this country must be tremendous, and travel, in any way, impossible. We supposed that we were about ten days' journey from the Cross Timbers, and on the waters of Red River. I had a horse, and each of my companions a mule, and although we were in the midst of enemies, we had little fear of not reaching the United States in safety. Besides Lewis and myself, our little party consisted of Irwin, Ish and Gillett. Irwin was an Englishman, who had just come by land from California —a brave, good-humored man, and not much afraid of anything save wild animals. Ish and Gillett were young men, from Missouri, who had been hired in Santa Fe by Harris. The latter was a mere boy, the former was much of a man, brave as a lion, active and industrious in the woods. Each man had a gun, and, with the exception of Irwin, a pistol or two. He, however, made up for this apparent deficiency, by bearing a double-barrelled English fowling-piece.[32] We had, likewise, a plenty of ammunition and Spanish blankets.

I cannot wonder that many men have chosen to pass their life in the woods, and I see nothing overdrawn or exaggerated in the character of Hawk-eye and Bushfield.[33] There is so much independence and self-dependence in the lonely hunter's life— so much freedom from law and restraint, from form and ceremony, that one who commences the life is almost certain to continue in it. With but few wants, and those easily supplied, man feels none of the enthralments which surround him when connected with society. His gun and his own industry supply him with fire, food and clothing. He eats his simple meal, and has no one to thank for it except his Maker. He travels where he pleases, and sleeps whenever he feels inclined. If there is danger about, it comes from enemies, and not from false friends; and when he enters a settlement, his former life in the woods renders it doubly tedious to him: he has forgotten the forms and ceremonies of the world; he has neglected his person, until neatness and scrupulous attention to the minutiae of appearance are wearisome to him; and he has contracted habits unfit for polished and well-bred society. Now, he cannot sit cross-legged upon a blanket; and instead of his common and

32. I have been unable to further identify any of these men. Irwin settled for awhile at Van Buren, Arkansas—Walter Lee Brown, "Albert Pike, 1809-1891," unpublished Ph. D. dissertation, University of Texas, 1955. Ish was not an uncommon name in Missouri (see for example, St. Louis *Missouri Gazette*, November 2, 1816, and the *Missouri Intelligencer*, August 7, 1829).

33. Hawk-eye is James Fenimore Cooper's noble frontiersman, Natty Bumppo, the hero of the *Leatherstocking Tales*. Pike had probably read *The Last of the Mohicans* (1826), and *The Prairie* (1827) in which the aged Hawk-eye journeyed to the Upper Missouri to flee civilization.

luxurious lounging position, he must be confined rigidly to a
chair. His pipe must be laid aside, and his simple dress is exchanged for the cumbersome and confined trappings of the
gentleman. In short, he is lost, and he betakes himself to the
woods again, for pure ennui; and the first night on which he
builds his fire, puts up his meat to roast, and lies down upon the
ground, with the open sky above him, and the cool, clear,
healthy wind fanning his cheek, seems to him like the beginning of a better and freer life.

13.—We started this morning early, and at noon we reached
another and still larger branch of the Brazos, running the same
course, (to the south-east).[34] We crossed it, and rested on the
north bank, near a large hole of water in the bed of the river,
but which was so immensely salt that our animals would not
drink it. I tasted some of it from the tip of my finger, and it is
no exaggeration when I say that it was as salt as the water of the
ocean. It was, in fact, perfect brine, of a deep dirty yellow color,
so strongly was it impregnated with salt. After stopping two
hours, we went down the river a short distance, among the
mesquito bushes, and Lewis shot a young doe, and Ish an old
buck. We cut up and packed the meat, crossed the river, and
kept on towards the south-east, which course we had pursued
all day. Just at night we came upon the river again, crossed it,
and encamped on the other side of it, in a small thicket of
bushes. This afternoon we had seen an abundance of horse
tracks, and marks of lodge-poles, and we concluded that there
must be a village of Comanches not far above where we were
encamped. Here we dug several holes in the bed of the river,
which was a hundred yards wide, and contained water in holes.
It was all alike salt, and we found it impossible to drink it.
We foolishly cooked part of our deer and ate it; and, more
foolishly still, some of us added salt, of which I had a little in
my pocket. At dusk we put out our fire, and would have slept
well, had we not dreamed of drinking huge draughts of water.
Once in the night I conceived myself lying flat by a river, with

34. This, as will become clear, was the Salt Fork of the Brazos, a name
which Pike and his party bestowed upon that stream. Donoghue, "Explorations
of Albert Pike," p. 136.

the water touching my lips, but entirely unable to get a drop of it into my mouth. Traveled east about eighteen miles.

14.—Left the river early, and bore to the north-east. About ten in the forenoon we came in sight of the river again to the right of us; descended into a deep narrow valley running into the river at right angles, and containing the bed of a little stream, which we followed up for two miles, partly searching for water, and partly because unable to cross it. Found no water; crossed it high up, and took our course again. About two in the afternoon, we came upon the river again, still to the right, and running a course parallel with us; bore down towards it, and came upon a deep, rocky hollow, running into it, and containing water in holes. Tormented with intense thirst, and with the heat of the day, we were rejoiced at finding water, and not more for ourselves than for our animals, who were trembling under us with weakness, and wearing that dim glassy look in their eyes which they always have when suffering from thirst. Drove them down the sides of the cañon, at the risk of their necks, and followed them. We found the water very salt, but still we could drink it. It seemed as if our animals would never become satiated with the water; they returned to it again and again, and stood pawing in it whenever they were allowed to get to it, until after dark. The quantities which we ourselves drank of it were immense. The large wooden Comanche bowl, which Irwin bore, and which held about a pint and a half, was but a single draught for either of us, and for half an hour it was hardly out of the hands of one of us before it was in those of another; and so salt was the water, that it had hardly passed down our throats before we were as thirsty as ever. Before we slept that night, I hesitate not to say, that we each drank three gallons of this water. After smoking, eating and drinking, we slept, only disturbed by the noise of a bear, who came tumbling down the side of the hollow, close to us. We traveled this day about twelve miles to the north-east.

15.—This morning we turned to the east and left this river, which we there named the Salt Fork of the Brazos, or in good Spanish, 'The Brazo Salado.' Part of the morning we traveled in a high prairie, or table land, and we then came to a place where this table sunk down abruptly into a lower country; here we descended into a long, narrow valley between the abrupt sides of the upper table land, which seemed, to look back upon them, to be mountains rising out of the plain. The country ahead, too, was very hilly and broken. About ten we arrived at a large clear limestone spring of water, where we stopped and drank plentifully; from this spring, a small stream of water ran down the valley, in a course nearly north-east. We followed the valley down, and crossed this hollow about forty times. The valley was full of horse-tracks and signs of Indians; and still, the temptation of a large catfish or two which we saw in the spring under the shelving rocks, was enough to induce us to fire a shot or two at them, which, however, was unsuccessful. About two miles below the spring, we encamped on the edge of the branch, in green, heavy grass, and close to an abundance of hackberry trees, with good fresh water. The valley was here running a course nearly north-east—and after dinner, we continued that course, until, weary of crossing the creek, we bent more to the east and left it to our left; crossed the point of a hill and left a high and conspicuous conical hill to the right, about six miles beyond which we emerged from the broken hills into the mesquito, covering the bottom on the edge of another river, about as wide as the Salt Fork, and of the same character.[35] Just on the descent to the river, was an old enclosure which had been built by the Comanches, of brush, and a circle surrounded with converging poles, which reminded me of the threshing floors of the New Mexicans. Passing through the mesquito, we reached the river, and found water, but salter, if possible, than the former. While we were sitting on our animals, watching them put their mouths to the water and refuse it, Lewis raised a laugh, by observing, that if Tom Banks reached that river, he

35. Donoghue ("Explorations of Albert Pike," p. 137) suggests that this may still be the Salt Fork of the Brazos. Earlier that morning, when Pike "turned to the east and left this river," Donoghue thinks that Pike had just crossed the Salt Fork below the point where it makes a large bend to the northeast. Later in the afternoon, Pike recrossed this bend as it dips south. It is also possible, however, that Pike left the Salt Fork just before it turned to the south, and that he had now reached North Croton Creek. The map of Pike's route in George Wilkins Kendall, *Narrative of the Texan Santa Fé Expedition . . .* (New York, 1844), suggests this.

would have salt tea enough,—alluding to his verbiage about Saltillo. This branch ran the same course as the former, and we supposed, joined it not far below. Crossed it and went up to the high mesquito prairie on the other side of it, and encamped without water. We now supposed ourselves to be on the north side of Red River, but we were immensely out of the matter. Traveled this day about eighteen miles; gained perhaps twelve, east.

16.—Our route this day, lay in the forenoon through a level prairie covered with mesquito bushes. We now began to hope that we should soon arrive at the open prairie. But at noon we came upon a break of the prairie into low, uneven ground, and saw away in front of us what appeared to be a large river. Here, Lewis went out, killed a deer, and brought it in whole. After dinner, I delayed in camp until the party were two miles ahead. About three miles from camp, we passed a small hill with a pile of stones on the summit,—probably the fruits of the superstition of the Comanches. At night, we encamped on a small branch of salt water which runs into the river. Here we saw a bear, but could not get a shot at him. To-day traveled about fifteen miles north-east.

17.—Crossed the river, which is about twenty yards, or perhaps thirty, wide—sandy, and with little water, like all the rest; and like them, too, running to the south-east.[36] After crossing the river, we continued on about three miles, and crossed a branch of the same stream, running with clear but very salt water through a grassy valley. After crossing, we kept up the branch for some distance, and ascended into the prairie, which was still clothed with mesquito bushes. Here we tried in vain to kill a deer, and stopped at noon on a deep hollow, with brackish water. In the afternoon, we kept on through the prairie, and towards night, came upon a hole of muddy water, beat up, as well as surrounded, by innumerable horse tracks. Here we concluded to pass the night; and immediately on stopping, Ish pointed out to us four or five wild horses, very quietly feeding not far from the water. Lewis and he accordingly went out with the intention of killing one; and after several shots,

36. North Croton Creek?

succeeded, and returned to camp, bearing a portion of the animal. Fire had been made in the mean time, and every man was soon busily employed in roasting horse-meat. Before we had time to eat, however, a sudden trampling was heard approaching—and we stood to our arms, when suddenly about a hundred horses came careering down towards the water. They had approached within thirty yards of us before they discovered us, when, with a general snort, they galloped swiftly by us. As they passed, Ish discharged his big gun, which added wings to their terror, and they were soon out of sight and hearing, and we returned to our cooking. Upon eating our meat, we found it far from unpleasant. It was tender, sweet and very fat; and on the whole, is far preferable to the meat of a lean deer. The choice piece in a horse, is under the mane; and this we left roasting under the coals, wrapped in the skin until the morning. After this, two or three of us went out on the track of the horses, and about two hundred yards from camp we found a beautiful young roan filly, dead—the effects of Ish's big gun. Of this animal, we took a small portion and returned to camp; and for the sake of satisfying my curiosity, I took with me the tongue. This part of the beast, I found not very palatable.

It seems astonishing, that from the few horses introduced so short a time since, into America, by the Spaniards, there should now be such immense herds in the prairie, and in the possession of the Aboriginals. Hardly a day passed without our seeing a herd of them, either quietly feeding, or careering off wildly in the distance. They are the most beautiful sight to be met with in the prairie. Of all colors, but most commonly of a bay, and with their manes floating in the wind, they present a beautiful contrast to the heavy, unwieldy herds of buffalo, which seem, even at their best speed, to be moved by some kind of clumsy machinery. Some old patriarch always heads the gang, and possesses the command over them. We were witnesses on one particular occasion to an example of communication between these animals, which proves them possessed of something nearly allied to the power of speech. We had seen a herd feeding at a distance, and we watched them to see what effect would be produced upon them, when they should receive our smell in the air; or, as hunters say, the wind of us, which was blowing across our path in their direction. On feeling it, they started in a slow trot, headed, as usual, by a noble-looking old patriarch. Three only of the whole herd were bold enough to separate and take another direction. On discovering this defection of his troops, the old chief turned back, and the whole herd halted. Trotting briskly to the three deserters, he communicated with them for a moment or two, and probably finding remonstrance unavailing, started back and put his followers in motion, quickly accelerating their gait to a gallop. You may see the leader sometimes before, and sometimes behind his troops, biting them and urging them on, by every means in his power. As to the tale of their keeping one of their number as sentinels, I believe nothing of it. Their acute smell gives them sufficient warning, and does away the need of a sentry. We traveled to-day about fifteen miles in a course nearly east-north-east.

18.—Left camp in the morning, after a hearty meal of horse-meat, and traveled through a high mesquito prairie. The bushes, however, began to grow thinner and smaller, and we now hoped to reach speedily to the high open prairie, an event which we anxiously looked for. About noon, we fell off from the prairie into a bottom of good land covered with thick hack-berry trees, and in a short distance, came upon a creek about twenty yards wide, running clear water, but salt. This is a branch of Red River.[37] Here we nooned, and for the first time saw a flock of wild turkeys, out of which we killed one. Leaving our camping ground, we crossed the creek and kept down it some distance, and then turned to the east. Towards night, we struck another branch, and followed the bed of it to the mouth, where it joined the creek on which we nooned, and here we encamped.[38] The water of the creek which ran rippling over the stones, reminding us of the clear streams of our own country and the mountains, was very salt, but there was a small tide of good water (that is, not too salt to drink) in the bed of the creek. Here we ate our turkey, with the addition of a little

37. South Wichita River?
38. North Wichita River and the Wichita?

horse-meat to relieve the dryness of it. This day we traveled perhaps fifteen miles east-north-east.

19.—This morning we finished our horse-meat, and followed the course of the creek two or three miles, and found sweet water under a bluff rock in the bed of the river. We had, for several days, been tormented by constant thirst; for salt water satisfies a man only while he is drinking it. We now drank enough to satiate us, and took a general smoke upon the occasion. We then struck into the prairie, and Lewis killed a fat buck. We then turned down to a branch of standing water, and nooned; and in cooking our dinner, we set the long grass of the bottom on fire, and had a noble blaze and smoke. We ate our dinner, and left it burning, not without apprehensions of its being observed by Indians. We still kept on our course through the mesquito prairie, and towards night descended into a hollow, and hunted water, but were driven out by the gnats and musquitoes without finding any. On emerging again from the hollow, we came upon an old Comanche village, which must have contained, when occupied, at least five hundred souls. After traveling through the prairie until nearly night, we found a hollow of good, and, for a rarity, perfectly fresh water. Here we encamped, and in the night were awakened by the snorting of one of our mules. After gathering our arms and waiting some time for an attack, we discovered that the cause of the alarm was simply a deer or two, whistling at a distance. Traveled this day about eighteen miles east-north-east.

20.—After traveling about five miles in a broken prairie country, we discovered two or three buffalo ahead of us, and Lewis and Ish went on and wounded two of them, one of which, an old cow, ran up into the prairie and fell. She was too poor for us to touch, and we left her lying there. We were now fairly in the broad open prairie, and among the buffalo; and to the wanderer in the prairie, nothing is so inspiriting as the thought of the immense herds of these animals which are found on its broad bosom. Their numbers are truly astonishing. You may see them for whole days on each side of you as far as your sight will extend, apparently so thick, that one might easily walk for miles upon their backs, listlessly feeding along, until they take the wind of you, and then moving off at a speed, of which the unwieldy animals seem hardly capable. Wherever they have passed, the ground looks as if it had been burnt over.

Except in their faculty of smelling, the buffalo is the most stupid animal in the world;[39] and if you will creep towards them, and obtain two or three shots at them before you are seen, you may then rise and fire half a day at them: they will only look stupidly at you out of their little eyes, and now and then utter a grunt. But when they have once smelt the blood of a companion, they are apt to abscond. When an old bull is shot in any vital part, and the hunter remains unseen, he will run a little way, and then stand and bleed to death; but let him once see the hunter, and become enraged, and it seems impossible to kill him. I have seen them live for a length of time which seemed astonishing, when ball after ball had been shot into their heart and lungs. A cow will commonly stand when shot, until she bleeds to death. The enraged old bull, making fight, has rather a formidable appearance, shaking his huge head, matted over with hair, and glaring with his little twinkling eyes. A large herd of them would make a tremendous charge upon a body of horse, if they could be brought up to it. Nothing could stand against their hard heads, which a rifle bullet will not enter at a distance greater than ten steps. Like all other animals, they take especial care to defend their young; and you may frequently see in the prairie rings perhaps fifteen or twenty feet in diameter made by the buffalo. They place their calves in the centre, and tramp round them during the night, to protect them from the wolves.

The flesh of an old bull is the worst meat in the world during the summer and autumn; and that of the fat cow is undoubtedly the best. I know of nothing edible, which I would not exchange for the hump ribs of a fat buffalo cow.

After leaving the old cow, we went on to a small hollow bordered by cottonwood and willows, and encamped in the bottom of the hollow. We had traveled this forenoon in a course

39. Pike's observations about the buffalo were verified by later visitors to the Plains. Walter Prescott Webb, *The Great Plains* (New York, 1931), p. 41, finds that "it is described by all observers, from Catlin on, as a stupid animal, the easiest victim to the hunter. . . ."

nearly east-north-east thirteen miles, and we now determined to change our course and turn to the north. We supposed ourselves to be on the north side of Red River, and were desirous of reaching the Washita. Accordingly, in the afternoon we traveled in a north course about eight miles, and encamped in the open prairie, on the edge of a hole of water. We saw in the evening, plenty of scattering bulls, all with their faces turned to the south, and we knew that the cows could not be far behind them. We likewise saw a herd of elk trotting off at a distance; and at night, we made a fire, for the first time, of the dry ordure of the buffalo, which is the common fuel in the prairie. It makes an excellent fire, and has saved me from freezing to death several times. Here we heard also for the first time, the buffalo grunting about us in the night. Traveled this day in the whole, about twenty-one miles.

21.—Early in the morning, we came suddenly upon a broad river with bluff banks, running in a course nearly east. Here, then, was Red River at last, which we thought was far behind us. Now, however, there could be no dispute. Here it was, a broad sand bed, more than a mile wide, with not a drop of water visible, and with a high prairie on each side—while the only thing to relieve the monotony, was a few hackberries growing under the bluffs. We crossed the river and found a thread of salt water just under the opposite bank. Here were plenty of new roads, made by the buffalo in crossing the river. On ascending the bluff, we came again upon a high prairie covered by numerous villages of prairie-dogs, who sat chattering at us from their holes. This singular little animal, which has no resemblance to a dog except in the name, is to be found in villages throughout the whole prairie, and always in the highest part of it, where they must dig to an immense depth to reach water. They are about as large as a gray squirrel, of a brown color, and shaped nearly like a woodchuck.[40] They are always found in villages, and there is commonly one hole which has five times the quantity of earth piled around it that any other house in the village can boast of. They have many enemies. The rattle-

40. Pike's description of the prairie dog is a good one. Webb, in his *Great Plains* (p. 39), calls this animal "the squirrel of the Plains."

snake lives in the same hole with them and devours them; and the little brown prairie wolf and the tiger-cat lie in wait for them at their very doors. You will frequently, too, find owls nestled in their holes. We stopped at noon in a small low place full of buffalo wallows. There had been water here, but it was here no longer. We found a hole, at length, about as large as my body, and scraped a small hole, from which I obtained a draught or two of mud and water, which left my throat plastered over with the former substance. We ate our last venison and went on. In the afternoon we saw some cows; and towards night my horse began to fail, and we turned down to a small creek, timbered with hackberry, for the purpose of encamping, and Lewis and Ish killed three cows and a yearling calf. The water on which we encamped was both muddy and salt. Traveled this day about fifteen miles in a direction nearly north.

Thus it will be seen, that from our departure from the Del Resgate branch of the Brazos river, we had traveled about one hundred and forty miles when we reached Red River, in a course generally north-east.

22.—Traveled generally this day in the prairie, now and then crossing a small creek, and encamped at night in an open place near a deep hole of water. This day we saw an abundance of cows, and heard them grunting about us at night. We were now in all the glory of a prairie life, with an abundance of buffalo, good water, and plenty of timber; and we lay down at night with a feeling of freedom and independence, which man does not always enjoy in a city. Traveled to-day about fifteen miles north.

23.—Early this morning, a band of buffalo came about us, and we lay in camp and killed two; took the tongues and the hump meat, and went on. About noon, we saw the first pecan tree which had greeted us, and we hailed it as something peculiar to home. You would have supposed that we had reached a house or city. We likewise found some scattering oak glades, and began to feel out of danger. Just after noon, we came upon a creek of good water, bordered with excellent grass, and determined to stop and recruit our horses. We turned down and encamped accordingly, after traveling this day about nine miles nearly north. Moccasin making and mending clothes occupied the remainder of the day; and not only at this time, but often afterwards, we had reason to rejoice that Irwin was with us to play the part of tailor, in which he was an adept.

24.—Lay by to-day, and in the evening Lewis and Ish killed one cow and a yearling, and wounded a barren cow; feasted upon marrow bones and hump ribs, and threw fear to the winds, very piously handing over the Comanches, with our good wishes, to his Satanic Majesty.

25.—Left camp, and, after proceeding about a mile, found our wounded cow, yet alive, and able to make fight; killed her and took the fleece. She was, to use a western expression, powerful fat. Plenty of meat packed now, every horse bearing a whole buffalo fleece; that is, all the meat on the outside of the backbone, hump ribs and side ribs. We crossed several creeks this forenoon, none of which were running; all, however, well timbered, and with good bottoms. Just before stopping at noon, Lewis shot an excellent buck, from his horse, and killed him in his tracks. We took his fleece likewise. Soon after, he killed a badger, and at the place where we encamped, we killed three raccoons. We stopped at a pond of water on the bank of a small creek, and I think I never enjoyed any experiment in epicurism so well as I did the mixture of buffalo and deer meat which we had here, and for several days after, in abundance. I have forgotten where we encamped this night, but I think that we made, this day, about fifteen miles, in a course, as usual, nearly north.

26.—Traveled, this day, through the same kind of country as yesterday. Nooned on a creek of running water, after crossing one or two creeks in the forenoon. Directly after setting out again, we crossed another creek, and were keeping down it to the east, when we descried a range of hills to the north, and determined to keep our course until we reached them. We accordingly kept on across the prairie, and encamped at night on another small creek, where we hunted turkies unsuccessfully. Traveled this day about fifteen miles north.

27.—This day we passed through immense herds of buffalo, and, about three in the afternoon, ascending a table hill which lay in front of us, saw that there were no buffalo ahead. We kept on until the middle of the afternoon, and encamped near a pond of water, and not far from a deep creek. It soon commenced raining, and during the storm Lewis killed a cow, and we brought the meat into camp. Here we lay two days, when the storm ceased.

30.—Moved this morning about six miles, to the top of a hill to the north of us, and stopped again, our animals being worn out by the storm. We encamped in a grove of oak, and made our first oak fire. Towards evening Lewis killed four buffalo cows, and we again kept from starvation.

31.—Lay by this day; killed three turkeys, and had a change of diet.

Nov. 1.—This day we again turned our course to the north, through the prairie. For a mile or two I rode, but was obliged to dismount and drive my horse before me. At noon, we encamped on a small creek, and at night in the Cross Timbers on the edge of a deep hollow. This day, for the first time, we saw a few grapes. Traveled about twenty-one miles, N. E. by N.

2.—This morning I left my horse and went forward on foot, packing a blanket upon my back. From this day until the seventh there was little variety in our traveling; sometimes in the open prairie, and sometimes for miles in a tangled wilderness of scrub-oak, grapes and briars, which hardly allowed our mules to force a way through them. My ancles were frequently covered with blood, and nothing but my strong pantaloons of leather saved my legs from being served in the same manner.

On the seventh, towards night, we heard a gun fired to the left of us, and knew, by the crack, that it was a fusee or a musket.[41] We accordingly supposed it to proceed from a Comanche. Proceeding on, however, we came, about three of the afternoon, upon a deep river of running water, which we all took to be the Washita, but which Lewis concluded, from its size, it could not be. He supposed it to be Red River; and finding it impossible to cross it, we turned back sadly, and encamped about four miles from it. The expression of despair upon the countenances of some of the party was ludicrous.

8.—This morning we turned down the river, determined to go in upon it and cross it. We had not proceeded far when we

41. Flintlock guns, or fusils.

saw an Indian at a distance of about five miles, in the prairie. We still, however, kept down the slope of the prairie, toward the river, at a slow gait, expecting his approach, and in about half an hour he appeared within a quarter of a mile of us, coming through a small point of timber. When within two hundred yards of us he stopped. We motioned to him to come on, and after some hesitation, he did so. I asked him in Spanish if he could speak that language, supposing him to be a Comanche, for they generally speak that language. Thinking that I wished to know his nation, he answered, 'Wawsashy' (Osage). It was a pleasant sound to us, and seeing it confirmed by his single point of hair upon the top of his head, we shook hands with him, and inquired of him, by signs, where his camp was. He pointed to the top of the hill, and wished us to go there and eat, to which we agreed, being desirous of finding out where we actually were. Seeing me on foot, he gave me his horse to ride, and kept ahead of us on foot, chattering continually to us, and accompanying his orations with an abundance of signs. We soon knew for a certainly that he was an Osage, by the frequent garnishing of his discourse with the word *Wawsashy*, and by the terminations *iginy* and *oginy*, as well as the emphatic adjective *tungah*. After riding about three miles, we stopped upon the summit of the prairie, and kindled a small fire; and in the course of a half hour were joined by about a dozen more of the tribe, all armed with fusees, except one, who bore a rifle. Before they joined us, however, we saw them run two or three wild horses, which they do by taking stations, and pursuing wild animals in turn, until some one comes near enough to the prey to place a noose over his head, which noose is carried, attached to the end of a long and light pole or wand. After joining us, and before we started again, some of them managed to steal all our tobacco, except one small piece, and then offering me another horse to ride, we moved towards their camp. It was past noon when we reached it, for it was at least thirteen miles from the river. As we approached, the inhabitants of the village, who had been warned of our approach, not only by various strange shouts, but also by messengers, came out to meet us in great numbers; and after crossing a branch of the river, we entered the camp with our arms nearly shaken off at the elbows, by the rough, but friendly greetings of our new friends. Entering the village, which consisted of about thirty lodges, we were conducted to the chief's tent, where we found a young Frenchman, who could speak very good English. He informed us that this was the tent of the principal chief, and that our property would be very safe in it. We entered and shook hands with the chief and his subordinates, who occupied the interior. We bestowed ourselves in various positions upon the buffalo robes which were laid about the fire, and maintained a true Indian gravity, until they should see fit to address us. The young Frenchman then asked us where we were from. We told him, and he interpreted it to our hosts, who uttered the common exclamation, Huh! and listened till we should speak again. Give me an Indian for a listener always. We gave them some details of our route, to which they listened with surprise, and perhaps with incredulity. If so, they were too polite to show it. They had, as it appeared, been at our old camps, and taken us for Pawnees, for they know no other name for any wandering Indian, than Pawnee. After the conference was over, I produced my pipe and began to fill it. A half dozen pipes were immediately shown, and requests were made for tobacco, to which I was, of course, bound to respond, and we had a general smoke. We passed the remainder of this day and the next with them, and were called upon, every hour in the day, to go to some lodge and eat. In the course of the second day and evening, we ate fifteen times, and were obliged to do so, or affront them.

These Osages are generally fine, large, noble-looking men, supplied with immense Roman noses. Young Clarimore, the chief of the party, in particular, was a very fine, noble-looking fellow.[42] They are much more generous and friendly, too, than the Choctaws or Cherokees, in their treatment of strangers, and fed us bountifully on the meat of the buffalo, bear, deer and pole-cat; of the latter of which, however, we partook merely out of compliment.

42. Apparently the son of the famous Osage chief Claremore. See John Joseph Mathews, *The Osages: Children of the Middle Waters* (Norman, 1961), 417-418.

Their lodges, unlike those of the Comanches, are round, and not conical, and are not more than eight feet in height. The tops of them were formed of thin fleeces of buffalo meat, which was drying in the smoke, supported by the bent saplings, of which the lodges are built. We found that, contrary to our fears, we were upon the Washita, and in the edge of the Cross Timbers; a consummation which we had long been very devoutly looking for.

10.—Left the camp in company with the Osages, and traveled in a south-east direction about twelve miles, and encamped again with them.

11.—This morning, left the Osages. They had solicited us strongly to go on with them, and we would have been wise had we done so. Lewis, Irwin and Gillet exchanged their mules for horses this morning, but Ish kept his mule. Lewis and Irwin obtained young and unbroken wild horses, (or, as the hunters call them, mestangs [mustangs]) and Gillet got an old worn-out hack. At parting, the chief presented us with an abundance of good meat; and in return, we gave him a red and gaudy Mexican blanket; and after lingering behind his men, and shaking hands with us, he left us.

From this time till the night of the thirteenth, our route lay through the Cross Timbers and the Washita Hills; and on that afternoon, we turned down from the hills to the river. Crossed it and encamped on the north bank of it. These three days were the worst part of the route. The gravel wore our feet to the quick, even through our moccasins, and the bushes and briars offered almost insurmountable obstacles to our progress. Probably in these three days, we traveled fifty miles, and gained, upon a straight line, thirty.

14.—Left the Washita and struck out from it. From this day till the twentieth, we traveled nearly an easterly course; sometimes in timber, sometimes in burnt prairie. On the 19th, we had a snow-storm. We had crossed two running creeks about twenty yards wide, besides several small ones—all branches of Blue. On the twentieth, in the morning, we came upon a Delaware, who was hunting deer. He conducted us part of the way to his camp, and then left us to hunt deer a while, as he said;

but we never found his camp. I do not suppose that he intended us to do so. We obtained a small piece of tobacco of him, however, of which we had had none for six or seven days. Both of these days (the nineteenth and twentieth) we were without meat, not even a mouthful.

21.—This day, at noon, killed a small deer, and ate ravenously—eating the whole animal except one ham and one shoulder. From this day to the 23d, we kept nearly the same course, (east) and about noon of the 23d, we struck Blue, and kept down it, as we did also on the twenty-fourth, till, about noon, we found ourselves in the bottom of Red River, at the mouth of Blue. Here we encamped, and laid by this day and the next, 25th. From the crossing of the Washita to the mouth of Blue, we had traveled, I believe, nearly one hundred and sixty miles,—perhaps more. The distance, upon a straight line, is not more than one hundred and twenty miles.

On the 14th, we killed four old bulls. They were the last we saw: the same day we killed and ate an opossum.

On the 22d, Gillet killed his horse, and became my companion on foot. During these last days, the prairie had been on fire all around us; and I assure the reader that there is not the least danger of a person getting caught and burnt up by it. I can outwalk it two to one, even in a good wind; and I think I could save myself by running through the fire. The most serious calamity which had befallen me of late, was the loss of my last knife, which I left behind me on the 23d; and of course I had a fair chance of discover the true value of fingers in the woods.

The country was, as before, at times prairie, covered with long grass; or, where the fire had been, hard, black and dry. At times we passed through spots of oak timber, and now and then, a small patch of briars and scrub oak. The water was now all sweet and clear, and there was an abundance of it.

On the 25th, we lay by in the bottom of Red River, and Lewis killed an old bear and cub. Some turkeys, also, were unroosted by some of us, and we could have killed plenty of deer, had we wished. There can be no better place for hunting than this bottom; but for briars and vines, I take it to be the worst place on earth.

From this day until the 28th, we had every variety of traveling, except that which was pleasant and easy. We crossed Blue on the morning of the 26th, and then took nearly a north course. That night I felled a tree about a foot in diameter, with a tomahawk, for the sake of grapes. On the 27th, we encamped early, and cut a bee tree, obtaining a good quantity of honey to eat with our bear meat; and the next morning we struck the road which goes in to Fort Towson. Owing to our making a slight mistake, and taking the wrong end of it, however, we did not manage to reach that place. There is a conical bare mound called the Cadeau Hill,[43] near this place in the road, and also a timbered hill, both of which Lewis thought he would know, but did not. We followed the road about six miles in a northwest direction, and concluding that we were not getting homeward, we stopped and ate on the edge of the timbered hill; followed the road a little further until it vanished, and then we again struck an east course. Had we taken the other end of the road, we should have been spared some trouble.

On the morning of the 29th, our northward course brought us to the first fork of Boggy, where we cut a sycamore and crossed upon it; part of the log was under water, and it was altogether a slippery business, especially for Irwin, who had received a kick a day or two before, and was obliged to straddle the log, and as they quaintly call it in the west, 'Coon it across.' A lame leg is no great accommodation in the prairie. After crossing, we kept to the east, but soon found ourselves getting entangled in a bottom, and turned to the north again; and on the 30th, about noon, we reached the other fork of Boggy. Here we heard a dog baying, and the cries of Indians; and while we remained on the bank, Lewis went to find the Indians. He returned just at night, and, of course, we deferred crossing until the morning. Killed some turkeys, and contented ourselves. The next morning we cut a willow and crossed on it,

43. Today's Sugarloaf Mountain, in northeast Bryan County. W. B. Morrison, "Across Oklahoma Ninety Years Ago," *Chronicles of Oklahoma*, IV, 4 (March, 1926), 336.

and were then obilged to cut a road through the cane with knives. At noon we ate nothing; and at night we finished our turkeys.

Dec. 1.—In the morning we met a Choctaw, who informed us that there was a road not far ahead. We nooned, however, before reaching it; and after starting again, turned off of our course, to the sound of an axe, and found five or six Choctaws cutting a bee tree. We offered to buy some of the honey, but they refused to sell it, but tried to beg powder and balls. A Choctaw is, without exception, the meanest Indian on earth. About the middle of the afternoon we reached the road which runs from Fort Smith to Red River. We, however, not knowing that there was any such road, supposed it to run from the ford of Boggy to Fort Towson, on Red River, to which we wished to go; and we accordingly took the north end of the road, being then twenty-three miles from Red River, and the weather too cloudy and wet for us to see the sun, or to know our course. We traveled about sixteen miles after striking the road, and encamped in the rain, without food. From this time, we traveled from thirty to thirty-five miles a day, driving the wearied animals before us.

On the 2nd, I sold my rifle to the Choctaws, for about a dozen pounds of meat, and Ish disposed of his in the same manner.

On the 4th, we encamped with two or three Delawares, and Irwin sold his double-barrelled gun for meat likewise. Upon leaving the Delawares, the next morning, and striking across to the road, we took the wrong end of it, and following it eight or ten miles, came to the Kiamesia.[44] Here we encamped, and the next morning took the road again; and on the 9th, we reached, about noon, the house of a certain sub-agent for the Choctaws, called McLellan, an acquaintance of Lewis's, but whose heart was not quite big enough to allow him to invite us to dine with him. We accordingly went on to the ferry on the Porteau,[45] where we arrived after dark, and found a little Frenchman there, who had nothing to eat but pounded corn, and nothing

44. Kiamichi River.
45. Poteau River.

to cook it in but a kettle that held about a pint and a half. It took us about half the night to cook three kettles full of said corn, from each kettle of which, each man got perhaps six spoonfuls.

On the 10th we reached Fort Smith, and we must have made a most ludicrous appearance. Falstaff's ragged regiment was nothing to us. I had a pair of leather pantaloons, scorched and wrinkled by the fire, and full of grease; an old greasy jacket and vest; a pair of huge moccasins, in mending which I had laid out all my skill during the space of two months, and in so doing, had bestowed upon them a whole shot-pouch; a shirt, which, made of what is commonly called counterpane, or a big checked stuff, had not been washed since I left Taos; and, to crown all, my beard and mustachios had never been clipped during the same time. Some of us were worse off. Irwin, for example, had not half a shirt. In short, we were, to use another western expression, 'as pretty a looking set of fellows as ever any man put up to his face.'

From the crossing of Blue to the first crossing of Boggy, we traveled about fifty miles; thence to the second crossing, about twenty-eight; thence to the road about twenty-seven, and on the road, about two hundred miles. In the whole, then, we traveled from Taos about fourteen hundred miles, or about thirteen hundred from San Miguel, out of which I walked a distance of about six hundred and fifty miles.

I have been less exact in describing our route after crossing the Fore Washita, because Washington Irving, who was at the Cross Timbers on the Washita, not far from the time at which we crossed it, will describe that portion of the western world in a manner which would do shame to any poor endeavors of mine to convey an idea of it.[46] I can only regret that we did not meet him in the prairie for in such case, we could have given him more material for a description of the 'far west;' and I should probably have had our journey laid before the public by better hands than my own.

And now, in leaving this portion of my work, I beg to assure

46. Pike was mistaken. Irving never got as far south as the Fore Washita; their routes did not overlap.

the reader that if there be any errors to be corrected thus far, they are by no means intentional. He will please to recollect that I have written entirely from my own memory, aided by that of Mr. Lewis. I find also another difficulty in writing. After living in the West, where many things which are peculiar to a wild life are common and uninteresting, one is apt to hurry over the minutiae of them in laying them before a part of the public to whom they are strange and new. One can hardly realize that what is so common to him and every one around him, can be interesting to any portion of the public; and for fear of being tedious and prolix, he is, perhaps, brief and unsatisfactory. With this brief apology, I leave the recital of our adventures in the Western Desert.

The reader may wish to know what became of the party which we left. In the month of April, Mr. J. Scott, whom we had left with the party upon the Del Resgate fork of the Brazos, came into Fort Smith in company with two others of the party; and the account which he gives me of the route of the party after we left it, is as follows:—They kept down the river for about twelve days after our departure, and then struck a due north course to the Fore Washita, crossing on the way only one more branch of the Brazos, but having passed the mouths of three branches which put into the Del Resgate from the north. They crossed Red River near the mouth of the branch which I mentioned as the only branch of Red River crossed by us. After striking the Washita, they kept up it nearly to its head, then crossed to the Canadian, and followed it down nearly to its junction with the Arkansas. They passed the whole winter upon the Canadian, and Harris was at Fort Gibson in the month of January. In the spring they left the Canadian, and took a south course, crossed Red River, and about one hundred and fifty miles south of it, Scott and his companions left them, after Harris had in vain attempted to persuade them to remain. Some half dozen of the party, including Bill Williams, turned back, soon after we left them, and went back on foot towards Taos. Thus much for Caesar and his fortunes.

In the month of December, 1832, a party of twelve men left

Taos, to come into this country by the way of the Canadian. They had proceeded only about two hundred miles from Santa Fe, when they were attacked by the Comanches; two men were killed and several wounded; all their animals were killed, and they left their money and baggage, and kept on down the river on foot. Five of them soon after left the river, and struck for Missouri, where they arrived safely; the other five still kept on down the river, and three of them went ahead of the others and came in. One of the two who were left behind was named Wm. R. Schenck, a native of Ohio; he had been wounded in the leg, and as nothing has been heard of him or his companion, the probability is, that they died in the prairie. The reader will find, in this book, a few lines occasioned by the receipt of the tidings of his death.

Poems

THE ROBIN.
Written in New Mexico, on hearing a red-breast sing, the only one
that I ever heard there.

Hush! where art thou clinging,
And what art thou singing,
  Bird of my own native land?
    Thy song is as sweet
    As a fairy's feet
  Stepping on silver sand—
      And thou
      Art now
As merry as though thou wast singing at home,
      Away
      In the spray
Of a shower, that tumbles through odorous gloom;
    Or as if thou wast hid,
      To the tip of thy wing,
    By a broad oaken leaf
      In its greeness of spring,
And thy nest lurked amid a gray heaven of shade,
Where thy young and thyself from the sunshine were laid.

Hush! hush!—Look around thee!
Lo! bleak mountains bound thee,
  All barren and gloomy and red;
    And a desolate pine
    Doth above thee incline,
  And gives not a leaf to thy bed—
      And lo!
      Below
No flowers of beauty and brilliancy blow,
      But weeds,
      Gray heads,
That mutter and moan when the wind-waves flow:
    And the rain never falls
      In the season of spring,
    To freshen thy heart
      And to lighten thy wing;

But thou livest a hermit these deserts among,
And echo alone makes reply to thy song.

   And while thou art chanting,
   With head thus upslanting,
     Thou seemest a thought or a vision,
      Which flits in its haste
      O'er the heart's dreary waste,
    With an influence soothing, Elysian—
       Or a lone
       Sweet tone,
That sounds for a time in the ear of Sorrow;
       And soon,
       Too soon,
I must leave thee, and bid thee a long good morrow.
     But if thou wilt turn
      To the South thy wing,
     I will meet thee again
      E'er the end of spring;
And thy nest can be made where the peach and the vine
Shall shade thee, and leaf and tendril entwine.

   Oh! thou art a stranger,
   And darer of danger,
     That over these mountains hast flown,
      And the land of the North
      Is the clime of thy birth,
    And here thou, like me, art alone.
       Go back
       On thy track;
It were wiser and better for thee and me,
       Than to moan
       Alone,
So far from the waves of our own bright sea:
     And the eyes that we left
      To grow dim months ago,
     Will greet us again
      With their idolized glow.

Let us go—let us go—and revisit our home,
Where the oak leaves are green and the sea-waters foam.

Valley of Tisuqui, March 20, 1832.

LINES.

Written in Santa Fe, Noon of Feb. 15, 1832.

THE sun is dull, the mist amid,
That like a grief is shading him;
And though the mountain be not hid,
His distant blue is shining dim,
And marking with its outline deep
The paler blue that bends above.
The winds have fanned themselves to sleep,
And scarcely now their soft wings move,
With an unquiet slumberous motion,
Watched by the pale and flitting noon,
The wanderer of earth and ocean,
Whose stay all men desire, but none obtain the boon.

It is the hour of deepest thought,
When noise hath all the slumberous tone,
A dream-like indistinctness, fraught
With all which makes man feel alone.
It may be in the hour and time—
It may be only in the heart—
The cause that from the soul's abyme
Makes Time's old images to start;
When all that we have lost, or left,
Or loved, or worshipped, at our youth,
Comes up like an unwelcome gift,
With all the sad and stern reality of truth.

The stormy image of the past
Upon me at this time doth rise;
And, gazing in the distinct vast,
Dim shapes I see with saddened eyes,

Like those that I have known before,
Yet altered, as I too have changed,
And some that near my heart I wore,
And some whose insults I avenged.
Ah yes! I know that sad, fair face—
Thy matchless form—thy witchery—
Thy step of air—thy winning grace!
Ah yes! I see thee in the dim obscurity.

My grief has now become as still
As is the sunlight or this wind;
And yet it knoweth well to fill,
With shapes like these, the gazing mind:
And Memory yields not yet her power—
Not yet her serpent sting will die;
Life is compressed into one hour—
A moment—by her searching eye:
And then a little fiend sits near,
And chatters of the lost and dead,
And hearts for woe grown chill and sere,
And points to Friendship's grave, as I his blood had shed.

And Fancy—Memory's sister—weaves
No golden web of hope for me;
Or if she smile, she still deceives
With all a wanton's mockery.
She paints to me a fireless hearth,
Or, worse than any other sting
We feel upon the lonely earth,
Cold hearts, and colder welcoming;
Friends wasted by life's ebbing tide,
Like sands along the shifting coasts;
The soul's best love another's bride;
And other worldless thoughts that haunt like unformed ghosts.

Well, I have chosen my own long path,
And I will walk it to the death,
Though Love's lone grief, or Hatred's wrath,
My way and purpose hindereth.

It may be, when this heart is cold,
And it were vain to love or hate—
When all that malice knows is told,
Some better name may on me wait;
And as the misty mountain mane
Doth not forever shade its blue,
The gloom on me may not remain,
When life, and love, and hope, have nought with me to do.

AGAPOU PNEUMA.

THOU must have altered in the two long years
Which thou hast passed since I beheld thee, Ann!
For then thou wast just budding into life,
And Hopes, with fiery eyes, thy heart did fan,
And gray Grief's tears
Had not assailed thee. Thou wast very rife
With budding beauty, which is now full blown
In all the sunny spring of womanhood.
Thy spirit shone
Like an etherial angel's in thy face:
There was a proud and an impassioned tone
Within thy voice, that breathed from off the soul
A strong enchantment on a heart like mine.
Thou wast a glorious being in thy bud;
But in thy blossom, thou must be divine.
Oh! I can fancy thee in all thy power,
In all thy beauty and magnificence;
Thine eyes so beautiful, and so intense,
Raining into the heart their starry shower;
Thy raven hair shining above a brow
Replete with Italy and with divinity;
Thy form so slight, so very delicate,
Yet swelling proudly with thy uncontrolled
And uncontrollable spirit. Oh! how cold
Seems beauty to me, when I think on thee,
Thou beautiful and bright and fiery star!
And I afar

Bow down before thee, though I have no hope
To win or wear thee near my withered heart.

Thou wast too full of uncontrolled romance,
Too full of Poetry's impassioned trance,
Too full of soul, to live amid the world.
Thy body to thy soul was like a cloud,
In which the silver arrows of the sun
Stay not, but pass wherever they are hurled;
'T was like the clear transparent element,
That shows the emerald beneath it pent,
Nor robs one ray. Thy soul breathed in thy face,
And lay upon it like a visible mist.
Thou wast not fit for life's realities;
The world all seemed too fair unto thine eyes;
Thou was too full of hope, and faith, and thrust—
And art, perhaps, ere this, most undeceived.
Thy heavenly eyes, perhaps, have been, and are,
Dim with the dew which wastes away the heart—
And such a heart! Oh! it is sad to think
That all the richer feelings of the soul
Are but its torment; that the lustrous star
Which shines the brightest, soonest wastes away;
Yea—that the gifted soul, that will, must drink
Of poetry, romance, and glowing love,
Kindles a fire that must consume itself!
And thou wilt be unhappy. Never one
Was gifted with thy fervid, trusting soul,
And went through life unscathed and sorrowless.
And thou and I, too, soon will reach our goal.
The world, which ought thy glorious spirit to bless,
Will chill thee, Ann! and make thy heart grow cold;
And thou wilt never, save in grief, be old.
This, this it is, which makes me love thee. I
Feel that there is between my soul and thine
A sympathy of feeling and of fate,
Which binds me to thee with a deathless tie.
Time has already seen *my* heart decay,

Where Death has trod. Yet, though it wastes away,
Daily and nightly, still the core is left,
And burns for thee with all its former fire;
There is concentred all.

I would to God
Thou couldst be mine, Ann! for the few short years
Left me to live; that when my death was nigh,
Thou mightst be near me with thy glorious eyes,
Shining like stars into my waning soul—
Thy arms be wreathed around my neck—thy lip
Pressed to my throbbing brow—thy voice
Hushing Despair, and that unconquered fiend,
Ambition—till it were
No pain to die, and breathe upon the wind
My last low gasp. Methinks if thou wast mine,
I might forget the world, and wo, and care,
And let them wreak their worst on me: perhaps,
My heart might be too strong for them to crush:
It may not be.
My fate is fixed. I ask the world a boon,
I cannot, will not, Ann, demand of thee:
Henceforth I pray the world that it forget
That I have lived.

All that I now have left,
Is death and my own wo; and I will die,
Unknown, unnamed. The world shall not be nigh,
To mark the quivering lip—the stopping heart—
The closing eye—the fingers clenched in Death—
The last low moan, when with the parting shiver,
I murmur, *Ann*.

Arkansas Territory, 10th March, 1832.

THE FALL OF POLAND.

Written on receiving, in Santa Fe, the news that Poland had again fallen.

SHE hath sunken again into Slavery's tomb,
Like a thunderbolt quenching itself in the sea;
And deeply and darkly is written her doom—
'Her existence is done—she can never be free.'

From the darkness that shrouded her tomb she arose,
And, throwing her cerements of bondage aside,
She flung her defiance and scorn at her foes,
And her banner was spread, as of old, in its pride.

'T was the contest of right against all that was wrong;
'T was the strife of the brave for their life and their laws;
And every soul, to whose pulse did belong
One throb of nobility, prayed for her cause.

It grew like a stream in the rains of the spring,
Or the clouds of the thunder that rise in the west;
And wide and more wide, as the unfolding wing
Of an eagle, that springs from the hill of his rest;

Till there was not a heart, through which rushed the red blood
Of a Polack, that did not bound into her ranks;
Till all hands were united; till like the spring flood
Of a river she moved, overflowing its banks.

Then above her the old banner waved in the air,
Over city and plain, as had once been its wont;
And the souls of her mighty departed were there,
Like the shadows of gods leading on in the front.

But the fetters are bound on her limbs once again,
And red hot, as they clasp them, are quenched in her gore;
And down on her soul thunders misery's rain,
While the blackness of tyranny shadows her o'er.

Oh! shame on ye, once again, sons of the Gaul!
Ye had just become free, and ye might have been great;
Yet ye suffered the noblest of nations to fall,
And lie bleeding and tortured once more at the gate

Of the Wolf of the North, who, with fangs bloody red,
Yet mangles the corse of the stag he has slain;
Oh shame on your souls!—ye had better be dead,
Than defiled as ye are, by this cowardly stain:

When a word from your mouth, like the thunderbolt's flame,
Would have sent back the Wolf to his haunt in the snow,
And rendered the hater of Freedom as tame
As the worst of his serfs, that lies crouching and low;

When you might have been held like the gods of the world,
And your memory kept in its worship and love;
When, had you the shaft of defiance but hurled,
The thunder of God would have helped from above;

That then ye should stand like base cowards aloof,
While the blood of the brave spouted out of their veins;
While their fabric of freedom was shattered—its roof
Tumbled into the dust by war's tempest and rains.

Live on, then, foul slaves! Let your citizen king
Bind your hearts with the chains which ye unto him flung;
But this deed shall, a halo of shame, round ye cling,
Which shall never be lost while the world has a tongue.

February 1, 1832.

SONNET.

SHE is not beautiful—but in her eyes
  No common spirit shadows forth itself;
So mild, so quiet, so serenely wise,
  Yet merry, as of any dainty elf
That dances on the turf by star-lit skies.
And such a friend she is—so good and true—
So free from envy, scorn, or prejudice;
She is as constant as high heaven is blue;

She seems like some most gentle, lustrous star,
Which men *will* love, because it dazzles not.
And though I wear away my life afar,
Still, in this mountainous and savage spot,
I think of her, as one who soothed my care,
And did her best to keep me from despair.

Valley of the Picuris, September 2, 1832.

LINES.

Written on the Mountains west of the del Norte, April 10, 1832.[1]

THE sun's last light is in the sky,
Yet still his breath is on my brow;
And, warm as in death's mockery,
I feel it going past me now.
His dying breath still quivers up
Above the mountains' many crests,
Like ruddy wine within a cup,
That never from its motion rests.
The mountains in the south grow blue
And indistinct, like waning day;
And in the East, their snowy hue
Is changing into sullen gray:
All objects, while the shadows play,
Grow dim and indistinctly deep;
For Nature's eye is closed, and she inclines to sleep.

And sad, slow thoughts come on the heart,
Like bees that swarm, one with another,
Or waves that with incessant start
Chase, and destroy, each one its brother.
The dreams of hope, that daylight nursed,

1. There are some splendid mountains west of the Del Norte; and it was while encamped, with one servant, among them, that I wrote these lines. I pity the man who cannot feel the influence of sunset among the mountains. Were I given to a belief in presentiments and sympathies, I might strengthen that belief by referring to these lines. My sister died in March, and they were written in April of the same year.—PIKE.

Like other flowers beneath the sun,
Have fled like images accursed,
Or vanish slowly one by one;
And all the thoughts of wo, that rested
Like fiends asleep, within the breast,
Are now with wakefulness invested,
And wander in their wild unrest
Throughout the heart, which is their nest,
And worse than this, the wasting food
Of these, the vulture-eyed, and all their ravening brood.

The thought of home is ever there,
Like a sad bird with fixed eye
That never shuts, but on the air
Gazeth with deep intensity;
And when the hand of Death may seem
Upon the universe around,
As at this hour of coming dream,
When hushed is all the day's light sound;
When pine, and snow, and rock, and heaven,
Are shadowed by sleep's waving wing—
Sleep, so like death, that in the even
They seem the self-same sombre thing;
When all is thus, it can but bring
That lone-eyed thought to me again,
And on the heart it falls like a cold winter rain.

Perhaps the wing of death is there,
Fanning some soul which I have loved
Into the cold and desert air,
A sad thing from its home removed;
Perhaps they weep for one that's dead,
And think of me the absent, too,
While I have not a tear-drop shed,
As they, the sad, forsaken do;
And so, perhaps, when I return,
'Stead of the loved one's voice and eye,
I may but find the marble urn,

Death's sad and freezing mockery;
And so one other wound will be,
Upon the seared and shattered heart,
Which sorrow loves so well, it doth not thence depart.

'T is terrible to be alone
In the wide world, a homeless thing,
Like a last wave that makes its moan,
And rolleth to the land, to fling
Itself away upon the shore,
With nothing near to mourn its death;
But, like the eagle, far to soar,
While Death his full nest shattereth,
Then to return, and see it float
Away amid the torrent's white,
Perhaps to hear his young's last note,
To see his mate's last look of light;
Oh! this is wo's most wretched sight!
This is the last, the dying pang—
The breaking of the heart which long hath borne the fang.

This must I bear as I have borne
A hundred other woes beside;
And when the last lone hope is shorn,
That glimmering light, which, scarce descried,
Hath been my beacon-star of late,
Then I have done with all of life,
And nought remains to me of fate,
Save death to end the weary strife:
Yet still the branchless tree lives on—
The mastless ship still wends her way,
Nor mindeth wind, nor storm, nor sun;
So I, perhaps, may live my day,
Blind, blind of heart, as best I may,
And some, perhaps, may mourn my death,
When neither envy's fang nor hatred hindereth.

ON THE LOSS OF A SISTER.

Written on hearing of the loss of a Sister, who died
March—, 1832.

AND thou, too, O my Sister; thou art dead:
And desolation once again has sped
His fiery arrow at the lonely heart.
Thus one by one from me, alas! depart
The images that, in the memory stored,
I count and view, as misers do their hoard;
They that along the wide waste of existence,
Have been, and are, the gentle spirits, whence
I gather strength to struggle on with life.

The first fierce sudden stroke the heart that crushed—
The first wild feelings through the brain that rushed—
Are gone, and grief hath now become more mild;
And I have wept as though I were a child—
I, who had thought my heart contained no tear.
And I have but returned from deserts drear—
Prairie, and snow, and mountain eminent,
At my first step upon my father-land,
To feel the snapping of another band,
Of those that bind me slightly to the world.
And thou! whose rainbow spirit now hath furled
Its wings, and gone to quiet sleep within
The dimness of the grave—amid the din
Of calumny which rose around my name,
When I left foes the guardians of my fame—
Amid the sneer, the smile, the slander rank,
Thy love, thy confidence, thy faith ne'er shrank.
Yea, when I tore asunder the few ties
Which bound me to the land of sunny eyes,
And broke the bands I could no longer bear,
Of poverty, enthralment, toil and care;
When love, and hope, and joy were changed to dreams
And fantasies, that, with their starry gleams,

Like things of memory, come upon the soul;
Then, then, my sister! did the big tear roll
Down thy pale cheek for me, thy only brother
Thy love hath been like that of my dear mother;
And it hath fed my heart with gentle dew,
And on my shadowed soul its soothing hue
Lay like the sunlight on a broken flower.
Yea, in the darkness of full many an hour,
When I have climbed above surpassing mountains,
Where from the deathless snows break out cold fountains;
When storm hath beat upon me; when my head
Hath made the ground, the rock, the snow, its bed;
And I have watched cold stars career above—
Then, then my comforter hath been thy love.
When I have felt most sad and most alone;
When I have walked in multitudes unknown,
With none that I could greet for olden time,
Or in those silent solitudes sublime,
Where even echo shuns the loneliness,
And ceases with abundant voice to bless;
When I have thought that I was all forgot
By ancient friends—or if in one lone spot
Within the heart I still was kept in mind,
It was as one disgraced, deluded, blind;
Then, more than ever, then, in the intense
And overpowering wo, thy confidence,
Thy faith, and love, my comforters have been,
And weaned me from myself and from my spleen.
For friends—but I reproach them not, nor heed them now—
What there is left of life, with changeless brow,
And with unquailing heart, I can perform—
Front the world's frown, and dare its wildest storm,
Live out my day, and fall into my grave,
Nor even then the help of friendship crave,
To hide my bones.
And yet—hush, heart! tell not thy weakness; let
False friends not know that thou hast ever wet
My eyelids with a tear for their neglect.

Why do I speak here of myself? Oh! grief
Is egotistical—and finds relief
In sad reflection, even on itself.
Well, thou art dead; and thou didst for me plead,
In all the fervent spirit of thy creed;
And happily didst sink to thy last sleep,
Trusting to rise at sounding of the deep
And awful angel-trumpet. Be it so;
For me, I have yet more of life to go.
Perhaps, ere death shall close my quenched eyes,
I yet may sleep beneath my well-known skies—
Weep o'er the graves that my affections hoard,
Veiling the eyes and hearts I have adored;
And if, perchance, some one or two are left,
Sire, mother, sisters, take them to my heart,
Shield them, defend them, that when I shall die,
Some one above the wanderer's grave may sigh.

Arkansas Territory, Jan. 12, 1833.

TO A———.

THESE lines are to thee; and they come from a heart,
Which hath never to thee spoken aught but the truth,
And which fain would, ere life from its fountains depart,
Speak to thee of the sorrows which clouded its youth.

And think not 't is only to show a fair rhyme,
Or a glittering thought to the eye of the world;
Oh no! 't is a motive more purely sublime;
My wings of ambition forever are furled.

'T is my love, my devotion, which *will* find a tongue,
And utter its thoughts before life and I sever;
'T is the heart which was bruised, and then wantonly flung
On the shore of life's sea, to be trampled forever.

For its words, and its thoughts, and its feelings have been
Misconceived, misconstrued, and traduced for long years;
And 't would fain, from the general calumny, win
One heart, that might water its grave-sod with tears.

For the world, I defy it and dare it; it hath
No power, no terror, no lash, over me;
I ask not the light of its smile in my path,
And its pity or frown might as well urge the sea.

I owe it, and ask it no favor; full well
I have proven its friendship, its mercy, its love;
But thou hast upon me a charm and a spell,
That through life and in death will be able to move.

I would show that the heart which the world hath reviled,
Whose passions have been like the waves of the sea,
Whate'er hath been—how ungoverned and wild—
Hath been constantly true in devotion to thee.

That devotion to thee, love, hath never been told:
Perhaps 't was unnoticed; the feeling most deep
Has the semblance of something unfeeling and cold;
The frief most o'erwhelming but seldom can weep.

And readier tongues spake their tale in thine ear,
And told thee their love with full many a sigh:
Perhaps thou wast dazzled by that and the tear,
And read not my love in the heart and the eye.

I told not my love—it were cruel to ask
One like thee, with misfortune and sorrow to wed,
To wear away life as an incessant task,
And pillow on Poverty's bosom thy head—

Till I turned from the green and the delicate lanes
Of home, love and joy, which were darkened with gloom,
And shivered, unflinching, the multiplied chains,
Which are woven round all when the heart is in bloom.

Since then, day by day, my lone heart hath decayed,
With a slow, but a certain, and deadly decline;
O'er its waste and its wilderness riseth no blade,
Which may say with its greenness—'Wo! all is not thine.'

And though I must die ere my deity sphere
Be revealed from the storm which holds heaven at will,
I *must* turn to the place where it ought to appear,
And worship its light till my pulses be still.

It may be that I am to live till my cup
Of affliction be filled and o'erflow at the brim;
Till the mist and the blood from the heart shall rise up,
When its last hope is gone—its last vision is dim;

Till thou hast become, in thy beauty, the bride
Of some other less wild, and less passionate lover;
Then the beacon is merged in the hungering tide—
Then the heart hath been crushed, and its struggle is over.

Arkansas Territory, Feb. 12, 1833.

SIMILES, IN TWO SONNETS.

ABOVE me are the dazzling snows; around
The mountains bend, high, rocky and eterne;
Anear the rattling rivulet doth sound,
And far below, it hath the bosom found
Of a bright lake, that seemeth not to spurn
One ray of sunlight from its gentle presence,
But doth embody all, and seemeth changed
To sheeted light by Sol's etherial essence.
O silver star! for whom doth ever burn
The altar of my soul's idolatry!
Let thy bright arrows sink into the sea
Of my sad soul, until it gently calm;
And though thou canst but people a lone dream,
Oh soothe me like an angel's silver palm.

And close beyond, the mountains gray upstream,
Like cloudy shades, into the upper air.
Perpetual watchers do the giants seem
Of the lake's quiet. Lo! their heads are bare
Beneath God's presence, which is mighty there,
In the etherial, keen, thin element.
A floating cloud hath down from heaven bent,
And on the hill-side feeds the springing leaves,
And into water-drops its soul doth weave,
Feeding the streams. O lady of my love!
Be thou, though absent, like the silver cloud,
Over my soul. Oh may thy spirit move,
Feeding its dark and parched wilderness!
And once, or ere I die, touch, transport, bless!

Mountains of Xemes, April 15, 1832.

A Mexican Tale

I t was just at night when I began to descend the last mountain between the village of San Fernandez, in the valley of Taos, and that of El Embudo, twenty-five miles from it, and to which I was now approaching. I had ascended these mountains in the midst of a fierce storm of snow, which, as night came on, had lulled, leaving the wind still blowing heavily through the mountain pines.[1] As I descended, the darkness and the cold both grew more intense and palpable. Well wrapped, however, in blankets, and trusting implicity to our sure-footed mules, we descended the mountain, not swiftly, but safely. At times the descent was so precipitous, that I was only kept from falling by the aid of the deep saddle, and the broad wooden stirrups of my friend, the worshipful Don Pedro Vigil, who, owning the best house, the best horses, and the prettiest wife in the valley of San Fernandez, had kindly supplied us with mules and a guide. So soon as I arrived at a part of the hill whence the descent was less rapid and dangerous, I put my mule to the best speed which I could accomplish by means of the long and heavy iron spurs which I wore, at each application of which, my mule uttered a groan, accompanied by a sensible increase of speed. Crossing the small river, which, running out of a narrow cañon or valley to the eastward of the road, supplies water to the inhabitants,[2] and which, frozen as it was, caused to my mule more fear with its perilous slipperiness, and to me, more difficulty, than all the voyage beside—crossing this, we heard the baying of dogs, to us a welcome sound, and were soon within the village. Neither then, however, with its still, sombre, dungeon-like appearance,

1. Pike traveled through Embudo on his way to Santa Fe in early December of 1831, shortly after his arrival at Taos.
2. The Río Pueblo.

nor on the following morning, as it lay in the midst of the valley, with the hills rising all about it, bare, red and desolate, and frowning gloomily over the monotonous whiteness of the plain —neither at one time nor the other, had it much of attraction for us. But I have seen it at another time, and under happier auspices; in the early autumn, when the corn and wheat were ripening over the whole valley, and when the mountains, partially clad in green, had not the same gloomy look as in the depth of winter, and when the river sparkled and rattled as it ran towards El Embudo, or the tunnel, the passage through the rocks, whence the village derives its name.

As we entered the village, everything save the bay of the dogs was silent; no merry lights gleamed from the casements, and the houses, as they stood huddled together like so many brick-kilns, had a certain churlish and inhospitable look. As we had no visions which might prove realities, of anything here in the shape of a merry tavern, with its good supper, good beds and jolly landlord, we agreed to apply at the best house in the village,—and we were not long in instructing our guide to that effect. Accordingly, turning into a roughly fenced enclosure, we found ourselves in front of a house, which, with its piazza in front, seemed superior to the habitations around it. Here our guide knocked at the small and only window to be discovered, and after various invocations to 'La Santa Maria,' and other saints of both sexes, he succeeded in arousing those within, and requested admittance in the name of the party. 'Adios!' was answered in a shrill voice, 'there are no men in the house, and you have frightened us already. We cannot admit you.' In this extremity, our guide bethought himself of the only sure means of obtaining an entrance. 'Pero, Señora,' (but madam), said he, 'they are Americanos, and they pay well.' I am not prepared to say which clause of this speech produced the effect, whether our character as Americans, or as good pay-masters; but of a certainty, the folding doors were soon wide open, and the lady of the house received us in her kindest manner. Passing through the sala, or long hall, which was garnished with vast quantities of buffalo meat, in thin, dry fleeces, as well as with huge strings of onions, and of red and green pepper, besides numberless saddle-trees, heavy bridles, and not a few buffalo robes, we entered the small square room which was the winter residence. In one corner of it stood the little fireplace, like a square stove, open on two sides, and filled with small sticks of pine set upright and burning, filling the room with all heat and comfort. Round the whole room, except the part occupied by two mattrasses [sic], was a pile of blankets, striped red and white, answering the purpose of sofas. High up on the walls were various small looking-glasses, pictures of saints, wooden images of the Saviour, and wooden cruifixes, interspered with divers roses of red and white cambric. These, with two or three wooden benches which served for both chairs and tables, completed the furniture of the room. The inmates of the house were but two. The mistress of it was a woman of about thirty years of age, of features which, as I discovered in my autumn visit, were not unpleasing, when left to themselves, but which at this time were hideously bedaubed and ornamented with red earth, which, as well as the white chalk-like earth, is the common rouge and paint of the females in the villages. Her hair lay smooth behind, disdaining that luxury, the comb. Her calico dress, with its short bosom and scanty pattern, was ungraceful in the extreme; and her feet appeared beneath it in their primitive nakedness. The Indian girl who appeared now and then, as she moved in and out the kitchen, was dirty in the extreme, clad only in a chemise and petticoat, as dirty as herself. Divesting ourselves of our blankets and extra clothing, we gave ourselves up entirely to the influence of the fire and the hopes of supper—for your mountain storm is a strange sharpener of the appetite. Contrary to our fears, supper came in a reasonable space of time, and we did good justice to the pounded dry buffalo meat, the beans and the blood-red dish of meat and pepper, all of them inseparable from a New Mexican table, and forthwith consigned ourselves to the blankets and mattrasses of our landlady.

On seating ourselves by the fireside the next morning, we found ourselves favored with the company of our hostess's father. A quaint looking old man was Don Diego, with his little sharp hat and little sharp chin, with short leathern breeches, gray stockings, and Apache moccasins, together with his coarse rough frock of woollen fabric. During the age of preparation neccessary, as I before hinted, to prepare a meal, upon me, as the only linguist of the party, fell the task of conversing with the old man—and sooth to say, I found him neither a foolish nor an uninteresting companion. Among other matters, I was struck with one legend which the old man related to me, and for the real truth of which he vouched. It struck me, not on account of any peculiar novelty in the incidents or the catastrophe, but because it goes far to prove the fact, of which we are getting every day more and more convinced, that there is more of romance in real life than in fiction, as also that the fire of passion and the depth of affection can exist under the most adverse circumstances, and in the roughest and most uncultivated breasts.

It is now several years since a mounted man was seen, just at the close of a fine day in August, to ride over the last small hills of the rocky barrier to the south of El Embudo, and approach the village, followed by two or three pack mules and a Spanish servant. The sun was just approaching to the western mountains, filling the sky with the splendid flush of loveliness, which rendors the sunset scenes of New Mexico unsurpassed even by those of New England. Over the whole sky, even to the tops of the eastern hills, the clouds were full of surpassing brilliancy and beauty. Hues of every shade, from the lightest silver to the deepest purple, and at every instant changing, gathered in the heaven, as the sun slowly fell behind the mountains. The valley, into which the trader was now entering, was but scantily greened over with grass and a tall dry weed which, even in summer, has a look of barrenness; but just around the village, which, low, dull, and silent, lay in the centre of the valley, the level expanse of wheat and corn gave it an appearance of fertility, which in truth it hardly deserves.

The trader, as he approached the town, seemed an object of curiosity to various individuals who were to be seen seated at the doors of the houses, all of them, of both sexes, with their never-failing companion, a segar of *punche* (their country tobacco) rolled in a slip of corn-husk. At this time, which was just at the commencement of the American trade to the country, the common people were not so well accustomed to the sight of Americans as at present. Then, the high hat, the long coat, the boots, the full pantaloons, seemed to them odd and *outre;* and they gazed upon the wearer as a singular curiosity. Amid various ejaculations—for the New Mexicans are not a people to restrain or hide their surprise or admiration—the foreigner moved steadily through the town towards the outer edge of it, obedient to a mute sign of direction given by his servant. One group, particularly, by which he passed, seemed interested by his arrival. There were two old men with their dress of leather and coarse woollen, a woman with her hair turned gray, and one of middle age, a young man, and a girl of some fifteen years. In the door-way, too, stood an Indian girl with her Nabajo blanket, black, with a red border, just around her middle, and answering for a gown.

'Mira! Don Santiago!' said one of the old men to the other—'there comes one of these strangers that have arrived now for years to our land.' 'Yes, brother,' was the answer, 'and no doubt he comes well laden with goods to fish away the *pesitos* (little dollars) of us poor.' 'And a good exchange,' resumed the other, 'to barter our musty gold and silver for the useful and beautiful things he brings. Every pelayo[3] has his hands full of dollars, and his legs cased in leather—ay, and his back, for not till now has he been offered a shirt.' 'As to your gold, Amigo Ramon,' answered Don Santiago, 'I know and see but little of it; but what little silver I have, Valgame Dios y La Virgen![4] is better bestowed in my big chests than in the pockets of that picaro.'

'Nay,' interrupted the oldest woman, 'they are no picaros, these Americans. I have been told by the Doña Imanuela, in Santa Fe, that she would place her dollars in their hands without counting them, and have no fear of losing one. Nay, compadre, an American cannot steal.'

'Quien sabe?' (who knows?) ejaculated the old man, 'every rascal has a good face till he is found out.'

3. See note 17 of the second "Narrative."
4. "Good God and the Virgin!"

'And then they are such ingenious men!' went on the dame,
'Tata Dios![5] such strange things as they know how to make,—
they know everything,—calico and balls of thread, and a thousand things more strange.'

'And, Señora,' said the young man, 'what beautiful guns—
not like our old fusees—some with two barrels, and some that
have no flints. Nay, it is true, Inacia! Have you not seen them,
Tata Ramon?'

'Yes, indeed I have—and so strange they are, too! Ah! they
are great men, these Americans! they can all read and write
like a priest. Lastima! (pity) that they are heretics.'

'And so beautiful,' timidly said Inacia, 'y tan grandotes!'

'Ay, indeed,' spoke again the old woman, 'they are all white
and beautiful; but, que les perdon Dios![6] they are not Christians
—they have no religion.

'Y tan bravos! (and so brave) said the young man. 'Son
Diablos, (they are devils) and have no fear. Well, the dollars
that I have are few; but they will be fewer when I have seen
the inside of this American's trunks. I want some powder, and
some calico for a jacket.'

'And I,' said Don Ramon, 'want some tobacco. It is ten times
as good as punche; and besides, look at my shirt-sleeve! I don't
intend to wear a blanket next winter, either.'

'Well, do as you please,' said Don Santiago, 'I am content to
wear a blanket like my father before me, and a woollen shirt
like my grandfather. Valgame la madre de Dios y los Santos! it
takes more than one sheep to buy a big coat of these heretics,
and I will fill the purse of none of them, malditos sean sus
cuerpos.'[7]

'Vamos,' (uttered with a peculiar Indian-like tone, and without sounding the final s) said Don Ramon as he rose to depart,
'what will you bet that you don't put ten dollars in the purse
or pocket of this American before he leaves El Embudo?'

5. *Tata* is a word of endearment which Mexican children call their mothers
and fathers—much like our *mama* and *papa*. Pike uses this frequently, just as
the New Mexicans probably did. *Dios* means *God*.
6. "Pardon them God!"
7. "Curse their persons."

'Adios!' (sounded like the 'Vamos') 'Adios hombre; not ten clakos—not ten jolas!'[8]

'Que me apuestas?' (what will you bet?)

'My wife here and Inacia are foolish, and will perhaps buy something; but I, not a clako!'

'Que me apuestas?'

'Que te apuesto? A hundred cigarritos.'

'A hundred! Vamos a ver! And of tobacco.'

'Well, of tobacco. Que diablo! ten dollars!'

'At any rate, Don Santiago, you will go and see this American; may be he brings some news from the villa; and, at any rate, he will not ask you to buy of him. Come, take your stick, and let us go.'

'Let us go, husband; I want some thread,' said the middle aged woman.

'Do, father,' said another voice, 'let us go.'

And go they did. The old man took his stick, which mere habit, and not age, made him use, and his wife deposited in her bosom several of the bright inmates of a big purse, which, in its turn, was the inmate of a big chest in the corner of the room.

Even according to this conversation was then the state of affairs in New Mexico.[9] It was supposed that an American could be guilty of no crime—no meanness. Did he want a store?—rooms in abundance were offered him gratis. Did he eat and sleep at a Spanish house while traveling?—no pay was received; and everywhere the people possessed that character of hospitality which they still preserve, at a distance from the large towns. In fact, I have never, at a single door, requested food and lodging, by the untranslatable expression, *tengo posada?* (literally, have I a tavern?) without being promptly answered in the affirmative; that is, in the little country settlements. The dim mists were gathering thickly around the dark brows of the mountains, blending the gloomy pines into one undistinguishable mass, as the party entered the house where the trader had stopped. It was the same house in which I afterwards slept, and which bore

8. "Clakos," meaning *tlacos*, and *jolas* are fractional currency. A *tlaco* would be worth about one cent today. *Jolas* were even more diminuitive.

9. In this curious sentence, Pike seems to be saying: "As this conversation illustrates, thus was the state of affairs in New Mexico at that time."

then, as it does now, the reputation of the best house in the village. Passing through the sala, or long hall, in which then the family resided, they were ushered into the winter room, now occupied by 'Caesar and his fortunes.'

A country store, including everything saleable, from a salt-kettle to a yard of tape, were nothing to the contents of the six trunks, with which young Jones was to make or mar his fortune.

Don Ramon was the first applicant; and the ice once broken, the business went on fluently. The powder, the shoes, the handkerchiefs, were soon purchased with little chaffering; but buying the big coat was not to be lightly hurried over. The price, however, being reduced to twelve dollars the yard, Don Ramon counted them down upon a trunk, and made no further purchases. The females, however, had, like our own fair, a genius for shopping; and to make a purchase, it was absolutely essential to see the contents of all the trunks. During all this time, the father was standing by the merchant, sturdily, however, maintaining his resolve of making no purchases. Catching an opportunity, while Don Ramon left the room, he demanded to see some cloth for a capote. The merchant showed him a cloak ready made. He bought it. 'Buy some tobacco, compadre,' said a voice from the sala, 'a hundred cigarrones, you know, of the best ojas, and of tobacco.'

The young man bought his powder, his red crape shawl to serve as a girdle, and a few other articles; and then a silken scarf and some ribbons, and a quantity of very small beads.

'Do you wear a scarf and ribbons?' said the provoking Don Ramon.

Rafael blushed, and so did Inacia. The trading was over. Let us leave the narrative a little.

Rafael Mestes was, in the judgment of Inacia Martin, the most pleasing young man in the valley of El Embudo; or, indeed, between Santa Fe and Taos. He was of the middle size, rather slightly but still firmly built, and possessed of all the ability of the *leon* of his mountains.

His eye, like those of all his people, was keen and black; and his face, though by no means singular or striking, might be accounted handsome. Mixing in his veins the blood of the Spaniard and the Indian, he possessed the energy and the indomitable fierceness of both races, united to the simplicity of character, which, as yet, had met little to corrupt it. He had been, from his youth, a herdsman and shepherd; and winter and summer he and his herds were to be found in the deep, narrow and rich valleys of the mountains.

He was the best rider, the best thrower of the *lasso,* and the best hunter in the valley. He could pick up a dollar from the ground with his horse at full speed. He could rope a running horse by either foot, or a buffalo by his horns, and throw him. And when he shot at one of these animals, his arrow fell out on the other side. Not that he could not use a gun; but for running buffalo, both Spaniards and Indians prefer the bow and arrow, and the lance. His bravery was undisputed. Alone he chased the leon, the tiger-cat, and the grizzly bear. And no Apache or Comanche ever kept long the cattle of which they might have robbed him. Neither does this sum up his good qualities; he was the best dancer in the fandango, the best fiddler, and the best improviso singer from the valley of Taos to the city of the Holy Faith.[10]

10. The Mexicans are great improvisators; but their poetry which they thus manufacture is truly despicable. In the south, I believe, it is better. They know but little about poetry, or anything else, in New Mexico, except their catechism; but here is a small article, which I have heard them sing.

Which, translated, runs thus:

A MI SEÑORA.	TO MY LADY.

El dulce bien por quien suspiro,
    Solo eres tu.
	The sweet delights for which I sigh,
	    Alone art thou.

El don supremo a quien aspiro,
    Lo tienes tu.
	The supreme gift—the mark so high—
	    That holdest thou.

Tienes mi pecho adormecido,
    Lo causas tu.
	My heart is sleepless—it is thine—
	    That causest thou.

Mira mi llanto enternecido!
    Lo enjugas tu.
	Witness this tender grief of mine,
	    That scornest thou.

El tiempo fué de mis pasiones,
    Una ilusion;
	My passions' hour has been to me
	    Illusiveness.

Y tus ingratos procederes
    Lastiman hoi mi corazon.
	And ah! ingratitude from thee
	    Tortures the heart it ought to bless.

Adonde estan tus juramentos?
    Tu tierno amor, tu firme fe?
	Where are the oaths which thou hast made—
	    Thy tender love, faith ne'er to fade—

Que es de aquel llanto enternecido!
    Onde esta? Onde se fué?
	The impassioned tears, which thou hast shed?
	    Where are they gone? Where are they fled?

[continued]

Inacia was young and pretty. As to accomplishments, a New Mexican girl has none. She could knit a glove or a stocking, and cut corn-husks into slips for smoking, and work various articles in beads.

In the jarabes, or singular dances of the fandango, her first partner was always Rafael. The first glass of the aguardiente, or white brandy, or of the vino del Paso, generally touched her lips. His hand was always ready at shawling and unshawling; and various little ornaments always marked his return from a journey to Taos. In return, the little bundles of ojas[11] which he took into the mountains for smoking, were always cut by her hand; and his guaje, or little gourd, was always filled by her, with the best punche. His stockings were all knit by her; and the little riband braided of beads, from which hung the little silver saint, was put round his neck by her hand. Born and brought up together, the course of their affection had known no ebb and flow. They were not sufficiently refined and sentimental, not to know that they loved each other, and nothing had taught them to conceal it. At least, if there was anything more than simplicity and nature in the matter, the old man who told me the tale could not describe it to me; for he had no idea of anything like love in a novel.

It was a bright and sunny morning, when, on the second day

There is a splendid piece of poetry, which one or two men in the country can sing. The story is, that La Pola was the mistress of Bolivar. The air to which it is sung is a superb minor, and it always gave me a thrill at hearing it.

> Colombianos! la Pola no existe:—
> Con la patria su suerte llorad;
> A morir por la patria prendamos,
> Y su muerte juremos vengar!
>
> Por las calles, y al pie del suplicio,
> 'Asesinos,' gritaba, 'temblad!
> Consumad vuestro horrible atentado!
> Luego viene quien me ha de vengar.'
>
> Y volviendose al pueblo, le dice:
> 'Pueblo ingrato! Ya voi espirar,
> Por salvar vuestros caros derechos:
> Tanta injuria podreis tolerar?
>
> 'Un Lapon, un Carib, un Calmuc,
> Las virtudes sabran respetar:
> De Colombia, los hijos valientes,
> Solo mueren por su libertad.'

after his arrival, the trader's mules were seen wending their way out of the village at their accustomed pace, and, crossing the river, were soon buried in the bosom of the mountains on the path which leads to Taos. There is no season of the day so exhilarating as sunrise. The heart will feel sleepy at noon, and melancholy at sunset; but not at sunrise. Everything seems to feel the influence of the young day except a mule; *it* is always the same, with its long pacing gait, and its ears tossing backward and forward.

At about the same hour, Rafael might have been seen emerging from the small low but neat cabin of his mother; and, after mounting his little fleet mare, taking the road which led in an opposite direction. His dress was now altered from the wide pantaloons, open on the outside of either leg to the knees, and gaily ornamented with a profusion of buttons, to the herdsman's common ones of leather. His jacket, too, of blue cloth, had given way to the short frock of gray woollen. His red

---

This is not all of it, but it is all which I can remember. I subjoin a translation, not aiming in it at rhyme.

> Colombians! the Pola exists not:—
>   With her country her fortunes lament;
> Learn to die for the rights of your country,
>   And her death let us swear to revenge!
>
> Through the streets to the foot of the scaffold,
>   She cried, 'Fear and tremble assassins!
> Your horrible action consummate;
>   Soon will come one who is to revenge.'
>
> And, turning to the people, she sayeth:
>   'Ingrates! I am now to expire,
> For saving your rights and your freedom:
>   Such wrong ye can silently bear?
>
> 'The Laplander, Carib, Calmuc,
>   The virtues, perchance, may respect;
> Ye alone, valiant sons of Colombia,
>   For your freedom are known to expire.'

The reader who has perused the *Bravo* of our countryman Cooper, has seen a heading of a chapter in that novel entitled part of a boat song. It is singular that the New Mexicans have a song commencing in the same way. I could have had it all written for me, but not intending, when I left Santa Fe, to come into the United States, I neglected it. The Spanish song begins thus:

> 'Soi pescator del hondo,
>   Fideli;'

and every verse ends with 'oye mi linda!' In it the lover describes himself as a fisherman, whose bait 'es el amor.'—PIKE.

11. *Hojas*, or leaves.

sash had disappeared likewise; but his head was left as usual for the weather to do its worst upon. His fusee[12] was set in front of him, and supported by a strap depending from the horn of the saddle. His bow and quiver hung at his back; and these, with a long rope coiled in front of him, and a small axe behind him, were the arms and implements of his calling. Arriving at a deep hollow which runs across the road about a hundred yards from the village, he alighted, and, seating himself upon a rock, seemed to await the coming of some one. Nor was he detained long; a light step was soon heard approaching, and Inacia descended into the hollow. Saluting each other by the title, brother and sister, and by the embrace and kiss so common among the Mexicans, they sat down together, and she inquired—'And how long hast thou waited for me here?'

'It is but a moment. Were it an hour, I am paid. But tell me, is your father well, and your mother?'

'They are both well, Gracias a Dios! and may he give them a thousand years of life! But you seem sad, and your eye is wandering; are you sick?'

'No,' said the young man, smiling, 'I was only engaged with my own fears: may they prove empty! Hearken, Inacia. I have no fear that you will ever prove faithless: why should you? We have been brought up together; our mothers are comadres, (sponsors,) and you can never know me better than you do now. But still, I have strange fears; I had bad dreams last night, and awoke frightened, thinking that a bear was tearing you from my arms. Ave Maria purisima! Your father loves you; but he loves money better. Nay, be not angry; I know what I say. Oye! Your father does not love me; I know not why: nor your mother. I cannot tell whence danger and disappointment are to come; but old Juan de Dios Lopez looks upon you with a loving eye—and he is rich. Perhaps, they may come from him. Beside, these Americans who come to the country—these beautiful, rich and brave—they, like everything else, may love Inacia, and your father may give you to one of them. Virgen bendita! I rave at thinking of it. But, Inacia, never become the bride of any but me. Look at these hands: they are brown with

12. A flintlock gun, or fusil.

toil; they can labor for two as well as for one, and God will guard and prosper us. He loves his children.'

'And why, caro hermano, should you fear that I will wed either our neighbor Lopez, or any of these strangers who frequent our country with their rare treasures? Have we not lived together and known one another long? ay, many years?'

'And have I not said, mi alma! that I do not distrust, nay, have never distrusted you? but the entreaties and severity of thy parents might do much with thy gentle spirit.'

'Have you never marked, Rafael, how thy gentlest sheep will prove bold in the defence of her weak young? and even the turtle dove which we hear moaning in the mountains like wind in the pine-tops—she, more gentle still, will not flee from man when her young are in the nest. And am I weaker than they, if they would force my heart?'

'Well, my sweet Inacia! thou has shown to me that my fears are weak and simple; but, querida, when the turtle dove is attacked by the hawk or the bald eagle, she has been known to take refuge in the bosom of man. My arm is strong, and wo to any who would ruffle a feather on the wing of my white dove!'

'Nay, now I should of right chide thee, Rafael, that thou thinkest so illy of my parents; but let it pass, though perchance it may be construed into a want of duty to those who love thee and reared thee in the true faith; if so, I may but do penance.'

'And sit upon a tombstone? I wonder what crime thou hadst ever committed, to pass thine hours in so gloomy a place.'

'Hush, Rafael—all commit many sins.'

'And some have better, and strange to say, more lenient confessors that we; in truth, our Padre teaches us by precept better than by example. I doubt, sometimes, Inacia, of the doctrines preached to us by such men as he; the stream that runs through a muddy soil, becomes after a space, itself foul. I have talked with these Americans, Inacia, whom we call hereges,[13] and they have told me many strange things, which—but I forget:—lo, the sun is two hours above the hills, and yet thou knowest not why I called thee here. You have kindly promised to make me a broad cinta to support my saint, for this round my neck is, to

13. *Herejes,* or heretics.

say the truth, something worn. Here is the chaquina[14] (small beads) with which to weave it; wilt thou do it for me?'

'Why not?'

'And, Inacia, here is something which, when thou wearest, thou wilt remember the giver. Say not a word; I'll not hear it. Come—the sun calls me sluggard; one embrace, and I go to the mountains. Have care of yourself till I return, lest you be sick. Adios mi vida!'

After the embrace, he threw himself upon his mare, held out his hand, as a last farewell, and bounding up the bank, rode swiftly off. Inacia stood silently watching him, till a small ridge sloping off into the bosom of the mountains, hid him from her sight; then, as a big tear gathered slowly and fell from her black lashes, she turned silently homeward. The village was silent, as common, and as she passed through it to the home of her father, hardly an individual met her eye.

The house into which she entered was like all around it, a small building of mud. At each end of it was a room projecting into the street beyond the body of the edifice to a line with the piazza, which stood in front of the sala. The walls, as I have said, were of large square bricks of mud, and above them, small timbers were laid across, projecting out to the distance of a foot or two from the building, and which, placed near together and covered to the depth of two feet with bricks of mud, formed the roof. The thick, heavy door was roughly carved, and the square windows were paned with the mica of the mountains. Everything was quiet about the house; four or five oxen and cows were lying about in the sun chewing their cud; and the jackass, just eased of his heavy load of pine sticks, was munching his husks contentedly at the door; two or three dogs were basking in the sun under the heavy wain of pine, which, with its pine wheels and pine axletree, looked to the eye like a useless pile of lumber. Even the hens had caught the infection, and went quietly about without their endless cackling; and the half dozen pigs which were staked close to the house to keep them out of

14. Probably a misprint for *chaquira*, a word first used in Peru to mean glass trade beads, but which was also used in Mexico. See Francisco J. Santamaría, *Diccionario de Mejicanismos* (Mexico, D. F., 1959), p. 362.

the corn were too luxurious to utter a grunt. Within, her mother was busily twirling the distaff and making yarn by the slow process of a former age, still common in New Mexico. Her father was smoking his cigar of corn-husks.

In the country in which every man, though he be a fool, has a small sprinkling of the knave, it cannot be supposed that Don Santiago Sandoval had escaped the general contagion. Not he; he had even been an Alcalde, which title generally implies a greater knave with a better opportunity, and a wider flight for his genius.

Men did not cry out against him, or point to him as an example to be shunned, and by which their children might take heed to their steps. No; he had no such reputation. He had been a man of much *diligencia*,[15] as the Spaniards call a faculty which they possess and exercise,—in our language, *swindling*. He had, perhaps, been bribed once or so. He had once had a chain upon his leg for a little time; 'but other reputable men had done the same—nay, worse. For example, there was Juan de Dios Lopez, and Juan de Jesus Ortis; they had been in prison for stealing horses and sheep; but Tata Dios de mi alma! such men always became rich, and flourished in the world.' This was by way of moral to their children.

No remark was made, or question put, when Inacia entered; and she sat down quietly to her knitting, in the still manner which characterizes the females of her country. Although we may reasonably suppose, that Love, who works more changes, and produces more strange effects, than Prospero's 'quaint and dainty Ariel,'[16] had lent to Rafael something of exaggeration, and a little vain fear, when he supposed that all things which looked upon Inacia must love her, yet natheless, she was a pretty, almost a beautiful girl. There is no taste in the dress of a New Mexican female—not a spark—and they never develope any thing of that grace of bust and outline, which enchants us in our own delightful girls. But without the aid, or rather with the disadvantage of dress, detracting from her natural beauty,

15. For example:—a man steals your horse, and gets you to give him five or six dollars for finding him. This is *diligencia*.—PIKE.
16. A reference to the wondrous "airy Spirit" of Shakespeare's *The Tempest*.

Inacia was far from homely; her eyes were keen, black and vivid; her face was oval and delicate; her mouth small, and lips beautifully thin—and a thin delicate lip well befits a black eye and jet locks. Her skin was tinged with the hue which the sun gives to all he loves to look upon warmly, and her small and round, yet delicate form, seemed to have hardly support enough in a taper foot and slender ankle which might have become Titania.[17] Were I to detail the conversation, which after the entrance of Inacia served to wear away the monotony of the forenoon, I should most certainly wear away the patience of my readers. Suffice it to say that it turned upon the crops, cattle, and in a word, upon all possible subjects except politics—that is a matter in which this isolated and unimportant, as well as uninterested people have nothing to do. Noon, that unwearied traveller, had arrived, perhaps passed, when the tramp of a horse was heard approaching; and the rider dismounting, entered the door, uttering as he did so, a benediction. He was the priest to whom belonged the spiritual charge of the village of El Embudo, as well as of the Jolla[18] and some others. As he entered, he was saluted by the master of the house with the title, *Tata Padre,* and by the mother more respectfully, as *Padre Santo.* His hat and cane were officiously taken charge of, and after seating himself on a pile of blankets, and wiping the sweat from his brow, he received and returned various enquiries after health, and started various topics of conversation, which, so far as I know, are common to all nations.

The Frai Luis Muro was about thirty years of age, of features coarse, and sensual, but regular; stoutly and firmly built, and of the medium height. Had he not been a priest, his character for virtue would have been little respected. He was grievously addicted to various sins; and among them was numbered the love of good liquor, and, at times, a forgetfulness of his vow of celibacy. Had he not been a priest, however, he would have been only a bon vivant, and a very good fellow, as the world of

17. Titania is queen of the fairies in Shakespeare's *A Midsummer-Night's Dream.*

18. La Joya, present-day Velarde, is located a few miles south of Embudo.

New Mexico goes, and no crime or sin would have been laid at his door.

To say the truth, the Padre Muro was infinitely superior to many or most of his brethren, who, in general, are in that country hardly as well educated as a boy of eight years in ours. Now the Frai Luis had been educated at the college of Guadalajara, and was a tolerable scholar in Latin and Greek. He was also well versed in the now exploded systems of natural philosophy and chemistry; and was in fact a man of no mean talent —and of no great sanctity.

During a pause in the conversation, which had continued for some time after his entrance, the eye of the Padre fell upon the cloak which had so lately elicited the dollars of Don Santiago.

'What, hermano,' said he, 'you have purchased a new capote! Did you not say that one of these strangers, these Americans, had been here of late?'

'Some such thing has happened, father, as you mention; and of a truth, I did improve the opportunity to lay aside the blanket and to wear the cloak.'

'And to lose,' said a voice from the door, 'a hundred cigarros of tobacco to me, which you are not to forget to pay, or I to claim. But, father, pardon me! My first salute was due to you.'

'You have no pardon to ask, Don Ramon! What of these hundred cigarros?'

'A wager, father, that he would not put ten dollars into the purse of this American.'

'And he—when did he go from here?'

'This morning, after the sun rose.'

'Did you talk with him while he was here?'

'Yes, father, he slept at my house.'

'And what said he?—do you remember?'

'Yes; much that it is not meet for me to repeat to you. These strangers are a bold and careless race; and of a truth they pay little respect to our holy church. They neither cross themselves nor tell the rosary—nay, nor remove their hat as they pass a crucifix.'

'It is true, hijo. I have seen some of them. They do not scruple even to attack our faith with argument; and if they are allowed to enter and reside thus in our country, I fear for the consequences. There are some among us already touched with heresy. I have heard of some bold speeches of a youth of El Embudo, and grievous shall be the penance with which he must atone. I speak of young Rafael Mestes—nay, it may be that unless he make full acknowledgement and reformation, I shall call upon the Gefe Politico to forward him to Mexico, there to learn the true doctrine.'

'Nay, father,' said Don Ramon, 'I hardly think that your power extends so far; and neither do I imagine that Rafael has merited any such penance. The boy may have had some thoughts, that certain matters in the existing state of the church might be altered for the better; and truly, father, I have had a shrewd leaning to the same opinion myself. For example, it seems to me that those who are our teachers should themselves be men of exemplary lives. How, for example, am I to take warning not to brutalize myself with liquor, when he who is my adviser, finds a difficulty in standing upright, and hath his words one standing in the way of the other? It seems, too, at times, to my mind, that we who are the most concerned in the matter, should have the right of examining the credentials of those, who claim to be our guides, and of looking into the book whence they derive their doctrines.'

'It is soon proved, Don Ramon!'

'Nay, father, I meant not to enter upon an argument in this matter; to doubt of one side is not to defend the other. Of these Americans, father, I have only this to say,—receive your tithes, and leave them in peace; your flock is not about to receive doctrines from them; although were we all like them, neither we nor you might be the worse. They too are Christians, and have their Padres, and do them reverence, and are never misused by them; and perhaps, as the sacred Scriptures may be read by him who runs, they who, to a child, can read it, may be more probably in the right way than we who never see it. But with regard to Rafael, should you oppress him, men might say that you did so, distrusting the goodness of your cause. Would we punish men—would you punish me because I in my heart preferred a monarchy to a republic? Nay, father, let him talk; they that heed him are few; they that he will convert are fewer. By the way, father, do you know of the reply which a Nabajo made not long ago to the Padre Sanchez?'

'Not I.'

'The Padre urged him to become a Christian. "No," said he, "God made me for a Nabajo; he does not want me to be a Christian." "But," said the old man, "now he has brought you here as a prisoner, purposely to give you an opportunity to become a Christian." "No, no," was the answer; "he did not make me for a Christian. Look here; he made a horse for a horse, and a mule for a mule; he made you to be a Christian, and me to be a Nabajo." What do you think of that?'

'I think that the Padre had better have left him alone.'

'He did, and acted wisely; but tell me, Padre, when will you celebrate mass?'

'Early in the morning, to-morrow; to-day I must see to the arrangement of the coming tithes; at the utmost, they are no immense matter, and if I lose half of them, as I do of the primicias, (first fruits), I may sit down with nothing.'

'I have not forgotten that I owe you six sheep of the primicias, which you may receive at any day. In the mean time, let us together pay a visit to our neighbor Lopez; if you will accompany me, we will not be detained long.'

With a promise to Don Santiago that he would return to dinner, the Frai Luis accompanied him to the house of him who has been already once or twice mentioned in this narrative by the name Juan de Dios Lopez. This man was about sixty years of age. His hair had not yet lost any of its original blackness, but his beard, always half an inch long, was of a dirty gray color; his eyes, small and half shut, were set deeply behind his cheek bones; his nose, thin and straight, projected over his mouth. Add to this a small figure, and a stooping, shuffling gait, with a certain fiendish and beastly expression of countenance, and you have the Señor Lopez. Besides tilling his ground, he at times brought up from the Paso del Norte, chocolate, sugar, wine, and whiskey, which he vended to his neighbors. It was the latter of these articles which caused him the present visit.

Upon their entrance into the house of this worthy, and after the usual salutations and embraces, a cuartillo of aguardiente, or grape whiskey, was at the instance of Don Ramon produced and placed upon the table, and the priest was not slow in testing its virtues.

'Gracias a Dios!' was his first expression, as he put down the glass after taking a long draught; 'Gracias a Dios! there is no water in that.'

'No, Señor Padre,' said Lopez, 'it is of the vintage of Velarde, of whom you may have heard. He is not the man to vend bad wine or whiskey; and far and near his vintage is known and in repute.'

'And worthily, too, if all his liquor hath such a gusto as this.'

'But, father,' said Don Ramon, 'how is it that our self-denying and mortifying church alloweth our teachers to partake of the juice of the grape, while of things, as it seems to me, yet more innocent, they are denied them the partaking?'

'It is, hijito, hard to find, in the whole range of creation, comforts more innocent and edifying than the juice of the grape, whether simply expressed in wine, or sublimated in aguardiente. And doth not St. Paul say to Timothy, that he hath license to take a little wine for his stomach's sake?—which word *kardia*, signifying in the Greek as well heart as stomach, I take to imply, that Timothy was of a diffident and timorous disposition, and that in order to give him courage to preach in public, the Apostle prescribed wine, which, as all men know, maketh the fearful bold. Hast thou not marked me when I have risen with a dry throat, and a heart on which the dew of wine hath not fallen, how I have hesitated and stammered and failed to edify my hearers? And again, when the naturally slow blood hath been quickened by the generous liquor, hast thou not seen how powerfully I have uttered the truths of our holy faith, and caused the hearts of the wicked to tremble?'

'I have, indeed, seen at times, father, that thou wert more powerful and edifying at one time than at another, but never till now have I known the cause. So let us take one other draught, and search for the bottom of the cuartillo. It may be, that when this is out the Señor Lopez will act the part of a kind host, and at his own expense replenish the measure.'

'He shall, or I will lay on him the malediction of our holy church, and that is not to be lightly incurred.'

'That it is not, father; and yet these heretic Americans thrive well under it. But tell me, father, how is it with these fasts, which come so often, and act so roughly both with body and soul? It strikes me that they are far from being of an edifying quality.'

'In sooth, hermano, thou art right. Our church, (thou art discreet), our most holy church is like some tall and venerable trees—she hath, clinging to her, some useless vines, which might be lopped off, and the tree flourish all the better. I doubt if my hungering for a day either please or benefits our Father in heaven.'

'Nor I; but, father, these penances and mortifications of the body and soul, are they, too, not included in the same reasoning? they most surely cannot benefit God, more than a burnt offering.'

'Brother Ramon, thou art one who loveth to dive too deep into these matters; pearls are only found in shallow water, and he who trieth the deep water worketh in vain. But here is one thing in which thou canst dive as deep as thou pleasest. Our host hath complied with thy hint, and hath set before us another measure of Velarde's vintage.'

The crafty Don Ramon, who, as the reader will have seen, was a sceptic upon the most received points of his religion, had drawn the Frai Luis into this discourse in order to elicit from him his opinions upon such articles of their belief as he was inclined to doubt, in order to indulge his malicious propensity, not openly—for that he might not dare to do—but covertly, by secret sneers at the pastor of his neighbors, and by laughing in his sleeve at the hypocrisy of the priest, and the folly of his dupes; perhaps, too, having some fears that he was not altogether right in his scepticism, he wished to learn the true belief of a man whom he knew to be well learned, and interested in maintaining the belief which he professed.

Whatever might have been his object, it was fully accomplished; for after their host had left the room, and the liquor began to work more powerfully on the strong brain of the priest, his companion drew from him, one by one, his most secret feelings and opinions.

Like a great proportion of the priests in Mexico, as well as in all other catholic countries, the Frai Luis, from despising many of the tenets he was obliged to teach, and by sophistry to defend, had, by degrees, arrived at the conclusion that the whole foundation of his faith was alike futile; and the number of Spanish translations of Volney's ruins[19] had rendered him a convert to the faith, or rather, absence of faith, of that ingenious writer. Leaving him, therefore, and Don Ramon, to pursue their conversation, which only ended when the utterance of the priest became embarrassed, and his tongue tied by the potent liquor, we will follow the step of their host after he left them to themselves, as we have before mentioned.

First, however, I have to say, that the reader is not to suppose that the picture I have drawn of the Frai Luis Muro is to be considered as anything less than a true picture of one half the priests in New Mexico. The priests of Santa Fe, of Taos, of San Miguel, and other places which I could mention—were name of avail—are all notorious gamblers, and scruple not to cheat in this branch of their sacred profession. The priest of Serolleta[20] is rarely seen except disguised with liquor, and the priest of Taos scruples not to intoxicate himself at a fandango. As to their deism, several of them have Volney in their libraries, and as to their chastity, they make no profession of it, and speak of their mistresses and their amours as a matter of course. Thus much by way of explanation.

When Lopez left his house, he bent his course directly towards that of Santiago Sandoval. There was a more than usual attempt at splendor in his appearance this morning; a pair of American shoes in the place of the common Comanche moccasins; a new black silk handkerchief rolled round his hat; and some other unimportant alterations in other parts of his dress.

When he entered the house with the usual salutation, Buenos

19. *Les Ruines, ou méditations sur les révolutions des empires* (1791), by Comte Constantine François de Chasseboeuf de Volney.

20. Perhaps a misprint for Sebolleta (or Cebolleta), a settlement north of the Indian Pueblo of Laguna. It is doubtful, however, that this community had a resident priest at this early date.

dias le de Dios, everything was as when the priest left it. Inacia was still knitting; her mother twirling the spindle, and her father occupied with his eternal cigar.

'Busy as common, comadre!' said Lopez as he entered, addressing the mother, 'late and early I can find you at work.'

'Yes, compadre,' was the answer. 'It behoves me to be busy; there must be blankets for my husband to take to Sonora in the spring, and they are not found growing on the bushes.'

'You say true, comadre! I sold my mules last year at a good price to these Americans; and those that I and my brother, your husband, shall bring from Sonora next summer, will pay us still better.'

'Ah,' replied the woman, 'you are rich, and the bigger the snow-ball, the faster it gathers and increases. We are poor, and must be content with an humbler profit.'

'True; I should lie were I to call myself poor. I have flocks of sheep and herds of cattle in the mountains. I have land enough to bring me every year, a hundred fanegas of wheat, and I have a good house; and yet, with all this, I have never taken me a wife.'

'And why not? There are girls enough. The woman whom you marry will live respected and happy; but perhaps you look for one who is rich. Is it so?'

'No; she whom I would marry must be young, handsome, and good tempered; and I am too old to get such an one.'

'Adios! you are far from old,' exclaimed the mother.

'Shu!' cried the father, as if chiding a mule.

'You was born the same year with me,—que diablo! am I old? Valgame la madre de Dios!'

'Vaya en hora buena,' (pronouncing it as vaya ena uena) replied Lopez—'perhaps then you will do me the favor which I am about to ask.'

'Who knows?' replied the father. 'What is it?'

'I have been thinking for a week that I had better marry.'

'Bueno!'

'And I thought that when I go to Sonora, I had better have some one to leave in my house and to take care of matters; people are very roguish, compadre!'

'Very true.'

'And besides, I am getting old, and I want some one to tend me when I am sick.'

'Um!'

'And, you know I ought to write a letter, to be polite, asking for the maiden whom I wish to marry.'

'Shu!—people at our time of life do n't stand so much upon politeness; it will do well enough for boys.'

'I thought so—and so I have come myself and saved the trouble of writing a letter. I thought it useless to stand upon ceremony when I wished to marry the daughter of my compadre.'

'Que?'

'And so if you will give me Inacia, I think we can be happy together. I have known her from a baby, and I shall be like a father to her.'

'Certainly I will give her to you,' said the father, 'and you shall be married whenever you see proper.'

'And,' said the mother, 'Inacia will be the prettiest bride, and the happiest wife in the valley of El Embudo.'

'Mother, I'll never marry him,' was the first expression which broke from the lips of Inacia. Her voice in the matter had been considered a thing of no importance; and it had all been settled without once appealing to her; of course all were astonished when they heard these words issuing from the lips of her who had before this ever been obedient to their slightest sign. There she sat, pale as death, with her temples swollen, and her eyes bright and keen, with the fierce, lowering look of an angry Spaniard.

'Inacia,' said her father, 'you shall marry him.'

'Oh father!' she cried, 'do not say so. What fault have I committed that you should at once make me miserable for life, and shorten the existence which you gave me. When you have been sick, have I not spread and smoothed your bed and pillow? I have prepared your food, and fed you as if you were an infant. I have watched by your bedside night after night, and wept over you as you slept. And when have I ever offended you? I have watched your eye to learn what you wanted before you spoke; and now, for the love of God, do not render me forever wretched.'

'Nay, Inacia,' said the mother, 'how canst thou be wretched; this is a girlish whim, and no more.'

'Nay, mother, it is more—much more. Rafael and I have pledged ourselves to one another before heaven, and God will punish me if I break that vow; and you will not force me to incur his anger.'

'And who bid thee incur his anger?' said the father. 'Did I pledge thee to this wretch, Rafael?'

'And, daughter, he is but a herdsman,' said the mother, 'and is reported to be a heretic.'

'They who call him heretic belie him; and though a herdsman, he is honest, bold, and faithful.'

'He is a cuzco, a chucho, a mal-criado, a picaro,' said old Lopez; implying by these epithets, a general assortment of disgraceful and mean qualities.

'Listen, father, and you, mother,' said Inacia, rising and standing erect on the floor—her face now flushed, and her frame quivering; 'I hear you vilify Rafael and make no answer, because you are my parents; but tell that reptile to take heed how he gives a loose to his tongue. A stone from a weak hand will crush a scorpion. Tell him, too, that I am pledged to another; and that if God gives me my reason I will never break my vow. Tell him that I detest and abhor him; and that I would spit upon him, could I thus slay like the centipede. Ai Dios!'

With the last word, clapping both hands upon her head, she fell forward into the middle of the floor, and lay as dead. Remedies were applied to bring her out of her swoon, and while this was being done, Lopez silently and unceremoniously departed, determining within himself, as he did so, to accomplish his purpose at all hazards. Inacia lay for an hour or two nearly senseless; and when she did recover her faculties, she was so pale, so weak, and so languid, that her parents, who sincerely loved her, and no doubt consulted what they took to be her welfare in determining on this marriage—her parents placed her in her bed, and promised not to urge the marriage.

On arriving at his home, Lopez, who imagined that in the

cold parting from the parents of Inacia, he saw the downfall of his hopes, threw himself upon a pile of blankets and mused a long time. He then rose and called the Indian girl. 'Where is the Padre?' said he.

'He fell out of his chair, and is now in bed asleep.'

'Where's Don Ramon?'

'He has gone home, Señor.'

'Mal rayo abrasa!'[21] muttered he. 'Well, go and get me some dinner, and make haste; and whenever the father wakes, let me know. Do you hear?'

'Yes, Señor.'

It was three or four hours before the priest awoke. During this time, except the short space occupied in eating, Lopez walked the room, muttering to himself, now curses against Rafael, now against the priest. The latter, however, carefully uttered sotto voce. At length the firm step of the priest was heard to approach; and lifting the curtain which covered the doorway, the Frai Luis entered the apartment with his face flushed, and his eyes red—but betraying in no other way the effects of the late debauch. Saluting his host in his common bland but firm tones, he seated himself, and proceeded to strike fire and light his cigar with the coolness of one who knew himself welcome.

'Will you smoke, Don Juan de Dios?' said he, holding towards his host a small package of paper cigars. 'These are of the best tobacco of Vera Cruz, and of a flavor something superior to our punche, which, of a certainty, is rather tasteless.'

Lopez took his cigar and lighted it in silence. He then rose, and drawing a measure of wine from the large earthen jar which contained it, he set it before the Frai.

'Drink, father,' said he, 'and then I have something for thy private ear, and which closely touches the interest of the church.'

The Frai drank a huge draught, and then looking into the eye of his host, he said 'Proceed.'

'Thou knowest Inacia, father?'

21. This curious expression, if Pike has recorded it faithfully, may mean "evil misfortune surrounds us."

'I have marked her for a pretty maiden, and a close attendant at the mass.'

'It is rumored, and with much seeming of truth, that she is about to wed the herdsman, Rafael Mestes.'

'And how doth this affect the church?'

'Every way. He is, as it is well known, a favorer of these heretic Americans, and hath much communion with Ramon Bernal, who is well known to be attached to strange and sceptical opinions; and surely it affecteth the church that he should be allowed to wed one who is so disposed to the truth as this Inacia.'

'Still,' replied the father, coldly, 'I see no danger in this. She may convert her husband from any misgivings which he may have in this matter; and if not, why even let him remain a heretic. Such as he shake not the pillars of the church.'

'Nay, father, but these Americans are a bold, and fearless, and dangerous people. Should their opinions and faith gain ground, where wilt thou be?'

'The Americans have priests.'

'But, father, I, as thou knowest, am a zealous and faithful servant of the church. I pay my tithes and primicias regularly; and I lean not to any new opinions. This thou knowest; and I, to say truth, I would fain wed with this Inacia.'

'Still, Don Juan, I do not see that my duty to the church calls upon me to interfere in this matter.'

'But, father, if I can show thee that it is for thy interest to do so, then, as a pious servant of the church, thou wouldst, perhaps, see thyself called upon to interfere; for thou and the church are one.'

'And how showest thou that it is for my interest? How provest thou this?'

'Thus:—if thou wilt use thy influence with the girl, and win her consent to marry me, I will bestow upon the church through thee, three ounces of gold and a jar of Velarde's best vintage.'

'This, indeed, alters the matter. Hast thou spoken to the parents in this matter?'

'This very day, and had their consent; but the tears of the girl

turned them again; and I fear me that I am now defeated in my
hopes.'

'Nay, son! let us hope better things. What I can do for thee,
con licencia de Dios, shall be done. Truth it is, this Rafael is an
arrant heretic, and ought not be suffered to wed with one so
pious and fair as Inacia. To-morrow I will talk with her touching this matter; and now let us discuss the merits of another
modicum of thy liquor.'

'At your pleasure, father! Serve me but in this, and henceforth command me. I have set my heart on this marriage.'

We will not accompany them through their debauch; nor
will we disgust our readers with the conversation which passed
between the priest and Inacia on the following morning. Suffice
it to say, that he held forth to her in turn, exhortation, entreaty,
and threatening. He warned her of the sin of disobeying her
parents, and of the still greater enormity of marrying or loving
a favorer of heretics. He threatened her with the anger of the
church and of God, until Inacia, weary and frightened, yielded,
and consented to marry Lopez. The day was appointed. At the
end of a week the marriage was to take place, and she promised
her parents that if she were alive on that day she would wed the
man whom they had urged upon her.

Rejoiced at this promise, and thinking her happiness now on
the eve of completion, her parents commissioned the priest to
make it known to Lopez, and to request his attendance to receive from the mouth of Inacia her promise to be his bride.
The Frai, elated by his success, and already grasping his reward,
hastened to bear the message.

It is needless to describe the joy of Lopez at receiving it.
Neither is it necessary to relate the manner of the parting of
these two worthies, when, half an hour afterward, the priest put
foot in the stirrup for the village of the Jolla, which parting was
accompanied by many mutual expressions of endearment; on
the part of Lopez, too, of reverence and thanks, and on that of
the Frai, of kind condescension and fatherly affection, all too
supremely ridiculous to translate. At length, with a promise
on the part of the priest that he would attend on the day appointed for the marriage, he rode off with his three ounces of

gold in his pocket, and a servant bearing a large jar riding behind. Neither is it needful to describe the meeting of Lopez
and his bethrothed—and how, with the powerful command over
her feelings, which all women, at times, know how to assume,
she calmly told him that she would become his bride on the
day appointed.

The reader will now allow me the privilege of passing over
four or five days, and taking up the narrative on the day before
that appointed for the marriage. He is likewise requested to allow the scene to be changed a little, and transferred into the
bosom of the mountains, about fifty miles to the north and east
of El Embudo. Let him imagine, then, that he is standing in a
deep, narrow cañon, between two immense ranges of mountains which gird the sides of the hollow, and meeting at each
end, seem to forbid either ingress or egress. Around their feet
the tall dark pines stand up in thousands from among the
abundant rocks, but grow thinner as the eye glances upward,
leaving the bleak summits of the mountains to stand red and
bare in the sight of heaven. Let him also imagine the valley
itself to be thinly covered with tall pines, among which the
grass is green and luxuriant. On one side of the valley runs a
clear stream of cold water, perhaps twenty yards wide, rattling
over the rocks, or standing in little pools beneath the fir-trees.
Such was the valley in which Rafael was herding his cattle. Just
in the centre of the valley stood a small edifice, built conically
of poles after the fashion of the Caiawas, and covered with
snowy skins. Just opposite the tent were the remains of an old
dam, seeming as if nothing short of man's ingenuity could have
constructed it, although it was, in fact, the work of that singular
animal, the beaver; and the fresh cut willows along the bank,
and here and there a path from the water, showed that the
community had not yet been extirpated, or obliged to trans-
migrate. Spread along the valley was a goodly number of beeves
and sheep feeding quietly or lying in the shade; around the
tent two or three skins of the grizzly bear and of the mountain
deer were stretched and drying in the sun. The little mare was
feeding not far from the door, and his dog tigre was coiled up
and lying in the door-way. Rafael himself might have been seen

a little farther up the valley, gliding carefully along the bank of the stream, and angling for the delicious little trout, which abounded in the clear elemental rivulet.

While he was thus employed, a man came winding slowly down from the hill at the western end of the valley, and approached the tent. His mule seemed jaded and hard ridden; and he himself was dusty, and bore other signs of travel and weariness. He was met by Rafael, and as he dismounted, greeted openly and kindly as an old acquaintance.

'Como te vas compadre?' said Rafael, holding out his hand.

'I am well, gracias a Dios!—and you?'

'And what brings you here, Jose? it is long since you have been in this cañon.'

'It would have been longer had you not been here. I come to bring you tidings which closely concern you.'

'What tidings? Oh, speak out. Do n't bring tidings, and be afraid to tell them.'

'Well—they say that he is a raven who croaks ill news; but I must tell you that Inacia Sandoval is to be married to-morrow.'

'How? To-morrow, do you say? And to whom?'

'To old Juan de Dios.'

'To him? And why not come sooner to inform me of it. Had it been your case, I would have ridden night and day to have told you of it.'

'It was only yesterday at noon that I returned from Taos. I have not failed in my friendship.'

'Well! forgive me, Jose. But tell me, how came it about, and after her vow to me?'

'Her parents and the Padre persuaded her to it.'

'Ay, so I told her. God's curse upon the priest and the parents; but I will see her before this marriage, and face this proud and drunken priest. If they push me too far, I may stand at bay and gore them. I might as well die at any rate as be a cowherd, whom every rich man can trample. Good bye, and thanks, Jose. You cannot go to El Embudo so quickly as my little mare.'

'But the cattle!'

'Ay, the cattle; let them take care of themselves. Part of them belong to Lopez; let him come and herd them.'

He caught his mare, saddled her, and rode swiftly off in the direction by which Jose had entered. It was now noon. Night overtook him as he reached the foot of the highest mountain on his road, and it was late when he crossed it. The wolf yelled from among the pines, and the wild cry of the leon was heard at intervals ringing from the caves and rocks. Over hill, rock, and stream, however, his sure-footed mare kept her way in the dim path, which was hardly descried by the starlight, and about sunrise on the next day he reached the main road from El Embudo to Santa Fe. Just at the point where the path in which he had been journeying meets this road, the latter enters a narrow passage between the hill on one side and some immense piles of rocks on the other, extending, perhaps, fifty yards, and just wide enough for one man to pass on horseback. As Rafael wound round the point of rocks at the entrance, and turned abruptly into the pass, he saw that in front of him a man had stopped, blocking up the way with his horse, and employed very leisurely about some repairs on his saddle. He was of a tall, bulky frame, clumsily made, and sitting heavily in the saddle. His horse, too, was taller and larger than the horses of the country; and both by his bridle and saddle as well as by his dress, the stranger was evidently an American.

'Make way there,' cried Rafael, sharply, 'and let me pass.'

'Diablo!' was the answer, in a strange kind of jargon, as the stranger turned in his saddle, showing a heavy, good natured face and large blue eyes. 'You might get your head broke, man, if you should not pay a little more respect to people.'

'Nay, Señor,' replied Rafael humbly, 'I meant no affront; but if you knew all, you would excuse me and let me pass.'

'All what, man? What is the matter with you?'

It is needless to repeat Rafael's brief and somewhat unintelligible tale, which he was obliged to repeat and explain to Lem Carpenter before he was allowed to pass on his way. Lem was a Kentuckian and a blacksmith, who, from the spirit of curiosity, had come to New Mexico, and from the spirit of gain, had remained there. He was undaunted as a lion, and ready to follow his feelings in any enterprise into which they chose to lead him; and the consequence was, that he very often found himself in a scrape.[22]

When Rafael had made his story clear to Lem, which, considering that the latter was no classical scholar in the Spanish, was done in a marvellously short time, he was encouraged by an assurance that all would go well; and Lem moved onward, directing him to follow.

After leaving this pass they wound a short time among small hills, following the course of a little brook of water, and soon came in sight of the village. A few people were gathered round the door of a house which served as a church, at the sight of which Rafael spurred forward eagerly towards the village. Lem, however, overtook him in a moment, and catching his animal by the mane, forced him to ride a little more moderately. On reaching the door of the church, Lem dismounted, and signing to Rafael to remain in his saddle, he entered into the church with his never failing companion, his rifle, in his hand. His entrance disturbed the ceremony which the Frai Luis had just commenced, and the priest's voice hushed as the careless American walked heavily towards the altar with his hat upon his head. Unmindful of everything about him, he drew the pale and weeping Inacia aside, and whispered with her a moment; then, suddenly grasping her by one arm, he bore her towards the door. Some of the bystanders attempted to interfere; but Lem threw them rudely aside, and continued his course. Handing his burden to the expectant Rafael, he pointed to the mountains, and Rafael, with a brief expression of thanks, darted forward again, and was soon out of sight. Some motion was made to follow him; but it was quickly prevented by Lem, who, placing himself in his saddle, menaced any one with death who should dare to stir. He maintained his place steadily for two hours or more, as if he were on guard, in spite of the maledictions of the Frai Luis, few of which, though delivered in very excellent Castillian, did he understand, and none of which did

22. Lemuel Carpenter moved to California from New Mexico in the fall of 1832 and remained on the West Coast. A biographical sketch by Iris H. Wilson will appear in a forthcoming volume of LeRoy R. Hafen (ed.), *The Mountain Men and the Fur Trade of the Far West.*

he care for. He then turned his horse's head towards Taos, and moved steadily out of the village. In the mean time Rafael pursued his swift course towards the cañon. He rested there a day and night; and then, leaving his old encampment, he struck by a wild and narrow pass through to the valley of the Picuris, a small stream which runs out of the mountains near El Embudo. From the eastern extremity of the valley, there is a pass by the head of the river to the valley of the Demora, on the eastern side of the mountains, and at the western extremity a road goes into the valley of Taos.[23] At the time in which the scene of our tale is laid, the valley of the Mora—a large, spacious, and good plain—was uninhabited; and consequently there was but little travel through the valley of the Picuris except by Comanche traders, and the Apaches of the mountains. The Mora, as it is commonly called, has, since then, been settled by the Mexicans, and its inhabitants, after remaining there some years, were forced to vacate the valley by the incursions of the Pananas or Pawnees.

Here, then, Rafael established himself. He built a hut, and soon had it covered with skins. The flesh of the bear, and of the black-tailed deer, was to be had for the asking; and the sly little trout could always be obtained from the sparkling stream. They dwelt here happily for a month, until they began to imagine themselves secure from pursuit. Hunting, fishing, and dressing the skins for their house, occupied them both; and Love, the strange wizard, made the valley as pleasant to them, and as free from loneliness, as if it had been peopled with multitudes. Although Rafael was something of a sceptic in matters of the Romish faith, still there was something in the quiet, patient and constant piety of Inacia, which commanded his respect. The old superstitions implanted in his mind kept still hold upon him, as they do more or less upon every mind; and perhaps the very idea that he was superior to her,— (a sceptic *will* have a feeling of superiority)—perhaps this very feeling enhanced and increased his love for her. The passion of Love may be more sublimated, more delicate, and more fastidious, in the more enlightened classes of society; but I doubt whether true,

23. See note 6 of the second "Narrative."

deep devotion—that love which teaches one to die for another—be not more frequently met with in the simple, uninstructed portion of the world to which Rafael and Inacia belonged. After being in the valley nearly a fortnight, Rafael returned alone to the old encampment which he had left, and drove home to his new camp nearly all the cattle and sheep which he had been herding; and in the course of another fortnight, he missed early one morning, some dozen of his best cattle. Horse tracks were seen further up the valley; and the robbers, whoever they were, had gone out towards the Demora. Rafael would have considered it a degradation to have lost a cow from his herd, even had the whole Pawnee nation taken it from him. He immediately mounted his mare, and pursued; and about eight miles from his camp, he overtook four Apaches, very leisurely driving his cattle before them. Without a word, he prepared himself to retake them. His only arms were his bow and arrows, and his keen knife. Drawing his bow from its leather sheath, he fitted an arrow to the string, and spurring his animal, while he directed her by the pressure of his legs and the swaying of his body, he rode swiftly up, and before the Apaches were fully aware of his approach, he was within six or eight steps of the hindmost; and drawing his arrow to the head, it passed through the back of the Indian, and fell from his breast. He immediately dropped forward upon the pommel of his saddle-tree, and his horse ran wildly on in the path, frightened at the convulsive grasp of the dying man, who still clung to the beast with all the tenacity of an Indian. The first arrow had hardly left the string, when another was drawn from the quiver, and directed against a broad chested Indian who had turned half way in his saddle and was looking back. It struck him in the side, and he reeled and fell from his horse. Unless one has seen the rapidity with which an Indian or a Spaniard sends arrow after arrow, it is difficult to conceive of it. As the two remaining Indians wheeled and came towards him, another arrow struck one of their horses in the breast, and he fell forward, entangling his rider with the stirrups; and the remaining horse, taking fright at the dead body which lay in the path, stopped, and putting down his head, refused to stir an inch—and the rider was forced to dismount.

Rafael sprang to meet him, dismounting likewise, tossing his bow and quiver aside, and grasping his keen knife. As they met, they grappled with each other, and for some time seemed equally matched. The Indian was a stouter and stronger man than the young herdsman—an advantage which was nearly made up for by the superior tenacity and spring of nerve and muscle in Rafael. They struggled for some time, each attempting to throw the other, or to employ their knives, which, however, soon fell from their grasp upon the earth. They fell together at length, and lay turning and rolling upon the ground like two serpents. The dust rose thickly around them; and just as Rafael felt his own grasp begin to relax, and that of his adversary tighten, and just as by one sudden exertion he had thrown him from him, and they lay side by side, he felt the clench of his foe relax upon his throat, and something warm gushed over him. He sprang to his feet; and as he did so, he saw close by him upon his knees, the Indian who had been crippled by the fall of his horse. He had crawled to them, and by mistake, had struck his knife to the heart of his comrade instead of his foeman. He despatched his remaining adversary, and then very leisurely scalping them in the fashion of the Comanches, that is, the whole head over, he mounted his mare, and without washing himself, proceeded towards his home.

Driving his cattle slowly before him, it was late in the day before he arrived near his camp. On approaching, he thought it singular that his dog came not out to bark at the tramp of the horse, and that Inacia came not running to meet him as was her wont. He dashed past his cattle, and rode hastily to the door of the hut. It was wide open; but within, all was still and desolate. His faithful dog was lying dead across the threshold, with several arrows sticking in him. The fire was still burning in the middle of the hut, adding, if possible, to the utter loneliness of the place. Rafael sank down, and hid his face in his hands awhile; then rising and dashing the tears from his eyes, he took a measure of the corn which he had brought thither for his own use, and bore it to his mare who stood patiently at the door. 'Eat, my life,' said he—'eat; it may be the last meal I shall give you.' He sat down again and waited silently till she had finished her corn, and then tightening the girth, he sprang into the saddle, and started quickly, but like one whose thoughts were calm and collected, towards the path which led across the mountains and towards El Embudo. It was nearly noon of the next day when he overtook the party which had taken his bride. It consisted of Lopez and several of his relations, and of the father of Inacia. He came upon them just as they were turning into the main road at the entrance of the narrow pass which I have before mentioned. As he came up, they bent their bows; but he made no answering sign of hostility. On the contrary, he gave signs of peace, and they, somewhat awed by his unnatural quiet, and by the deadly paleness of his face, here and there spotted with blood, suffered him to approach closely. 'Listen,' said he, in the calm tone of despair. 'You have taken my bride from me. She is mine in the sight of God. But it is useless to contend against a host. Suffer me to bestow upon her one embrace, and I pledge my honor not to molest her more.'

A brief consultation was held between Lopez and her father, and then she was placed upon the ground from before the saddle of the latter. The party formed a ring around her and Rafael, and she rushed into his arms. Long, long was that last embrace, and but few words were spoken, when, with a motion like thought, Rafael buried his knife in her bosom. She staggered back,—smiled upon him, and fell. The whole party rushed immediately upon him; but with the spring of a tiger-cat, he grappled with the old Lopez, and, though a dozen mortal wounds were given him with their long, slender spears, he quit not his hold until he had buried his knife two or three times in the body of his foe.

Three crucifixes are carved in the rock just at the entrance of this path; and upon the top of it, above them, stands another of wood, set in a pile of small stones; and every one who passes is requested, by the inscription, to say an Ave Maria for the rest of three souls which departed there.

Poems

Oh, who with the sons of the plain can compete,
When from west, south and north like the torrents they meet?
And when doth the face of the white trader blanche,
Except when at moon rise he hears the Comanche?

Will you speak in our lodge of a bold Caiawah?
He is brave, but it is when our braves are afar;
Will you talk of the gun of the Arapeho?
Go—first see the arrow spring off from our bow.

The white wolf goes with us wherever we ride;
For food there is plenty on every side;
And Mexican bones he has plenty to cranch,
When he follows the troop of the flying Comanche.

The Toyah exults in his spear and his shield,
And the Wequah—but both have we taught how to yield;
And the Panana horses our women now ride,
While their scalps in our lodges are hung side by side.

Let the Wawsashy boast, he will run like a deer,
When afar on the prairie our women appear;
The shaven scalps hang, in each lodge three or four—
We will count then again, and ere long there'll be more.

The Gromonts came down—'t is three summers ago—
To look for our scalps and to hunt buffalo;
But they turned to the mountains their faces again,
And the trace of their lodges is washed out by rain.

The Spirit above never sends us his curse,
And the buffalo never gets angry with us;
We are strong as the storm—we are free as the breeze;
And we laugh at the power of the pale Ikanese.[1]

1. IKANESE is the name by which the Comanches designate the Americans.
The Gromonts [Grosventre] of the prairie are a band of the Blackfeet, or, as the
Spaniards call them, Patos Negros. The Shoshones are the Snakes.—PIKE.

Let them come with the pipe; we will tread it to dust,
And the arrow of war shall ne'er moulder with rust:
Let them come with their hosts; to the desert we'll flee,
And the drought and the famine our helpers shall be.

The mountain Shoshones have hearts big and strong;
Our brothers they are, and they speak the same tongue:
And let them in battle but stand by our side,
And we scorn Ikanese and black Spaniard allied.

Oo-oo-ha! Come out from the Brazos Cañon![2]
Let us range to the head of the salt Semaron!
For our horses are swift, and there's hair to be won,
When the Ikanese waggons their track are upon.

SONG OF THE NABAJO.

Who rideth so fast as a fleet Nabajo?
Whose arm is so strong with the lance and the bow?
His arrow in battle as lightning is swift;
His march is the course of the mountainous drift.

The Eutaw can ride down the deer of the hills,
With his shield ornamented with bald-eagle quills;
Our houses are full of the skins he has drest;
We have slaves of his women, the brightest and best.

Go, talk of the strength of a valiant Paiut;[1]
He will hide in the trees when our arrows we shoot;
And who knows the wild Coyotera to tame,
But the bold Nabajo, with his arrow of flame?

The Moqui may boast from his town of the Rock;
Can it stand when the earthquake shall come with its shock?
The Suni may laugh in his desert so dry—
He will wail to his God when our foray is nigh.

2. Cañon.—pronounced *canyone.*—PIKE.
1. The Paiuts live to the west of Santa Fe. So do the Coyoteras, who are the terror of the trapper. The Moqui (pronounced *Mokee,*) and the Suni (*Sunee*) live near the Nabajo.—PIKE.

Oh, who is so brave as a mountain Apache?
He can come to our homes when the doors we unlatch,
And plunder our women when we are away;
When met he our braves in their battle array?

Whose mouth is so big as a Spaniard's at home?
But if *we* rush along like the cataract foam,
And sweep off his cattle and herds from his stall,
Oh then to the saints who so loudly can call?

Up, then, and away! Let the quiver be full!
And as soon as the stars make the mountain air cool,
The fire of the harvest shall make heaven pale,
And the priesthood shall curse, and the coward shall wail.

And there will be counting of beads then to do—
And the Pueblos shall mount and prepare to pursue;
But when could their steeds, so mule-footed and slow,
Compare with the birds of the free Nabajo?

LINES.

Written on hearing that Wm. R. Schenck, my companion for three
or four months in the prairie, had been wounded by the Comanches,
and left alone to die.

The sun is waning from the sky,
The clouds are gathering round the moon,
Bank after bank, like mountains high,
And night is coming—ah! too soon.
Around me doth the prairie spread
Its limitless monotony,
And near me, in its sandy bed,
Runs rattling water, like the sea,
Salt, salt as tears of misery;
And now the keen and frosty dew
Begins to fall upon my head,
And pierces every fibre through—
By it my torturing wound with misery is fed.

And near me lies my noble horse:
I watched his last, convulsive breath,
And saw him stiffen to a corse—
And knew like his would be my death.
The cowards left me lying here
To die; and now three weary days,
I've watched the sun's light disappear;
Again I shall not see his rays—
On my dead heart they soon will blaze;
O God! it is a fearful thing,
To be alone in this wide plain,
To hear the raven's filthy wing,
And watch the quivering star of our existence wane.

Yes; I am left alone to die—
Alone! alone!—it is no dream;
At times I think it is—though nigh,
Already dimly sounds the stream;
And I must die—and wolves will gnaw
My corse, or ere the pulse be still,
Before my parting gasp I draw;
This doth my cup of torture fill—
This, this it is which sends a thrill
Of horror through my inmost brain,
And makes me die a thousand deaths.
I value not the passing pain,
But I would draw in peace, my last, my parting breath.

And here, while left, all, all alone
To die—how strange *that* word *will* sound—
O God! with many a torture-tone,
The fiends of memory come around.
They tell of one, untimely sent
Unto the dim and narrow grave,
By honor's laws—and friends down bent
With grief, that I, the reckless, gave;
And bending from each airy wave,
I see the shapes I loved and lost

Come round me with their deep, dim eyes,
Like drowning men to land uptost,
And here and there one mocks, and my vain rage defies.

O God! my children. Spare the thought!
Bid it depart from me, lest I
At last to madness should be wrought,
And cursing thee, insanely die.
Hush! for the pulse is getting slow,
And death, chill death is near at hand.
I turn me from the sunset glow,
And looking towards my native land
Where the dim clouds like giants stand,
I strain my eyes—if I perchance,
Might see beneath the still, cold moon,
Some shape of human kind advance,
To give a dying man the last, the dearest boon.

In vain!—in vain! No being comes—
And all is lone and desolate;
Deeper and darker swell the glooms,
And with them Death and eyeless Fate.
Now I am dying! Well I know
The pangs that gather round the heart;
The brow's weak throb has ceased to glow,
And life and I are near to part.
I would not ask the leech's art—
For death is not so terrible
As 't was. And now, no more I see;—
My tongue is faltering;—'t is well—
O God!—my soul!—'t is thine—take it to thee.

Ark. Territory, March 20, 1833.

THE LIGHTNING.

The breath of the ocean my cradle is,
Which the sun takes up from the blue abyss;
And the upper cold gives it shape and form,
And it peoples itself with living storm.

And when it has reached the upper air,
I hold its helm while it wanders there;
And I lie in the shade of the lifted sail,
And steer my boat before the gale.

I coil myself like a quivering snake,
Invisible on a chaotic lake;
And I stay unseen in the chasms of cloud,
And the vapors that even to earth are bowed.

I look on the stars with my glittering eye,
And they hide away while the clouds go by;
And while my eye and form are unseen,
The meteors down to my palace lean.

And when my cradle is shaken by wind,
And moon and stars are eyeless behind,
Oh then I quiver, and mankind see
Me lose invisibility.

I look in the eye of the winged stars,
And they wheel away their orbal cars,
And hide afar in the depths of heaven,
Like water-drops by the tempest driven.

I look on the sun—and he hideth under
The misty plume of my servant, Thunder;
And the moon shuts up her arching lid,
And the eye by which the tides are fed.

I take the form of a fiery adder,
And dash myself down the heaving ladder
Of cloud, till I hiss on the ocean's breast,
And it foams and awakes from its azure rest.

I take the form of an arrow of flame,
And I pierce the clouds and make darkness tame;
And the flap of night's dark drifting sail,
Shakes down to the earth the glancing hail.

I dash myself against rifted rocks,
And the echoes awake and come in flocks;
And each with his hoarse and rattling tongue,
Throws back the challenge the thunder flung.

And often when heaven's unstained floor
Is as far from dim as the inmost core
Of an angel's heart, I am seen to glide
From the lid of the west;—thus the cheek of a bride

Will blush when her lover's step is heard;—
And then, like the wing of a heavy bird,
My voice of thunder afar wakes,
And the dim sunset his pinion shakes.

And there all night I am seen to quiver,
Like the pulse of an adamantine river,
That out of the depth doth come and go—
And my cradle of cloud is unseen below.

I am hidden in earth, and air, and water;
I am parent of life, and king of slaughter;
I green the earth—I open the flowers,
And make them blush by the lip of showers.

I am the heart's etherial essence,
And life exists not, save in my presence;
I am the soul of the mighty earth,
And give its children their vital birth.

I go to the heart of the hidden rocks,
And my touch awakens the earthquake shocks;
I am the soul of the flowers and buds,
And I feed them with air and water-floods.

I am eternal, and change forever;
I wander always, but dissipate never;
Decay and waste no power possess
On me the deathless and fatherless.

Unelemental, immaterial,
Less gross than aught that is etherial,
And next to spirit in rank am I;
While matter exists I can never die.

SONG.

The day hath passed, love, when I might
   Have offered thee this heart of mine,
As one whose yet unclouded light
   Was pure, love, pure and bright, as thine:
When, though I gazed on thee, as him
   Who gazeth on a distant star,
Thy brilliant eye could not grow dim,
   In shame for me, thy worshipper.

Yet still, although it be but shame
   To be beloved by such as I,
That love will shed its saddened flame,
   Knows no decay, can never die.
Its soul of fire hath no decline;
   For rocks check not the swelling river;
And though thou never canst be mine,
   I'm thine, love—thine alone, forever.

The Inroad of
The Nabajo

It was a keen, cold morning in the latter part of November, when I wound out of the narrow, rocky cañon or valley, in which I had, for some hours, been travelling, and came in sight of the village of San Fernandez, in the valley of Taos.[1] Above, below, and around me, lay the sheeted snow, till, as the eye glanced upward, it was lost among the dark pines which covered the upper part of the mountains, although at the very summit, where the pines were thinnest, it gleamed from among them like a white banner spread between them and heaven. Below me on the left, half open, half frozen, ran the little clear stream, which gave water to the inhabitants of the valley, and along the margin of which, I had been travelling. On the right and left, the ridges which formed the dark and precipitous sides of the cañon, sweeping apart, formed a spacious amphitheatre. Along their sides extended a belt of deep, dull blue mist, above and below which was to be seen the white snow, and the deep darkness of the pines. On the right, these mountains swelled to a greater and more precipitous height, till their tops gleamed in unsullied whiteness over the plain below. Still farther to the right was a broad opening, where the mountains seemed to sink into the plain; and afar off in front were the tall and stupendous mountains between me and the city of Santa Fe. Directly in front of me, with the dull color of its mud buildings, contrasting with the dazzling whiteness of the snow, lay the little village, resembling an oriental town, with its low, square, mud-roofed houses and its two square church towers, also of mud. On the

1. Pike is here describing his own arrival at Taos, which he approached from the East through the valley of the Río Fernando de Taos.

147

path to the village were a few Mexicans, wrapped in their striped blankets, and driving their jackasses heavily laden with wood towards the village. Such was the aspect of the place at a distance. On entering it, you only found a few dirty, irregular lanes, and a quantity of mud houses.

To an American, the first sight of these New Mexican villages is novel and singular. He seems taken into a different world. Everything is new, strange, and quaint: the men with their pantalones of cloth, gaily ornamented with lace, split up on the outside of the leg to the knee, and covered at the bottom with a broad strip of morocco; the jacket of calico; the botas of stamped and embroidered leather; the zarape or blanket of striped red and white; the broad-brimmed hat, with a black silk handkerchief tied round it in a roll; or in the lower class, the simple attire of breeches of leather reaching only to the knees, a shirt and a zarape; the bonnetless women, with a silken scarf or a red shawl over their heads; and, added to all, the continual chatter of Spanish about him—all remind him that he is in a strange land.

On the evening after my arrival in the village, I went to a fandango. I saw the men and women dancing waltzes, and drinking whiskey together; and in another room, I saw the monti-bank open. It is a strange sight—a Spanish fandango. Well dressed women—(they call them ladies)—harlots, priests, thieves, half-breed Indians—all spinning round together in the waltz.[2] Here, a filthy, ragged fellow with a half shirt, a pair of leather breeches, and long, dirty woollen stockings, and Apache moccasins, was hanging and whirling round with the pretty wife of Pedro Vigil; and there, the priest was dancing with La Alte-gracia, who paid her husband a regular sum to keep out of the way, and so lived with an American. I was soon disgusted; but among the graceless shapes and more graceless dresses at the fandango, I saw one young woman who appeared to me exceedingly pretty. She was under the middle size, slightly formed; and besides the delicate foot and ancle and the keen black eye, common to all the women in that country, she possessed a clear

2. The attendance of all classes at the *fandango* was noted by most American visitors. See, for example, Gregg, *Commerce of the Prairies*, p. 170.

and beautiful complexion, and a modest, downcast look, not often to be met with among the New Mexican females.

I was informed to my surprise, that she had been married several years before, and was now a widow. There was an air of gentle and deep melancholy in her face which drew my attention to her; but when one week afterward I left Taos, and went down to Santa Fe, the pretty widow was forgotten.

Among my acquaintances in Santa Fe, was one American in particular, by the name of L——.[3] He had been in the country several years; was a man of much influence there among the people, and was altogether a very talented man. Of his faults, whatever they were, I have nothing to say. It was from him, some time after my arrival, and when the widow had ceased almost to be a thing of memory, that I learned the following particulars respecting her former fortunes. I give them in L.'s own words as nearly as I can, and can only say, that for the truth of them, he is my authority—true or not, such as I received them, do I present them to my readers.

You know, said he, that I have been in this country several years. Six or eight years ago, I was at Taos, upon business, and was lodging in the house of an old acquaintance, Dick Taylor.[4] I had been up late one night, and early the next morning, I was suddenly awakened by mine host, Dick, who, shaking me roughly by the shoulder, exclaimed, 'Get up, man—get up—if you wish to see sport, and dress yourself.' Half awake and half asleep, I arose and commenced dressing myself. While employed in this avocation, I heard an immense clamor in the street; cries, oaths, yells, and whoops, resounded in every direction. I

3. Mr. L. may be Alexander Le Grand, a fascinating frontiersman with careers in both New Mexico and Texas. He and Pike were later remembered to have been "friends and intimates in New Mexico." See William Waldo, "Recollections of a Septuagenarian," Missouri Historical Society *Glimpses of the Past*, V, 4-6 (April-June, 1938), 90-91. That Le Grand was in New Mexico during Pike's stay, there can be no doubt. In Taos, on February 20, 1832, he translated a letter for John Gantt. Ritch Papers, no. 129, Huntington Library, San Marino, California.

4. Richard Taylor, a Kentucky merchant, came to New Mexico at least as early as July of 1827. Report of foreigners who arrived at Santa Fe, July, 1827, in Weber, *The Extranjeros* (Santa Fe, in press). In December of 1831, Taylor married María Sandoval at Taos. Chávez, "New Names in New Mexico," *El Palacio*, 64, 11-12 (November-December, 1957), 377.

knew it would be useless to ask an explanation of the matter
from the sententious Dick; and I therefore quietly finished
dressing, and, taking my rifle, followed him into the street. For
a time, I was at a loss to understand what was the matter. Men
were running wildly about—some armed with fusees, with locks
as big as a gunbrig; some with bows and arrows, and some with
spears. Women were scudding hither and thither, with their
black hair flying, and their naked feet shaming the ground by
their superior filth. Indian girls were to be seen here and there,
with suppressed smiles, and looks of triumph. Men, women,
and children, however, seemed to trust less in their armor, than
in the arm of the Lord, and of the saints. They were accordingly
earnest in calling upon Tata Dios! Dios bendito! Virgen purisima! and all the saints of the calendar, and above all, upon
Nuestra Señora de Guadalupe, to aid, protect, and assist them.
One cry, at last, explained the whole matter,—'Los malditos
y picaros que son los Nabajos.' The Nabajos had been robbing
them; they had entered the valley below, and were sweeping
it of all the flocks and herds—and this produced the consterna-
tion. You have never seen any of these Nabajos. They approach
much nearer in character to the Indians in the south of the
Mexican Republic than any others in this province. They are
whiter; they raise corn; they have vast flocks of sheep, and large
herds of horses; they make blankets, too, and sell them to the
Spaniards. Their great men have a number of servants under
them, and in fact, their government is apparently patriarchal.
Sometimes they choose a captain over the nation; but even then,
they obey him or not, just as they please. They live about three
day's journey west of this, and have about ten thousand souls
in their tribe. Like most other Indians, they have their medicine
men who intercede for them with the Great Spirit by strange
rites and ceremonies.

Through the tumult, we proceeded towards the outer edge
of the town, whither all the armed men seemed to be hastening.
On arriving in the street which goes out towards the cañon of
the river, we found ourselves in the place of action. Nothing
was yet to be seen out in the plain, which extends to the foot
of the hills and to the cañon, and of which you there have a

plain view. Some fifty Mexicans had gathered there, mostly armed, and were pressing forward towards the extremity of the street. Behind them were a dozen Americans with their rifles, all as cool as might be; for the men that came through the prairie then were all braves. Sundry women were scudding about, exhorting their husbands to fight well, and praising 'Los Señores Americanos.' We had waited perhaps half an hour, when the foe came in sight, sweeping in from the west, and bearing towards the cañon, driving before them numerous herds and flocks, and consisting apparently of about one hundred men. When they were within about half a mile of us, they separated; one portion of them remained with the booty, and the other, all mounted, came sweeping down upon us. The effect was instantaneous, and almost magical. In a moment not a woman was to be seen far or near; and the heroes who had been chattering and boasting in front of the Americans, shrunk in behind them, and left them to bear the brunt of the battle. We immediately extended ourselves across the street, and waited the charge. The Indians made a beautiful appearance as they came down upon us with their fine looking horses, and their shields ornamented with feathers and fur, and their dresses of unstained deer-skin. At that time, they knew nothing about the Americans; they supposed that their good allies, the Spaniards, would run as they commonly do, that they would have the pleasure of frightening the village and shouting in it, and going off safely. As they neared us, each of us raised his gun when he judged it proper, and fired. A dozen cracks of the rifle told them the difference; five or six tumbled out of their saddles, and were immediately picked up by their comrades, who then turned their backs and retreated as swiftly as they had come. The Americans, who were, like myself, not very eager to fight the battles of the New Mexicans, loaded their guns with immense coolness, and we stood gazing at them as they again gathered their booty and prepared to move towards the cañon. The Mexicans tried to induce us to mount and follow; but we, or at least I, was perfectly contented. In fact, I did not care much which whipped. The Nabajos seemed thus in a very good way of going off with their booty unhindered, when suddenly the scene was altered. A considerable body, perhaps sixty, of the Pueblo of Taos, a civilized Indian who are Catholics, and citizens of the Republic, appeared suddenly under the mountains, dashing at full speed towards the mouth of the cañon. They were all fine looking men, well mounted, large, and exceedingly brave. These Pueblos, (a word which signifies tribes—of Indians) are in fact, all handsome, athletic men. There are about a dozen different tribes around here, each having a different language, and all very small in number. The Taos, the Picuris, the Poguaque, the Tisuqui, the Xemes, the San Domingo, the Pecos, (the two latter, however, though they live fifty miles apart, all speak the same language),[5] the San Ildefonso,[6] and one or two others; all these are close here. You need not go more than seventy miles from Santa Fe to find any of them. Some of their towns were formerly much larger than at present—for example, that of the Pecos tribe. Half their town is fallen to ruin. The wall which originally surrounded it, is now at a distance from the one little square which composes the present town. I say square, but it is an oblong, about forty yards by fifteen, surrounded by continuous houses of mud, three and four stories high, to which you generally ascend by ladders, and go down again from the top. Everything is built for the purpose of defence. There is but one passage from the oblong, and this is about six feet wide. When the Spaniards first came up above the Pass [El Paso] and conquered the Indians, and founded Santa Fe, these tribes rose against them and drove them again below the Pass. Only the Pecos and San Domingo tribes remained faithful, and they were nearly exterminated by the other Indians, on account of it. In the Pecos tribe, there are not more than fifteen or twenty men.[7] The Santa Fe tribe went

5. Pojoaque, Tesuque, Jemez and Santo Domingo. Pecos and Santo Domingo Indians do not speak the same language. Had Pike said Pecos and Jemez, he would have been correct.

6. The Abiquiu.—PIKE.

7. Once the largest Pueblo settlement, Pecos declined in population throughout the eighteenth and early nineteenth centuries, until its final abandonment in 1838. Contrary to Pike, Comanches and disease were the cause of this. Neither Pecos nor Santo Domingo remained loyal to the Spaniards during the 1680 Revolt. Alfred Vincent Kidder, *An Introduction to the Study of Southwestern Archaeology with a Preliminary Account of the Excavations at Pecos* (New Haven, 1962), pp. 83-87.

into the mountains, and has disappeared, mingling, perhaps with the Apaches. Another tribe is the one which the Indians and Spaniards call the Montezuma tribe. I cannot say, whether this be their proper name, or one which they have learned from the Americans; but the latter supposition would be improbable. This, too, is a small and diminishing tribe; they live in the mountains not far from Taos, and never intermarry with any other tribe. They worship a large snake, whose teeth, I suppose, they have extracted, and rendered it harmless. Not long ago, it was lost, and after a time, it was discovered by some of the Pueblo of Taos, who knew it by some ornaments it wears. They gave notice to the Montezuma tribe, and their priest came and took it back. But I am tiring you with this verbiage; shall I go back to my story?

'Ho,' said I, 'go on with your account of these Indians first.'

'Just as you please. They likewise keep a continual fire burning in a kind of cave; every year, a man is placed there to take care of it; and for the whole of that year, he does not see the sun; —they bring him food, wood and water. I have never seen this, but creditable Spaniards have told me that it was all true, and I am far from being inclined to doubt it.[8] You will see between this and the Nabajo country, remains of vast buildings of rock and mud, which were evidently used for temples—by their insulated position, and their entire difference from the other ruins around them. One of these places, about two days' ride from here, is under a mountain, in which, they say, treasures are hid. In fact, many things concur to prove these Indians to be different from our Indians, and even from the Eutaws—(or, as the Spaniards write it, Llutas)—from the Apaches and from the Comanches. Their dances are very graceful and considerably complicated, and as regular as our contra dances; much handsomer than any dances and xarabes [jarabes] of these vagabond Mexicans. But sooth it is, they are accompanied by the same monotonous *hu a ha, hu a ha,* which all Indians sing, so far as

8. The legend about the "Montezuma tribe" was a common one, but usually credited to Pecos Pueblo where Montezuma was said to have been born. See, for example, Gregg, *Commerce of the Prairies*, pp. 188-190. See also, Benjamin M. Read, "The Last Word on 'Montezuma,'" *New Mexico Historical Review*, I, 3 (July, 1926), 350-358.

I have ever seen them. I might say, too, that they have very little of that sententious gravity and unbending sobriety of appearance generally ascribed to Indians. They laugh, and chatter, and play; but to do all Indians—Mr. Cooper, and Heckewelder,[9] and any other person, to the contrary notwithstanding. The Osages play with their children before white men, laugh, chat and joke; the Choctaws laugh so much as frequently to appear silly; and you may look in vain for those specimens of dignity and gravity which are told of in many veritable books. Not that I mean to say that they are never grave—sometimes they are; but generally, an Indian is the most merry and apparently light-hearted thing in the world. Do you think that they are like Chingachgook, who would not embrace Uncas till they were alone by their camp-fire?[10] No. An Osage chief will fondle his child, toss it in the air, and chatter to it like a childish woman, talking baby talk. So will a Comanche, or a Crow, or a Snake, and they are the gravest Indian I ever saw. But I was speaking of the difference between them and our Indians. They have woven blankets—heaven knows how long; and they have, and had before this continent was discovered, a considerable knowledge of pottery; witness the vessels of cookery, and also the bottomless jars, which they put one upon the other for their chimneys. They are probably a mixture of the Mexicans, (whether these latter were originally Phoenicians, Egyptians, or Aboriginals,) and of the Northern and Eastern Indians—the fiercer and ruder tribes who inhabit to the north, east and west of them. The Mexicans, in my opinion, penetrated at some day—heaven knows how long ago—into the United States, and were repulsed, leaving those fortifications, hieroglyphics, and other matters so curious to the learned. They likewise came towards the north and left colonies in New Mexico; but the cold kept them from going farther; they were no people for mountains and deserts. I incline to believe that they were

9. A reference to James Fenimore Cooper and John Gottlieb Ernestus Hecke-welder, a missionary whose *An Account of the History, Manners and Customs, of the Indian Nations, Who Once Inhabited Pennsylvania. . . .* (Philadelphia, 1819), Pike had apparently read.

10. A reference to a scene at the close of chapter XIX of James Fenimore Cooper's *Last of the Mohicans.*

Phoenicians; at any rate, they were an insulated portion of the human race, entirely distinct from, and far superior to, the natives of the east and north, as well as of California. As to the story of the Nabajos having a part of a Welsh bible, and a silver cup, it is all a matter of imagination. To be sure they have beards, and are whiter than the surrounding Indians, and they do speak a language which nothing can learn, and which is marvelously like the Welsh,[11] in the respect of guttural and nasal unpronounceables. So much for Indians—and since I have ended where I began—with the Nabajos—I will return to my narrative.

'Upon seeing the Pueblo of Taos, between them and the mouth of the cañon, the Nabajos uttered a shrill yell of defiance, and moved to meet them. Leaving a few men to guard the cattle, the remainder diverging like the opening sticks of a fan, rushed to the attack. Each man shot his arrow as he approached, till he was within thirty or forty yards, and then wheeling, retreated, shooting as he went. They were steadily received by the Pueblo, with a general discharge of fire-arms and arrows at every charge, and were frustrated in every attempt at routing them. Several were seen to fall at every charge; but they were always taken up and borne to those who were guarding the cattle. During the contest, several Mexicans mounted, and went out from the village to join the Pueblos, but only two or three ventured to do so; the others kept at a very respectful distance. At length, finding the matter grow desperate, more men were joined to those who guarded the cattle, and they then moved steadily towards the cañon. The others again diverging, rushed on till they came within fifty yards, and then converging again, charged again, charged boldly upon one point; and as the Pueblo were unprepared for this manoeuvre, they broke through, and again charged back. Drawing them together in this way to oppose them, nearly two thirds of the cattle were driven through the line, goaded by arrows and frightened by

11. Many early explorers and travelers in the West entertained the idea that a tribe of Welsh Indians lived in the West. The Hopi Indians were often thought to be this tribe. For a thorough discussion see David Williams, "John Evans' Strange Journey," *American Historical Review*, LIV, 2 & 3 (January & April, 1949), 277-295, 508-529.

shouts. Many of the Nabajos, however, fell in the melée, by the long spears and quick arrows of the Pueblo. In the mean time, I had mounted, and approached within two hundred yards of the scene of contest. I observed one tall, and good looking Spaniard, of middle age, who was particularly active in the contest; he had slightly wounded a large athletic Nabajo, with his spear, and I observed that he was continually followed by him. When this large chief had concluded that the cattle were near enough to the mouth of the cañon to be out of danger, he gave a shrill cry, and his men, who were now reduced to about sixty, besides those with the cattle, gathered simultaneously between the Pueblo and the cañon. Only the chief remained behind, and rushing toward the Spaniard who had wounded him, he grasped him with one hand and raised him from the saddle as if he had been a boy. Taken by surprise, the man made no resistance for a moment or two, and that moment or two sufficed for the horse of the Nabajo—a slight made, Arabian looking animal—to place him, with two or three bounds, among his own men. Then his knife glittered in the air, and I saw the Spaniard's limbs contract, and then collapse. A moment more sufficed for him to tear the scalp from the head; he was then tumbled from before him to the ground, and with a general yell, the whole body rushed forward, closely pursued by the Pueblo. In hurrying to the cañon, the Nabajo lost several men and more of the cattle; but when they had once entered its rocky jaws, and the Pueblo turned back, still more than half the plunder remained with the robbers; fifteen Nabajos only were left dead; and the remainder were borne off before their comrades. The Pueblos lost nearly one third of their number.

'It was this fight, sir, this inroad of the Nabajos, which brought me acquainted with the young widow of whom we have spoken before. She was then an unmarried girl of fourteen; and a very pretty girl too was La Señorita Ana Maria Ortega. I need not trouble you with descriptions of her; for she has saved me the trouble by appearing to your eyes in that sublime place, a fandango—when you first saw the charms of New Mexican beauty, and had your eyes ravished with the melody and harmony of a Spanish waltz—(I beg Spain's pardon)—a New Mexican waltz.'

'Which waltz,' said I, 'I heard the next morning played over a coffin at a funeral; and in the afternoon, in the procession of the Host.'

'Oh that is common. Melody, harmony, fiddle, banjo, and all —all is common to all occasions. They have but little music, and they are right in being economical with it; and the presence of the priest sanctifies anything. You know the priest of Taos?'

'Yes. The people were afraid to get drunk on my first fandango night. I was astonished to find them so sober. The priest was there; and they feared to get drunk until he had done so. That event took place about eleven at night, and then aguadiente [sic] was in demand.'

'Yes, I dare say. That same priest once asked me if England was a province or a state. I told him it was a province. He reads Voltaire's Philosophical Dictionary, and takes the old infidel to be an excellent christian.[12] Ana Maria was his god-daughter, I think, or some such matter; and I became acquainted with her in that way. He wanted me to marry her; she knew nothing of it, though; but I backed out. I did not mind the marrying so much as the baptism and the citizenship. I do n't exchange my country for Mexico; or the name American for that of Mexican. Ana was in truth, not a girl to be slighted. She was pretty, and rich, and sensible; her room was the best furnished mud apartment in Taos; her zarapes were of the best texture, some of them even from Chihuahua, and they were piled showily round the room. The roses skewered upon the wall, were of red silk; and the santos and other images had been brought from Mexico. There were some half dozen of looking-glasses, too, all out of reach, and various other adornments common to great apartments. The medal which she wore round her neck, with a cross-looking San Pablo upon it, was of beaten gold, or some other kind of gold. She had various dresses of calico and silk, all bought at high prices of the new comers; and here little fairy feet were always adorned with shoes. That was a great extrava-

12. Apparently a reference to the controversial Antonio José Martínez, a broadminded eighteenth century type of liberal who would be excommunicated in 1857. E. K. Francis "Padre Martínez: A New Mexican Myth," *New Mexico Historical Review*, XXXI, 4 (October, 1956), 265-289.

gance in those days. Ana Maria had no mother when I first saw her; but she was still wearing the "luto"[13] for her, and she had transferred all the affection to her father, which she had before bestowed upon her mother; and when the knife of the Nabajo made her an orphan, I suppose that she felt as if her last hold upon life was gone. She appeared to, at least.

'Victorino Alasi had been her lover, and her favored one. He had never thought of any other than Ana Maria as his bride, and he had talked of his love to her a hundred times. But there came in a young trapper, who gave him cause to tremble, lest he should lose his treasure. Henry, or as he was most commonly called, Hentz Wilson, was a formidable rival. Ana knew not, herself, which to prefer; the long friendship and love of Victorino was almost balanced by the different style of beauty, the odd manners, and the name American, which recommended Hentz. Her vanity was flattered by the homage of an American, and Victorino was in danger of losing his bride. The bold, open bearing of Hentz, and his bravery, as well as his knowledge, which, though slight at home, was wondrous to the simple New Mexicans, had recommended him, likewise, to the father. Just before, his death suspended, for a time, all operations. They had each of them made application by letter (the common custom) for the hand of Ana Maria. In the course of a fortnight after the inroad of the Nabajo, each of the lovers received, as answer, that she had determined to give her hand to either of them who should kill the murderer of her father. And with this, they both were obliged to content themselves for the present.

'Directly after the inroad, I came down to Santa Fe. The Lieutenant Colonel of the Province, Viscara, was raising a body of men to go out against the Nabajo,[14] and repay them for this

13. Mourning dress.

14. The account which follows is based on Governor Antonio Vizcarra's campaign of 1823. Pike's informant has some of his facts straight. The group did leave in the summer, in late June. After some of the party turned back it numbered about 1,350 men, and did travel by way of Jemez Pueblo, crossing the Río Puerco on its way into Arizona. See David M. Brugge, "Vizcarra's Navaho Campaign of 1823," *Arizona and the West*, 6, 3 (Autumn, 1964), 233-244, for the best account of this expedition. Pike's romantic episode may or may not be true, but the statement that only fifteen men advanced against the Indians is absurd.

and other depredations lately committed upon the people, and he was urgent for me to accompany him—so much so, that I was obliged to comply with his requests, and promised to go. Troops were sent for from below, and in the course of four months, the expedition was ready; and we set out upon the Nabajo campaign. We were a motley set. First there was a body of regular troops, all armed with British muskets and with lances. Here, there was a grey coat and leathern pantaloons; there, no coat and short breeches. But you have seen the ragged, ununiformed troops here in the city, and I need not describe them to you. Next there was a parcel of militia, all mounted; some had lances, some, old fusees; and last, a body of Indians of the different Pueblos, with bows and shields—infinitely the best troops we had, as well as the bravest men. Among the militia of Taos, I observed the young Victorino—and Hentz had likewise volunteered to accompany the expedition, and lived with me in the General's tent.

'It was in the dryest part of summer that we left Santa Fe, and marched towards the country of the Nabajo. We went out by the way of Xemes, and then crossing the Rio Puerco, went into the mountains of the Nabajo. We came up with them, fought them, and they fled before us, driving their cattle and sheep with them into a wide sand desert; and we being now out of provisions, were obliged to overtake them or starve. We were two days without a drop of water, and nearly all the animals gave out in consequence of it. On the third day, Viscara, fifteen soldiers, and myself went ahead of the army, (which I forgot to say, was thirteen hundred strong). Viscara and his men were mounted. I was on foot, with no clothing, except a cloth round my middle, with a lance in one hand, and a rifle in the other. That day I think I ran seventy-five miles, barefooted, and through the burning sand.'

'Viscara tells me that you ran thirty leagues.'

'Viscara is mistaken, and overrates it. Just before night, we came up with a large body of Nabajos, and attacked them. We took about two thousand sheep from them, and three hundred cattle, and drove them back that night to the army. The Nabajos supposed, when we rushed on them, that the whole of our force was at hand, and they were afraid to pursue us. But it is the battle in which you are most concerned. When we attacked the Nabajo, they were drawn up, partly on foot, and partly on horseback, in the bed of a little creek which was dry. It was the common way of fighting, charge, fire and retreat; and if you have seen one fight on horseback, you have seen all. I observed, particularly, one Nabajo, upon whom three Pueblos charged, all on foot; he shot two of them down before they reached him. Another arrow struck the remaining one in the belly. He still came on with only a tomahawk, and another arrow struck him in the forehead. Yet still he braved his foe, and they were found lying dead together. I could have shot the Nabajo with great ease, at the time; for the whole of this took place within seventy yards of me.

'In the midst of the battle, I observed Victorino and Hentz standing together in the front rank, seeming rather to be spectators than men interested in the fight. They were both handsome men, but entirely different in appearance. Victorino was a dark-eyed, slender, agile young Spaniard, with a tread like a tiger-cat; and with all his nerves indurate with toil. His face was oval, thin, and of a rich olive, through which the blood seemed ready to break; and you could hardly have chosen a better figure for a statuary as he stood, now and then discharging his fusee, but commonly glancing his eyes uneasily about from one part of the enemy to the other. Hentz, on the contrary, was a tall, and well proportioned young fellow, of immense strength and activity; but with little of the cat-like quickness of his rival; his skin was fair even to effeminacy, and his blue eyes were shaded by a profusion of chestnut hair; he, too, seemed expecting some one to appear amid the enemy; for though he now and then fired and reloaded, it was but seldom, and he spent more time in leaning on his long rifle, and gazing about among the Nabajos.

'On a sudden, a sharp yell was heard, and a party of Nabajos came dashing down the bank of the creek, all mounted, and headed by the big chief who had killed the father of Ana Maria. Then the apathy of the two rivals was at once thrown aside. Hentz quickly threw his gun into the hollow of his arm, examined the priming, and again stood quietly watching the motions of the chief, and Victorino did the same. Wheeling round several times, and discharging a flight of arrows continually upon us, this new body of Nabajo at length bore down directly towards Hentz and Victorino. As the chief came on, Victorino raised his gun, took a steady, long aim, and fired. Another moment, and the Nabajo were upon them, and then retreated again like a wave tossing back from the shore. The chief still sat on his horse as before; another yell, and they came down again. When they were within about a hundred yards, Hentz raised his rifle, took a steady, quick aim, and fired. Still they came on; the chief bent down over the saddle-bow, and his horse, seemingly frightened by the strange pressure of the rider, bore down directly towards Hentz, who sprang to meet him, and caught the bridle; the horse sprang to one side, and the wounded chief lost his balance, and fell upon the ground. Losing his hold upon the horse, he dashed away through friend and foe, and was out of sight in a moment. The Nabajo rallied to save the body of the chief, and Viscara himself rushed in with me to the rescue of Hentz. But the long barrel of Hentz's rifle, which he swayed with a giant's strength, and in which I humbly imitated him, the sword of Viscara, and the keen knife of Victorino, who generously sprang in the aid of his rival, would all have failed in saving the body, had not a band of the gallant Pueblo attacked them in the rear and routed them. Hentz immediately dispatched the chief, who was, by this time, half hidden by a dozen Nabajos, and immediately deprived his head of the hair, which is more valuable to an Indian than life.

'After our route in the sand desert, the Nabajos sued for peace, and we returned to Santa Fe. Poor Victorino, I observed, rode generally alone, and had not a word to say to any one. Although formerly, he had been the most merry and humorous, now he seemed entirely buried in sorrow. He kept listlessly along, neither looking to the right hand or the left, with his bridle laying on the neck of his mule. I tried to comfort him, but he motioned me away. I urged it upon him, and he answered me gloomily, "Why should I cheer up? what have I to live for? Had I lost her by any fault of my own, I would not have thought so hardly of it; but by this cursed old fusee, and because another man can shoot better than I—Oh, sir, leave me to myself, I pray you, and make me no offers which do me no good. I think I *shall* be happy again, but it will be in my grave, and Dios me perdone! I care not how soon I am there."

'As I fell back towards the rear where I generally marched, Hentz rode up by me and inquired what the young Spaniard had said. I repeated it to him. "Do you think he is really that troubled?" inquired he. "Yes," said I—"the poor fellow seems to feel all he says." Without a word, Hentz rode towards him, and reining up by him, tapped him on the shoulder. Victorino looked fiercely up, and seemed inclined to resent it, but Hentz, without regarding the glance, proceeded with a mass of immensely bad Spanish, which I know not how the poor fellow ever understood. "Here," said he, "you love Ana better than I do, I know—you have known her longer, and will feel her loss more; and after all, you would have killed the chief if you could have done it—and you did help me save the body. Take this bunch of stuff," holding out the hair, "and give me your hand." Victorino did so, and shook the offered hand heartily; then taking the scalp, he deposited it in his shot-pouch, and dashing the tears from his eyes, rode off towards his comrades like a madman. So much for the inroad of the Nabajos.'

'But what became of Victorino?' inquired I.

'He married Ana Maria after she had laid aside the luto, (mourning,) and two years ago, he died of the small pox, in the Snake country. Poor fellow—he was almost an American.'

Poems

HOME.

THOUGH the heart hath been sunken in folly and guilt—
Though its hopes and its joys on the earth have been split—
Though its course hath become like the cataract's foam—
Still, still it is holy, when thinking on Home.

Though its tears have been shed like the rains of the spring—
Though it may have grown loath to existence to cling—
Oh, still a sweet thought like a shadow will come,
When the eye of the mind turns again to its Home.

Though the fire of the heart may have withered its core
Unto ashes and dust—though the head have turned hoar
Ere its time, as the surfs o'er the breakers that foam—
Still, a tear will arise when we think upon Home.

TO THE MOON.

Oh quickly rise,
Thou lovely and surpassing moon!
And look into mine eyes,
Ere sober night too swiftly hies;
Grant me this boon.

Here I have kept,
Watching for thy delaying light,
(While others lay and slept,)
As I at other times have wept,
And called daylight.

Yea, I have lain,
And eastward turned my anxious gaze—
But all thus far in vain;
Not yet thy brilliant silver rain
Hath shot its rays.

The evening star
Chid me to go unto my bed—
  Saying, 'she's yet afar,
  And hours will pass, or ere her car
    Be upward sped.'

And she hath set
Behind the western hills; and thou
  Hast not uprisen as yet,
  And trampled with thy silver feet
    The anarch brow,

That doth uplift
Upon the far and eastern marge
  Its high and snowy drift,
  The elements' eternal gift—
    The constant targe

At which are sped
And shivered all thine arrow-gleams—
  By which, likewise, are fed,
  And sent along their rocky bed,
    The mountain streams.

Ah! here she comes!
The stars, her ministers, grow pale,
  As upward from gray glooms,
  The queen of majesty illumes
    Rock, hill, and dale.

Thy light is pure
As love of children, gentle moon!
  Sorrow, it well can cure,
  And from its winter sadness lure
    The heart most lone.

Now I can sleep,
If thou wilt but vouchsafe to shine
  From thy untrodden deep,
  And pleasantly mine eye-lids steep
    In light divine.

The stars that peer
Behind their dimness at thine eye,
And humbly sit and steer
Their orbal boats around thy sphere,
Love not as I.

Adieu, adieu!
For now my lids begin to droop,
And from thy kingdom blue,
Sleep's gentle and bewitching dew
Doth kindly stoop.

So now, good even!
My worthless hymn of praise is sung;
In truth my heart is given,
O silver nautilus of heaven!
Upon my tongue.

Santa Fe, March 10, 1832.

LINES.

Written in the Vale of the Picuris, Sept. 3, 1832.

THE light of morning now begins to thrill
Upon the purple mountains, and the gray
And mist-enveloped pines; and on the still,
Deep banks of snow, looks out the eye of day;
The constant stream is plashing on its way,
As molten stars might roll along the heaven—
And its white foam grows whiter, with the play
Of sunlight, that adown its bed is driven,
Like the eternal splendor from God's forehead riven.

And tree, and rock, and pine, are wreathed now
With light, as with a visible soul of love;
The breeze along the mountain sides doth blow,
And in and out each grass-enshaded cove,

Marking the darkness from those dens remove,
And be dissolved within the splendor shower,
Which raineth to the depth of each dim grove,
And under all the rocks that sternly lower,
And even in the caves, and jagged grots doth pour.

Yet here and there, is a plume of mist,
Whose only care is up the hill to float,
Until the sun be broad and fair uprist;
And then the unseen angels, that take note
To steer in safety this etherial boat,
Will turn its helm to heaven's untroubled seas,
Where its white sail will glimmer, like a mote,
One moment, and then vanish: now the trees
Through it are seen, like shadows through transparencies.

And now the dew from off the flower-bells,
And from the quivering blades of bending grass,
Begins to rise invisibly, and swells
Into the air—(the valley's silent mass)—
Like to the incense which to God doth pass
From out the bruised heart; the cricket's hymn—
The anthem from bright birds of many a class—
All people with their influence, the dim
Soul's solitude, in this most brief, sweet interim.

And Sorrow, though she be not wholly still,
Hath yet a certain gentle look and kind,
And mingling with all nature's joyous thrill,
Breathes a delicious feeling on the mind—
A soothing melancholy, hope-inclined—
Like the dim memory of a saddened dream,
Which made the heart once weep itself stone-blind,
And now doth like both pain and pleasure seem,
Until we know not which the feeling we should deem.

But Sorrow will full soon regain her own,
Although this golden and delicious calm,
Hath made her gentle as the water-tone,
Till she doth sleep, like Peace, with open palm,
And closed eyelid, and enfolded arm;
Soon Memory beneath her eye will sting,
And like a fiend that does his best to harm,
From the dark past will gather up, and bring,
Full many a torturing, and half-forgotten thing.

And she will point to home and hope forsaken—
And friends grown old, perhaps inimical;
And Love beneath her eye again will waken,
From troublous slumber; and again will fall
Foul Poverty, that hid with icy pall
My hope and happiness and father-land;
And I once more shall stand amid them all,
Cast them aside with an unflinching hand,
Shiver my household gods and mid the ruins stand.

O thou, New England! whom these jagged rocks—
These chanting pines—this stream of fluid light—
These mountains. heaved at first by earthquake shocks,
And now defying them—this upper white
Of snow, which beards the sun—this vale so bright—
And all the thousand objects here in view—
Make now most present to the memory's sight
Thy hills—thy dells—thy streams—thy ocean blue—
Thy gorgeous sky, and clouds, of such surpassing hue.

Oh! I have left thee—and perhaps forever,
Land of the free, the beautiful, the brave!
It was a mournful hour which saw me sever
The ties which bound me unto thee, and brave
The exile's woes, and seek an exile's grave.
And now my heart is all—ay, *all* thine own;
Again above me thy hoar forests wave;
Again I hear thy ocean's measured tone;
I live with thee, and am with all the world alone.

And spite of thy unkindness, I am proud
To be thy son; yea, proud of thee and thine;
Although thy failing, prejudice, hath bowed
My highest hopes, and taught lone grief to twine
Around my heart, as doth the poison-vine
Around the oak, rotting it to its core—
Yet still I love thee, and my heart is thine.
And while my feet sound sadly, and forlore,
I pace, and think of thee, and on thy glories pore.

And here, beneath these mossless rocks and grey,
I think of those most venerable aisles,
Where I have passed of many a holy day,
Into the sanctity of ancient piles,
To sit and hear thy faith—of those green isles
Gemming thy bays, and quiet ocean-nooks—
Of the bright eyes, and cheeks enwreathed with smiles,
Which make thee famed for beauty's starry looks—
And more than all, I think of quietude and books.

And still, all this is like the lightning, shot
Athwart the visage of the midnight gloom;
One moment dazzling—the succeeding, not:
And when I think of one of thine, with whom
The hours seemed winged with joy's all sunny plume,
Then, then the torturing fiends again have power—
Then from the darkness of my mental tomb
Thy star doth wane, the clouds about me lower—
And on me comes anew, the dark and fearful hour.

What is there left that I should cling to life?
High hopes made desolate, while scarce expanded—
A broken censer, still with odor rife—
A waning sun—a vessel half ensanded—
Life's prospects on grey rocks and shallows stranded—
A star just setting in a midnight ocean—
A smoking altar broken and unbanded,
Lit with the flame of poetry's devotion—
A bosom shattered with its own disturbed emotion.

This scene, for once, has made my sorrow calm;
And I do thank it—though old Time may mar
Full soon his work. And Hope has held her palm
Like an old friend to me, and set her star
Once more upon the waves of life afar;
And though it sink full soon, nor ever lift
Again its eye above the stormy bar,
Yet still I thank her for the passing gift,
Though henceforth eyeless, on life's stormy waves I drift.

Farewell to thee, New England! Once again
The echo of thy name has touched my soul,
And it has vibrated—oh! not in vain,
If thou and thine shall hear it. Now the goal
Is nearly reached—the last expiring coal
Is trampled. Lo! ere all of life be done,
And ere the wind doth o'er my dead brain roll,
Thou hast the last monotony of one,
Who has been—is—will be—and that for aye, thy son.

HOME.

Full many a tongue,
Liquid as may be, hath its praises sung;
From his around whose lips the fond bees clung,[1]

Unto the wood-thrush wild—of 'Home, sweet Home.'
'T is an old theme; yet if it can impart
Some new, fresh feelings, ever to the heart,
It may be thought of, when that heart is rife;
Words are but feelings, and so home is life.
Why is it that whate'er we hear or see,
'Minds us of home, with a strange witchery?
Because the heart is to the harp most like—
The simple Jewish harp—which, though you strike

1. If Xenophon did not write the praises of home, he ought to have done it.—PIKE.

A thousand notes, hath still its undertone,
The key-note of them all; and long and lone
That tone is heard, after *they* all are dead.
The sound of rain upon the humble roof—
('T is an old thought, I know, that needs no proof,
But I do use it, since its force I feel.)—
The sound of music, following on the heel
Of priests, as worthless as the music is—
The fairy foot that glances past the door,
The eye, that nothing seems but love to pour
From all its deep, black, keen intensity;—
One brings to memory
The rains, that oft have lulled me unto rest,
In the old mansion, after from the west,
Them rising slowly up, I had beholden,
And covering with their frown the bright and golden,
But dying smile of the chill-hearted sun—
Of the small stream, that near the old house run,
As if a smile of friendship there had fallen,
And coursed along—the fields with gray rocks wallen,
And every old and much familiar thing,
That seemed to watch and love me, slumbering;
The other seems the breathing of the flute
Of my old friend, so rich, so round and clear—
(Yet sweet as 't was, when all its tones were mute,
His voice was still more pleasant to my ear);
The last—but that's a dream—
Yet it may seem,
That one may keep alive a sunny dream
Within the few green places of his heart,
Where Want and Wo long since have wiled themselves,
Like the ice-worm of Taurus.
        God of heaven!
Never from me let that fond dream be riven:
The dream of hope, love, joy and home, again,
As to the dry grass doth a summer rain,
Doth unto me a new existence prove.
It is like some lone, silver, sad-eyed dove,

Sitting amid the elements' commotion,
And fanning with her wings the angry ocean,
Until she makes herself a quiet nook,
Quiet as heaven. It is like some sad book.
Of beautiful words, in which the angry reads
Until, within his heart, new thoughts it feeds,
Till, as the book is, he is quiet too.
It is like anything most sweet and strange,
Which can our angry, tortured passions change
Unto more mildness, in its soothing way.
It is the theme which keeps me from despair;
That, be my grief or sorrows what they may,
Their sepulchre, their burial clothes are there.

Santa Fe, Jan. 5, 1832.

TO THE PLANET JUPITER.

THOU art, in truth, a fair and kingly star,
Planet! whose silver crest now gleams afar
Upon the edge of yonder eastern hill,
That, night-like, seems a third of heaven to fill.
Thou art most worthy of a poet's lore,
His worship—as a thing to bend before;
And yet thou smilest as if I might sing,
Weak as I am—my lyre unused to ring
Among the thousand harps which fill the world.
The sun's last fire upon the sky has curled,
And on the clouds, and now thou hast arisen,
And in the east thine eye of love doth glisten—
Thou, whom the ancients took to be a king,
And that of gods; and, as thou wert a spring
Of inspiration, I would soar and drink,
While yet thou art upon the mountain's brink.
Who bid men say that thou, O silver peer,
Wast to the moon a servitor, anear
To sit, and watch her eye for messages,
Like to the other fair and silver bees
That swarm around her when she sits her throne?

What of the moon? She bringeth storm alone,
At new, and full, and every other time;
She turns men's brains, and so she makes them rhyme,
And rave, and sigh away their weary life;
And shall she be of young adorers rife,
And thou have none? Nay, one will sing to thee,
And turn his eye to thee, and bend the knee.
Lo! on the marge of the dim western plain,
The star of love doth even yet remain—
She of the ocean-foam—and watch thy look,
As one might gaze upon an antique book,
When he doth sit and read, at deep dead night,
Stealing from Time his hours. Ah, sweet delay!
And now she sinks to follow fleeting day,
Contented with thy glance of answering love:
And where she worships can I thoughtless prove?
Now as thou risest higher into sight,
Marking the water with a line of light,
On wave and ripple quietly aslant,
Thy influences steal upon the heart,
With a sweet force and unresisted art,
Like the still growth of some unceasing plant.
The mother, watching by her sleeping child,
Blesses thee, when thy light, so still and mild,
Falls through the casement on her babe's pale face,
And tinges it with a benignant grace,
Like the white shadow of an angel's wing.
The sick man, who has lain for many a day,
And wasted like a lightless flower away,
He blesses thee, O Jove! when thou dost shine
Upon his face, with influence divine,
Soothing his thin, blue eyelids into sleep.
The child its constant murmuring will keep,
Within the nurse's arms, till thou dost glad
His eyes, and then he sleeps. The thin, and sad,
And patient student, closes up his books
A space or so, to gain from thy kind looks
Refreshment. Men, in dungeons pent,

Climb to the window, and, with head upbent,
Gaze they at thee. The timid deer awake,
And, 'neath thine eye, their nightly rambles make,
Whistling their joy to thee. The speckled trout,
From underneath his rock comes shooting out,
And turns his eye to thee, and loves thy light,
And sleeps within it. The gray water plant
Looks up to thee beseechingly aslant,
And thou dost feed it there, beneath the wave.
Even the tortoise crawls from out his cave,
And feeds wherever, on the dewy grass,
Thy light hath lingered. Thou canst even pass
To water-depths, and make the coral-fly
Work happier, when flattered by thine eye.
Thou touchest not the roughest heart in vain;
Even the sturdy sailor, and the swain,
Bless thee, whene'er they see thy lustrous eye
Open amid the clouds, stilling the sky.
The lover praises thee, and to thy light
Compares his love, thus tender and thus bright;
And tells his mistress thou dost kindly mock
Her gentle eye. Thou dost the heart unlock
Which Care and Wo have rendered comfortless,
And teachest it thy influence to bless,
And even for a time its grief to brave.
The madman, that beneath the moon doth rave,
Looks to thy orb, and is again himself.
The miser stops from counting out his pelf,
When, through the barred windows comes thy lull—
And even he, he thinks thee beautiful.
Oh! while thy silver arrows pierce the air,
And while beneath thee, the dim forests, where
The wind sleeps, and the snowy mountains tall
Are still as death—oh! bring me back again
The bold and happy heart that blessed me, when
My youth was green; ere home and hope were vailed
In desolation! Then my cheek was paled,
But not with care. For, late at night, and long,

I toiled, that I might gain myself among
Old tomes, a knowledge; and in truth I did:
I studied long, and things the wise had hid
In their quaint books, I learned; and then I thought
The poet's art was mine; and so I wrought
My boyish feelings into words, and spread
Them out before the world—and I was fed
With praise, and with a name. Alas! to him,
Whose eye and heart must soon or late grow dim,
Toiling with poverty, or evils worse,
This gift of poetry is but a curse,
Unfitting it amid the world to brood,
And toil and jostle for a livehood.
The feverish passion of the soul hath been
My bane. O Jove! couldst thou but wean
Me back to boyhood for a space, it were
Indeed a gift.

        There was a sudden stir,
Thousands of years ago, upon the sea;
The waters foamed, and parted hastily,
As though a giant left his azure home,
And Delos woke, and did to light up come
Within that Grecian sea. Latona had,
Till then, been wandering, listlessly and sad,
About the earth, and through the hollow vast
Of water, followed by the angry haste
Of furious Juno. Many a weary day,
Above the shaggy hills where, groaning, lay
Enceladus and Typhon, she had roamed,
And over volcanoes, where fire upfoamed;
And sometimes in the forests she had lurked,
Where the fierce serpent through the herbage worked,
Over gray weeds, and tiger-trampled flowers,
And where the lion hid in tangled bowers,
And where the panther, with his dappled skin,
Made day like night with his deep moaning din:
All things were there to fright the gentle soul—

The hedgehog, that across the path did roll,
Gray eagles, fanged like cats, old vultures, bald,
Wild hawks and restless owls, whose cry appalled,
Black bats and speckled tortoises, that snap,
And scorpions, hiding underneath gray stones,
With here and there old piles of human bones
Of the first men that found out what was war,
Brass heads of arrows, rusted scimetar,
Old crescent, shield and edgeless battle-axe,
And near them skulls, with wide and gaping cracks,
Too old and dry for worms to dwell within;
Only the restless spider there did spin,
And made his house.

      And then she down would lay
Her restless head, among dry leaves, and faint,
And close her eyes, till thou wouldst come and paint
Her visage with thy light; and then the blood
Would stir again about her heart, endued,
By thy kind look, with life again, and speed;
And then wouldst thou her gentle spirit feed
With new-winged hopes, and sunny fantasies,
And, looking piercingly amid the trees,
Drive from her path all those unwelcome sights—
Then would she rise, and o'er the flower-blights,
And through the tiger-peopled solitudes,
And odorous brakes, and panther-guarded woods,
Would keep her way until she reached the edge
Of the blue sea, and then on some high ledge
Of thunder-blackened rocks, would sit and look
Into thine eye, nor fear lest, from some nook,
Should rise the hideous shapes that Juno ruled,
And persecute her.

      Once her feet she cooled
Upon a long and narrow beach. The brine
Had marked, as with an endless serpent spine,
The sanded shore with a long line of shells,
Like those the Nereids weave, within the cells

Of their queen Thetis—such they pile around
The feet of cross old Nereus, having found
That this will gain his grace, and such they bring
To the quaint Proteus, as an offering,
When they would have him tell their fate, and who
Shall first embrace them with a lover's glow.
And there Latona stepped along the marge
Of the slow waves, and when one came more large,
And wet her feet, she tingled, as when Jove
Gave her the first, all-burning kiss of love.
Still on she kept, pacing along the sand,
And on the shells, and now and then would stand,
And let her long and golden hair outfloat
Upon the waves—when lo! the sudden note
Of the fierce hissing dragon met her ear.
She shuddered then, and, all-possessed with fear,
Rushed wildly through the hollow-sounding vast
Into the deep, deep sea; and then she passed
Through many wonders—coral-raftered caves,
Deep, far below the noise of upper waves—
Sea-flowers, that floated into golden hair,
Like misty silk—fishes, whose eyes did glare,
And some surpassing lovely—fleshless spine
Of old behemoths—flasks of hoarded wine
Among the timbers of old shattered ships—
Goblets of gold, that had not touched the lips
Of men a thousand year.

           And then she lay
Her down, amid the ever-changing spray,
And wished, and begged to die; and then it was,
That voice of thine the deities that awes,
Lifted to light beneath the Grecian skies,
That rich and lustrous Delian paradise,
And placed Latona there, while yet asleep,
With parted lip, and respiration deep,
And open palm; and when at length she woke,
She found herself beneath a shadowy oak,

Huge and majestic; from its boughs looked out
All birds, whose timid nature 't is to doubt
And fear mankind. The dove, with patient eyes,
Earnestly did his artful nest devise,
And was most busy under sheltering leaves;
The thrush, that loves to sit upon gray eaves
Amid old ivy, she too sang, and built;
And mock-bird songs rang out like hail-showers spilt
Among the leaves, or on the velvet grass;
The bees did all around their store amass,
Or down depended from a swinging bough,
In tangled swarms. Above her dazzling brow
The lustrous humming-bird was whirling; and,
So near, that she might reach it with her hand,
Lay a gray lizard—such do notice give
When a foul serpent comes, and they do live
By the permission of the roughest hind;
Just at her feet, with mild eyes up-inclined,
A snowy antelope cropped off the buds
From hanging limbs; and in the solitudes
No noise disturbed the birds, except the dim
Voice of a fount, that, from the grassy brim,
Rained upon violets its liquid light,
And visible love; also, the murmur slight
Of waves, that softly sang their anthem, and
Trode gently on the soft and noiseless sand,
As gentle children in sick chambers grieve,
And go on tiptoe.

          Here, at call of eve,
When thou didst rise above the barred east,
Touching with light Latona's snowy breast
And gentler eyes, and when the happy earth
Sent up its dews to thee—then she gave birth
Unto Apollo and the lustrous Dian;
And when the wings of morn commenced to fan
The darkness from the east, afar there rose,
Within the thick and odor-dropping forests,

Where moss was grayest and dim caves were hoarest,
Afar there rose the known and dreadful hiss
Of the pursuing dragon. Agonies
Grew on Latona's soul; and she had fled,
And tried again the ocean's pervious bed,
Had not Apollo, young and bright Apollo,
Restrained from the dim and perilous hollow,
And asked what meant the noise. 'It is, O child!
The hideous dragon, that hath aye defiled
My peace and quiet, sent by heaven's queen
To slay her rival, me.'

        Upon the green
And mossy grass there lay a nervous bow,
And heavy arrows, eagle-winged, which thou,
O Jove! hadst placed within Apollo's reach.
These grasping, the young god stood in the breach
Of circling trees, with eye that fiercely glanced,
Nostril expanded, lip pressed, foot advanced,
And arrow at the string; when lo! the coil
Of the fierce snake came on with winding toil,
And vast gyrations, crushing down the branches,
With noise as when a hungry tiger cranches
Huge bones: and then Apollo drew his bow
Full at the eye—nor ended with one blow:
Dart after dart he hurled from off the string—
All at the eye—until a lifeless thing
The dragon lay. Thus the young sun-god slew
Old Juno's scaly snake; and then he threw
(So strong was he) the monster in the sea;
And sharks came round and ate voraciously,
Lashing the waters into bloody foam,
By their fierce fights.

        Latona, then, might roam
In earth, air, sea, or heaven, void of dread;
For even Juno badly might have sped
With her bright children, whom thou soon didst set
To rule the sun and moon, as they do yet.

Thou! who didst then their destiny control,
I here would woo thee, till into my soul
Thy light might sink. O Jove! I am full sure
None bear unto thy star a love more pure
Than I; thou hast been, everywhere, to me
A source of inspiration. I should be
Sleepless, could I not first behold thine orb
Rise in the west; then doth my heart absorb,
Like other withering flowers, thy light and life;
For that neglect, which cutteth like a knife,
I never have from thee, unless the lake
Of heaven be clouded. Planet! thou wouldst make
Me, as thou didst thine ancient worshippers,
A poet; but, alas! whatever stirs
My tongue and pen, they both are faint and weak:
Apollo hath not, in some gracious freak,
Given to me the spirit of his lyre,
Or touched my heart with his etherial fire
And glorious essence: thus, whate'er I sing
Is weak and poor, and may but humbly ring
Above the waves of Time's far-booming sea.
All I can give is small; thou wilt not scorn
A heart: I give no golden sheaves of corn;
I burn to thee no rich and odorous gums;
I offer up to thee no hecatombs,
And build no altars: 't is a heart alone;
Such as it is, I give it—'t is thy own.

DIRGE.

Over a Companion, buried in the Prairie, July 5th, 1832.

THY wife shall wait,
　　Full many a day, for thee;
And when the gate
　　Turns on its unused hinges, she
Shall ope her grief-contracted eye,
Nor leaving hope to die,
　　Longingly for thee look,

Till, like some lone and gentle silver brook,
That pineth by the summer heat away,
And dies some day,
   She waste her mournful life out at her eyes.
Vainly, ah! vainly we deplore
Thy death, departed friend: no more
   Shalt thou enjoy the spirit of known skies;
The barbed arrow hath gone through
   Thy fount of life,
And now the veined blue
   Hath faded from thy clay-cold cheek, and thou,
   With stern and wrinkled brow,
Like one that wrestled mightily with death,
   Art lying there.
   Whether, above the skies,
Thou treadest heaven's floor, (as was thy creed),
   Beneath God's lightning eyes,
   Happy indeed,
(As hope, weak-winged, should ever try to soar),
   Or, buried there,
Taking thy dead, eternal sleep,
   Shalt only rise in atoms to the air,
   (As thinks despair),—
Howe'er it be, we take our last adieu.
   Lie there, pale sleeper!
Lie there! we weep for thee within the heart:
   Our fount of grief is deeper,
For that it riseth not into the eyes.
Thy grave is deeper than the wolf can go,
And wheels have rolled above thee; so farewell!
   Farewell! for soon,
   With sad and solitary tune,
The echo of our voice will leave thy grave.
   Again, again,
   Farewell!

Refugio

IF there is any one thing calculated to disturb my patience, (and I confess that I am no rival of Job,) it is to be misinformed in distances when I am traveling. I cannot conceive of anything more perfectly calculated to destroy a man's good humor, than to expect to ride or walk three miles, and on the contrary, to find it lengthen out to ten. After the expiration of the three miles, your whole aim is to reach the stopping place; you become insensible to the beauties, if there are any, of nature around you. Every time your horse stumbles, or you hit your toe, you wish the road, guide, director and all, at the—worst place which your principles allow; and in fine, you get to be a remarkably well refined specimen of a man *non compos mentis.* Such, at least, was my condition, as I approached Santa Fe, for the first time. Leaving La Cañada de la Santa Cruz, or the valley of the Holy Cross, in the morning about ten of the clock, we moved sturdily towards the city of the Holy Faith, distant about twenty-five miles. We had already left the snow behind us, and were now traveling over the hard, frozen ground. We were told, at starting, that it was five leagues to the city, and after traveling nearly that distance, we inquired of the guide, 'How far now?' 'Cosa de media legua,' (about a mile and a half). It was then a little over ten miles. In the course of two or three miles more, I inquired again. It was now 'quizas legua y media,' (perhaps four miles and a half.) I had a great idea of shooting him. At length, getting utterly out of patience, with the cold wind increasing every moment in intensity, I inquired again. Poking out his chin and pouting out his lips, as if to indicate the place, he said it was 'mui cerquita,' (close at hand.) 'Is it half a league?' inquired I. 'Si es lejitos.' Now, lejitos and cerquita are the exact antipodes of each other; but I have always observed, that in that country, when you are told that a place is cerquita, it is proper to lay in three days' provision. I have been told that a place was three leagues off, when it was two days' journey. At length, surmounting a small eminence, our guide turned, with an air of immense importance, and ejaculated—'Ai esta!' There it was, sure enough; and I now saw the perfect propriety of General [Zebulon] Pike's description of it, viz.—that it resembled a fleet of flat boats going down the Mississippi. It looks like a whole city of brick-kilns. The mile between us and it was soon passed over, and we descended a small elevation, and entered the city. For about two hundred yards, we kept along a narrow street, with a continuous row of mud buildings on one side of it, and a meadow on the other. This discovery of the meadow, however, was subsequently made; for just then, it was getting too dark to discern objects particularly well. Now and then, at the sound of an American's voice, a door was opened, and a head protruded for an instant, and then again all was dark; for scarcely ever does the glimmer of a candle shine through the small, square windows of that part of the villa. Leaving this street, we turned short to the right, and entered the public square. All here, too, was dark and desolate. We crossed it, and our guide, stopping before one of the doors in its continuous wall, commenced interrogating a person who was passing, in immensely bad patois, as to the possibility of finding a boarding house. The answer was, in good plain English, 'I do n't comprehend you;' and making ourselves known to our countryman, and committing ourselves to his guidance, we were soon safely established in the comfortable house of Don Francisco Ortis.[1]

On viewing the city, the next morning, I found that there was something more of splendor here than in Taos. There is the public square, surrounded with blocks of mud buildings, with porticos in front, roughly pillared, and mud-covered. The windows have a wooden grating in front, which no doubt renders them exceedingly fine and very comfortable. The panes in the square are of glass; in the other parts of the city, gen-

1. Of a prominent Santa Fe family, Ortiz had been elected to the First Territorial Deputation in 1825.

erally of the mica of the mountains. In one corner of the square is the jail and guard room—for the soldiers here serve as jailers, and were to be seen crawling about, nearly as ragged as a French beggar, and adding greatly to the splendor of the square. Within forty yards of this square there is another, called the muralla, surrounded, likewise, by buildings, which on one side are fallen to ruin.[2] It is used as a wheat-field, and belongs to the soldiers who have their dwellings around it. Except in these two squares, the houses are placed anywhere, in an admirable disorder. The little stream which runs through the town waters their fields. It was once much larger than at present; for when the Indians were driven from the Valley of Santa Fe, they retreated to the lake in which this river and the Pecos both rise, as well as the little creek of Tisuqui, and attempted to dam up the river of Santa Fe, and starve out the inhabitants; and they nearly succeeded. This lake is on the summit of one of the highest mountains in the vicinity of Santa Fe.[3] It is about sixteen miles, perhaps more, from the city, and never opens until July. It is always full, and fed with constant springs. The people of Santa Fe, a few years since, employed an Englishman to open it, agreeing to pay him two thousand dollars for so doing, which money was to be raised by subscription. When it was nearly finished he demanded a part of the money, in order to pay his workmen, and other expenses. They refused to advance a dollar until it was finished; and he swore that they might finish it for themselves. Since then, the work has remained as he left it, needing about a month's labor to finish it, and by giving the city a greater supply of water, to increase the extent of arable land, and of course, the size of the city. In the course of the first week of my residence in Santa Fe, I became acquainted with

2. The *muralla* was a defensive wall which was crumbling by the time that Pike saw it. Perhaps he mistook an open area near the wall for a plaza.

3. There is some truth to this story. The Indians cut off the Spaniard's water supply during the siege of Santa Fe in the Pueblo Revolt of 1680, but they accomplished this by closing off canals in Santa Fe itself. Since they held the part of the city along the Río de Santa Fe, they had no need to go to the mountains. See Charles Wilson Hackett (ed.), *Revolt of the Pueblo Indians of New Mexico and Otermin's Attempted Reconquest, 1680-1682* (2 vols. Albuquerque, 1942), I, 101. The Pecos does not have its source in the same lake that feeds the Río de Santa Fe. Pike's subsequent story about the Englishman does not have any basis in fact.

several of the great men of the province, and it is but fair that you, kind reader, should enjoy the benefit of their acquaintance. Briefly then:

Santiago Abreu, the present Governor of the Province of New Mexico, is, of course, the most distinguished man in it. At the death of his father, he was left in possession of a small property, which belonged in common to him and his two younger brothers; this property he gambled off, and made his first entrance into public life in front of the Governor's coach, with his brothers standing as footmen behind. After this, he passed some years in abject poverty, supported chiefly by Americans; and two or three years ago, when an American died there who had brought out a small stock of goods, Abreu bought his goods on credit, sold them for cash, and, gambling with the money, won about three thousand dollars. This made him a great man. He was then chosen Delegate to the Congress; and while in the city of Mexico, his letters were opened in the Post Office, at Santa Fe, by the post master, Juan B. Vigil, who sent copies of them back to Mexico, where they were versified and published. Last year he was appointed Governor. He is ignorant, deceitful, mean and tyrannical.[4] Every New Mexican, however, is deceitful and mean. Juan B. Vigil was formerly custom-house officer, and was deprived of office, citizenship, and the privilege of entering a church, for peculation and fraud. He now lives very comfortably upon his booty, has a church of his own, and gets along very well without the citizenship.[5]

Francisco Rascon, the second Alcalde, was punished, when in the Pass, for stealing the ornaments from the image of the Virgin Mary.

4. Santiago Abreu had become Governor in the spring of 1832, while Pike was still in New Mexico. He had been elected deputy to the Congress in Mexico City in 1824, but there is no evidence that his attainment of political office was as dramatic as Pike believed. Abreu had served as customs collector before becoming Governor—an honest one apparently—and was thus in disfavor with American merchants. See, for example, (St. Louis) *Missouri Republican*, November 14, 1837.

5. Juan Bautista Vigil y Alarid became the last Mexican Governor of New Mexico when Manuel Armijo fled before the Army of the West in 1846. Vigil had been dismissed from his job as customs collector in 1826 for abusing his office (Report of the legislative committee to Governor Antonio Narbona, January 11, 1826, Mexican Archives of New Mexico, Santa Fe). Whether his punishment was as severe as Pike claims is not certain.

I do not know anything against the first Alcalde, the Secretary and the Assessor, except that they take bribes whenever they can get them; that is nothing, however, in New Mexico.

The Regidor, or Assistant Alcalde, Miguel Sena, has only perjured himself three times, to my own knowledge, and put his father in jail once: but even the New Mexicans call him a great rascal.

The former Governor, Chares [Chávez],[6] has been seen to steal a dollar at a monti-bank. He is, however, too stupid to be capable of committing sin.

Juan Ortis,[7] another great dignitary, very pious, and formerly Alcalde, stole several pair of shoes from an American, a year or two ago.

So much for my acquaintances, the great men of the province. As to the common herd, they are rather better; they have some generosity and hospitality. They will all lie and steal, to be sure, and have no idea of gratitude. There is neither honor among the men nor virtue among the women. In fact, honor in New Mexico would be apt to lie on the owner's hands. Character is a mere drug, a valueless article; and he who has little of it is as well off, and as rich, as he who has much. The men most in honor now in that country are such as have either stolen, perjured or dishonored themselves. One, in particular, in San Miguel, had been confined under the regal government nine years, for stealing, and only a year or two ago was taken in irons to Santa Fe, for stealing mules; and he—he is more powerful and respected in his town than the head Alcalde.

Among the Americans with whom I became acquainted, shortly after my arrival in Santa Fe, there was one in particular who excited my interest and won my esteem. And here I beg leave to remark, that in what I am about relating, I shall, for reasons which will doubtless be obvious to all who follow my brief tale to the conclusion, conceal the actual names of the

6. José Antonio Chávez had occupied the Governor's Chair from the spring of 1829 to the spring of 1832. Of a prominent New Mexico family, he had served in a number of public offices. Lansing B. Bloom, "New Mexico Under Mexican Administration," *Old Santa Fe*, I, 3 (January, 1914), 266.

7. Juan Ortiz, Francisco Rascon and Miguel Sena were all prominent officials, apparently holding the offices which Pike ascribes to them. Whether their transgressions were real remains speculative.

persons interested in it. Most of the circumstances are facts, although the time at which they actually occurred was a little anterior to the date of the tale. Most of them are facts, and the actors yet alive.

The name by which my new acquaintance was known by the Mexicans was Refugio, and by this appellation I shall designate him, whenever I have occasion to mention his name at all.[8]

He was a native of some one of the Eastern States. I never perfectly learned his history, for he was, in general, of a reserved and abstracted nature, and seldom spoke much of himself. I do not know that this proceeded from any desire to conceal any part of his life or history; on the contrary, he always seemed to me to be careless about it. But it was only when required, for the sake of elucidating or explaining any circumstance which occurred in conversation, that he spoke of himself; and he then did so in the same manner as he would have done of any other individual, and mentioned any fault or folly as unhesitatingly as he did anything on which he might have been inclined to boast. What I did learn, was, therefore, learned at different times, and in detached portions. His parents were in moderate circumstances, and his father was a farmer, who, possessing strong and good sense, and a common education, early took care to bestow upon his son the benefits of erudition, of which he knew the value; and in the country where learning is common and easily obtained, the excellent talents of Refugio, and his constant and intense application, soon stored his mind with the riches of ancient and modern lore. About the time that Refugio commenced the study of the law, his circumstances became involved, and after various ineffectual struggles to extricate himself, he left his home, and bent his steps to the far West. The idea of a wild and lonely life struck his fancy, which was now morbid from disappointment and sorrow, and he embarked in a trip to Santa Fe, with the purpose of going from that place into the northern mountains, and there hunting beaver. On arriving, however, in the territory, he was disgusted with the tiresome, dull, monotonous nature of a wood life, and with the in-

8. I have been unable to identify Pike's "Refugio." Clearly, much of the plot is fanciful, although it may be based on a real incident.

sipid and tedious companions with whom it brings a man in contact—companions gathered from the lowest ranks of society, that is to say, in general, when in the woods, only remarkable for ribaldry, profanity, and constant quarrel and jar, and when out of them, like sailors in port, for revelling, drunkenness and a senseless scattering of their hard-earned wages. He therefore remained in Santa Fe, and, perhaps, enjoyed as much solitude there as he could have done in the woods. He resided alone, and had his meals brought him by a native of the country; and at almost any hour of the night or day, you might find him in his room, reading, writing, or, more commonly, immersed in reflection. His excellent knowledge of the Spanish, which he spoke superbly, made him be generally employed as an interpreter in the courts of justice, and as a transactor of business for the Americans, a business which was, at that time, abundantly lucrative; and his carelessness, as to consequences, when determined upon any line of conduct, and his independence in asserting and maintaining the rights of those for whom he was acting, rendered him feared and respected by the dispensers of justice, (they call it justice,) in the city; and his constant accommodating disposition, his known talents, and quick retribution when he felt himself aggrieved, made him respected by the Americans. He was a thin, spare man, with a bold, intellectual, but melancholy cast of countenance. His eyes were deep and black, but not vivid, unless when he was excited by passion, and had, except then, the peculiar look which accompanies the eyes of all who are short-sighted.

As I said before, I never made inquiries of him respecting his former history, but after my acquaintance with him had continued some three months, and we became somewhat intimate, he gave me the liberty of ransacking what he called his chaos of papers. I have always been sorry that I never copied any of them. They consisted chiefly of poetry in fragments, thrown about in careless disorder. His writing was to him—so it seemed to me— like a conversation with himself, an embodying and expressing of unformed and floating thoughts, under the concentration of mind which the action of writing called forth. From these I became convinced, that among other things of which his separation from home had bereft him, had been that first, greatest passion, love. I think he had been unfortunate in fixing his affections where they were not answered or rewarded.

There is one circumstance which, perhaps, it were better to leave untouched, but it is my purpose to delineate an actual character, and neither to extenuate or exaggerate in what I have to relate. Refugio was a bold and unwavering infidel. Of this I became aware casually; for he never disputed in my hearing upon the matter, although I had several times given him occasion, and though others had spoken harshly of those who, like him, were blind to the true faith. By such remarks his spirit was never stirred, and no answer was ever elicited. After I became acquainted with his disbelief, he was, perhaps, a little less cautious in expressing his sentiments before me, but still I could never induce him to dispute with me. He seemed to be totally convinced of the correctness of his views, and the strength of his objections, and being aware that the diffusion of his unfaith would neither help the cause of morality or happiness, to the commonalty of mankind, he of course had no motive for disputation. He was no bigot in his creed, no vulgar railer, no causeless and wanton shocker of the feelings and prejudices of others —and this made him respected, even by the most zealous and bigotted of his countrymen in New Mexico. I think that his mind was continually occupied with the past. For the future, he seemed to have no care, though a love of home, and a hope of returning there, never seemed to leave him. He would sit and muse for hours together, without speaking, and would then, perhaps, break his silence by some wild, abrupt remark, on some singularly deep and strange metaphysical thought, which seemed to come from him unconsciously; and then, without a moment's hesitation, he would plunge into some remote subject, or acute train of reasoning or observation, as if he desired to remove the effect of what he had unconsciously uttered. Perhaps I am delaying too long in describing his character. It is natural for one to suppose that what interests himself should likewise interest his readers,—the true cause of prosing and weariness in writing. From such evil fortune, may heaven shield us.

In the latter part of February, Refugio informed me that he

had agreed to accompany another American to Chihuahua, for the sake of seeing the lower country; and in the course of a day or two, he called upon me to take leave of me. The pack mules of the merchant, Donaldson, were already on the road, and he was on his way out of the city, to overtake them. He shook hands with me kindly, and wished me every kind of prosperity. He told me that it was improbable that he should return to Santa Fe. 'Heaven knows,' said he, 'what will become of me, or where my destiny will lead me. I am a leaf the wind blows on his unsteady currents, and as I have never yet been fortunate, it is highly improbable that I ever shall be so. Farewell! and now and then remember me in your dreams.'

On arriving at a little village about one hundred miles this side of the Pass, Donaldson was taken sick, and Refugio delayed with him some days. In the mean time, the pack mules went on under the protection of the convoy of Mexican soldiers, then stationed at the villages of the Rio Abajo, as it is called, half way between the city of Santa Fe and the Paso del Norte, to escort passengers, and defend them from the attacks of the Apaches, who were, at that time, committing depredations on the inhabitants of the country; for they break out of the mountains, now and then, and use their good allies, the denizens of the Mexican republic, very roughly. They are, in fact, a powerful tribe, and extend from the vicinity of Taos all along the chain of the Cordilleras, to near the city of Mexico. I have heard them computed at fifteen thousand warriors, but I cannot vouch for the correctness of the statement: I hardly think that it is much exaggerated. They will come down and rob the people, to the very gates of Durango and Chihuahua, and when the soldiers come out of the country below, to oppose them, they retreat to the mountains, and as soon as the soldiers return, they follow on the track, and about the time that they enter the city, the Indians are robbing outside of the gates, driving off cattle, and depriving of their hair the loyal subjects of Sant' Ana. They are the more dangerous, on account of using poisoned arrows, the least scratch with which is certain death. They gather and confine a number of rattlesnakes, centipedes and scorpions, and tease them until they become furious. They then kill a sheep, and, taking out the heart, throw it, with the blood yet circulating in it, into the midst of them. Every fang and sting is immediately fastened upon it, and after leaving it there for a time, they take it out and place it in some vessel. In a day or two it becomes a green mass of corruption, and in it they dip the points of their arrows.[9]

When Donaldson recovered from his illness, two other Americans came down from Santa Fe, and the four started together to go on to the Pass, through the Jornada de la Muerte [Jornada del Muerto], or the journey of death, a distance of ninety miles, entirely without water. Of the two men who joined them, Waitman and Everton, I know but little, and, in fact, never saw them save once or twice. They were common, gross, sensual men, who would never have been admitted to the society of such men as Refugio, except in a country where all distinction among Americans is confounded. They started together, all mounted on good mules, and well armed.

It was a chilly night in the beginning of March, (for in that mountainous region the nights are always cool); the moon had not yet arisen, but her light was beginning to brighten a little in the dark and changing clouds, which covered the sky from the eastern to the western mountains;—the west wind came sweeping down in fitful gusts, from the icy peaks beyond the Del Norte, across the desolate plain of the Jornada de la Muerte, which lay barren and desolate as a desert; a few tall weeds raised their heads above its red, hard surface, and sighed as the wind went by, with a singular, desolate sound of mourning;—here and there a cedar stood—low, ragged and gnarled, with its long and grotesque branches dimly seen through the obscurity of the cloudy night;—the wolf was heard howling about with his multitudinous noises, and the collote, or prairie-wolf was barking, off in the distance, towards the mountains. In the midst of all this dreariness, a Mexican gentleman was traveling hastily towards the Pass, (now but a few miles distant), attended by three or four servants, when suddenly the mule upon which the

9. Snakes, Mohaves and Shoshones reputedly used this method of obtaining poison, although they found rattlesnake venom sufficient in itself. Robert Glass Cleland, *This Reckless Breed of Men: The Trappers and Fur Traders of the Southwest* (New York, 1950), pp. 40-41.

gentleman was mounted and riding ahead, stopped, and putting
her head down, snorted loudly, and refused to proceed. In vain
did the rider attempt to get her to go on; he turned her out of
the road, but still her only motions were retrograde; and at
length, by her violent springs and prancing, he became in im-
minent danger of being dismounted. He therefore directed his
servants to lead the way, but their animals had likewise caught
the infection, and refused to go on. He then ordered a servant
to dismount, and see what there was in the road to frighten the
mules. Proceeding cautiously forward for perhaps a rod, the
servant was frightened by some object which lay in the road,
and which proved to be a man's hat. A little farther on, a mule
was found, with the rope which was attached to her neck tangled
in a ragged cedar. All the party now dismounted, and commenced the search in utter silence. Some moments were passed
in this manner, when a sudden and shrill cry from the eastern
side of the road drew all to the spot whence it proceeded. 'Aqui,
Señor! Venga par aca!' (Here, sir! Come hither!) As the gentleman approached within four or five feet of the group of servants,
he felt his feet detained by some tenacious and slippery substance, the nature of which he was at no loss to divine. Just at
this moment the moon broke forth from behind the hills, and
gave a dim, gloomy light through the medium of the clouds,
discovering the body of a man lying upon his face, upon the dry
grass and weeds of the plain. He was dead—entirely dead; but
the blood was yet undried on the hard earth. When they turned
him over, it was seen that one of his hands was still clenching
a part of the hair reins of the bridle. There was a wound in his
back, made by a bullet, and the gun had been discharged so
near him as to burn his clothes. Besides this, there was a deep
stab behind the shoulder; and one of the servants, in treading
about, discovered a broad and long knife lying near the body.
It was at first conjectured that the Apaches had slain the American—for such he was—but this idea was untenable. There was
his mule—his gun—his hat—everything belonging to him—and
his scalp was untouched: and they remembered that a lone
American had passed them the day before, going out of the up-

per edge of the Jornada. Of course, therefore, it was conjectured that his own countryman had been his murderer.

After much difficulty, the corpse was bound upon a mule, and conveyed into the Pass, where it was identified as the body of Donaldson, and the two men, Waitman and Everton, were arrested on suspicion; for it was easily proved that they had entered the Jornada de la Muerte in company with the deceased, and that they had arrived at the Pass only a short time before the corpse, perhaps three hours. The affair was taken up by the few Americans residing there, and the two men were committed to prison, heavily ironed.

The body of the unfortunate merchant was buried upon a hill near the town,—for the people are too pious to permit a heretic to be buried in holy ground, and to be pounded down after the fashion of true believers,—and the grave was afterwards guarded for two or three nights, to prevent the Mexicans from opening it to obtain the sheets in which the corpse was wrapped.[10]

In the course of a fortnight the trial of Waitman and his accomplice was had, and proof enough was adduced to show them guilty. They, accordingly, confessed the crime, but, at the same time, implicated Refugio, and accused him of striking the blow with the knife. They pointed out his initials on the handle of the knife, and not a doubt remaining on the minds of the Alcalde and of the Americans present, of the guilt of this unfortunate man, orders were immediately sent up to Santa Fe, for his arrest and coveyance to Chihuahua. Waitman allowed that he shot Donaldson in the back, as he was riding ahead, and that the mule of the deceased, frightened by the report, threw him off to the ground, where he was finished by the knife of Refugio. When asked for the motives he said that there were none but the desire of money, of which the deceased had a considerable sum about him.

Upon the arrival of this news at Santa Fe, great commotion was excited. Refugio was taken, ironed heavily, and chained to

10. Josiah Gregg, in his *Commerce of the Prairies* (p. 185) also records that Americans were buried on a hill near Santa Fe, and notes the danger of the corpse's "shroud" being robbed.

a post in the public square. Every one supposed him guilty, but
when he was examined, a day or two after his apprehension,
many were induced to alter their belief; his appearance was so
much like that of an innocent man—he told his own story so
clearly, in the same quiet, melancholy manner which commonly
characterized him—and he seemed so unconcerned about his
fate. He stated that on first entering the Jornada he had been insulted, and forced into a quarrel by Waitman; that Donaldson
had taken the part of the latter, and that consequently, he had
returned to Santa Fe. He referred them to the short time which
elapsed after his departure from the last village till his return
thither, and stated that the knife with which he started from
Santa Fe was stolen from him a day or two before entering the
Jornada.

Against all this was the testimony of the two murderers. Refugio was again taken and chained to the post, and kept there for
the space of two or three weeks. His conduct while there has been,
and is, matter of astonishment and admiration to the Spaniards.
They speak of him as a wonderful man. Chained there in the
hot sun for so long a time, fatigued, wearied, starving,—nothing
conquered his spirit. The dignitaries of the place, (of whom I
have given the characters), were mean and Mexican-like enough
to insult, scoff at and misuse him; but they repented of it. His
splendid knowledge of their language, and perfect command
of his faculties, enabled him to overwhelm them with a flood of
scorn and biting satire, which caused even the populace to
pursue them to their houses with hisses. So terrible was his
anger, that the Spaniards took him to be deranged; and it was
only when some one of his few remaining friends went to see
him, that he seemed again himself. Then he would converse as
before his disgrace, and seem not to feel the intense degradation
of his situation; and then only, the terror-stricken dignitaries
of New Mexico could venture through the square, without
feeling the terrible lash of his tongue.

He had been confined about three weeks, when, as I was
standing conversing with him, a band of about twenty soldiers
rode into the square, and surrounded us. The chains were struck
from his hands, and half a dozen of the soldiers, grasping him in

the same manner as they would a sack of corn, proceeded to bear him towards a mule, which stood with its aparejo,—its leather rope, &c. all ready for packing him to Chihuahua. So sudden was the motion of Refugio, that I know not how he accomplished it, but there was a loud cry, and I saw one soldier dashed against the post, bleeding at the mouth and nose, and another fifteen steps from him, with one arm bent under him, as though he had been thrown upon it; and Refugio stood erect, grasping the heavy musket of one of the soldiers, and bidding them all stand off at their peril. At this moment Viscara rode into the square:—another instant, and a half dozen bullets would have been lodged in the body of Refugio, (that is, if the soldiers could have hit him;) but at the cry, 'El teniente coronel!' each man bared his head, and awaited the approach of Viscara. He was immediately accosted by Refugio. 'Sir,' said he, 'call off your dogs, and thank Heaven that none of them are dead. What! do you imagine that I am to be bound upon a pack-mule, like a bag of wheat, and taken thus to Chihuahua? I thought that *you*, at least, knew me better. Dead, you may take me so, but alive you cannot, and you know it; and you and the fools with whom you are associated know that I am innocent. Kill, then; I have two or three friends who will not fail to avenge me.' By this time some half dozen Americans had gathered around, who were mostly friends to Refugio; and Viscara knew their stuff too well to despise it. He well remembered the time when a house was barricaded against his troops —and when they fought, the Americans would have whipped his troops to death. They have had plenty of examples to teach them the nature of the Americans. Milton Sublette, (who deserves to be remembered for his courage), is the man who, three or four years ago, when a pack of beaver belonging to him was confiscated, and lay in the public square, under a guard of five or six soldiers, and in front of the guard-house, went out and tumbled over the fifteen or twenty packs which lay upon it, then, throwing is own upon his left shoulder, and grasping his long, keen knife in his right hand, he threatened any one with instant death who should dare to pursue him. He bore his pack of beaver to the house where he boarded, and threw it upon the roof, and that night took it to Taos.[11] A few such examples make men careful.

'Refugio,' said Viscara, 'if you will give me your word of honor, that you will not attempt to escape from my soldiers, I give you mine that you shall be conveyed honorably and decently to Chihuahua.'

'I ought to do no such thing,' was the bold answer; 'I have the power of life and death in my own hands, and am not inclined to ask favors. But I answer you as a man of honor, which is more than can be said of any other contemptible New Mexican, and I will therefore accept your pledge, and give you mine.'

'Give up the musket, then, Refugio; and as that soldier who lies there bleeding at the mouth seems rather unfit for service, you can take his mule and ride it; my word is pledged for your being treated well.'

'Very well; but do not hurry me. As to the musket, there it is,' throwing it down, 'but I have something yet to say to my friend. Your men can wait for me a while.'

Drawing my arm through his, he walked to the outside of the soldiers, and we finished our conversation. 'And now,' said he, 'farewell! I suppose that the two miscreants will hang me, for in this country they are not over scrupulous in examining and weighing anything which is in favor of an American. But if I can once see them face to face, I will wring the truth out of them; I think I can make them quail a little; I have always thought that I possessed, in a considerable degree, the faculty of obtaining an influence over mankind—that is, if I chose to exert it. Generally, however, it has been too unimportant an object for me to take the requisite pains. But if I can do nothing with them, at least, the cowardly and despicable slaves of Chihuahua shall never have the pleasure of seeing me hung; I will take my own time and way to leave the world. Thank God, my parents will never hear of it, for none here know my true name.

11. The story of Milton Sublette's siezure of his furs, and defiance of Mexican authorities in the spring of 1827, must have been popular among the Americans. Gregg immortalized the story in his *Commerce of the Prairies*, while Pike's earlier version of it has gone virtually unnoticed. A biography of Sublette by Doyce B. Nunis appears in LeRoy R. Hafen (ed.), *The Mountain Men and the Fur Trade of the Far West* (Glendale, 1966), IV, 331-339.

Not that I have committed any crime, to make me ashamed of it, but I wished not for them and the world to hear of me only as an unfortunate and disappointed man. Life has long been wearisome to me, but the hope of one day seeing my home, and the want of sufficient cowardice to enable me to put an end to myself, have kept me struggling along with the world. I am not afraid to die. Men say that I shall recant and be terrified on my death bed. It may be so; at present I have no fears of dying; I have been too wretched, my hopes have been to often crushed, for me to wish to live or to be afraid to die.'

'Have you never thought, Refugio, that it might be that your doctrines and your unfaith have been the chief cause of your gloom and disquiet?'

'No—I know they are not; it is my nature; I am not deceived in myself; I have studied my own heart long and intimately, and I know its powers and its strength, as well as its springs of action. Abstract argument will never prove to me that any particular creed can render a man gloomy and sad. One creed may have a greater tendency that way than another, and perhaps mine in a superior degree; but Chatterton, Savage, and Henry Neele[12] were as deeply involved in melancholy as Byron and Shelley. No, it is the nature of man and his disappointments. But we must part. Whether I am destined to go down to the grave with obloquy, and the imputation of guilt resting on my name, or not, you at least will believe me innocent. God bless you:—we part forever.'

Directly after this, the cavalcade passed out of the city, and took the road to the Pass. Another party of troops received him at the Rio Abajo, and continued with him to the Pass, and there delivered him to another, which took him to Chihuahua. When he arrived there, he was emaciated, by fatigue, to a skeleton; but still he preserved the same unconcerned boldness which had marked his deportment in Santa Fe. A day or two after his arrival, he was brought to trial, together with Waitman and Everton. The latter were first tried and condemned on their own

12. A reference to Thomas Chatterton, an English poet who committed suicide in 1770 at age eighteen, and Richard Savage, an unhappy English poet (d. 1743). I have been unable to identify Henry Neele.

confession, and then their evidence was brought forward against Refugio, together with the other circumstances which conspired to show him guilty. He then rose, and supporting himself with difficulty, requested the permission of the court to address a few words to the prisoners. It was cheerfully accorded him. As he commenced speaking, his tones were low and faint, but as he proceeded, his voice fell more and more distinctly upon all ears, and the earnest and rich modulations of its sweet tones thrilled like the notes of an Æolian harp. His pale face became flushed, and his frame seemed to acquire an intense strength. 'Men,' said he, 'what have you against me, that can urge you to seek for a life which is now ready to be rendered up to the God who gave it. Have I wronged you? Have I broken your peace of mind, or ruined your prospects, that you desire to send me to the scaffold, and to leave disgrace and shame resting darkly upon my name? Be not deceived; nay, quail not, hide not your eyes, and turn not away your heads. Be not deceived; the God in whom ye believe will avenge me. Ye will go down to the grave with the curse of a double murder resting on your souls, and ye cast away—if your creed be true—every hope of a reconciliation with God. Posterity will know that I was innocent. Who will believe, who does believe, even now, your tale? Look at me. Am I a man, I, who scarcely live now, to take away the life of a fellow being for the sake of a little gold? Am I the man to raise a knife against him? am I the dastard to strike him in the back? am I the wretch to associate with *you* in an act of murder? For my life I care nothing—*that* is valueless. For my fame, my good and honest name only, have I a care. Let that be unstained, and I am content to stand upon the scaffold with you, to die with you, and to pollute the air with you. Have you the heart to see a fellow man, whom you know to be innocent, writhing in the torture of death and dishonor, turning his last look at the sun, and quivering with the last gasp of death, to satisfy your revenge? If ye have the courage, why not look me now in the eye? Am *I* guilty, am *I* abashed at the eye of any mortal, and, more than all, of *yours?* Hearken! If there be indeed a future state of retribution, as ye both believe, it shall be your chief torment, that even in death ye insulted and contemned the Lord God

Omnipotent; that ye dragged a man, who was entirely innocent, upon the scaffold with you? And how will ye, who cannot bear the glance of *my* eye, how will ye look into the countenance of an offended and a terrible God? And what will ye gain? Will I die by your side? No, never! Death will do his work on me ere the time; or if not, I can do it on myself. Will men believe me guilty? Not they. When they learn that I was absent but one day after entering the Jornada de la Muerte, and that I reeturned to the village above it before the murder was committed, who will not see that I was innocent? and what court would condemn me, except in a country where no foreigner need hope for justice?' Here he was interrupted. A stir was visible among the judges, and the eldest of them spoke; for what Refugio said was interpreted as he spoke.

'Señor Refugio,' said he, 'this court can hear no imputations upon itself, and you are allowed to make none.'

'I stand corrected, señor! the truth should not be told at all times.'

'Where is the evidence of your so speedy return to the village?' again demanded the judge.

'At home—who was to bring him here—and how was an American to obtain anything which might aid him in saving his life and his honor? They are not here. But let me proceed.'

'You cannot do so; you have insulted the court, and if you die, your blood be on your own head.'

'Who says that I shall not do so? Listen to me, countrymen! I adjure you by all your hopes of heaven! I adjure you by your parents, wives and children! by your manhood! by your good feelings which are not yet extinct! by all that is sacred and dear to you! to rise and declare the truth. Now, by the God of heaven! you *shall* look me in the face for one moment. I command you to lift your eyes to mine; and if you can, after that, still declare me guilty, be it so, and I am content.'

Struck by the earnestness of his address, the men both lifted their eyes to his, and for a moment or two were unable to withdraw them. The intense, deep wo which reigned there had yielded to a blaze of terrible light which seemed to illumine the whole of his transparent features. Fixing his gaze steadily upon them for a space, he essayed to move towards them, but swayed and fell, and the blood burst forth from his lungs. The event would still have been doubtful, although the moving lips and the restless gaze of both the prisoners seemed to indicate the failure of their vindictive resolution, when a sudden tumult arose without the court. Two Mexicans—their mules covered with foam and themselves with dust—rode up to the door, and rushed into the presence of the judges, and demanded to be sworn. They had heard that their evidence would save the life of Refugio, and they had come to give it in. They deposed, that during the time of his absence from their village he could not have entered more than twenty miles into the Jornada de la Muerte.

'At what time did he leave the village?' inquired the chief judge.

'At sunrise, Señor; and returned again before sunset.'

'Do you know this knife?'

'Yes, Señor; it is the knife which the Señor Refugio had when he arrived at my house,' answered one of the men.

'You are sure it is his knife?'

'Si, Señor; but I will tell you; that American in the black coat took it from the sheath, when it hung up in the room, while Refugio was out.'

'Why did you not tell Refugio of this?'

'Señor, what had I to do in making a quarrel between two friends? I thought that it might be only a joke. How could I imagine that an American would steal a knife?'

'Take up the unfortunate man and bear him to my house,' said the chief judge. 'Father,' added he, to a gray-headed old man, wearing the tonsure, who sat by his side, 'will you accompany him, and see that the French surgeon attends to him?'

Refugio was raised by the nervous arms of four servants; and as they were about bearing him past the box in which the prisoners sat, the old priest ordered them to stop. The prisoners looked with troublous eyes upon the body. The blood was abundant about his mouth and upon his breast; his black hair was wet with sweat, as though it had rained upon him, and his eyes were closed. Suddenly, the deep, solemn tones of the Padre were heard. 'Men,' said he, 'I charge you, in the name of the living God, whom Christians and Heathen worship, to lay your hands here in his blood, and declare that he was guilty; and wo! wo! unto perjury!' Waitman alone moved to do so; and just as his hand touched the body it quivered. The wretch fell back to his seat, and his whole vindictive courage giving way to terror, he muttered, 'He was innocent.'

What remains of our tale can be told in a few words. The two prisoners were forwarded to Mexico, and either there or on the road, they escaped from prison. Refugio recovered partially from his sickness, and likewise went to the south, and I have since then heard nothing from him. He is probably dead ere now. But his memory will long live in the country which witnessed his sufferings, his disgrace, his undaunted boldness, and his final triumph.

Poems

The spirit in my soul hath woken,
   And bids me speak to thee again;
And silence, many a day unbroken,
   Must cease, although it cease in vain.
As life approaches to its goal,
   And other passions seem to die,
The thoughts of thee that haunt the soul
   Decay not, sleep not, death defy.

Love's busy wings delight to fan
   A heart that hath been worn to ashes,
And, aided by thy spirit, Ann,
   Beneath his eye that heart still flashes.
Oh! why doth Love build up his nest
   A ruined palace aye within,
Hiding within the poet's breast—
   Why seeks he not a home more green?

He hath no alcyon power, to still
   The passions of the trampled heart,
Rob of its pain the torture-thrill,
   Bid sorrow, want, and pain depart:
Oh no! he adds a fiercer pang
   To every wo which rankles there,
Sharpens the scorpion's fiery fang,
   Adds wildness unto terror's glare.

Yet still, I love thee, and forever—
   No matter what or where I be;
The blow which shall existence sever,
   Alone can end my love for thee.
I love thee as men love but once—
   As few have loved, can love a woman;
It seemeth strange, this perfect trance
   Of love, for one that is but human.

But thou wast rich, and I was poor;
 I never spake my love to thee;
And I could all my wo endure,
 Nor ask thee, Ann, to wed with me.
To wed with me!—it were to wed
 With Poverty, and Want, and Wo:
Rather than this, from thee I fled,
 And still a lonely outcast go.

But day by day my love hath grown
 For thee, as all things else decline;
And when I seem the most alone,
 Thy spirit doth commune with mine.
I have no portion with the world,
 Nor hath the world a part with me;
But the lone wave, now shoreward hurled,
 Will turn, yea, dying, turn to thee.

I make to thee, thy love, no claim;
 I ask thee but, when I shall die,
To lay the world-forgotten name
 Within thy heart, and o'er it sigh.
Think that the love which I have felt,
 To which existence hath been given,
Has been as pure as stars that melt
 And die within the depths of heaven.

Fare thee well—it is for ever!
 Thou hast heard my dying words;
Till the cords of life shall sever,
 Till the serpent Wo, that girds
The exile heart, its strings have broken,
 Bruised and crushed and shattered it;
Until this, to thee are spoken
 All my words—my dirge is writ.

Ark. Territory, April 20, 1833.

FANTASMA.

I sit, unconscious of all things around,
Gazing into my heart. Within its void
There is an image, dim and indistinct,
Of something which hath been—I know not which,

A dream, or a reality. In vain
I seek to force it take a visible form,
And be condensed to thought and memory.
At times I catch a glimpse of it, behind
The clouds and shadows, which fill up the chasm
Of the dim soul. And when I seem to grasp
The half-embodied echo of the dream,
When it hath almost grown an audible sound,
Then it retreats, hunting the inner caverns
And undisturbed recesses of the mind—
Recesses yet unpeopled by quick thought,
Or conscience, hope, live fear, or memory—
And there they hide. Now, while I separate
Myself yet more from my external life,
And turn within, I see those floating thoughts
Quiver amid the chaos of the heart;
And slowly they assume a more distinct
And palpable appearance. One by one,
Dimly, like shadows upon ocean-waves,
For a brief moment they are memory.

I see a boy, reading at deep, dead night;
The lamp illuminates his pallid face,
Through the thin hand which shades his deep, black eyes,
Half bedded in the clustering, damp, dark hair.
He closes up the book, and rising, takes
A step, a tottering step, or two, and speaks
In low and murmuring tones unto himself:—
'The fountain is unsealed; this "annciente rime"
Hath shown my powers to me—hath waked the tide
Of poetry, which lay within the soul.
Henceforth I know my fate; the latent love,

Now well revealed, of wild and burning song,
Will render me unhappy: until now
I have not known the bent of my own mind.
And now I look into it, as a new
And unexhausted treasure. Burning words,
Wild feelings, broken hopes, await me now.
Oh! what a curse this gift of song will be!
'T will quicken the quick feelings, make still less
The power of grasping happiness, give strength
To every disappointment, wo and pain.
If I win fame, ever unsatisfied;
If not—but I shall win it—and in vain.
Oh! what a curse, indeed, were prophecy,
And knowledge of the future. Could the soul
Exist, and know what waits it, with no wing
Of hope to shade it from the blasting eye
Of hot despair? Well, be it so; the gift
Must be received. Passion will have its way,
Although the heart be shivered by its wild

And stormy course. Although the eyes grow dim—
Dimmer than mine; although the unripe buds
Of happiness are shaken from the stems
Fed by the heart, and choak its fountains up
With their decaying blights; yea, though that heart
Be like a house deserted—with the doors
And windows open to the winter wind—
The lamps extinct, the moonlight shining in
Through barred casements and wind-moven blinds,
With ghastly eye,—passion will have its way.'
I see him hide his face within his hand.
Was it to weep? It might be. He was young,
And tears flow freely at the spring of life.
In after years the desert is less moist,
The fountains of the heart are deeper, or
More choked and more obstructed. He was young,
And had not known the bent of his own mind,
Until the mightly spell of Coleridge woke

Its hidden powers, as did the wondrous wand
Of God's own prophet the sealed desert-rock.
He saw his fate; he knew, that to a mind
Enthusiastic, wayward, shy as his,
It is a curse, this love of poetry;
It is a thing which on the heart doth brood,
Unfitting it for aught but solitude;
Unfitting it to toil and jostle with
The busy world, and gain amid its crowd
The scanty pittance of a livelihood.
He knew all this, and wept—who would not weep?

That shadow vanishes, and like a man
Standing anear one broad monotonous sea,
And gazing to its distant space, and void,
And chasmal indistinctness, I behold
Another shadow, gathering in the vast,
Wherein are stored old dreams and antenatal echoes.
And now its images and thoughts take shape.
I see the boy sit in a crowded room.
His eyes have still that look of wasting gloom
And lustrous deepness; still his cheek is pale,
His lips are thin and bloodless, and his form
Is wan and wasted; bright eyes bend on him,
(That might make summer in the wintry heart;)
Transparent checks are flushed, whene'er his voice,
With its low murmuring, is heard, as 't were,
In lone communion with himself—for praise
Has fed his eager spirit with her rain
Of dangerous sweetness. Songs of wild and fierce
And energetic things, or low and sweet
Eolic tones, but unconnected with
Himself, unegotistical, had won

Praise and a name for the enthusiast boy.
But, with the same intense and constant look
With which men gaze within upon their soul,
And with a deep expression of devotion,

He gazed continually there on one—
One that knew not his love, but stealthily
Uplooked at him, and seemed to him more cold
Because she loved him. Oh! the power of love
Is terrible upon the poet's heart.
The quick and fiery passions there that dwell,
And quiver, serpent-like, make too his love
As wild, intense, unmingled as themeselves.
The boy tells not his love—
Not even when from out his wasting heart
The passions will have vent, and he doth breathe
His feelings to the world—this one remains
To feed that heart with its destroying dew.
'T is only when the passions of the soul
Have lost some fierceness, and become more tame,
Not in the first intense, enthralling gush,
That men write down their soul in measured rhyme.
After a space, it is some sad relief,
To weigh and ponder it in different ways—
To view it in all lights—in short, to make
Poetry of our feelings and our heart.

I lose the shadow:—will its place be filled?
Darker and darker the chaotic vast;
And now upon its eyeless surface, moves
The half-embodied spirit of a dream,
Like an unshapen dread upon the soul,
A heaviness which hath no visible cause.
When will the dream arise from out the chasm,
And be revealed?—oh when? I cannot yet
Express it to myself. Again the vast
Quivers like clouds that are by lightning shaken.
And now more clearly I behold the dream—
The shadow comes distinctly to mine eyes.
I see the boy stand in a crowded street:
The shade of manhood is upon his lip;
His thin form has grown thinner, his dark eyes
More deep, more melancholy, more intense.

No muscle moves upon his pallid face;
His brow contracts not, though its swollen veins
Show that the stream of passion or of wo
Beats fastly there. Full listlessly he leans
Against the pillar of a noble dome,
Holding no converse with the crowd; his eyes
Look inward, there communing with his spirit.
Another shadow rises. Ah! it is
That lady of his love; I see her pass

By the enthusiast boy: and now I see
Him, by the sympathy which doth connect
His soul with hers, raise up his dark, sad eyes.
They meet his idol. Now his pallid face
Is flushed, his frame is shaken, as it were,
With a quick agony; the gouts of sweat
Stand on his brow. Like one who talks to spirits,
His lips part and emit a stifled sound.
One sad, mute gesture is his last farewell.
The hand of poverty has chilled his hopes,
Closed up their rainbow wings, and bid them brood
No more upon his heart, to comfort it.
Weary of toil and care, he leaves his home,
To seek in other climes a fairer lot,
And friends less faithless, and a world less cold.
He hath not told his love; he hath not asked
The idol of his soul to wed with want,
And poverty, and pain—perhaps remorse.
He leaves his home, henceforth to be a leaf,
Wandering amid the currents of the air,
Or of the trackless sea—a fallen blight—
An aimless wave, that tosses on the ocean,
Bearing a star within its heart of love.

Gone like the spirit of an echo;—gone
Into the shapeless chasm of the soul.
But still the cone of one white, glittering star
Lightens the dim abyss of memory.

Another shadow rises, and behind
The wild chaotic darkness waits to whelm
That shadow like the rest. I see a desert;
And in it is that boy, now grown a man:
Strange alterations have been on his soul;
His sorrows still are there, but kindly now,
Like ancient friends, they people his lone heart.
Like shadows round the roots of wasting trees,
Feeding them with an influence of love,
The sorrows feed his soul, and make it calm.
He has communed with nature, in her moods
Of stern and silent grandeur, and of sweet
And calm contentment, and of bold
And barren loneliness—conversed
Most intimately with his wasted heart,
And tracked its hidden fountains to their head;
And like sick men, that watch their frame decay
With strange and silent quietude, so he
Has watched those fountains, choked with blighted hopes,
Or sublimated unto unseen dew,
By passion's constant and devouring fire;
Has watched that heart, once verdurous, waste away,
Shedding no tear, nor feared to meet with death.

Henceforth he hath no hope;—a still despair,
A quiet, lone monotony of heart,
A strong, unsatiated wish of change,
A carelessness and scorn of all mankind,
But not a hate, and deep within his heart
A love of beauty and of poetry—
This is his nature.
I lose the shadow, and the chasmal shades
Throng from the void, filling the inner heart.
The quivering star of memory is extinct;
The echo rings no longer on the sea
Of dreams and past realities. So be it—
It is a lesson of another boy,
Whom not his crimes or follies, but the tide

Of his quick passions ruined. Let, henceforth,
None be like him. If ye are born to toil,
Wear out your hearts, and let not poetry
Enter and nestle there:—it is a curse.

Ark. Territory, May 10, 1833.

BALLAD.

Written on leaving New England.

Farewell to thee, New England,
  Farewell to thee and thine;
Farewell to leafy Newbury,
  And Rowley's woods of pine.

Farewell to thee, old Merrimack,
  Thou deep, deep heart of blue;
Oh! could I say, while looking back,
  That all, like thee, are true!

Farewell to thee, old Ocean,
  Gray father of the waves;
Thou, whose incessant motion
  The wing of ruin braves.

Farewell to thee, old Ocean;
  I'll see thee yet once more,
Perhaps, or ere I die, but not
  Along my own bright shore.

Farewell, the White Hills' summer snow,
  Ascutney's cone of green;
Farewell Monadnoc's regal glow,
  Old Holyoke's emerald sheen.

Farewell to hill, and lake, and dell,
  And each trout-peopled stream,
That out of granite rocks doth swell,
  And ocean-ward doth stream.

Farewell to all—both friends and foes—
  To all I leave behind;
I think not now of wrong and woes:
  A long farewell, and kind.

I go to live—perchance to die—
  Unknown, in other climes;
A man of many follies I,
  Perhaps, but not of crimes.

I have a pride in thee, my land,
  Home of the free and brave;
Still to thy anciant motto stand,
  Of 'Honor or a grave.'

And if I be on ocean tost,
  Or scorched by burning sun,
It still shall be my proudest boast,
  I am New England's son.

So a health to thee, New England,
  In a parting cup of wine;
Farewell to leafy Newbury
  And Rowley's woods of pine.

SUNSET.

A Fragment.

SUNSET again! Behind the massy green.
  Of the continuous oaks, the sun has fallen,
And his last ray has ceased to dart between
The heavy foliage, as hopes intervene
  Amid gray cares. The western sky is wallen

With shadowy mountains, built upon the marge
  Of the horizon, from eve's purple sheen,

And thin gray clouds, that daringly uplean
Their silver cones upon the crimson verge
    Of the high zenith, while their unseen base
Is rocked by lightning, which will show its eye
    Soon as the night comes. Eastward you can trace
No stain, no spot of cloud upon a sky
    Pure as an angel's brow;
    The winds have folded up their quick wings now,
And all asleep, high up within cloud-cradles lie.

Beneath the trees, the dark and massy glooms
Are growing deeper, more material,
    In windless solitude; the flower-blooms
    Richly exhale their thin and unseen plumes
Of odor, which they gave not at the call
    Of the hot sun; the birds all sleep within
Unshaken nests—all but the owl, who booms
Far off his cry, like one that mourns strange dooms,
    And the wild wishtonwish, with lonely din.
There is a deep, calm beauty all around,
    A massive, heavy, melancholy look,
A unison of lonesome sight and sound,
    Which touches us till we can hardly brook
Our own sad feelings here;
It cannot wring from out the heart a tear,
    But gives us heavy hearts, like reading some sad book.

Not such thy sunsets, O New England! Thou
    Hast more wild grandeur in thy noble eye,
More majesty upon thy rugged brow.
    When sunset pours on thee his May-time glow
    From his flush heart, it is on proud and high
Gray granite mountains—rock and precipice,
    Upcrested with the white foam of the snow—
    On sober glades, and meadows drear and low—
On wild old woods of savage mysteries—
    On cultivated fields, hedged with gray rocks,
And greening with the husbandman's young treasure—

On azure ocean, foaming with fierce shocks
Against the shores which his dominions measure—
   On towns and villages,
   And environs of flowers and of trees,
Full of gray, pleasant shades, and sacred to calm leisure.

And when the sunset doth unfold his wing
   Upon thy occident, and fill the clouds
With his rich spirit, on thy eves of spring,
He is a far more bold and gorgeous thing;
   He sends his flocks of colors out in crowds,

To sail with lustrous eyes the azure river
   Of thy keen sky, and spirit-like to cling
   Unto its waves of cloud, and wildly fling
Themselves from crest to crest with sudden quiver.
   Thy sunset is more brilliant and intense,
But not so melancholy, or so calm,
   As this which now is just retreating hence,
Shading his eye with gray and misty palm,
   Lulled into early sleep
   By thunder from the western twilight deep,
Now 'neath the red horizon moaning out his psalm.

Ark. Territory, May 10th, 1833.

LINES.

[In one month I shall be in the prairie, and under the mountains
in another.]

ONCE more unto the desert! who
   Would live a slave, when he can free
His heart from thraldom thus? O who?
      Slave let him be.

Once more unto the desert! now
   The world's hard bonds have grown too hard.
No more, oh heart! in dungeons bow,
         And caves unstarred.

Heart! bid the world farewell: thy task
   Is done;—perhaps thy words may live;—
Thou hast no favor now to ask,
         And few to give.

Thou hast writ down thy thoughts of fire,
   And deep communion with thine own
Sad spirit; now thy broken lyre
         Makes its last moan.

Thou hast laid out thy secrecy
   Before the world, and traced each wave
Of feeling, from thy troubled sea
         Unto its cave,

Within thy dim recesses, where
   The feelings most intense are hidden;
Thou hast outborne thence to the air
         Thy thoughts, unbidden.

And now unto the desert. Why!
   Am I to be a slave forever?
To stay amid mankind, and die
         Like a scorched river,

Wasting in burning sands away?
   Am I to toil, and watch my heart
And spirit, hour by hour decay,
         Still not depart?—

To pour the treasures of my soul
   Upon the world's parched wilderness,
And feel no answering echo roll
         My ear to bless?

Once more unto the desert! There
 I ask nor wealth, nor hope, nor praise,
Nor gentle ease, nor want of care
   On my dark ways;

Nor fame, nor friends, nor joy, nor leisure—
 Here I must have them all, or die,
Or lead a life devoid of pleasure—
   Such now lead I.

No life of pain and toil for me!
 Of home unhoped for—friends unkind!
Better the desert's waveless sea,
   And stormy wind.

Better a life amid the wild
 Storm-hearted children of the plain,
Than this, with heart and soul defiled
   By sorrow's rain.

Out to the desert! from this mart
 Of bloodless cheeks, and lightless eyes,
And broken hopes, and shattered hearts,
   And miseries.

Out to the desert! from the sway
 Of falsehood, crime, and heartlessness;
Better a free life for a day
   Than years like this.

Once more unto the desert, where
 My gun and steed shall be my friends:
And I shall ask no aidance there—
   As little lend.

Farewell, my father-land! Afar
 I make my last and kind farewell.
I did think to have seen thee—ah!
   How hopes will swell!

Farewell forever! Take the last
   Sad gift, my father-land, of one
Struck by misfortune's chilling blast,
       Yet still thy son.

Farewell, my land! Farewell my pen!
   Farewell, hard world—thy harder life!
Now to the desert once again!
       The gun and knife!

Ark. Territory, May 25, 1833.

Appendix

CRAYON SKETCHES AND JOURNEYINGS

Letter 1[1]

I ought perhaps to explain the title which I have seen fit to give the numbers that I propose now and then to present to the readers of the Pearl. They are intended to be precisely what the title imports,—mere rough sketches, from memory too, of a journeying from St. Louis to Santa Fe, and through various parts of New Mexico, performed by the author in the year 1831. I shall not be scrupulous as regards the manner of the sketch. It may be simple description, and it may sometimes be combined in a tale. In the present number I can only present my readers with the former.

I must apologise for the frequent use which I shall be obliged to make of the personal pronoun 'I.' It sounds harshly on the ear, I confess—and it is somewhat of an offence against modesty —but nevertheless, necessity has no law.

I have often regretted, and I doubt not that I shall always regret, not having pencilled down my first impressions of the great West and its people, when they were fresh in my mind in all their novelty and strangeness. Then, I could have written down their slight peculiarities, their quaint, and to an eastern ear, singular expressions—all that strikes a stranger as novel and uncommon. Now, it has all become familiar to me. The slight shades of difference have become imperceptible, gone, lost, in the void filled with things forgotten. The west has now become a home to me. Its people have become familiar friends—I am even as they, and their peculiarities are no longer marked—I have lost the power of describing them.

Without troubling the reader by asking him to follow me in

1. *The Boston Pearl and Literary Gazette*, November 8, 1834.

my devious course across the United States, and without detailing the causes which influenced my actions, let him suppose me at St. Louis in the state of Missouri, in the month of August, 1831, ready to start for Santa Fe—one of a company of thirty men.[2] It is not the purpose of these numbers to describe towns and cities. They rather incline to take our readers into the depths of the sea-like prairies—into the sublimities of forests and mountains, and thither therefore let us go.

We left St. Louis on the 10th of August, and took up the march in detached parties for Independence, on the western border of the state, where we were to rendezvous, and whence we were to go forth into the desert. Only once or twice in my life have I felt so free, as I did the morning after leaving St. Louis, when I mounted my horse and with my gun before me set out on my ride for the day. There is a freedom of mind, a buoyancy of feeling, a separating and detaching one's self from the world, when for the first time we sleep on the broad bosom of our general sepulchre, the earth, or watch all night the keen stars which in their turn seem to watch us—when for the first time we depend upon our horse and gun, and feel that they not failing us we are independent. Little did I then think of the cold and weariness and hunger which we were to encounter. Well it was for me—well it is for the general family of mankind that the future is to them an unrevealed, and a sealed book.

It is impossible for me, at this day, to speak of the state of Missouri in any other than general terms. I was struck with the general appearance of prosperity throughout the whole state— with the neatness of its farms, the intelligence and hospitality of its inhabitants. Proud of their descent from the sons of 'Old Virginia and Kentucky,' or themselves natives of one or the other of those states, most of them have much of the chivalrous, open, and hospitable nature which belongs generally to the sons of the 'Old Dominion' and Old Kentuck.' I love a western man. There is so much open, brief, off-hand kindness—so much gen-

2. This party was captained by Charles Bent, who would later become the first American governor of New Mexico. See Harold H. Dunham, "Charles Bent," in LeRoy R. Hafen (ed.), *The Mountain Men and the Fur Trade of the Far West* (Glendale, 1965), II, 27-48.

uine honesty, excellence of heart, and steadiness of purpose in them, that they always claim, from him who knows them well, the utmost affection and respect. You, who have never left the shores of the Atlantic, cannot appreciate, you know nothing about their character. Perhaps, reader, before we part, I may attempt to make you acquainted with some of them.

It was in Missouri that I first saw a prairie of any extent. There is no sight on which the broad sun looks, that is more beautiful and more magnificent. You emerge from a deep, heavy body of timber, of that solid, massy, continous greenness, that we never see in the east, and you gaze upon a broad, undulating plain, covered with grass mingled with flowers of the most gaudy colors,—extending away—away—north, south and west— with here and there a long line of timber on the edge of some water course, or a solitary grove standing like a lone castle in the garden-like greenness around it. Let not the reader imagine, however, that there is in *these* prairies any of that illimitable extent of vision which he has upon the ocean. By no means. The horizen is rather limited, because the prairie is generally a succession of long, undulating, swelling ridges—and in travelling over them you are like one riding over the long, heavy swells of the sea—at one moment you see only to the summit of the next ridge, and at the next you have a broad sea of a thousand colors before you.

It was in these prairies that we saw in its utmost perfection the mirage, which afterward, when I was hungering and thirsting, deceived me often with the empty promise of water. In the prairies in Missouri you may see it every day, when the sun shines, and most beautiful it is. You will see, far ahead, upon a long ridge, a running flame, and a smoke, as though the grass on the ridge were burning. It will curl, and wave, and float up spirally and quiver, till the deception is perfect—and then it will vanish, and down below in the hollow you may perceive a broad, rippling lake of water, or on the ridge a thick green grove of trees—promising shelter and fire for the night. The illusion is perfect—so perfect that I would have wagered any sum that the first of these unreal phantom groves which I saw was a real, good, bona-fide bunch of trees.

I missed in these prairies the brilliant sunrise and the gorgeous twilight of New England. In the prairie there is little of the splendor which you see in both, in that land of the brave and free. On the tall mountains of the Del Norte I have often watched the sun go down, and the thick clouds that enveloped him rise in thin fleeces up into the dark blue heaven and assume all the colors which in New England float out of the heart of the dying sun—but in the prairie there is little of this. The sun rises with little brilliance, and he sinks into his temporary grave with a small portion of that varied glory with which the country of my birth accompanies his set. Still sunrise is a stirring and beautiful sight even in the prairie. You lie down, with a broad bed of grass and flowers beneath you, and the pure dew bathing your forehead during the night. Day light spreads over the heaven, and you awake—you dash your hands in the grass and with the dew you wash yourself—you are on your horse—and then up comes the sun—broad, bright, and like a sphere of white fire—unaccompanied with the gorgeous heralding of the colored clouds. He sets in his own simple and stern majesty—the king of heaven—no pompous heraldry announces his death to the earth below—but he sinks to his grave like a warrior, silently, and in quiet calmness. You see no flushing of the sky—no piling together of the red clouds—and yet there is something indescribably grand in a sunset on the prairies of Missouri. It has always seemed to me like the burial of a conqueror—in his naked, simple glory—undirged—ungloried—buried with his own grandeur—and it alone about him—and then if from some simple cottage—half hid—in the green prairie, you hear the tones of a lonely flute ringing over the plain which is almost a desert, the charm is complete.

The whole of our company did not travel together from St. Louis to Independence. There were something like fifteen of us together for the first two thirds of the way—men from every corner of the union, and some from other and more distant countries. For example, there were three of us Yankees from Massachusetts—there were two from Virginia, one from Georgia, &c. &c. Then there was a little Frenchman on whom we had conferred the dignity of cook. He had been a sergeant in the army which marched into Spain to put down the Cortes—and he had with him his sword—his commission as sergeant in that immense expedition, and another as lieutenant in the National Guards during the *Trois Jours*.[3] I wish I could remember his name. He was an adept at every thing. Not a word of English spoke he—but we could converse in Spanish, which he spoke tolerably well. He sang us the Marseillois[4] and the Parisienne, and played the flute. He acted as tailor and made himself a blanket capote, and when we reached Santa Fe he turned confectioner. He was *one* specimen of the Frenchman. Old Charles, or Rael, was a Prussian, born at Cologne, or some place near the border of France. He was a perfect specimen of the old soldier—and we made him *cook primo*. He was dirty, shrewd, and thievish. He had fought both for and against Napoleon, and talked half a dozen languages, all at once. For example *'para, questo, ca!'* He was more of a Frenchman, however, than anything else. He was a second specimen. Then there was Batiste something, a little, imbecile, one-eyed Canadian,—useless as a pine stick, except to drive an old white mule in a pair of shafts, with a little swivel behind, on which he sat a-straddle; from morning till night. I remember, (to exemplify the man,) that, one day, being on guard in the heart of the Indian country, and wanting to light his pipe, he struck a straw in the touchhole, clapped some tow in the pan, struck fire, and commenced lighting, when bang! went his old musket, with a bullet and a dozen buck shot in her. He used to sing us Canadian boat songs. They might have sounded well to Thomas Moore, Esq. on the St. Lawrence, but to me they are only one grade above an Osage war song. Next came Antonio, a tall, black, scowling Catalonian —lazy and useless—and then a New Mexican Spaniard whom I then thought the best rider I had ever seen. After he joined us we soon had all our mules broken, but before, we had some amusing scenes, and one or two broken heads. A number of mules were purchased, after we had been three or four days from St. Louis, and such of the men as had no horses, under-

3. Pike refers to the 1823 French invasion of Spain on behalf of Ferdinand VII, and the July 25-28, 1830 revolt against Charles X, which placed Louis Philippe on the French throne.

4. The "Marseillaise," the French National Anthem.

took to ride them. They were perfectly unbroken, and for two or three mornings we had a most ridiculous scene. None of the men knew how to manage the animals, and they were generally no sooner on than off. One poor fellow was no sooner on his mule's back, than he was seen describing a somerset—pitching probably in his fall plump upon his head. Another would go up into the air as straight as an arrow, and a light on his feet. Others would stick on, and the mules taking the bit in their teeth, would run with them a mile or two like incarnate fiends. It is very little use to try riding a mule with an American saddle and bridle. You want a deep Spanish saddle, a heavy double cast bridle with which you can break your animal's jaw—and then you can ride.

Alas, it is sad to think how the thirty who composed that party have scattered. One was drowned the next winter in the mountains north of Santa Fe. Some are in that city—some are trapping—some are in California—some are in Sonora—one at the coppermines—some in Chihuahua—one in San Juan de Dolor[es], or some other *hacienda* in the centre of Mexico— some are in Missouri—one poor fellow was killed a year or two since in the prairie—others are, heaven knows where. No two of them are left together. Yet such is our journey through the world. We rush onward—the currents of circumstances whirl us away from our friends, and we see no more of them. We form new connections—and the cold hand of time takes the memory of our old friends from us.

I think it was on the tenth of September, that we finally left all settlements behind us, and took up our regular march toward the desert. It is, if I remember aright, something like a hundred and seventy miles from Independence to the Council Grove, (so called because the Spanish and American Commissioners met there to settle the boundry line between Mexico and the United States,)[5] and having arrived at this grove we considered ourselves fairly started. The grove itself is no way remarkable, except that it is nearly the last one on the road. It is principally hickory timber, and all the men were employed for a day or

5. This is not correct. George C. Sibley and his United States survey party of 1825 named the Grove in honor of a council with some Osage Indians.

two in making gun rods. Here we first began to stand guard, and a blanket began already to be comfortable in the evening.

I am convinced that the whole country now composing the great American Desert, was once covered with water. This great prairie rises gradually from the Mississippi to the Rocky Mountains—and even at the Council Grove must be three or four thousand feet above the level of the sea.[6] Yet there is a high bluff above the grove, (which itself is on a very small stream), with a low, perpendicular front, and some fifty feet high. On the face of this bluff are evident marks of the water, and on the summit are shells and water worn rocks in abundance. I have seen cavities in large rocks, on the side of the Rocky Mountains, at least ten thousand feet above the sea, filled with little pebbles, manifestly washed in there—and the valley of the Del Norte, on the sides of the mountains, to the height of two hundred feet above the level of the stream, (perhaps, twice as much), bears marks of a sea of waters too plain to be denied—even to columns of earth and rock thirty feet in height—perfectly insulated from the sides of hills, round, and worn in ridges by the action of the waters. There has been a time when only the summits of these mountains were seen above the ocean— and the great American desert was the bottom of a sea. So that it is perhaps with reason that we call this the New World.

6. Present-day Council Grove, Kansas, is 1,234 feet above sea level. Pike's observation that the Plains were once covered with water is correct.

CRAYON SKETCHES AND JOURNEYINGS

Letter 2[1]

Friend Pray,—I address this letter to you, so that if it should not seem worthy of publication, you can consider it as a private epistle to yourself. As *such* at least, it will give you some pleasure; and I shall value that more than any praise it might receive.

I think it was about the middle of October, or perhaps, not quite so late, when we reached the Arkansas, and I for the first time beheld that great river. With our reaching this river, commenced our troubles and vexations. Our oxen, from hunger and drought, began to fail, and we were, every day or two, obliged to leave one behind us. The hungry jaws of the white wolves soon caused them to disappear from the face of the earth, and by thus affording these voracious animals food, we had a continual train of lean, lank and gaunt followers, resembling Hunger-demons, following us stealthily by day, and howling around us by night. We ourselves suffered extremely from thirst, for as there was a wide low kind of 'bottom' (as it is called in the West) covered with long grass, on either side of the river, and not exceedingly pleasant to the traveller, we followed the road, which at the distance of about half a mile from the river ran along on the prairie summit of the bluffs. Add to this a constant, fierce, dry wind from the north, that blew upon us for a fortnight about this time, or somewhat before, making our very throats as dry as the 'Aunciente Marinere's.' On the Arkansas, however, we killed some fine buffaloes, and feasted regally on humps and various other savory morsels, which

1. *The Boston Pearl and Literary Gazette,* November 22, 1834.

230

Apicius[2] might have envied us. After following the Arkansas, about eighty miles, we forded it with our wagons, and took a more southerly course toward the Semaron [Cimarron River]. I think that it might have been between six and seven hundred miles from Little Rock, where we crossed the river, but I cannot tell. I am but a poor calculator of distances at the best. When we crossed, the water was nowhere more than two feet in depth, rather muddy, but sweet. After crossing, we travelled about twelve miles through the sand-hills, and then came into the broad and barren prairie again. The prairie, however, between the Arkansas and Semaron, (a distance, according to our route, of about a hundred miles), was not level, but rather composed of immense undulations, as though it had once been the bed of a tumultuous ocean—a hard, dry surface of fine gravel, incapable, almost, of supporting vegetation. The general features of this whole great desert—its sterility, dryness and unconquerable barrenness—are the same wherever I have been in it. Our oxen were daily decreasing in number, and our train of wolves enlarging. I can give the reader some idea of their number and voracity, by informing him, that one night, just at sunset, we killed six buffaloes, and having time to butcher and take to camp only three, we left the other three on the ground, skinned and in part cut up. The next morning there was not a hide, a bone, or a bit of meat, within fifty yards of the place. These wolves, however, very seldom attack a man, although I did know one who was *treed* by them in the mountains. They generally confine themselves to buffalo calves, and, in default of this more tender meat, to ham-stringing now and then an old buck, which they do very dexterously. I think that one of them would be a tough antagonist to a man—and I remember an incident told me by a gentleman named Smith, who had been an old journeyer through the prairie, which shows something of their strength. He had killed a buffalo at night, and on going to the body in the morning, discovered a large wolf with his head and shoulders entirely buried in the stomach of the 'corpse.' He resolved to go up behind the wolf, and stab him with his knife, but when

2. Apicius was a famous Roman epicure in the time of Tiberius, credited by historians with the invention of *pâté de fois gras*.

within about fifty yards of him, he found that he had left his knife at camp. Not to be *backed out*, he determined to jump on the wolf and break his back or choke him to death. He did jump on him accordingly, but instead of allowing his back to be broken, the animal began to *back out* himself, and Smith 'took the track back again,' (as they say in the West,) with all haste. He declares that he heard, for the first fifty yards, the teeth of the wolf snap together behind him at every jump. He distanced him, however, but thenceforward gave up the idea of breaking the backs of wolves.

After striking the Semaron, that saltest, most singular, and most abominable of all the villanous streams of the prairie, we went crawling up it for forty miles, with our jaded oxen, at the rate of about eight miles a day, and about the first of November we reached the middle spring of the Semaron.[3] Before reaching this point, my horse ran off in a storm, one night, and left me to walk the rest of my way to Santa Fe. I had no particular objection, for the Indian Summer was over, and it was altogether too cold to ride. Just before arriving at the middle spring, we sent off five men to go unto Taos, and bring out provisions and oxen. This reduced our company to twenty-five men. I will try and give you some idea of life in the prairie, by just describing our stay of one night at this middle spring. I think I shall hardly ever forget the place. The river, coming from the southwest, here made a bend and ran due east, that it, as nearly as I can recollect—running, in the *elbow* so formed, nearly to the feet of some bluffs of rock which were piled up on the north side of us, with just breaks enough between them for the wind to whistle merrily between their rough teeth. In front of us, to the south, (as we camped in the elbow), there was the narrow, dry sand-bed of the river, and beyond it a dry plain, stretched out as it seemed in an eternity of barrenness. We reached the spring in the middle of a light snow, accompanied as it had been heralded, by a keen, biting north wind, fresh from the everlasting ice-peaks that guard the springs of the Arkansas. We camped, and commenced gathering the dry ordure

3. The middle spring, which Pike subsequently describes, was a prominent point on the Santa Fe Trail.

of the buffalo for fuel—the only salvation of the journeyer in the prairie. We piled a quantity under the wagons, and with difficulty having satiated our hunger, I for one rolled myself in my blankets and coiled myself in the tent. As the hours of night wore away, the snow fell thicker, and the cold grew more intense. At half past one, I was called out to stand guard. I strapped my blanket round me, shouldered my gun, and was ready to stand as sentry till nine in the morning—for what purpose, the wise commanders of the party knew best. Indians never attack on such nights. I stood at the west end of the camp—in front of the tent belonging to our mess. On the east end was another tent, and by it a small fire, where the captain of our guard, quaking, half with cold and half with fear of Indians, *stood* guard *sitting*. For about half an hour, I paced back and forth on the rod and half of line allotted me—in snow about a foot deep. The storm was over, and the wind every moment grew more intensely cold. At length my feet forced me to the fire. I warmed them, and they were cold before I was at my stand again. I tried the fire again, but with no better fortune and then I resolved to build a fire for myself. I piled some of our fuel together, and sat down to watch it ignite. It was then about three in the morning—and in about an hour it gave me sufficient heat to keep tolerably warm by bending over it—which I did, with a sovereign contempt for every tribe of heathen Indian between the Mississippi and the mountains. In the morning my feet were so swollen that I could with difficulty move—and the reader, and you also, may judge of the degree of cold, when I tell you that a horse froze to death within ten feet of me. Great God! how those animals suffered. I have seen oxen come and stand by the fire, till it scorched the skin from them. You could not drive them away—and no wonder.

From this place we crawled on to the upper spring, forty miles farther, and here we left the Semaron. I have never seen it since, and I most devoutly hope never to see it again. The volcanic hills of the Semaron, at this point, are a curiosity. They consist of a mass of rocky fragments, which seem to have been thrown into the air from the level prairie by some ancient explosion or eruption—and such, no doubt, is the fact—for they consist of huge, unjointed, shattered, burnt rocks, and of large fragments of what seems like lava—and besides, the plain, to a considerable distance, is covered with lumps of scoriae and lava, as if they had been scattered there by the same explosion. After leaving this place, we had an inclined plane to travel on, sloping toward the Canadian, as hard as rock, and over which the wagons glided, almost without the need of exertion. The weather was moderate, and we met with no farther trouble, until we reached the Point of Rocks.

Letter 3[1]

Without boring your readers with any farther account of my marvellous adventures by prairie, and through storm, let me take you over a 'pretty considerable' spur of the Rocky Mountains, into the land of promise called *La Provincia Nuevo Mejico*. I delight to wander among the mountains, not only on the fleet wings of Fancy or Memory, but even when borne down the cold current of time, on the pinions of stern Reality. Not a very coherent figure that—but you know what I mean. In sober truth, there is to me, when I wander among the kingly cones of the mountains—those giants, wearing their stainless mantles of white snow over their broad shoulders of element-defying granite—there is something like a lifting in the mind of itself from and above the enthralling cares and the enslaving contingencies of the world, like that which we feel when we move like unimportant motes over the limitless desert of the ocean-like prairie, but with this one difference. In the prairie we are alone; we have that same desolate, companionless feeling of isolation, so well expressed by Coleridge. We separate ourselves from our companions, and turning our mind inward to a consideration of its own hidden joys or miseries—its memories or anticipations, we pass over the desert as men pass through a glimmering and lonely dream. But the mountains are our companions. We lose that feeling of solitude and oppression at the heart, and in its stead is an expansion and an elevation of the mind, as though the great spirit which, as Fancy might imagine, inspires the mighty mountains, was entering into the heart and

1. *The Boston Pearl and Literary Gazette,* January 10, 1835.

abiding there. You will understand all this, however, to refer
to a time when I was roaming about over these mountains, with
the cool air that came down from their icy foreheads tempering
the heat of summer—when I was perfectly at my ease, and had
no other care than to pass off an hour or so, and take my fill of
enjoyment from the glorious scene around me—and not to that
time when I made my first ingress into the Province of New
Mexico, starving, and through snow three feet deep. At that
latter time, that hideous old maid, Reality, clasped me to her
cold bosom, and her cry was 'aroint [begone] thee, Romance'—
and so she did, unless there might have been romance in the
sober and sad thought of bread, a fine fire and a blanket.

The valley of Taos into which I entered on the morning of
the twenty-ninth of November, 1831—if I mistake not—contains
the most northern settlements in the Republic of Mexico. It is
true that on some maps you will see, perhaps two hundred miles
to the north of this valley, some three or four villages marked
down, and distinguished by the names of sundry saints—but
they only exist upon those maps. The valley of Taos is large and
in summer, when all under cultivation, it is surpassingly beautiful; but when I entered it, it was a sight for Timon in his mis-
anthropy to have enjoyed.[2] I shall not describe it here, because
I have done it elsewhere. I have seen it stated that the valley
contains fifteen thousand inhabitants, but I believe it to be a
mistake. The principal village in the valley is *San Fernandez,*
which may perhaps contain a thousand souls. Besides this, there
are three or four other small villages, and some scattering settlements here and there. Perhaps the whole valley may contain
four or five thousand inhabitants.[3]

I well remember my first entrance into a Mexican mud-palace.
Passing through an opening wherein a folding gate of massy
pine was swinging, I found myself in a large court, surrounded
on three sides with buildings of mud, like arid walls, with here
and there a little square window, with panes of mica, and cross-

2. A reference to Shakespeare's *Timon of Athens.*
3. Pike's estimate is close. In 1822, the population of the *partido* or district
of Taos was 3,098 apparently not counting the Pueblo Indians who may have
numbered around 2,000. See Lansing B. Bloom, "New Mexico Under Mexican
Administration, 1821-1846," *Old Santa Fe,* I, 1 (July, 1913), 28-29.

bars of wood—resembling the windows and grates of a jail. Crossing the court, I passed under a long piazza, supported by rough pillars of pine, of about the same finish as the lumbering wheels and axles which lay about the yard—and thence I entered a dark passage, at the upper end of which hung a curtain. Raising this, I popped through a little square opening into the 'sitting room' of the then first Alcalde of *San Fernandez de Taos*. The Señor himself, a tall, pleasant looking old man, with grey hair—and his wife a busy and merry little old woman, greeted me kindly—for whatever vices that people may possess, they are at least hospitable. There is something ludicrous, even to me, in the reminiscence of that scene. I wish I were a painter, that I might send you a sketch of it *a la Hogarth*. Suppose you imagine it, and then you can sketch it yourself. I will just give you the outlines.

A room about fifteen feet square—with one little square window—a little furnace-like fireplace in one corner—piles of colored blankets all round the room—two or three huge chairs of pine—a low table of the same—and on the white washed walls various rough pictures—roses of red cambric, and crucifixes. Imagine then, *El Señor Alcalde* with a sharp nose and little keen eyes—half sitting, half reclining on the blankets, smoking a *cigarrito* of cornhusk—dressed in a short jacket of blue cloth with about a hundred buttons on it, short breeches—forgive the word ladies, or suppose it erased, and substitute *calzones*—long grey stockings, and moccasins. Opposite him is his lady, dressed like an American woman. Imagine then his son and that son's wife—the former a dandy, with his *chaqueta* of gorgeous yellow calico,—his *calzoneras* open at the side of the leg, of fine cloth, embroidered—*embuttoned*—shall I not coin too—and ornamented at the bottom of each leg with a broad band of morocco—the latter a belle with her *tunico* of silk, and her scarf shading her brow, and waving over her dark locks. And lastly, imagine my own individual self—just from the prairie—a tall, wild, smoked, Indian-like fellow. I think my dress would have excited considerable attention in your fair City of Boston. A cap of fur covered a long and tangled mass of hair—leggins of blanket protected my nether limbs—and thin moccasins my

feet—and round me was wrapped a buffalo robe, out of which
appeared my whiskered and mustachioed face, black as a Comanche's with pine smoke. Such apparitions, however, were common
there, whatever they might be at Boston, and so, without much
ceremony, and in consideration of my having bespoken a
sistencia[4] there for a day or two, I was soon introduced to my
first Mexican breakfast—and although the red pepper did scorch
my throat grievously, I did ample honor to mine host's viands,
and withal gave great satisfaction to mine inward man.

I was at San Fernandez a week—saw a fandango or two—and
then departed for Santa Fe, in company with three other Americans. As it is not my purpose to follow your journal makers and
men who travel for the end of making books, I shall not trouble
your readers with any very precise description of the route.
There was something of adventure in crossing the mountains
in a snow storm—and I assure you that the mountains between
Taos and *El Embudo,* are not to be lightly spoken of—neither
is a snow storm on them any thing very interesting or agreeable,
when one rides a mule.

There was nothing on the road which either excited my attention or would interest your readers, except the villages of
the civilized Indians. These excited many reflections. Scattered
here and there over the valley of the Del Norte—speaking different languages—they tell you silently but forcibly that these
tribes are the wreck and remnants of what they once were. I
wish [George] Catlin, the painter, or some one of equal talent
—some of our yankee painters would go into that country. On
the Del Norte he might find twenty tribes, all different,—noble
looking men. In the mountains there are multitudes—and between the Del Norte and the Pacific. If they wish for originality
and fame, there they may find both. Would I had been a painter!
A man possessed of talents, money and leisure, might tell the
world after two or three years' research in that country, things
to astonish it, and establish his own fame. He would stand at
Santa Fe or Taos, on the line of demarcation which separates
the Mexican Indian from the Aboriginal. Let me explain. It is
manifest to me—for shall I not have a theory too?—that the

4. A *sustancia,* or *substancia,* meaning sustenance.

North American Indian, that is, *our* [American] Indian, is the aboriginal of the country. I do not believe that they ever emigrated here. They all have the same signs—the same personal appearance, the same manners and habits. I believe that anciently a colony of Phoenicians settled in Mexico—I believe this from their astronomy, their temples, their pyramids, and their hieroglyphics. I believe it from their civilization; I believe that as this people increased, they extended themselves to the East, through Texas to the country on the Mississippi and the Ohio. I know that they extended themselves to the North, along the Del Norte, because the Pueblos of the Del Norte, are manifestly a mixed race, and differ from the tribes immediately to the north of them. On the Mississippi and Ohio they remained for a time, but were defeated and driven back by the more savage aboriginals, leaving behind them the mounds and fortifications which have puzzled all our antiquarians. All the tribes in the United States—the Blackfoot, the Wawsashy or Osage, the Keelatto or Crows, the Shoshonees or Snakes, the Apaches, the Eutaws, the Indians of the Prairie—all the tribes West of the mountains except perhaps the Nabajo, are manifestly one race; but on the Del Norte there is another and a different one.[5] Their women work at home, and their men in the fields. There is a great field in that land for the painter and the antiquarian. I cannot enter it—but I would that I could excite some friend to do it.

5. Pike's theories about the origin of the American Indian are inaccurate, but are of interest as representative of the type of speculation of his time.

A Journey to Xemes[1]

I left Santa Fe on a clear, cool morning in July, to wend my way beyond the Rio del Norte to an Indian town situated in the valley of the Xemes, and known by the same name as that little stream.[2] The sun was just lifting above the tall, dark green peaks of the hills to the East of Santa Fe, when I set forth from that city of mud. Often, while in that country, did I regret that Heaven had not been so kind as to make me a painter, that I might have embodied upon the canvas a hundred scenes of glory and beauty which met me in that unknown and unfrequented land. Here, it is true, were none of the towers and Moresco battlements—the courts and corridors, fountains and gardens of the Arabesque Alhambra. There was no Granada—there were no mementos of the conflicts of the Christian and the turbaned infidel. But in their stead were the forty languages, spoken by the fragments of subjugated nations—the rude architecture of the days of Montezuma—the mementos of a race as brave as the Moors, conquered, to, by the same stern and uncompromising bigots as those who tumbled the glory of Granada to the ground, and clothed the children of the victor Moor in sackcloth and ashes. Here it is true, were no mountains known in classic song, and hallowed and magnified by historic recollection and traditionary lore—no rivers on which the Caesar had encamped, and in after days the crescent dashed in battle against the cross—but here were mountains mightier than those of Europe, and the Del Norte rushing onward to the Gulf of Mexico. Here, too, were the descendants of Roderic and Pelayo, and

1. *The Boston Pearl*, February 20, 1836.
2. The narrator is travelling to the Indian Pueblo of Jemez.

perhaps of the Abencerrages,[3] mingled in blood with the children of the red hunters of the North. Here was the same language which echoed in the hills of Spain, and yet spoken by a people who called themselves republican. Here were the mountains, the mists and the thunder-storms—all food for the painter's art. Alas! how much of enjoyment was lost to me! and how often did I lament that it was so!

The City of Santa Fe lies in a kind of amphitheatre, being surrounded with mountains on all sides except the South. On the East lies the chain between the city and San Miguel—a spur of the Rocky Mountains—though those immediately in sight are not of great elevation. On the North are the barren hills of Santa Cruz, and on the West the taller mountains which extend along on either side of the Del Norte. On the South is a plain stretching toward the pass, and following the course of the river. The little tributary of the Del Norte which waters the city, called in the magniloquent manner of the Spanish nation and its degenerate scions, 'el Rio Grande,'—the great river—runs out of the hills on the East, through a narrow and rocky gorge, which rises rapidly into the bosom of the mountains.[4] Three miles up this valley an American had established a tan-yard, and three miles farther up, another had founded a saw pit. Above the latter place the valley became narrower, and ascended abruptly toward the top of a high mountain, on the summit of which is a lake, which feeds the Pecos and the Rio Grande.[5] At the saw pit I have often been in thunder storms— the thunder crashing like gigantic artillery, and the rain drenching, and the hail pelting me, while six miles below, at the city, all was sunshine and calmness. As you pass out of the city, to the South, winding about among the mud houses, disposed

3. Pike had apparently read Washington Irving's *A Chronicle of the Conquest of Granada* (1829) and *The Alhambra* (1832). Roderic was the Visigothic King of Spain who valiantly, but unsuccessfully, tried to defend the country from the Moors in 711. Pelayo was Roderic's successor, who held Austurias against the Moslems and is generally recognized as the founder of the Spanish monarchy. The Abencerrages are a storied Moorish family of Granada, which was massacred at the Alhambra by a rival family, just before the end of the Moorish period.
4. Río Grande, Del Norte, or Río Grande del Norte are all names for today's Río Grande. Pike has here confused this with the Río de Santa Fé.
5. Separate lakes feed the Pecos and the Río de Santa Fé.

irregularly here and there, the view to the South is shut out from you by the plain, which extends to the river, and seems like a ridge or low line of hills, setting in close to the bank of the stream. Just as the sun rose we crossed the Rio Grande, and urged our mules up the little bank, unto the outer portions of the city. My equipage was simple and my train small. Imprimis, there was myself, of whom we will waive description. Then there was a young fellow from San Juan de Dolor[es], a good natured, lazy, whistling, singing, talkative, cowardly, and knavish varlet, who filled the important function of squire, body guard, servant and chief of the commissariat, answering to the name of Manuel Jaramillo—most expert at packing a mule, throwing the *lazo,* riding an unbroken brute, hunting up a lost animal, and pouching his rations whenever they fell due and Heaven granted time to eat them. Manuel was a decent looking and decently attired vagabond, being about five feet eight in hight, stout, strong, browned with exposure and labor, with small feet, dark, quick eyes, and having a jest for every one he met, and a new song for every mile of the road. His *chaqueta,* or close jacket, was profusely supplied with lace— his *calzoneras,* or pantaloons, were superbly decorated with buttons—his *botas* were of the finest stamped leather which the artizans of Sonora could manufacture. Add to this that the accoutrements of his horse were chosen as much for gaud as for substantial use—his saddle cover being of stamped leather, richly worked with silk, and his *armas* of panther skin, while his bridle was made to jingle after the most approved fashion.

The remaining member of our party must not be lightly passed over. Although he had but little to say, and that very seldom, yet what he did say was much to the purpose—short and sententious; and he was equally ready in action as in speech.

This was my good dog Tigre,[6] who cared not whither he went, so that he followed after me, slept near me at night, and had his due allowance of meat to discuss at proper and reasonable times. Tigre was a most exceeding good watch dog, brave, vigilant and faithful, and many a night have I laid my head

6. Tigre also appears in Pike's story of "The Gachupin," wherein he belongs to another trader. Pike probably owned no dog while in New Mexico.

upon my saddle, in an enemy's country, with no living thing near me but him. He was a large, yellow, lion-like fellow, with long hair, curled and shaggy, like masses of raw silk. Poor Tigre! I gave him away when I left the country. They chained him up, but he moaned and whined after me with a despairing tone which I shall never forget. But to ourselves again. The remainder of our force consisted of three mules, those interesting and accomplished animals, two of which we rode, and a third we drove before us, ladened with two heavy trunks, containing an assortment of goods, with which to trade with the Indians of Xemes. As we intended, before returning to Santa Fe, to go from Xemes, under the Nabajo Mountains, to Sevolleta,[7] and knowing the aforesaid Indians—to wit, the Nabajo—to be not over scrupulous with regard to the law of nations or the rights of individual property, I bore with me a double-barrelled gun, and a pair of good, sizeable pistols, for which a man would have been puzzled to find room in his pockets; and Manuel was also armed with his bow and arrows, a tomahawk, and a fusil, one of those mementoes of the *Soldados* of Cortes, having a huge lock with all the machinery of it on the one side, and being infinitely more dangerous to him who should discharge it, than to him at whom it should be discharged. Add to this that each of us bore at his saddle bow a large gourd, shaped like an hour glass, and holding, at a moderate computation, about half a gallon each, filled with a liquor some scores of times stronger than spring water, and you will own that we were indifferently well supplied for our journey.

After we had left the city behind us some three or four miles, I stopped to gaze around me. The loftier peaks of the Eastern mountains had now, as the sailors say, 'hove in sight,' and their dark green crests of cedar-covered rock were wreathed with black thunder foam, continually rolling and fluctuating over them, mass within mass, of perfect, dense, almost frightful blackness—above which, like the light foam on the black waves of a midnight ocean, was a volume of white mist, glittering like

7. Cebolleta was a frontier community located some twelve miles north of Laguna Pueblo and was the scene of frequent Navaho attacks. Pike's "Nabajo Mountains" must be today's Sebolleta Mountains.

snow in the sunlight. At the lower extremity of the mountains a broad white curtain of mist was let down, shining and well defined at its outer edge, quite to the plain, while directly in front the blue sky was smiling. In the South, and a little to the West, was a high, round hill, on the road to Albuquerque, a place not distinguished for any thing except as being the bounds beyond which the dignitaries of Santa Fe banish the contemners of their authority. They forbid their coming 'abajo de la Canada, d'arriva de Albuquerque [below Santa Cruz de la Cañada and above Albuquerque].' While I was admiring the grandeur of the scene, I turned to observe what effect it had upon Manuel. He had valued the delay which I made only as it afforded him time to light his cigarrito, and so onward we marched, I wrapped in my thoughts and he in smoke. The castles which I occupied myself in building during the succeeding hour, were about as unreal and as easily dissipated as the fabrics which his smoke wove as it floated upward. I never did but one thing in my life which I had planned and intended doing long beforehand. That solitary exception was, getting married. I got to Santa Fe without intending it, and I got back without intending it. I have always been hustled about the world without the privilege of choosing where I should go, because instantaneous circumstances have decided my movements, and the consequence has been, that I, being the person most interested, have had the least option in the matter.

I was awakened from my reverie by a loud discussion going on near me. We had approached a mud palace, and three big dogs at once assailed Tigre. He, however, had one invariable rule in fighting. It was to deal with one at a time. When, therefore, they all leaped upon him, he confined himself to the biggest, and in a moment seized him by the side, skin, rib and all. A loud cry of torture followed the crash of the unlucky rib, and the discomfited combatant left the field. The second immediately came in for his share. Tigre seized him by the fore leg, and the sharp teeth passed through and through it, and he too howled, and limped off. The third attempted to make good his retreat, but Tigre turned his flank, seized him by the windpipe and left him for dead. That fight taught me a good lesson. It was to grapple with difficulties singly, and overcome them in detail. Men generally view them in the mass and are discouraged. When the result of the contest was seen, an irregular fire of very correct Castilian commenced from the house, I got out of the range of their shot as soon as possible. Manuel was not able to resist the temptation, but sarcastically advised the old man, who was chief spokesman, *to bark* for himself, if his dogs were killed, as it was the only business he was fit for.

About seven miles from Santa Fe we ascended unto the hills, and travelling among them for six miles farther, approached the Del Norte. The hills were formed of a dry, red, barren soil, unfit for cultivation. Here and there we came upon a *covval* [corral]—an enclosure for sheep, with a hedge round it, made of cedars cut down and heaped together. Beside these, there were no signs of any thing human. Every thing was wild and barren. The ground was parched and dusty for want of rain, and the tall weeds scantily covered the hill sides. After leaving the hills we arrived at a small village where a most ludicrous accident befel us. The mule which we had packed was a little, ungainly wretch, of a most crooked and morose disposition. To speak the simple truth, though somewhat irrelevantly, she was a perfect devil incarnate. About four miles from Santa Fe I rode aside from the path to obtain a near view of a singular hill to the left, and while delaying there, heard my squire raising a most terrific whoop, with as much earnestness and repetition as though a bunch of Flat Heads had attacked him. I hasted to the rescue, at the utmost speed of which my mule was capable—which was but slow withal—and found my paragon of squires busily attempting to disencumber *Mulita* of her packs. She had lain down out of sheer obstinacy, and refused to budge until we took off the packs and assisted her to regain her legs. We soon discovered that a mule is not exactly the animal to humor in that way. Afterward, and as soon as she came in sight of a hill, down she dropped, and the same farce of unloading was again to be enacted. My patience at length failed me—with which I never was over-stocked—and I resolved to try my obstinacy against hers. Down she fell again, set her ears forward, with a mulish expression of countenance which seemed to say, 'get me up if you can.' I dismounted, took my rope of plaited hide from my saddle bow, and directed Manuel to do the same. Each of us applied to the gourd for resolution, and then standing, one on each side of *Mulita,* commenced beating here where she lay, with the knotted ends of our ropes. For at least fifteen minutes we continued to ply our task, while all the answer we obtained was a groan now and then, as an acknowledgement of our favors, and a winking of both eyes every time the rope descended. After bearing it until the patience of a mule could endure no longer, she sprang up with one jump, and trotted on. She went on for about six miles without again taking lodgings, until we arrived at the little town of which I before spoke. In order to reach the village we had a broad ditch, about three feet deep, to cross, dug for the purpose of conveying water to irrigate the fields. Into this I drove *Mulita,* but she had no sooner got fairly in than down she dropped, on one side, covering one trunk entirely, and after remaining so for a moment, rolled over on the other side. I was strongly tempted to murder her, but though greatly enraged, could not help being amused at the diabolical revenge she had taken. Every thing was thoroughly wet, and each trunk weighed about four hundred pounds. With the help of three or four laborers who luckily were close at hand, I disengaged the trunks, had them safely landed, pulled her out of the water, set her on her feet again, packed the trunks on her, cut a long cedar pole, and ordered Manuel to drive her on. He beat her to a jelly before we reached a house, and zealously endeavored to break every bone in her body.

After our ignoble adventure in the ditch, we of course were forced to find some posada, whereat to remain a day or two, while we should dry our merchandise. Sooth to say, I was not at all unwilling to stop, in as much as the sun had by this time rendered the air hot and oppressive, and his rays glared up from the red soil until they almost blinded us. We therefore inquired for the best house in the place, and were pointed to one a little removed from the village, inhabited, we were told, by the Alcalde. Thitherward we went, and entering the narrow gateway unto the court, I ordered Manuel to unload and unsaddle our mules—for in that country every house is an inn—and proceeded to the sala, or long hall, which is always the Summer residence

We need hardly stop an instant to survey the exterior of the domicil. It was, like all the buildings in that part of the Mexican republic, built of bricks of mud, with a square court in the middle. Half a dozen donkies were chewing husks about the gate, and a pig or two were staked out in the field. The sala was a long room, with piles of colored *zarapes* or blankets about the wall, and an array of small looking-glasses, roses of cambric, and saints and crucifixes about on the walls. The description which Irving, in his Tales of the Alhambra,[8] gives of the lower class in Spain, will answer to perfection for the people of Mexico. They are a lazy, gossipping people, always lounging on their blankets and smoking the *cigarrillos*—living on nothing, and without labor. From morning till night they doze or chatter, and are seldom seen to do any thing; but when a fandango comes they are all life and bustle. At least two thirds of the days of the year are *fiestas,* or feast days, when their conscience would smite them if they were to work, and in that matter they are particularly chary of their conscience.

I had been among them some time, could speak their language fluently, and was therefore not afraid of an ungracious reception. I entered accordingly with the common salutation, 'Buenos dias le de Dios'—God give you good days—and was greeted with the cordiality of an old acquaintance. Nothing is such a passport to the common people as a knowledge of their language. They attach themselves at once to him who can speak it, and look upon him as a friend. Tigre followed me in, and two or three of his canine brethren seeing his boldness, sneaked in after him. A kick or two dispersed them, but the inmates of the house had far too much respect for me to eject Tigre—a mark of honor which caused him a tremendous fight in the afternoon, for he had no sooner put his nose out at the door than the whole brood attacked him, and he was compelled to whip them all before he could force them to treat him with proper consideration.

I was embraced and shaken by the hand in turn, by the

8. See note 3.

Alcalde, a hale, hearty looking old man—mistress, a thin-featured, acute old lady—his son, about my own age—the heiress of the family, a pretty, black-eyed damsel, dressed after the American fashion, and four or five of the neighbors. The only person who did not extend to me this courtesy, was a tall, half naked Indian, who was sitting half reclined on the blankets. He merely grunted out an 'adish!' and continued to smoke his pipe.

I do not intend to weary my readers if I have not already done so. Suffice it to say that I remained here two days. The old man told me long tales of the wars between the Spaniards and the Nabajo—the young man told me of hidden treasures, to be found in the bosoms of the mountains—the old lady told tales of superstition and diablerie—the daughter sang the rude ballads of her country, and even the Indian became talkative, and recounted the hundred wars of his nation, the San Domingo tribe, and their neighbors, in olden time. Of some of these *cuentas* I made memoranda, and one or two of them may perhaps amuse the reader, if they do not instruct him.[9]

9. Pike obviously intended to publish a sequel to this "Journey," but it does not appear in the remaining issues of the *Boston Pearl*.

TALES OF CHARACTER AND COUNTRY

Written for the Advocate.[1]

San Juan of the Del Norte

The Territory of New Mexico is the Siberia of the Republic. Extending from the Paso del Norte, that is, the point where the road from Santa Fe to Chihuahua crosses from the east to the west bank of the Rio Grando del Norte—the great river of the North, in latitude, I believe, about 33. n.—to the well known limits of our own vast territory on the North—it is almost entirely composed of mountains and deserts. The Del Norte runs in a south direction thro' it—and upon that river, and the small streams which run from the mountains into it, is the only arable land in the Territory. The climate in the northern part is cold and severe, and the husbandman only raises his crops by the most constant labor. At some other time, I may more fully describe the country, but at present I have said so much, only as the prelude to a simple relation which I am about to write.

When, two hundred and fifty years ago, the Spaniards sent a body of troops into New Mexico, accompanied by a large band of settlers, they found the whole country occupied by various tribes of Indians. These people were considerably advanced in civilization, and were in few respects like the wandering Arabs [meaning the nomadic tribes] of our part of the continent. Their villages were generally built in the form of a square—with continuous houses of mud—thick-walled, and of three or four stories. To the square there were but one or two narrow entrances

1. *The* (Little Rock) *Arkansas Advocate*, November 27, 1833.

—and the entrance to the houses was by ascending a ladder on the outside, and descending, thro' the roof, into the house. In this way every village was a fort. They cultivated the ground with much diligence, and depended principally upon their corn for their subsistence.

The Spaniards soon conquered many of these tribes, and reduced them to obedience—but, shortly after, they revolted, and were again reduced, after a bloody contest. In this last struggle, the only tribes that remained true to the Spaniards were the Pueblos of Pecos and San Domingo; and the consequence was, that they were almost entirely annihilated by their red brethren. The Pueblo *(tribe)* of Pecos now consists of about twenty men—and that of San Domingo of about a hundred.[2] The village of the latter is situated just where the road from Santa Fe to the Pass first strikes the Del Norte, about 25 miles from the former city. They have an Alcalde of their own people, and a Spanish priest, and are legal voters in all elections. This latter privilege has been granted them since the formation of the Republic.

Some twenty years ago, and before any American of the North had crossed the mountains, introducing with him the manufactures of France, England and the United States, and increasing ten-fold the comfort and convenience of the people—before the soldiers had learned any other cry than *Viva el Rei!*—when the men wore leather and coarse jerkins of frieze—and the women thought it no hardship to dress as poorly as their husbands—about that time, and of any sunshiny day, in any season of the year, you might have seen a little, lean, withered Spaniard, sitting at the door of his mud tenement, which stood near the Del Norte, just above the village of San Domingo. Had you marked his countenance, you would have observed a certain soured and melancholy look, which gave evidence that the Senor San Juan was not entirely at peace with himself, or in good humor with the world. His upper man was cased in a kind of jerkin of grey frieze, reaching below his middle, and disclosing his brown and shrivelled neck and breast. His nether extremities, as far as the

2. See note 7 of "Inroad of the Nabajo." Pueblo is better translated here as community or people, rather than tribe.

knees, were accoutred with breeches of deer-skin, ending in two points at each knee—ornamented with half a dozen huge metal buttons, and girt about his loins with a parti-colored belt, which had probably been the pride of his boyhood. Below these again, were the long, grey stockings, and the clumsy moccasins of the fashion of the Apaches—which, with a broad-brimmed sombre-ro upon his cranium, completed the attire of the venerable San Juan.

The domicil was a small, square building of mud—with thick walls—a flat roof, covered also with mud to the depth of two feet —a small, low door—and one little, square window, with panes of the mica of the mountains. Inside, there was the pile of coarse, colored blankets—the rough stool or two—the small, stove-like fire-place—and the dozen images, pictures of saints, crucifixes and roses of red cambric—all of which characterize the houses of the New Mexicans. Outside was a patient donkey chewing upon the argument of some withered weeds—a hen or two—a pig, staked at the door, to keep him out of the fenceless wheat-fields—and a cart, with two masses of pine timber for wheels, a huge log for an axle, and another for a tongue.

The reader will, I make no doubt, be glad to learn the cause which invested Don San Juan with the woful visage which he was wearing, of a fine, clear morning in August—and, certes, [certainly] I am nothing loth to inform him. San Juan had been, when young, the most merry and contented fellow in the world. His voice was the loudest in the quaint songs of the fandango, and he was held in high and deserved esteem by all the pretty Senoritas of the Village where he lived—for at that period of his life, he was—not a solitary recluse near the village of San Do-mingo—but a gay youth in La Canada de la Santa Cruz.[3]

In an unlucky hour he accompanied a trader to Sonora, and thence to Chihuahua. This was the destruction of the peace of our hero. The great wealth which he saw there, created in him an intense desire for riches—a morbid and dissatisfied state of mind—and he became dull and gloomy. He undertook to dig for silver ore in the mountains of Xemes, and spent in the pursuit

3. Present-day Santa Cruz, between Santa Fe and Taos, usually written "Santa Cruz de la Cañada."

the little money which he had gathered by untiring industry. Scheme after scheme he tried, and still he was as poor as ever—and at the age of thirty, he, wearied of the world—forsook it, like Childe Harold[4]—and retired to loneliness and obscurity, among the Pueblo of San Domingo. He raised a little blue corn—a little wheat—some red pepper—and some tobacco—and had he been contented, he might still have been happy. But "who can minister to a mind diseased?" Continual smoking had withered up his body, till he was as lean as Shakespeare's apothecary—and continual laziness had made his fields as lean and barren as the same apothecary's shop. There he sat—with his cigarrito in his mouth—his chin leant upon his two hands—surveying, with dolorous looks, the dismal expanse of his land, relieved here and there by a patch of greenness, which looked, amid the surrounding monotony, like a lonely isle in the ocean. His situation had, of late, been far from enviable. The Indians, who had at first welcomed him and assisted him in making his farm and house, had lost their esteem for him—for, industrious themselves, they despise an idler and a drone. They were to be seen at all times of the day, at work—naked except a cloth about the middle—and they naturally contemned their idle neighbor.

At present, however, Don San Juan gave indubitable proof that some matter of immense weight occupied his brain, and pressed like an incubus upon his spirits—for tho' his cigar still remained in the corner of his mouth, the smoke had long since ceased to pour its volumes from that vast cavity—while he sat there upon the tongue of his cart, with his nether limbs dangling ceaselessly in the air, and his head still sunk in his hands. At length he arose suddenly, like a man struck with a new idea—clapped his hands together—and commenced singing in a loud tone an old jarabe. After this burst of joy he again composed himself—drew a strip of corn husk from his pocket—produced his *guage* [guaje] or little gourd containing tobacco, from the same place, and carefully rolled himself a cigar—entered the house and lighted it—and then slowly proceeded towards the village of San Domingo.

4. Like many educated Americans of his day, Pike had read Lord Byron's romantic poem, *Childe Harold's Pilgrimage*.

It was a walk of about half a mile, and as he sedately pursued his way over the dry, red ground, a sudden burst of wild music, of the shrill, Indian flute, and drum, struck his ear, and he hurried on the faster. Entering the village, he found the Indians engaged in the mazy evolutions of their elegant dance—keeping time to a slow and melancholy, tho' wild tune, stongly resembling some ancient Scotch airs that I have heard. Both the music and dances of the Pueblos of New Mexico, are indeed totally different from the monotonous hu-a-hu and the irregular dances of our own savages. The same monotonous and gutteral chant which is used by all the Indians within the bounds of our States, is the only music of the Cumanches, Snakes, Eutas and Apaches, and all the tribes in the mountains, north of Santa Fe—at least, as far as I have been acquainted with them; but at the point where we first find the vestiges of the nations of Aztec and Anahuac, we see an utter difference in the music and dances, as well as the habits of the Aborigines.

After watching a little while the plumed and ornamented actors in the graceful and regular dance, San Juan went on to the lower part of the town and cautiously ascended a ladder to the first story of one of the houses, thence in the same way to another and another story, and thence descending by an aperture in the roof, he found himself in a large, low apartment, of which the only inmate was an old beldame occupied in cooking over a small fire. She turned to him as he entered, and without speaking, pointed to a low stool near the fire, and again turned her attention to the large earthen jar, with which she was busy, while she rocked to and fro, crooning at the same time a low song. It was with some embarrassment, that San Juan took his seat—for the old beldame was considered by the Indians as something of a sorceress—as partaking, in no small degree, of the character and attributes of the priestesses to whom they had paid deference, before the eloquence of the shaven monk and the fury of the priest-directed soldier had converted them to the pure and simple faith of Romanism. She was short of stature, withered and bleared—and, with her high cheek-bones, and black, tangled hair, resembled nothing so much as an old Arab woman. She was a Nabajo, who had been taken captive in a skirmish, and re-

tained as a servant, by one of the principal men in the Pueblo—
and in this capacity she had acted for some years. She was still
unconverted to their faith, and at stated times performed her
strange and mystic ceremonies to the great scandalization of the
Padre, who had remonstrated frequently with her master upon
the subject, but to no effect.

"Jaralista," said San Juan at length, with a desperate exertion
of courage, "have you been well since I was here last?" A kind
of assenting grunt, was her only answer; but it was enough to
encourage him to proceed. "Were I in your case," said he, "I
would be far from remaining a slave—you possess powers which
are more than mortal, and it is strange that one so gifted will
remain a servant."

"Ay," said the woman, "I do possess powers not given to others,
but what matters it? I may not use them for my own benefit."

"You might, perhaps, then do it for your friends, who might
in their turn assist you. Where are the ruins three days journey
from this, in the edge of your country. That mountain contains
great treasures, and you have the power to open it and to bring
them forth. Teach me to do it, give me the power to open the
wonderful door, and here are three dollars of pure silver, with
the King's head—Viva el Rei—stamped upon them."

"And do you think that I will open the treasures of my fathers
to thee—pitiful, base, priest-trodden slave! Get thee from my
sight, or I will exterminate thee. Fool, idiot, cur! Begone!

The poor Saint was confounded. He had not expected this
volley of wrath, and he hastened to escape the vengeance of the
enraged beldame. As he did so, he stumbled unluckily over a
large cat, which lay between him and the ladder, and fell; and
the hag still more enraged at the injury done her favorite,
rushed upon him and fastened her nails in his face, uttering at
the same time, low curses in the rough guttural language of the
Nabajo, which to him, sounded like the invocations of spirits,
and frightened into insanity, he freed himself from her clutches
by a desperate exertion, and mounting the steep ladder like a
cat, gained the open air.

The next morning early, San Juan mounted his donkey,
crossed the river in the ferry boat kept by the Indians, and took

the road which led towards the mountains of the Nabajo. His knife was in his belt, and his bow and arrows at his back. Other arms he had none, except you might give tht name to a mattock [a digging implement] which he bore with him. Towards night of the third day, he arrived at the place of his destination—a narrow valley between the mountains, which raised their barren crowns in every direction, around the green and solitary nook. In the midst of the valley, was a confused pile of ruins, where there had once been a temple, part of the stone walls of which were still standing, and various irregular piles of earth showed where the buildings of mud had stood.[5]

There are many such proofs in that Province or Territory, of the existence in it, at some former time, of a race of Indians more civilized than even the domesticated Pueblos. In different parts of the country there are the wild Apaches—the fierce and handsome Eutas—the more civilized, whiter, and bearded Nabajo, weavers of blankets, and herders of sheep, cattle and horses —free and independent. What caused the difference between these fierce tribes and the settled and quiet Pueblos?—There is but one solution. When the civilized and enterprising Mexicans grew strong[6]—and I stop not here to inquire from whom they were descended, whether from the Hindus, or the Phoenicians— they sent out various colonies, some of which reached to New Mexico, and taught the Pueblos the rude arts which they now possess—probably intermarried with them. These same Mexicans —natives of Aztec or Anahuac—penetrating into the country which we now inhabit, built the fortifications which we so frequently see, which have so much puzzled the brains of the learned and curious, and which—overpowered by their savage adversaries, the rightful owners of the soil—these colonist have left as their only memorials.

But to return to our neglected hero. So soon as night came on, he wrapped himself in his blanket, and, throwing himself on the

5. Pike may have reference to the ruins at Chaco Canyon, which he places in the mountains for literary effect, or to lesser known ruins in the Tunicha or Chuska Mountains.

6. By Mexicans, Pike apparently means the Aztecs or some other pre-Columbian aboriginal group in Mexico. Pike's theory about these Indians is interesting but inaccurate.

ground by his small fire, reclined, but not to sleep. While he lay there, with the magnificent mountains shooting up their tall snowy cones on every side of him, and with the thin vapor that curled around their heads hardly dimming the clear star-light—while nothing broke the silence of the fair night, except the far-off cry of the yellow *leon,* and the white wolf, and the constant music of the little tributary of the Del Norte, which ran [s]plashing at his feet, thoughts of seas of wealth—of stately domes and pleasure-houses—of power and grandeur fleeted thro' his brain like bright shadows, while he lay and watched the stars, and the cold presence of the mountains. At length the fire decayed, and its dying embers went sparkling out, and the cold wind began to moan, high up in the pines—and then he dozed, and opened his eyes again, and, fixing them steadily upon the opposite mountain, he was surprised to see a kind of glimmering upon the side of it. Watching it intently, he saw it increase, until a door in the side of the mountain opened, and a blaze of splendor burst from it, illuminating the whole valley. Within—for it was not more than one eighth of a mile from him—he saw great piles of gold, silver and jewels, shining in the light; and in the door-way stood a figure, dressed like a Nabajo, beckoning him to approach. He did so, with a mingled sensation of delight and dread, and forcing his way among the fallen masses of rock, he soon arrived at the door of the cavern. The Nabajo was no longer there, but a low music still lingered about its walls. He wandered about for a while tho' its recesses, and then loading himself with as much gold as he could carry, he turned reluctantly to leave the cave; but stumbled and fell on the threshold. The music changed to a trumpet-tone that rung fiercely thro' the cavern; and the ponderous door shut creakingly upon him, and held him with a powerful pressure between itself and the rocky face of the mountain. The pressure became excruciating and his agony intense. It seemed to him that every limb was pinioned fast, when a loud yell and a shout in the Nabajo tongue broke upon his startled ear. He looked about him. It was broad day-light; and he lay tied fast, with twenty Nabajos around him.

He was a prisoner to the Spaniard's foe; and his task was, to grind meal upon his knees till his death. *So much for a hankering after WEALTH!!*

TALES OF CHARACTER AND COUNTRY
NO. III
Written for the Advocate.[1]

The Gachupin

THE GACHUPIN.

For the truth of the following tale, I only vouch thus far. It was related to me by a very excellent and worthy friend, whose word I never saw cause to doubt. Such as he told it to me, do I give it to my readers. I relate it in the first person, and in his own words.

"Just after the execution of Iturbide, and the establishment of the Republic, I was in the village at the Pass of the Del Norte. Just at this time," (this was in 1831,) "it is amusing to observe the respect paid the memory of that weak Emperor, compared with the abuse which was then [1823] lavished on him. He is now eulogised as a patriot—he was then stigmatised as a tyrant, and so he was—but such a tyrant as befits this people. They have no such thing in their heart as republicanism; and not the People's love of liberty, but the revenge of Sant' Ana, tumbled Iturbide from his throne. But never mind him. I had travelled thro' the villages of the Rio Abajo, and the dreary Jornada de la Muerte [*Jornada del Muerto*], and was at length safely lodged at the posada of mine host, Don Vicente Jaramillo. Just then, an American was in good odor—they had not quite forgotten our services—and I was well treated, well fed, and had free access to every vineyard and wine-cellar on the banks of the Del Norte.

1. *The* (Little Rock) *Arkansas Advocate*, December 11, 1833.

257

I walked out one evening, far down the river, and delayed a good while, plucking the ripe grapes and peaches, and chatting with the pretty and lively paisanas, who were wandering about in the moonlight. Some of them even looked beautiful, in their quaint, old Spanish attire, with the thin shawls which covered their heads, tossed back from their foreheads, and floating out behind. It was near midnight, when I got back to the village; but I had no fear, for I was well armed, and accompanied by my faithful dog *Tigre,* who, you know, is a match for any Mexican.

As I was walking leisurely along, under a portico, which extended the whole length of the street, I was surprised at a singular grating noise, seemingly on the other side of the street. I stopped and listened, but was for a time uncertain whence it proceeded. At length I cast my eyes upward, and upon the roof of one of the opposite buildings, I saw a fellow, engaged in removing the rubbish from the rafters, thus making a hole, thro' which to descend into the house. I hesitated—should I cry out, he would escape. I placed myself at the door, and awaited my hero, with a good cudgel in my hand. In about half an hour, the door opened softly, and he came out, with his arms full of silver plate; and at the moment his head appeared, I lent him a blow upon it, which laid him across the threshold. The plate fell rattling on the ground, and half a dozen servants awoke at the noise and came bustling out. Upon seeing me, there was a tumult of fierce cries. 'Que hai? Maldito que sea su corazon!— Al suelo con el Americano!' *(What is the matter?—Cursed be his heart!—To the ground with the American!')* Sticks were brandished, and knives glittered. Nevertheless, I stood my ground, and Tigre growled and showed his teeth. In the mist of the clamor, a stern voice ordered silence. It was their master. "What is the matter?" said he.

"The matter is," I answered, "that your sleepy servants let thieves enter your house. Mend the hole in your roof—pick up your plate—and thank God, that you can yet eat out of silver, like your ancestors.

"But how?" said he, "pray explain."

"With all my heart. I saw this fellow working on your roof, and waited for him at the door."

"Pick him up, you rascals, and take him to jail," said the gentleman, "and pray, Senor, oblige me by entering my house and taking a little wine."

I did so, and that house was my home as long as I remained in the Paso del Norte.

You see, that, so far, I have used a very laconic brevity. I shall be diffuse enough presently. When I called upon Don Santiago Morela, the next morning, he introduced me to his daughter, and as you will allow that I have a very prepossessing appearance, (what the devil are you laughing at?) and a great deal of tact, I soon became acquainted with her. I hate descriptions, and I hate school boy sentiment. She was a beautiful Spanish girl. I give you no catalogue of her charms—but when I say, that with all my taste and fastidiousness, I fell over head and ears in love with her, you will acknowledge that she must have been beautiful. Her father was a Gachupin, that is, he was born in Old Spain; and tho' the sentence of banishment had been issued against all old Spaniards, now six months, still he had not removed. He was a man of much talent and a good education, and he had himself formed the mind of his daughter.

In short, I determined to declare my love to Isabel. I soon found an opportunity. We were alone in the room. Of all languages in the world, next to the Italian, I delight to make love in the Spanish. It has such a splendid vocabulary of terms, required in such matters, and it rolls from the tongue with such a liquidity. I opened my lips three or four times, but failed to speak. I used to talk love well enough in Baltimore, but this was another matter. Suddenly she placed her hand upon mine—I compressed my lips. She sighed—I bit them, till the blood started—and then she spoke, and the low tones of her voice sounded like music in the air. "Senor!"—and then she stopped. I looked in her face, and she blushed and looked down. "I wish to tell you a secret—I have thought of doing it for a good while," (I had been there a whole week), "and with you, I believe it will be safe—whether you grant my request or not." 'The Devil!' thought I 'is she about to woo me to my face?'—but I kept silence. "My father wishes me to marry this Alari, and, de veras [truly], I hate him, and"—(I mentally abjured all woman-

kind); "and—and—I love somebody else." 'Fire and torments!'—
I thought again. "Now do, my dear Sir,—do use your influence
with my father to prevent the marriage. He will listen to you
more than any one else. Indeed—indeed—if I marry Alari, it
will break Julian's heart, as well as my own."

Here was a consummation. After all, as Hajji Baba says, after
all, Minshallah! she had never thought of loving me. Alas! my
vanity, and my love!—both disappointed. But I have read Plato,
and am a philosopher of the first water.

"And who is Julian?" I inquired.

Her answer was too long and involuted to repeat. It contained a long description; but I knew whom she meant. It was
William Stanley—a young Virginian.

"Does your father know any thing of Julian?"

"No. I have only seen him twice. I was afraid to tell *him*."

Stanley was my particular friend, and for that reason I re-
frained from gaining her affections—I might have done it, you
know, (none of your laughing now, you rascally Yankee)! but
I would not. I laid a plan to bring him to live at our house, and
in the evening I went to find him. He was a young fellow, who,
being in Alabama the year before, had taken a fancy to see
Santa Fe. He was rich—had long since sold out the few goods
which he brought with him—and was now lounging about,
awaiting the return of the company to the United States.

I employed myself, after supper, in looking for him, but saw
nothing of him until after dark. The thought then struck me, to
seek him at the Monti bank. You are surprised that I should take
so much pains about the affairs of any body except myself. So
am I—*now*—but I liked Stanley, and hated Alari, who was a little,
conceited, mean Spaniard, in the regular habit of dining with
Don Santiago every day.

There was a woman dealing monti, with something like a
thousand dollars in silver and onzas,[2] piled up before her. Stanley, among a multitude of others, was betting. I watched the
game awhile, and then entered the next room, and commenced
a game of billiards with a young American. I was using him up

2. *Onza,* while usually meaning ounce, in this case probably refers to a gold
coin of high denomination known as an *onza.*

very fast. (you know how I play the game,) when the name
'Isabel', pronounced in a low voice, caused me to turn my head
cautiously. In a corner of the room were the Officer of the Customs, and the Comandante of the troops, in close council. The
American who was playing with me understood no Spanish.

"I think," said the Comandante, "that you hate Don Santiago,
and will aid me in any scheme to get him out of the way."

"Hate him!—Cien mil diablos!"—and the villain ground his
teeth. I knew him for the greatest rascal in New Mexico, and
that is a superlative recommendation. For a while, I could
distinguish nothing—and then the Comandante spoke again;

"I have the representation ready. With your signature and
mine, it will go. The sentence of banishment was passed six
months ago, and it shall now be fine and banishment."

"And what becomes of Isabel, when the father is banished? In
that case you lose her."

"Not I. Alari will marry her before that time."

"And what good—por el nombre de Dios!—will his marriage
do you?"

"Alari marries her for me—my thousand dollars pay him for
his bride. Do you understand?"

"Como no?" (why not?) and the villain laughed long and
long. I shuddered at their corruption—but they spake again.
'T was the voice of the latter.

"You have a rival. Did you see that American betting at the
bank? He and Isabel meet every day or two, in the vineyard."

All that followed this was indistinct. "Swords—servant—corner of the church of Our Lady of Guadalupe." This was all. I
had lost my game—carelessness, you know. I went into the monti
room. Stanley was getting up, and his servant was putting
money in a bag. I bowed to the two priests, who had been playing—took Stanley by the arm, and walked into the air. Oh! how
cool and delicious it came off from the mountains, and thro'
the vineyards, after we had breathed the polluted atmosphere of
the gambling room.

We walked towards the river. The moon was just rising. We
sat down on the bank of the stream, and I told him all that I
have now told you. He swore and raved. These Virginians are

as hot as pepper. Now *I* am cooler—I am a Marylander. I am like a cucumber—and never quarrel—more than three times a week. I am never rash;" (he had threatened to pull the Governor's nose, in Santa Fe), "and I soon brought him to his reason. In the mean time we had risen, and were going doucely along towards our homes, and I had just got him in a pretty good humor—he was as mild, as Bottom says, as any sucking dove,[3] he was cool—not Yankee cool—that's below zero—when out jumped three or four fellows from behind the corner of a church, with their swords drawn, and charged upon us. We were both well armed, and as they came on, we both fired our pistols, and down came one fellow, crying to a dozen saints that he was *muerto* (dead) and after two or three passes with our swords, the rest of them took to their heels, and left the valiant Comandante to get help as he could. So did we; but it turned out the next day, that we had only broken his arm.

Perhaps I ought to explain a little. By remaining in the country after the passage of the law banishing the Gachupins, Don Santiago was liable to fine, if not imprisonment.

The word 'Gachupin', which is applied to the Old Spaniards, is a word used by the Mexicans, when they first saw the Spaniards, to express what they took them to be—a new animal— man and horse joined.[4] And don't suppose that I exaggerate the depravity of Alari. Oh, no. Such examples of corruption are very common in this country, for a New Mexican is never known to possess either honor or virtue.

The next morning, according to promise, I introduced Stanley to Don Santiago, and he was invited to dine with us. After dinner, and over our wine (we had delicious wine), I engaged our host in a tete-a-tete. I inquired the character of Iturbide, and the incidents which led to his dethronement and execution.

"Iturbide," said he, "was a weak man, and tried to imitate

3. Pike is quoting Bottom, the weaver in Shakespeare's "*A Midsummer Night's Dream.*"

4. While Pike's version is more colorful, etymologists believe the word derives from the Portuguese *cachopo*, meaning child. It was applied to any Spaniard, but usually designated a recent arrival who had not yet learned the ways of the land. See Francisco J. Santamaría, *Diccionario de Mejicanismos* (Mexico, D.F., 1959), pp. 541-43.

Napoleon—a certain way for such as he to fall. He fell, not by the patriotism of the people, for that is a virtue which very few of this nation possess, but by the vengeance of Sant' Ana. That General, who is our bravest man, except his father in law, Guerrero, was in command of the division of the army stationed at Vera Cruz. He quarreled with another General, who was engaged to marry the daughter of Iturbide. Both were ordered to the presence of the Emperor—he heard their statements, and tho' Sant' Ana was plainly in the right, still he reprimanded him, and approved the conduct of the other. He was then weak enough to send for Sant' Ana, and to tell him privately, that no blame attached itself to him—that he was on the same footing as before. He then directed him to repair to his station, and to forget what had passed. He also inquired, in how many days he should reach Vera Cruz. Sant' Ana answered, that he was perfectly satisfied, that he intended to return the next morning, and without hurrying himself, would reach his post in three days. He left the city that night, and the next day, was in Vera Cruz —put his army in motion, who idolized him—raised the flag of the Republic, and tumbled Iturbide from his throne.[5] The people are already lamenting the Emperor—they are half sick of a republic. There is neither virtue nor knowledge among them, and they are not fit to be free."

The old man looked round as he concluded. Stanley and Isabel had left the room. 'T was my time to speak. I laid philosophy aside—told him every thing, and pleaded for Stanley. I am eloquent when I take a fancy to be so. You would have thought I was pleading for myself—and that night Stanley and Isabel were married. After all, disinterestedness is a pretty thing. I should have been tired of a wife by this time. I am glad that I acted so honorably by Stanley. The next day I had to kick Alari out of doors, to keep the Don from murdering him—another deed of charity on my part. *Voila la fin!*"

"Stop!" said I, "What became of all your friends?"

5. Antonio López de Santa Anna's revolt at Vera Cruz was the beginning of Emperor Agustín de Iturbide's downfall. This, however, is a garbled account of the events leading to Iturbide's demise. Guerrero was not Santa Anna's father-in-law, nor was a daughter of Iturbide involved in Santa Anna's rebuke by Iturbide.

"Now, who but a Yankee would go beyond a marriage for the end of a tale? They went thro' to the United States, with the wagon company, soon after the marriage, and are now living happily in Virginia. I had a letter from Stanley this spring. The Comandante broke his neck, running away from the Apaches. The Officer of Customs was hung for treasonous correspondence, and Alari obtained his place. He pretends to have forgotten the kick, and wants me to drink wine with him, every time I go down there. He would poison me, if he were not afraid that I should live long enough after the dose to send him to heaven."

Manuel The Wolf Killer

NO. VII

Written for the Advocate.[1]

It was of a clear, fine morning in the latter part of August, that I was wending my way slowly along, towards a small village between Santa Fe and the Pass [El Paso], and about one hundred miles from the latter.[2] Noon had passed, and the unpleasant heat of the forenoon had yielded to a cool and gentle breathing, which came calmly off the mountains west of the Del Norte. The greenness of summer had not yet begun to turn grey under the sullen footstep of Autumn—and all along the sides of the hills, and over the narrow valley between the mountains, in which I was travelling, were to be seen bright spots of verdure, relieving the dreary appearance of the red and barren soil. Not a cloud was to be seen in the firmament, which resting apparently on the grey cones of the mountains, both to the east and west, stretched peacefully above. Here and there the birds were busy in the cedars, and now and then one arose, and pouring out his heart in a song as he went, vanished in the blue

1. *The* (Little Rock) *Arkansas Advocate,* February 28, 1834.
2. The narrator, as the end of the story reveals, was traveling south. Although Pike tells this story in the first person, it is doubtful that he ever journeyed to El Paso. The town toward which the narrator was traveling can not be identified with certainty. The Chihuahua Trail ran most of its course along the east side of the Rio Grande. A point one hundred miles north of El Paso would place the narrator in the harsh desert of the Jornada del Muerto, clearly not the type of terrain he describes. Perhaps Pike meant to say one hundred miles from Santa Fe. If so, the story would have taken place at Casa Colorado (present-day Turn), or La Joya, between Albuquerque and Socorro.

distance. I was alone. My horse, like all the New Mexican horses, was a small, clean limbed, active animal, as sure footed as a mule. The road was principally level, and lay, as I have already said, between two ranges of mountains, which were perhaps thirty miles apart.

As I rode slowly along, in that kind of listlessness which a man is apt to fall into when alone, I was startled by a loud shout, far ahead of me, and to the right, followed by the clamor of a number of dogs. It was at that time considered dangerous to travel the road alone, on account of the Apaches, who had become very troublesome, not only robbing their allies, the Mexicans, of their supernumerary cattle, but also at times taking a scalp or two. But I had not supposed that there would be any danger until I should reach the *Jornada de la Muerte* [*Jornada del Muerto*], or Journey of Death, ninety miles above the Pass. I prepared myself, however, for the event, by loosing my pistols in my belt, &c. and stopping my horse. The noise approached, and directly a large, grey wolf dashed out of the cedars to the right—sprung across the road, and made towards the mountains on the left, closely followed by two or three dogs, and a hunter who ran with amazing speed after them. The ground to the left was rather open, and enabled me to watch the event of the chase. After running about half a mile from me, the dogs pressed the wolf so closely, that he turned to make fight, and was immediately pinned to the ground by the hunter, with the long spear which he carried, and he then, stooping down, deprived the animal of his scalp, and giving the carcass a kick, called his dogs, and came again towards the road. I waited for him to come up, and as he was about crossing the road before me, I addressed him courteously, in the common phrase of salutation. To this he made no reply, but looked up with a wild glare, held up the reeking scalp, and crossed the road into the cedars. I had sufficient time, however, to see that he was a tall, slender man, with a wild, keen eye, but with the rest of his countenance so disfigured by a thick, matted, black beard, as to prevent me from forming any judgment as to his features. He was dressed in a Nabajo hunting shirt of leather, fitting tight to his body and arms, a pair of leggings and of moccasins. His head was left entirely bare and unprotected—but so thick was the hair, that it might have defied both rain and sunshine to make any impression on his brain.

I had ceased to think about him, and was deeply buried in remembrances of olden time, when a hoarse, rumbling sound caused me to raise my head and look around. Far in the west, above the mountains of the Del Norte, I saw two or three white crests of foam, shining like the wing of the sea-gull. I knew the sign, and put my horse to better speed, for a thunder storm in the mountains is neither the warmest nor the pleasantest thing in nature, and I had yet fifteen miles to ride, before I should reach the village. The crests of foam rose higher and more numerous, and under them came the heavy thunderbanks. The lightning shot up ever and anon behind the mountains, and the thunder came louder and more frequent. In the mean time I had been gradually approaching the eastern mountains, and when within about ten miles of the village, the road ran directly under the steep crags, for the distance of four miles. Before I reached this point, however, the clouds, heaving slowly up, had rolled their black masses over one another, to the zenith. The lightning shot fiercely from cloud to cloud, and the wild wind moaned high up on the mountain. Then there came a sudden fierce flash, and my horse recoiled, for the thunder crashed among the rocks like a thousand cannon. Reining him up to the road again, I put him to his best speed. The rain began to fall, and the lightning grew more intense. The point of mountain ahead, which shot out into the plain, and round which the road went, was a high, abrupt pinnacle of rock, and as I approached it swiftly, I could see the lightning flash against it and recoil quivering. A vast body of cloud had gathered around the lone crag, and as I passed under it like the wind, I held my breath, fearing that some fragment would be shattered from it and annihilate me. A moment of suspense passed, and I was safe.

On passing this point, I was again in the wide part of the valley, and the six remaining miles were soon passed over. On arriving at the village, I dashed up to the best looking house I could see, threw myself from my horse, and entered the porch. On hearing the clatter of the horse's heels, an Indian girl made her appearance, inducted me into the house, and by means of various ejaculations and expostulatory cries, succeeded in raising a big, awkward fellow to take care of my horse.

On entering the little room at the extremity of the Sala—or long hall—I found the only inmates to be two women—one old and sour, the other young and pretty. I had entered the house with a particular prepossession against the whole country, the village and the house, and with a most determined resolution to be inveterately cross and sulky. The sight of a clear, black eye, and a beautiful foot and ancle, overturned all my resolves, and thawed all my perverseness. I attempted to render myself very especially amiable, and we had a long confab together, while the aforesaid Indian girl was getting my supper. The conversation was, at first, managed entirely by them—for I never try to stop a woman's tongue, any more than to drive a pig a certain way—and consisted entirely of ejaculations of astonishment, in the shrill tones of the mother and the liquid music of the daughter. At length I introduced a theme which is always close to the New Mexican's heart. I asked them, when would there be a fandango.

"Tomorow night," was the reply of the old woman. *"Ai Dios!* What a fandango! *Purisima Madre de Dios!*—and so many beautiful girls!"

"And the Priest?" said I.

"Oh yes. Our *Tata Padre* is a good Priest—he loves to dance. Yes, he will go." Et cetera. It is not worth while to detail the conversation.

The room was ornamented with roses, images, &c. as is common; but there was a long cord extending across it, to which was appended a great number of little tufts of wool. I did not exactly understand their use, but I made no queries touching the matter.

We all slept in the same room. I had placed my pistols under my pillow when I lay down, for I had learned by experience to distrust the people. I had slept awhile, and on waking, I saw that the young woman was still sitting at the fire, engaged in cooking. Her mother was on her pallet. "What was she cooking for," thought I to myself. "Her lover, perhaps," and I turned over to sleep again. Just then, I heard a heavy step, outside of the house, and the girl rose and left the room. I thrust my hand under the pillow, drew out a pistol, and again covered myself with the blanket, and pretended to be asleep. In a moment, she entered the room with a man, whom I immediately recognised for the Wolf hunter. He was dressed as when I met him. He walked to the corner of the room and there deposited his gun, which was an old American rifle, and his bow and arrows and lance, for he seemed to go fully armed. He then drew from his belt three wolf scalps, and hung them on the line, with the other bits of wool, with the nature of which I was now perfectly acquainted. During all this he said nothing, but as he returned towards the fire, his eye fell upon me, and he inquired fiercely;

"*Quien Tienes?*" Who have you here? Why don't you answer? Oh I see. Some favored lover. *Mal rayo abrasa?*[3] It is for this that I bear storm, wind, and fire."

He had drawn his long knife from his girdle, and was about throwing himself upon me. Had he done so, I should certainly have slain him, but the girl caught him by the arm, and whispered the single word, "Americano." It acted like a talisman. He dropped his knife and became apparently calm. For two or three hours he sat there with her—cold, quiet, and stern in manner—but when he spoke in answer to some affectionate question of hers, it was with an abrupt, startling incoherence of manner, which I took to proceed from the jealousy excited by my presence, though strangely enough, it did not appear to cause the girl any surprise or uneasiness. At length he took a light, and retired to another apartment, and his mistress took her place by the side of her mother. One room answers as a sleeping apartment in that country for a dozen, if necessary, of both sexes. I lay awake a long while, and had come to a firm determination not to close my eyes during the night—but weariness prevailed against wisdom. I fell asleep, and only awoke when the sun was shining brightly in at the little square window, and the whole family was up and busy. I saw nothing of the Wolf hunter. After a little time I obtained my breakfast, and prepared to

3. See note 21 of "A Mexican Tale."

start, but on bringing out my horse, I discovered that some unlucky slip or jar, the evening before, had so lamed him as to
render him unfit to travel. So, consoling myself with the reflection, *"La Providencia es grande,"* I sent for a horse doctor,
and made up my mind to lay by a day or two, and to eke out
my time as well as I could, with the scanty amusements of a
Mexican village. I do not pretend to say, that the promise of
the fandango did not in some measure tend to reconcile me to
my lot.

In a short time the Doctor made his appearance, and while
he commenced operations on the hoofs and joints of my horse,
I seated myself on a big stone in the yard, and opened a conversation with him. I found him as garrulous as the Barber of
seven brothers, immortalized in the wondrous tales of the reign
of the Calif Haroun Al Raschid;[4] and sooth it is, that words
are a commodity rarely lacked by a New Mexican.

"You may be sure, Senor Americano, that for no other man
in the world would I do what I have done for you. *Alma de
cielo!*—but no one can refuse to do anything for an American.
Now, a ragged Spaniard will employ the science of a *medico* for
half a dozen hours, and then goes off with a *"Dios lo paga!"* God
pay me, indeed! If I had as many lives as a cat, I should starve,
for *them.* But you Americans always pay like kings. A round
peso is the least that I get from you for such a job."

"You may be sure," said I, taking advantage of his want of
breath, "you may be sure that if your skill, of which I have a
high opinion, shall render my horse fit to travel, in three or
four days, I shall pay you well for your trouble."

"May you live a thousand years! And as to rendering him fit
to travel, who can do it better than I? *Primeramente,* I was born
in California—*segundamente,* I have a diploma from the College at Guadalajara—and *terceramente,* I saw Iturbide crowned,
being at the time surgeon to the fourth Regiment—and if all
that does not make me a doctor, I beg leave to know what
would?"

"Indeed," said I, "you have high claims, and that you are a

4. Perhaps a reference to a character in the *Arabian Nights.*

man of sense, is apparent from the value which you put on the American character."

"Yes, Senor," said *el Medico*, at the same time dropping the leg of the horse, on which he had been operating, and proceeding very coolly to roll himself a cigar, *"si, Senor,* I am always ready to serve your countrymen. Now, our Padre, who thinks that no man ought to get to heaven, without a special license from him, often rebukes me for the friendship I show the *cavalleros,* whom he is pleased to denominate heretics; but for myself, though I as much respect our Lady of Guadalupe, and all the Saints of the Calendar, as he, still the house in which I live belongs to any American."

Just then the Wolf hunter came out at the door, and muttering something in reply to the brisk salutation of the Doctor, passed out into the street, armed as on the preceding day—not, however, without a nod of respect to me.

"So you know Manuel?" inquired the Doctor.

"No," said I, "he knows me, as an American—I have no other connection or acquaintance with him."

"*Si—si—el pobre Loco* is a great friend to all the Americans."

"Why do you call him crazy?" inquired I—"and why is he a friend to all the Americans?"

"Oh, it's a long story to tell—but if you will wait till I finish with the horse, we will go to my house, take a cup of wine, and I will tell you all about it."

As I was exceedingly anxious to know more about Manuel, I made no scruple in accepting the offer of the *Medico.* He finished his operations in a marvellously short time; and we proceeded to his house, where over a jar of wine he recounted the following tale, which I shall give in his own words, only omitting sundry excursions which he made to this side and that of the main narrative.

"Three years ago," said he, "Manuel Baca was a lively, fine young fellow, as you might find between the Rio Abajo and Durango. He was decidedly the best hunter, and the most fearless rider, all along the valley of the Del Norte. He was the best dancer and fiddler too, and that, you know, is no small recommendation in our country. Manuel had been several trips to

Sonora, California, and Chihuahua, with some of your country-men—and one Senor Estanali (Stanley)[5] had given him a good rifle, which he valued next to his life, his mistress, and his little brother. This explains to you his attachment to the Americans. Manuel had one only brother, a child about six years of age, who had been left, by the death of both his parents, to depend on him for subsistence. *Maravillas de cielo!*—it was really a won-der to see how he loved the child! Wherever he went, little Jose was with him. You could always see him stuck up in front of him on his saddle, or held in his arms, as he went among the mountains on foot. Besides this child, there was one other being that he loved, and that was Juanita, who lives just across the road, in that little whitewashed house. It was predicted by every body that there would be a wedding—and it was said that the last trader who had passed through from Santa Fe, carried off several of Manuel's dollars in his pocket. Since matters have turned out as they have, there are plenty of people who say that they knew that she cared but little for him—but for my part, I always thought that she loved him. But when the man is killed, the whole world knew that the mule would kick.

"There was another, though, that loved him indeed, although he cared nothing for her, and that was Maria—she who lives with her mother in the house where you stayed last night. She and Manuel had been brought up like sister and brother, and he loved her like a sister, but no more. You will ask, how I know that she loved him, and I can tell you that a man does not graduate at Guadalajara for nothing. Well, so the matter stood, when one fine morning in August, just as the corn was getting fit to eat, Manuel went out to the mountains, to kill a bear, who had been thieving in the fields. Just as he was start-ing, he brought little Jose over to my house, to leave him with me and my wife—but the child began to cry and begged to go. I advised Manuel not to take him, but he could not refuse, and was forced to do it. He perched him up before him on the sad-dle, and set out. About ten miles from this place, there is a rocky gap in the mountains, about two miles long, with precipitous

5. Perhaps the veteran Santa Fe trader Elisha Stanley. Pike also mentions a young William Stanley in his story of "The Gachupin."

sides, and very deep. Just at the mouth of this gap, he came on the trail of the bear, and just as he came to a part of the pass where he could ride no longer, he caught sight of the bear ahead of them, rolling along very leisurely towards the upper end of the gap, where it closed up to the side of the mountain. Here then he dismounted, and expecting to kill the bear immediately, he tied the head of the horse to his knee, and sitting the boy down on a rock, told him to wait a little until he came back. He then pursued the bear, and soon came up with him, but in his hurry he shot him too far back. For a moment or two, the bear was undecided whether to make fight or to run, but at length came to the latter determination, and rushed off up to the gap, with all his speed. Excited by seeing the blood which his shot had drawn from him, Manuel followed on, forgetting the child. It was an hour before he overtook and killed him, and as soon as he became collected, he thought of his brother, and hastily returned down the gap. As he approached the bottom of it, he heard a long, loud yell, and a faint cry, as of a child in pain or terror. He rushed on and again came a loud yell—mingled of rage and grief. It was the savage cry of the white wolf. Two or three bounds, and he turned a point of rock, and had a full view of the scene. A large she wolf was uttering fearful cries, and tearing like a demon, the bloody corse [corpse] of his brother, and his horse was madly attempting to break his bridle, and snorting loudly with terror. Unable to shoot the animal, he rushed on—but the wolf did not flee before him. Turning upon him with her glaring eyes and bloody teeth, she sprang at him, like a panther, with a mad, wild howl. Though unprepared for the attack, Manuel dropped his gun and drew his knife, as she fastened upon his breast and tumbled him upon the rocks. His knife flew from his hand. The sharp fangs of the wolf were fastened in his breast, and she was only kept from fixing her teeth in his throat, by the blows which he aimed at her head. The blood ran from his breast and weakened him, when the thought struck him to turn upon the animal, and press her beneath him. He did so, and while she was struggling to escape from under him his hand fell upon his knife—and he buried it in her heart. There was a stifled cry—a shiver—and she

was dead—and Manuel arose and staggered to the corse of his
brother. He was dead, dead—and by him, lay a young wolf,
which he had found in straggling about the gap, and which he
had pounded with rocks for amusement—till the dam, attracted
by the cries of her young, had dealt out a terrible retribution
on the child.

"All that day Manuel did not return—and that night his horse
came home with the bridle broken, and the saddle under his
belly. The next morning early, we went out to search for Manuel, and Maria insisted on accompanying us. We found him
lying by the body of his brother, and senseless from loss of
blood. He was taken up and conveyed home, with hardly any
signs of life. During his recovery, Maria tended him like a
sister—but when after he became able to converse, he sent for
Juanita—she refused to go and see him. From that day to this,
he has been what you see him—mad—mad—and sometimes dangerous. The only person whom he seems to know is Maria—
and he cares only for her or an American. His whole business
is to hunt wolves, of which he destroys great numbers. Cold or
hot, rain or sunshine, it is the same to Manuel. You may hear
him and his dogs every day in the year. He lives at the house of
La Lupe, the mother of Maria, and you would be astonished
to see the affection which that good girl has for him. Let him
come home at what hour he will, she has his food ready—and
often has she been to the mountains, when he has been gone a
day or two, to find him, and bring him home. He is known every
where, as Manuel the wolf killer, and every body pities him,
and uses him well. This, Senor, is the whole of his story."

After the worthy little *Medico* had finished, I recounted to
him the conduct of Manuel the night before, as an explanation
of, and excuse for, my curiosity with respects to him.

"Yes, yes," said he, "you need be under no concern from
Manuel—he loves an American as well as myself. But now let
us take another *traguito* of wine, and go to the Alcalde's house.
Do you know, I left two fellows there, when you sent for me,
who were disputing about their father's patrimony. He had left
them one donkey and one ox—and the Alcalde was just deciding

that they should cut each animal in two, and each one take his half."

We went to the *Casa Consistorial*.[6] The Alcalde was as stupid as any legislator of a certain Territory, which shall be nameless, but he had good wine. I cannot now say exactly how I wore off the day—but at night I was at the fandango. There was a long-bearded, big fellow, scraping the violin, and another twanging the guitar, and in front stood another who sang the interludes to the *jarabes*, extempore, with a voice like clapping two shingles together. There were twenty girls, with every variety of dress, from the silk *tunico*, and the floating *reboso*, to the simple *basquina* and *camisa*, and those of dingy hue, disclosing, too, as much of their persons as the dress of a fashionable belle. Then there was a multitude of men—some in great pantaloons, ornamented with lace and a profusion of buttons—and some only in their leathern breeches and shirt—and the latter—the *camisa*, like that of the ladies, seeming to have a wonderful antipathy to clear water. Sometimes they were hugging each other, and whispering *double entendres* and inuendos, during the mazy evolutions of a *valse*, in which a black shirt sometimes made a very familiar approximation to a silk gown—for in their dances, rank and dress are counted as nothing. Sometimes they stepped a *jarabe*, without a blush at the vulgarity of the singer, and once they tried a contra dance, in honor of *El Senor Americano*, whose name had already been repeated some half dozen times in their songs.

After dancing a waltz or two—amusing myself awhile with the contortions of face exhibited by the singer, (the New Mexicans are peculiarly blessed with ugliness)—and breathing an abundance of smoke and *heavy laden* air, I made my escape and went home.

Maria had not been at the fandango. I found her sitting by the fire, waiting the return of Manuel. I went to bed and left her still there. I know not now long she waited, but he returned not that night.

The next day passed off, and the next night, like the former. The little *Medico* doctored my horse—the priest went to pray

6. The court house.

over a dead child, and the fiddles played a waltz before him—and I ate and drank and slept.

In the afternoon of the third day, the *Medico* informed me that my horse was well, and in the same breath, that he and Maria were going to search for Manuel. He requested me to go with them, and offered me a mule to ride and I gratified him by going.

I will spare the reader a long recital of the journey. Suffice it, that after the proper quota of kicks and curses, uttered respectively by the mule and the *Medico,* the saddle was put upon the back of a little dun, satanic animal, and I, with considerable haste and much fear and trembling, got into the saddle, and after three or four vigorous flings and jumps of the animal, we proceeded briskly onward. That non-descript invention of man, called a mule, is certainly possessed of more cunning, and a more diabolical nature, than is usually granted to a quadruped. There is something generous, noble, and proud in a fine horse, and you love him next to your mistress—but I should like to see any man feel affection for a mule—for its obstinacy, its revenge, and, in one word, for its mulishness. Every rod or two there was a *capriole*—and on every such occasion, the *Medico* very piously ejaculated, *"Ave Maria! Gran diablita!"* &c. though I had frequent occasion to believe that the villain was inwardly chuckling at my discomfiture. If so, I soon had my revenge—for just in the midst of a vigorous series of gymnastics, I gave the immense iron bit a pull to one side, and backed my mule up against his little horse, when with one kick she nearly demolished the steed, and tumbled the rider into the mud, and then sticking out her long ears, seemed to take a pleasure in being frightened. With many a malediction, and at the same time crossing himself, the Doctor righted his steed, and bestowed himself again in his saddle, and we proceeded, and my mule, seemingly satisfied with the mischief she had done, went quietly on, during the remainder of the route, at a swift pace.

We reached the mountains, and after a long search, found the object of our solicitude under a high crag of the mountains—bruised, bloody, and nearly dead. His head was fearfully cut, but he was perfectly in his senses, and he spoke faintly but rationally to us as we came up. The severe blow on the head, received by falling from the rocks, and the consequent loss of blood, had, as it frequently does, removed his insanity.

The firmness and devotion which had supported Maria through the long trial of her affection, did not desert her now, when most needed; but there was a quick, wild expression of rapture, strangely mingled with anguish, in her countenance, when he spake to her a few words of endearment—and her frame swelled with the excitement, which was at length relieved by a burst of tears.

Three months afterward, I returned from the Pass. I danced with Juanita, at the wedding of Manuel and Maria—and I drank my last cup of wine with my friend *El Medico*.

TALES OF CHARACTER AND COUNTRY

NO. X

Written for the Advocate.[1]

Trappers On The Prairie[2]

I wish I could have had Zimmermann in the great prairie, between this and the Rocky mountains, for about a month. If Providence had kept him from being devoured by the wolves, I think that in that time, I would have cured him of his vagaries for solitude.[3] Men think that when they have gone a mile into the woods, and seated themselves under a burnt stump for an hour or two, they have enjoyed solitude—but were they to try it in a bare and barren plain, where men wander for days and see neither a leaf, a stick, a tree, or a rill of water, they might take solitude to be another matter. There is a vanity and a pride too, in thinking that one's self is actully more miserable than the rest of mankind, and so because they are, or would be more wretched than the world around them, they love solitude. I have some idea of turning this into a metaphysical essay, but on consideration, it will be as well to defer that project until another time.

If then, gentle reader, you are not already tired of my ramblings, I shall beg your attendance a little, while I place under your eye certain personages and events, to which I am moved at this time to draw your attention.

It was a cool, clear, pleasant morning, early in October, that

1. *The* (Little Rock) *Arkanasas Advocate,* April 11, 1834.
2. Title added by the Editor.
3. Johann Georg Zimmermann, a Swiss physician and philosopher, with

a small band of trappers were encamped on the edge of the Semaron, close under the Rocky mountains. The country, which rises gradually from the edge of our settlements to the foot of these mountains, had here become so elevated, that it might with propriety be called a broad table land, or the first bench of the ridge of mountains. It still, however, preserved its character of a dry, level, gravelly prairie, perfectly barren and unbroken by any thing, save here and there a scanty patch of low weeds. The buffalo grass, at its best only attaining the length of an inch or two, was now dried by the heat into a fine, hairlike hay, exhibiting neither greenness or any other sign of life. Just at the moment when I open this brief story, the sun rose broadly and suddenly out of the plain, with the same distinctness that he does from the level ocean, and commenced lifting himself slowly in the heavens. His rays fell on no tree, no shrub, no spot of greenness, except on the edge of the little stream already mentioned, which, springing out of the mountains, runs through the prairie, and joins the Arkansas above its junction with the Canadian. It is in every respect a most singular river. I have crossed it many times, and have never found it more than thirty yards in width, and in most seasons of the year it contains very little water. To-day it may be in one place a perfect sand bed—dry, and covered with white salt, tasting precisely like Glauber's, and equally nauseous, while half a mile above, the water may be running clear, and a foot in depth. To-morrow the case may be reversed. Here may be water and there none. In short, the water is continually springing up and sinking again, and what renders it still more singular, is, that when the sand is dry, and you find water by digging, it will be very sweet and good, while the sand every way around, may be shining with salt. The Dead Sea itself, shows not an aspect of more sterility and desolation, than this river, and the desert of Zahara is hardly more barren.

Just on the edge of this river, were two or three fires, round which were reclined several individuals, dressed generally in leather—and colored by the sun and wind, till they were hardly distinguishable from the native children of the prairie. Their mules and horses were staked around them and their guns lay by them, while they waited the morning repast, which a Mexican servant was busily preparing at each fire. One man was stationed on the look-out below, and another above the camp—for a trapper's life, alway [s] one of great danger, and requiring constant precaution, is preeminently so on the Semaron and the Canadian. These rivers are a kind of neutral ground, occupied at various times by the Cumanches, the Pawnees, the Arapehoes, and the Caiawas—and the former river is also haunted by the Eutaws, and sometimes, though unfrequently, by the Gromonts [Gros Ventre] of the prairie. The Semaron has been especially dangerous on account of the Cumanches and Caiawas, two nations generally confounded, but entirely distinct, although they are frequently found robbing the Americans in company. A trapper knows, however, that these tribes seldom attack a camp unless at day light or just as the moon is rising—but the Arapehoes, who are a band of the Blackfeet, or as the Spaniards call them, *Patos Negros,* attack equally at all hours, and fight much more bravely than either those two nations or the Pawnees. The Gromonts, likewise, are no contemptible enemy, and also a band of the Blackfeet. The Eutaws are rather a timid race, although a much better looking Indian than any of the rest. The Blackfeet are the most determined enemies whom the trappers have to encounter, if we except some of the Indians to the west of the mountains. I say the most determined, because they keep up a constant warfare against them, and kill many men for them every year. The Cumanches, on the contrary, are a cowardly and skulking tribe, and only attack when they have ten or twenty to one. The scale of courage respecting these nations, and many others, is perfectly well understood and defined by the trappers—for while the nations already named, except the Blackfeet, are but little dreaded, they use rather more vigilance when among the Shoshones or Snakes, a large tribe, from whom the Cumanches, speaking the same language, are probably descended.[4] Then came the Black[f]eet, and then the Crows, or Keekatso, who are a small people, but exceedingly brave.

It is not therefore to be wondered at, that the small party of

4. Pike is correct. Comanches and Snakes are Shoshonean people.

trappers with whom we are concerned, should have used the utmost precaution, to guard against a surprize. Their life is always hard and dangerous, and it has struck me that there is a great similitude between their character and that of the sailor. There is the same indifference to storm and cold, and frequently to hunger—and when in port, if I may use the expression, the same disregard of money, and the same repugnance to "sailing again" before they have spent the last copper.

It seemed that they must have lately arrived at their camping ground, for their traps were tied up and lay round them, and the beaver skins which lay round the camp stretched on sticks were quite dry. Besides, had they been on trapping ground, every man would before that hour have been out, setting his traps.

There are probably as many brave men among the mountain trappers, as among the same number of men in any part of the world. Inured to danger, they soon learn to disregard it—and hearing the Indian yell frequently sounding around them, they soon learn to yell in their turn, and frequently to imitate the Indians in some of their barbarities. There is also a great fund of originality among them, and many men may be found there, who could at once convince the world that the characters of Hawk Eye and Mike Fink are by no means exaggerated.[5]

The person who appeared to be the commander of this company, was a middle sized, stout man, with a bold, rather handsome and expressive countenance, and which was more singular for one in his manner of life, a wooden leg. He had lost one "pin" some years before, without any possible fault of his own—for a half breed, I think, shooting at some person against whom he had a grudge, had missed his mark and broke the wrong leg. If Tom Smith thought that this way of breaking one's leg was unceremonious, he certainly found that the remedy was no less so—for as it was in the mountains, and as trappers are not generally accompanied by a medical staff, the leg was taken off with a handsaw, and seared with an axe. Tom, however, who

5. Hawk-eye is briefly discussed in note 33 of the second "Narrative." With the publication of Morgan Neville's *The Last of the Boatmen,* in 1829, Mike Fink was already entering the pantheon of American folk heroes.

was a man of the most dauntless bravery, and one of the most generous of human beings, still stuck to the old trade, and stumped about after beaver nearly as well as the best of his trappers.[6]

Near him was another individual, who, if this should ever meet his eye, will excuse me for mentioning his name, which I do with the utmost respect and friendship. Rhodes was and is, the best specimen of the old hunter that I have ever seen. Take him out of the woods, the prairie, and the mountains, and he languishes. He is like a transplanted exotic. He has been in the woods for many years, till that life is his element. He has traversed the country from the heads of the Arkansas and the Columbia to the mouth of the Del Norte, and is still, though old, a hale and hearty hunter. A few years ago, he took a fancy that no teeth were better than loose teeth, and so pulled out the seven or eight which he had left, and so remains without a "peg." It is a grievous trouble to him, whenever he is forced to assail a tough piece of buffalo bull or horse—but an antelope and bear he manages very well.

Then there was Tom Banks, an Irishman—and a most tremendous archer at the long bow. Tom was brave as a lion, too, or said he was, which is the same thing. It is almost always the case, that we have nothing but men's words for such matters. However, he was a merry, good-humored fellow, and like most of the children of St. Patrick, rarely objected to a mug of *posheen*.

Close by was old Jeru—the most comical and quizzical of all old Frenchmen—withered, lean, almost toothless—but with a soul as big as that of many a man of two tons—loquacious and given to sententious discourses.

Besides these, there were two Frenchmen, and one other personage too remarkable to be passed over. This was Bill Williams, the best trapper in the world—a tall, raw-boned, red haired, sharp and long-faced man, manifestly of Scotch descent. He is the best hunter I ever saw; and not only that, but the best man I ever saw for supporting hunger and thirst and putting the necessities of his comrades before his own.

6. Pike recounts some of Tom Smith's adventures in his first "Narrative."

"Bill," said the Captain, "did you see any trail of Camanches when you was out this morning."

"That's it again! Camanches! *Ka!* Don't you know how to pronounce that word yet? I'll be d--d if I don't teach you orthography, or leave your company."

"It is Camanches."

"There, again! once you have the bull by the horns you hold on like a toothache. *Oye Pedro! Nosese dice por Vmd Cumanches? Como se—se—no es Cumanche?*

"*Si Senor—*es Cumanche."

"Well, I give it up," said Tom, "and now answer my question."

"Pronounce right then, Tom, and don't disgrace yourself. No, I didn't see any thing, and what is worse, I didn't see any buffalo sign. Tom, you watch them fellows—you Tom Banks I mean—them fellows that are cooking. They'd steal anything. They'd steal a man's character and keep it by 'em till they wore out their own."

"No buffalo sign."

"No. It will be horse or beaver soon—and I go for beaver. Here comes a hawk. I'll have him stewing in the pot now directly."

He raised his gun as the hawk came sailing by, and without dropping it after firing, squinted along the barrel to see what effect his shot had produced. Unlike Leather Stocking's shot at the pigeon, it did *not* kill the bird, but he was just as well satisfied as if he had.

"There," said he, "I think I disturbed his movements a little. He don't sail quite so well as he used to. He sails sort of cat-e-corner'd now."

"Well, load your gun again, and we'll have some buffalo for breakfast yet"—said Tom, "and make no noise about it. Don't you see them moving about two miles down the river."

"Ay, ay" said Bill, after taking a deliberate look—"there comes our cattle sure enough."

"The sight of buffalo is always an inspiring one to men in the prairie. It is not only the best meat in the world, but when it comes, it is in abundance—and the hunter with his herds of buffalo around him feels perfectly independent. It is, therefore, no wonder that our band of trappers who had been travelling over the barren country between the Canadian and the Semaron, eyeing also for several days the ribs of their mules and horses, which they began to fear they might in a few days be gnawing—it is no wonder that they were in raptures at the sight of a large herd of those unwieldy animals feeding slowly along on their way to the south. The Frenchman jabbered and the Spaniards no less, while the Americans put themselves in fighting array.

"Bill," said the Captain, "how shall we take them?—crawl up, or give them a run?"

"Any how—but I'll tell you. Hush your bawling mouth"—to a Spaniard who was running about like a crazy man, crying, *"cibolo—cibolo"*—for which he obtained, beside the reproof, a smart rap on the head from Bill's gun-stick, *"calla tu boca, bestia!* Doesn't every body see that they are *cibolos*—and attend to cooking that antelope that it cost me three hours hunting yesterday to kill. I'll tell you how to do it. Let's you, old Rhodes, Tom Banks and I crawl on 'em and get a shot or two—and then these Spaniards and that *Pueblo* can run them on horse-back. You see they can come down in the bed of the river and the buffalo won't mind 'em."

This plan was agreed to, and the four already mentioned commenced their progress towards the buffalo. By taking advantage of the inequalities of the ground, and keeping close to the river, they were able to approach within about four hundred yards of them without being observed. They then commenced advancing upon their hands and knees, moving very slowly, and stopping occasionally, so as not to excite suspicion. Now and then an old bull would lift his head, and look suspiciously at them, but soon satisfied that there was no danger, he always returned to his food. The bulls, as is often the case, were in the front, and the hunters were obliged to delay until the cows should come up—the latter being, in autumn, by far the best food. An accident, however, soon occurred that favored their plan—for an unlucky calf, straying towards them was surrounded by at least a dozen large white wolves. It raised a piteous cry as they commenced ham-stringing it, and a number of cows came rushing to the rescue. All the four discharged their guns and one or two of the animals were wounded—but as the hunters were out of their sight, and made no noise, the troop evinced no disposition to flee. Another discharge followed, and one or two fell—and several of the old bulls came grunting about with great curiosity—but so soon as one of them smelt the blood of the fallen animals, he tossed his head high in the air and started off in a great hurry, as though he supposed that he might be apt to get himself into trouble by remaining. The whole herd followed—and just then the two Spaniards and the *Pueblo* rushed out upon them, on horseback, armed each with their bows and arrows, and the latter with a long, slender lance, with a staff about twelve feet in length.

When the buffalo saw these formidable enemies close upon them, their exertions for escape were redoubled. The cows shot ahead, and the bulls, always slower, fell in the rear—and, passing them by, the hunters urged their horses close along side of the cows. The bulls immediately scattered in every direction over the plain, and left a clear field for the battle. As each hunter rode up within three or four feet of his victim he drew his bow to the arrow-head, and without watching its success, sped on after another. The *Pueblo* in particular, whose horse seemed perfectly trained to the sport, managing him by the pressure of his legs and the sway of his body, without touching the bridle, after striking down one buffalo with his lance, and finding some difficulty in extricating it, betook himself to his bow, and at his first shot his arrow passed thro' his victim and fell out on the other side. Five or six buffalo were killed in this way, and several wounded—and the herd was now fleeing in every direction. The Americans still stood on the bank of the river, watching the chace [chase], when the *Pueblo* came directly towards them, in full run after a fine cow. As he approached the party, Bill cried out—*"Lazalo, Manuel—Lazalo."*—To sling his bow over his shoulder and uncoil a long and smooth hair rope from the front of his saddle, was with the agile Indian the work of not more than a minute—then gathering it into two or three coils, and holding the remainder of it in his left hand, he gave his horse the spur. When within about ten feet of his victim, he commenced whirling the rope about his head, and then launching it through the air, it fell directly on the horns of the animal. At the moment it fell, his horse obedient to his motions sprang to the left, and darted ahead of the buffalo on that side, bringing the rope from her horns round her hind legs, and tumbling her violently upon the ground. With one jerk of the rope he extricated it from her horns and she rose again. The manoeuvre was repeated several times—until the animal stood still and absolutely refused to stir. He then despatched her with a single arrow.

The dexterity of the Spaniards and some of the Indians in such matters is truly astonishing. It is no uncommon thing for them to lay a dollar on the ground, and retiring to the distance of a hundred and fifty yards, put their horse in a swift gallop, and pick up the dollar as they pass. I have heard many anecdotes of their skill, in every thing relating to horsemanship—and perhaps the two following may not be uninteresting. The best horseman and *lazero* that I ever saw, is [Antonio] Viscara, the Commandant of New Mexico. He is a native of some State south of Chihuahua, and has one or two brothers. One of them is, I have heard, even more skilful than the Colonel, his brother. This man was returning, some years ago, from Durango to New Mexico, and stopped one evening at a *corral*, full of unbroken horses. Several Spaniards were standing around the *corral* (or inclosure,) roping the horses and taking them out, to break them for riding. He entered into conversation with them, and they inquired where he lived. He said, in New Mexico. Now the inhabitants of the lower and the western country look on the New Mexicans as inferior in horsemanship, and in truth they are so—particularly to the people of California and Sonora. They thought therefore to have some amusement, and asked him if he would not like to rope a horse? He said, that he did not care—he would try. They gave him a *lazo,* and asked him what horse he would choose. He told them that it made no difference—and they pointed out to him a large black horse, which they had been trying in vain to catch, and one of the best, as well as most unruly of their animals. A bad horse will frequently watch and avoid the rope. Viscara accordingly took his stand clumsily, but when the animal came running round in the crowd, he threw the rope rapidly over his head, and bringing it at the same moment behind him, threw him down and broke his leg. They were obliged therefore to take him into the prairie and shoot him. Thinking it, however, a mere accident, they pointed out another, which he threw down, breaking his neck. They then exclaimed in surprize—"you are a native of New Mexico, are you!"

"I did not say that I was. I *live* there."

"Where was you born then?"

He named a certain *hacienda*—and they inquired his name. When they learned it, their mortification and vexation was extreme, for every one knew, by report, of the Viscaras.

The other anecdote is a brief one. In some battle before the Revolution of Iturbide, a Mexican, whirling his *lazo* over his head, rode up to a field-piece, and throwing his rope over the mouth of it, while the other end was attached to his saddle, put spurs to his horse and carried the cannon safely off. This I believe to be a fact.

But to return to our trappers. After the *Pueblo* had slain his animal, Bill gave a long yell to recall the others, and the hunt was ended. The remainder of the day was spent in slicing the meat very thin and hanging it about their camps to dry in the sun—an operation which the aforesaid sun performs very suddenly, aided by the keen, dry prairie wind, for in a day or two the meat becomes so dry that it is easily pounded into powder.

During the two or three days employed in this business, Bill was far from idle. Every day he was far out in the prairie, for he is the most restless man in the world. At one time you might see him cracking away at the little prairie-dogs, whose villages are abundant in those high plains, tho' what on earth they do for water is a mystery. At another, squatted on the ground waving a red handkerchief over his head to entice the antelope, and at another, merely pacing about with no ostensible purpose— keeping always a sharp look-out for the Indians. A man or two by themselves suit them exactly, and the carrying off a ranger a year ago was no strange occurrence. By the way, I do not know that any thing has ever been heard from that man, but two reasons incline me to think that they killed him. The first is, in 1831 the small pox was among the mountain Pawnees, and they swore vengeance against the whites for carrying it among them; and the second is, that when the wagon company was on its way from St. Louis to Santa Fe in 1832, the son of a Pawnee chief came into their camp, or up to their wagons, and was conversing with some of them, when a Pueblo Indian, returning among some Spaniards in the same company, shot him in the back and killed him.[7] I should imagine that the Pawnees, naturally enraged, would glut their revenge whenever they had an opportunity.

Bill and Tom Banks were out on a hunt, the second morning after the buffalo chace [chase], and after getting to the distance of three or four miles from camp, they alighted by a hole of muddy water in the prairie, and sat down to rest; after leading their horses down into the hole, which was a small hollow with abrupt sides, deep enough to conceal them from sight. While they sat on the edge of the hollow, there appeared a scattered number of buffalo running exactly against the wind—a sure sign that there were Indians near. The buffalo were not more than a mile from them, and they had barely time to get into the hollow, when something like twenty Indians made their appearance, mounted, and dashing at full speed after the buffalo. Their glittering spears—their shields ornamented with red cloth and feathers, and their picturesque and wild attire, render the prairie Indian a noble spectacle.

"Tom," said Bill, "what Indians are them chaps? I think they must be Eutaws by their feathers. Now if I was a limner [painter] I'd make my fortune."

Tom's bravadoes had fled, and he was quaking and trembling with fear. He did, however, muster up energy enough to say;

"I think they're Eutaws."

"Well, I'll never trap another beaver if they are. They're Cumanches—for the Eutaws wear whiter skins—they get deer plentier. Don't they ride well any how? There goes down a buffalo. I wish I could get one of them fellows in about a hundred and twenty yards—I'd make him hop."

"I hope they won't come that near."

7. The same story is told by Josiah Gregg, *Commerce of the Prairies,* edited by Max L. Moorhead (Norman, 1954), p. 216.

"I dare say. Well, a man don't look so beautiful when he's scared. I wish you'd keep your jaws together, for by the Lord! they can hear 'em chatter two-thirds of the way to camp, and I'll bet on it."

It is a rule with an Indian not to kill more meat than he can can use. Seeing them, therefore, stop short at one buffalo, Bill judged immediately that it was a war party. Had they been hunters, laying up meat for the winter, they would have kept on killing. The animal was soon cut up and packed, and the party were shortly out of sight. Our two hunters then ventured out and returned to camp. On their report, two of the party went down the river to reconnoitre, and discovered by the smokes that there were a good number of the Indians. They returned therefore, and preparations were immediately made for moving. They travelled all that night and the greater part of the next day, and camped again in a small grove which lay on both sides of a deep hollow, running up into the mountains towards the head of the Arkansas. As night approached the scouts again brought news that the Cumanches had followed them and were encamped about three miles below. It therefore became evident that they would be attacked, and the question was how best to defend themselves. The plan was at length determined on, and when night came it was put in execution. Fires were lighted, as was common, in the camp, and leaving the *Pueblo* in it, the whole party proceeded with their animals to thread the narrow and difficult hollow. After going about five miles, they halted in a place which two men could have held good against a hundred, and all the Americans returned towards their first camp. About half a mile from it, in the hollow, was a place where there was a sudden ascent capable of being defended with great effect. At the foot of this they built a small fire, and then concealed themselves above.

An hour or two of anxious suspense passed away, and then the report of the *Pueblo's* rifle was heard, followed by a long loud yell. Two or three discharges of fusees followed, and then one more crack of the rifle—and all at once another loud yell arose higher up the river. The party still lay silent—nothing was seen of the *Pueblo,* and it was soon evident by the continual glare and report of fire arms, and the mingled yells and shouts, that some way or other there was a general fight below.

This, of course, they were utterly at a loss to comprehend—and waited in great surprise [suspense?] for the arrival of the *Pueblo*. He appeared at length at the fire below, and bounded up the rocks, and a few words explained the whole matter. The trappers had been watched by two parties—one of Cumanches and the other of Eutaws, and as there happened just then to be some feud between the nations, their meeting was the signal for battle. After detailing this matter, the *Pueblo* tossed three scalps towards Bill, and inquired if it was *bon*. Bill turned them over with great curiosity, and holding them by the long black hair, said with a strong expression of disgust at the people to whose heads they had not long before been respectably appended;

"Yes—I'll swear to the creturs being Cumanches. That *Pueblo* takes off a scalp scientifically. I have seen some of these yellow villains that would use the dullest knife they could find, on pur-pose; and saw into the back of the neck, so as to get all the skin on the head. Ay, ay, they're Cumanches to a sartinty. *C'est bon, amigo*—and it is a devilish deal better than most of us would have done in the same case."

The noise of the battle began to approach, and it was soon made manifest that one party had driven the other into the narrow pass—whichsoever it was, it was alike necessary that they should be hindered from passing on.

"Stand to your traps, my boys," cried Bill—"two or three of you be ready to roll rocks when they begin to come up here—and Tom Smith and Rhodes, you help me pepper 'em."

In a moment or two there was a rush of dark bodies towards the fire, and the *Pueblo* cried out that they were the Cumanches. While they stood within the light of the fire, two or three rifles were fired from above, and every shot told. For a little while they were irresolute, but the Eutaws came pushing on, and they were obliged to aim at the ascent. As soon, however, as they be-gan to climb it, the heavy rocks poured down upon them, and foiled at every point, they turned to pay, and mingled man to man with the Eutaws. Not one escaped.

In a few moments the pass was still again, and then a single Eutaw appeared at the fire, and held his hands up, crossed one over the other. The *Pueblo* was ordered to inquire what he wanted, and the answer was, to smoke a pipe with the Americans. After some consultation, this was agreed to. The first man who descended was the *Pueblo*, and for half an hour he was busy in hunting out those Indians who had been shot by his party, and scalping them. The Eutaws seated themselves around the fire, and the Americans likewise. The great pipe was produced, and a long smoke was had. Then a quantity of buffalo meat was cooked, and the two parties, after their repast, took different directions.

Index

Index

Excluding Pike's poems.